Magweza
Zibere
Mazimbe
Mhathlehuru
Maringe
Chigeza
Doperakondo
Nyamutatu
Bvuterevadzimu
Musita
Mukukurajecha
MAZIVANDADZOK
Dangadema
Katuri

Mawisire
Pengapenga
Magocha
Machera
Matangi
Magondo
Zimedzanyika
Bengwa
Nyanjuzi
Dzivarenjuzi
Manyoka
Chemhindo
A

LIGHTNING'S EGGS

DanTs Media Publishing 2019
www.danielmutendi.co.zw

Edited by Grace N'senda
Cover design by Walt Barna

First Printed in 2019

ISBN 978-1-77929-439-5

Daniel Mutendi

Special thanks to my proofreaders and preliminary editors;
Tsitsi Mutendi and Fearless Mutendi.

Sincere gratitude to my inspirators;

Bambo Samere Mutendi
Enginas Mutendi (VaChimedza)
Catherine Mutendi (Mai Dolla)
The Mutendi Clan

For my wife Tsitsi Mutendi and our kids;
Jasmine Mufaro Mutendi
Daniel Djimon Mutendi
Nyasha Maia Mutendi

It is a foolish leaf that detaches itself from a healthy branch to try to attach itself to another tree

Glossary

Baba – Father

Bamukuru – Short for *babamukuru* – A father's older brother or an older sister's husband

Bamunini – Short for *babamunini* – A father's younger brother or a younger sister's husband.

Chapungu - The bateleur eagle

Chimandamanda – A marriage ceremony where the groom brings a cow to his in-laws that is then slaughtered and fed to both families present. In doing this, the groom would be thanking his in-laws for the opportunity for him to marry a virgin

Chiverera, - a big male baboon that walks alone in the wild.

Dzvatsvatsva – A spider-like creature that runs around fast on the ground usually seen at night near bonfires

Gota - A room reserved for an unmarried young man.

Hweva – (Morning Star) The brightest star that rises in the east a few hours before sunrise and continues to be seen even when the sun has just risen

Mahewu – A fermented sweet-sour drink made from mixing ground millet or sorghum, and leftover granules of *sadza* with water and leaving overnight to ferment.

Mai – Mother

Mainini - A mother's younger sister or a wife's younger sister

Makondohwe – Rams

Mashavi-shavi – A black and white bird believed to be messengers of evil spirits

Mbira – A musical instrument played by using thumbnails to hit the keys

Mbuya – Grandmother

Mhondoro – A spirit medium embodied by a lion, usually with a dark or very light fur

Mubobobo – A charm that makes it possible to sleep with women without their knowledge and consent

Muchakata – A type of tree

Mugwatikwati - A type of a tree

Mukoma – An older brother

Munyamagundure – A type of fruit tree that grows in the wild

Mupani – A type of a tree

Mutondo – A type of tree

N'anga – A dealer in medicines and charms, sometimes with powers to decipher messages from the spirit world

Nduma – Love token

Ngororombe – A type of dance

Ngozi – The spirit of a dead person that comes back to avenge by haunting those responsible for their death.

Roora – Dowry

Sadza – The staple food of most of Southern Africa, made from maize/corn meal

Sekuru – Grandfather or mother's brother

Shezhu – A bird that can guide people to beehives.

Svukukuviri – A mythical two-headed snake

Tezvara – Father-in-law

Tsikamutanda - A witch hunter

Vatete – A father's sister or a husband's sister

Chapter 1

The three men had been sitting quietly for a while, each one buried deep in his thoughts.

"Kriiiiiiieeeeeeeiiii!" a screeching owl is heard nearby. Muzanenhamo is irritated. He uses a dry stick to poke into the fire and remove the excess ashes from the glowing coals. The burning *mupani* logs produce cracking sounds, and sparkling embers explode in every direction. The fire that seemed to be dying is reignited so much that the three men begin to shuffle uncomfortably in the searing heat. Muzanenhamo throws the stick he was using as a poker into the fire and watches it wither as it is consumed by the lashing flames.

"Kriiiiiiieeeeeeeiiii!" the screeching owl is heard again, this time closer to where the three men are sitting. The screech is pitched so high it is piercing right through their eardrums. Muzanenhamo draws in some thin phlegm, which keeps rolling out of his large nostrils. He shakes his head in irritation.

"This is not good," he mumbles scornfully as the owl lets out another loud screech, breaking the silence of the night.

Muzanenhamo takes out a small container made from a goat's horn that contains his powdered tobacco from his sling bag and tips it in the center of his palm before he sniffs it all up. His brother-in-law, Chafunga remains silent just staring listlessly into the burning fire. His thoughts seem to have wandered somewhere very far away. Muzanenhamo suddenly utters,

"When I went to take a bath in the river this afternoon I saw two snakes fighting. I could have easily killed them because they were fighting right near the pathway, but for some reason, I felt drained, and I just could not do it. I knew there and then that this was definitely a bad omen. Now I have no doubt that this owl has been sent to end it all." He carries on mumbling as he lists other mysterious events that occurred before him over the past few days, which seemed to confirm the imminent approach of a great tragedy. His nephew, Chengetai who was sitting beside him, kept nodding his head and grunting in affirmation to everything his uncle mentioned. Chafunga would at times pay attention to what was being said, but he would then quickly get sucked back into his own mind.

This went on deep into the night, until just before the first rooster had begun his alarm. Even though it was spring, the breeze that was blowing that night made it feel like the middle of winter. The heat from the mupani fire warmed the men from the front, but their exposed backs were frozen stiff. Muzanenhamo would at times turn to give his spine to the fire to warm it up. Chafunga got up to fetch more firewood and took his time before going back to the fire. He hoped that by the time he got back, his brother-in-law would have changed the depressing subject of bad omens. But when he got back, he found Chafunga going on about the notorious *mashavi-shavi,* the evil birds, which perched and sung for a long time at his home a few day that had passed. He said that he tried to shoo them away, but they kept coming back and perching themselves in the big tree that was behind his yard, singing their eerie songs. Chafunga had no option. He just had to sit through the agony and tolerate the depressing words.

On this day, before the sun had set, Nyaradzo, Chafunga's pregnant wife started experiencing cramps. She initially thought that she was getting into false labor because she still had a whole good month to go before her due date. Before this development, Chafunga was meant to go back to his village in Dangadema, but now he could not leave his wife in such a state. This was Nyaradzo's first pregnancy, and by law, it was required that the delivery had to take place at her parent's home. So a few days ago, Chafunga brought her back to her village to fulfill this law. That morning when she had gone into labor, the elders quickly arranged that she be taken to the well-known village midwife, Mbuya Nyamukuta who happened to be Nyaradzo's paternal grandmother. Mbuya Nyamukuta lived far from where Nyaradzo's parents stayed. The elders instructed Muzanenhamo Jr. (Nyaradzo's brother) and his nephew Chengetai to accompany Chafunga and his wife to the midwife's home.

By the time they arrived at her home, Chafunga was carrying Nyaradzo on his back, as she could no longer walk from the pain. It was difficult for him to carry an eight-month pregnant woman on his back, but he had no other way to get her to the midwife. It was not her weight that he was concerned about, but the difficulty of balancing her on his back as he walked. Since the first day they met, he had not seen Nyaradzo in such pain, looking so helpless. This had shocked him to the marrow, and it had gotten him anxious as they sat by the fire, waiting for her to give birth. He was agitated and concerned by Muzanenhamo's consistent babbling. This was not the time to talk about bad omens and all.

Inside the kitchen hut, the effects of the medicine Nyaradzo had taken were starting to show. Mbuya Nyamukuta had ground a chunk of a *mugwatikwati* root and mixed it with leaves of different plants and put these ingredients in a clay pot, half-filled with goat milk. She stirred quickly with a wooden spoon and asked Nyaradzo to drink the medicine while she applied some of it on to her clitoris, and some deep into her birth passage. This was a catalytic medicine that would force the uterus to spit out the fetus even though it was way before the time for the baby to be delivered. From Mbuya Nyamukuta's examination, there was imminent danger that Nyaradzo's baby would die in the womb if it were not quickly taken out. Nyaradzo began sweating, and her eyes were popping out of her sockets in pain. She began to pant heavily. The light coming from the fire at the center of the hut exposed a swollen blood vessel on Nyaradzo's wet forehead. Beads of sweat trickled down her face. She let out a sudden loud scream while holding her back with her left hand as she pivoted the rest of her body with her right hand on the floor.

"Hey! What is wrong with you? Do you seriously want to broadcast to all those hungry witches out there that there is fresh blood in this hut? Please, please I beg you, can you shut up and keep your voice down, huh?" Mbuya Nyamukuta curtly whispered. She was trying to keep herself calm, but agitation ended up forcing her to raise her voice, and this seemed like an instruction to Nyaradzo to increase her pitch.

"Nyaradzo, remember we are surrounded by witches in this area, and at this point, you know you and your baby are extremely vulnerable to them. Can you please just shut up and let us get through with this quickly. Bite your teeth and take a deep breath," she tried again to calm her down, but Nyaradzo seemed not to have even heard one word. She kept on screaming. When Chafunga heard the screaming, he immediately stood up, but Muzanenhamo quickly reminded him that the job at hand was for women, and all he could do was just sit and wait for word to be sent to them from the hut. Chafunga felt silly and helpless at the same time. He remained standing and taking in the pain of the assault from the screaming that kept going on and on. Sometimes it was loud, but from time to time, it would sound like the whimpering of a dog in the cold. This carried on until it was almost dawn.

All the while, Nyaradzo would sometimes go on her knees and keep like that for a period before lying on her side, assuming the fetal position. When she laid on her back, the women who were with her in the kitchen would turn her around. They kept struggling to keep her voice low. Just after the first rooster had beat itself with its muscular wings and sounded a high pitch alarm to notify the world that the sun was making its way up, Nyaradzo gave birth to a healthy baby boy. The women were delighted that the baby was well and that it showed no sign that it was meant to stay in its mother's womb for another full month. All the screaming that had defined the night immediately died. The youngest woman from the hut was sent to inform the men who were by the fire that the clan of the Monkey had been blessed by the addition of another boy. Chafunga leaped for joy and gave his brother-in-law a firm handshake as they congratulated each other.

"Ummnn, so you've decided to start by getting a boyfriend for my wife!" Muzanenhamo said, with his nostrils filled with ground tobacco. The men laughed in relief. The bad omens that had hounded their night seemed to have disappeared with the dawn.

Nyaradzo asked Mbuya Nyamukuta if she could hold her baby. She immediately held him close to her bosom and sighed in relief. She felt a surge of love as she saw his eyes try to look up at her. Exhausted from the night's events, she leaned on the wall of the hut on her back. She smiled as she looked at the baby, a lot of love showing in her tired eyes. She then asked her grandmother to move closer to her. She wanted to whisper something to her. The old woman dragged herself carefully closer to Nyaradzo. Nyaradzo whispered into her ear, moving her head carefully to avoid disturbing the peaceful baby. Suddenly, the old woman jerked in surprise, moving her head away from Nyaradzo and putting her hands together on her chest as she looked at Nyaradzo. She quickly erased the shocked look, as wisdom commanded her to swiftly restore her dignity. None of the other women who were in the hut heard what she had been told. A few moments later, Nyaradzo told the women that she needed to close her eyes for a bit so that she could take a short nap. She closed her eyes to sleep, still holding her child in her hands. Her drowsiness seemed to have rubbed off onto her child, who immediately fell asleep too. The women took this moment to take turns to go outside to get some fresh air and do other things.

Before too long, the baby started stretching and kicking. He burst into tears, indicating that he wanted to be fed.

"Hey you, daughter of the Lions, wake up and feed your baby," Mbuya Nyamukuta said as she shook Nyaradzo. Nyaradzo does not answer. She tries again, but no response comes from Nyaradzo. By this time, the baby's cry had augmented.

"Nyari, you are going to drop that child!" the old woman screamed as she took the child from Nyaradzo's chest, but Nyaradzo does not move. Mbuya Nyamukuta feels Nyaradzo's hand and finds it cold. Slowly like a chameleon, she lays her palm close to Nyaradzo's heart and does not feel any vibration. Nyaradzo's body had turned to stone now. The old woman shoots from where she sat, holding the baby close to her; she suddenly screams and wails while circling around the hut. Like a relay, the screaming passes on to the other women who go berserk and throw themselves on to the wall and floor of the rondavel. What was this that the ancestors had done now?

Chapter 2

Chafunga was a twenty-two year-old man. He lived in the Kingdom of Dangadema under King Zihwe, and he was also a young warrior under this king. He had first seen Nyaradzo one day when she visited her aunt, who was married and now living in Dangadema. She had come from the Kingdom of Musita, where she stayed with her parents. At this time, Nyaradzo was just a sixteen-year-old girl. Chafunga and Nyaradzo had fallen in love with each other on the very day that they had first met. However, it had to take over two summers for Nyaradzo to finally agree to be Chafunga's girlfriend and for him to pay his dowry for her to the Lion clan of Musita.

Nyaradzo was a tall, beautiful, and well-built girl. Many boys and men had fallen in love with her, especially those from her home area in Musita. Even though all these men wanted her, she became notorious for rejecting and not even tolerating or entertaining love proposals from them. Her parents would often receive a lot of gifts, mostly from wealthy men who desired to win her heart in marriage. Many of them were hugely disappointed when word spread that some simple guy from the Monkey Clan of Dangadema won Nyaradzo's heart and married her.

When Chafunga took the trip to his in-laws to deliver the dowry, his brother and his mother's brother accompanied him. Before long, the *chimandamanda* ceremony was held at Nyaradzo's parents' home. For this ceremony, the groom has to bring a cow that is slaughtered and fed to both families present. In doing this, the groom would be thanking his in-laws for marrying a virgin. Nyaradzo was then taken to Chafunga's home where many people celebrated. The celebrations were held at Chafunga's brother's house because their parents had long passed. Many people congratulated Chafunga for having married the most desired bachelorette. All these happenings did not sit well with the king of the land, King Zihwe.

King Zihwe was largely feared by many throughout the kingdom of Dangadema. This king ruled his subjects with such a heavy hand that most of them loathed him. All that he wanted to happen would happen, regardless of how it affected his subjects. No one would dare to challenge whatever he declared. The sentences that he passed for most of his offenders were mostly death sentences, or when he was lenient, the offender would be asked to leave the kingdom for good. He was so cruel that none of his three wives had conceeded to marrying him. The girls' parents feared the repercussions of denying the all-powerful king his desires, so they forced their daughters to marry him. The people of Dangadema felt that they had been unfortunate with their leaders. King Zihwe's father had also been a feared and cruel leader during his reign. To them, this meant that the prospects of getting a good shepherd for them would be very far into the future, especially if Zihwe's ancestors were to bless him with long life. This hurt them also because a lot of the other kingdoms surrounding them lived in peace and were blessed with wise and caring leaders.

King Zihwe was a physically strong man who during wartimes would lead his armies from the battlefronts. He was very confident in himself when it came to fighting. Many said that he had acquired a powerful charm that sharpened his fighting skills. He had a big scar on his left cheek that he earned during one of his fighting escapades. Even though he had that big scar on his face, he was still attractive. Actually, many women admired how he was built.

During the first days that Nyaradzo visited Dangadema, King Zihwe heard of the stunning girl who had visited his kingdom. He sought to see her for himself, and when he did see her, his heart also fancied her. He then planned to get her to be one of his wives. If Nyaradzo had been a resident of Dangadema, it would have been effortless for him to do this. All he would have needed to do was give out a command, and so it would have been. Anyway, the king realized that if he were to forcefully take Nyaradzo to be his wife, he risked taking his kingdom to war against King Musita of the Musita Kingdom. At that time, he had just come out of a battle against some kingdoms from the east of Dangadema. He emerged as the victor, and he wanted to rest himself and his troops. He did not fear going to war with Musita or any other kingdom. With this on his mind, he decided to try his luck by approaching Nyaradzo and declaring his love for her the way other men were doing. To him, being the king meant that chances that Nyaradzo would agree to his proposal were high.

To Nyaradzo, all men were just the same. Her mother had told her that real good men were scarce, therefore if her heart had fallen for any man, she needed to give herself good time to learn about this man until she was satisfied that she could live with him for the rest of her natural life. Because of this,

Nyaradzo refused to give her heart to the boys and men of Dangadema, and her story spread throughout the whole kingdom. It was even whispered that Nyaradzo had told the king to reserve his heart for his three wives at the palace. Nyaradzo was described by some, as a sweet baobab fruit. No matter how much it is hit by clubs, it remains holding onto the parent tree, refusing to fall down to the hungry boy.

Chafunga did not relent in his quest to have Nyaradzo as his girl. His heart told him that the girl loved him. Musita was quite far from Dangadema, but to a man, a place is only too far away if the girl he loves does not live there. He paid numerous visits to the Musita. Many of his early visits were almost in vain because Nyaradzo was haughty. This, therefore, made it very difficult for Chafunga to see or talk to her. She would give reasons such as her eyelashes, or her fingernails being sore, so consequently, she could not walk to go and speak to Chafunga. Chafunga kept on trying his luck. Each time he got the chance to look directly into Nyaradzo's eyes, he saw the overflowing love that was in her heart. Eventually, Nyaradzo agreed to be his girl.

Two of the king's nephews, the sons of one of his sisters, were his informants. They were always updating the king on new developments. King Zihwe was surprised and deeply indignant to learn that she had given her heart to Chafunga. He wondered why Nyaradzo had refused to be his wife. He was the king, and he was way better than Chafunga, a mere junior warrior from many of his regiments with nothing to his name! How could this be? Chafunga had no cattle. He was one who struggled to till his land. He would wait for his older brother to finish tilling his fields and then lend him the cattle to till his own land. This meant that for many planting seasons, his crops would be harvested much later than those of most people in his province. His plants would be stunted. Zihwe wondered why Nyaradzo's parents had allowed her to be taken by a man who had no cattle kraal at his home. As he kept thinking about this, he was much troubled. So much that he developed insomnia, but he could not think of what to do about the issue.

The attention and affection that Nyaradzo got from the boys and men of Dangadema were also not well received by a lot of the girls in this land. When Nyaradzo was brought by her people to be left at her new family's home, the emission of jealous engulfed a lot of the girls in the village. As a result, it took Nyaradzo long to make real friends amongst the girls in Dangadema. Various speculations about why she had no friends circulated. They surmised that she was very arrogant and that she was a witch. They also said that she did not want to hang out with other young women because her goblins did not permit her to do so as they also needed her to play with them. When she would go where a group of young women would be gathered, she would notice that they would quickly leave one by one until she would be the only one left there. This did not bother her too much. She just ended up doing what she had to do on her own. On days that she desired to talk about women stuff, she would go and spend time with her aunt, her father's sister who lived close to her home in Dangadema and whom she had visited when Chafunga first saw her.

The other thing that made her life in Dangadema difficult was that during this time, her husband Chafunga had days when he and the other warriors in his regiment would be required to go away for further training to keep them fit and ready for wartimes. There were times when he would spend a lot of time constructing buildings at his homestead in preparation for his growing family. There were days when he would go deep into the forests with his friends to hunt some prime animals to provide delicious food regularly to his young bride. All this meant that there were many times that Nyaradzo was left at home alone. On days such as these, she would rise early in the mornings to go and work in her groundnut field. She would only go back home when the sun would be hitting just above the forehead (around mid-morning) to cook some food for herself. She would then do other chores like decorating the walls of her huts with red soil and ashes to paint different patterns and motifs. In the late afternoons, way before sunset, she would go down to Chengura river to take a bath.

"*Sekuru*, have you noticed that your bird is almost always alone these days? It is actually depressing, I feel sorry for her," this was Shupai, King Zihwe's nephew talking to the king as they were walking around the king's residence.

"Oh come on Shupai. Are you still talking about that lost soul? My heart stopped wishing for her a long time ago before her parents even received those very few goods from their poor-in-law," the king answered, laughing.

"Anyway, I decided to inform you, just in case you are not aware of what goes on in your kingdom. It is the visitor who notices the cobwebs in the home." Shupai then said.

"But just out of curiosity, why is she living on her own when she has a husband? A new one for that matter." The king wanted to know.

"Aa-ah, *sekuru*, that young man is like a *dzvatsvatsva* which cannot stay at one place and gets to many places in a short space of time. He finds great pleasure in moving around the entire kingdom and hearing people heap praises on him for having won the girl who refused even the king's hand in marriage," Shupai sneered, at the back of his mind knowing exactly what his words were doing to King Zihwe's big fat ego. For a moment he felt proud of his privileges of being the king's nephew, one of the very few people who could say what they wanted to the king and get away without any harm going their way. Any other person would have been killed for saying such words to King Zihwe. After this short discussion about Nyaradzo and Chafunga, the two went on to discuss different things, but for the king, the thought of being the laughing stock of his kingdom all because of Nyaradzo's refusal to be his wife and falling for simple Chafunga had begun to seriously erode his ego. By the time the two men went their separate ways, his mind had wandered very far away.

During the days that followed, the king announced to his chiefs and guards that he wanted some time to be a *chiverera*, a big male baboon that walks alone in the wild. They left him to be on his own as he had requested although they kept their ears wide open to make sure that he was okay all the time. During these days, King Zihwe studied all the activities and routines that were carried out by Nyaradzo. He got to know the times that she went to her field and the times that she went to take a bath.

On one of those days, he planned to accidentally bump into Nyaradzo on one of the pathways. Nyaradzo got out of the path and knelt on the grass, looking down as was required by the law in Dangadema when a woman was in the presence of His Royal Highness, the king.

"Please stand up and relax. You can talk to me while standing," the king said with a fake smile and tone of politeness lacing his words. Nyaradzo remained in her position without saying a word.

"I said you can stand up and speak to me. Nothing will happen to you. I am the law, so no one will take you to court for speaking to me while standing, okay?"

Nyaradzo responded, saying,

"You may speak to me, my Lord. It does not matter that I am kneeling like this. I am just like all your other subjects, so speak to me, my Lord. I will listen."

Zihwe tried to tell her that she was very different from the other subjects and that he had not stopped loving her even though she had refused to be his wife. He said many other things, but as he said these things, he began to feel very foolish. He thought that he was mumbling many silly words and making himself appear like a big idiot in front of the girl he loved. He ended up leaving Nyaradzo, still kneeling and going his way, cursing himself for being a foolish king. He wondered what it was that made him blush and behave silly whenever he began to speak to Nyaradzo. He was the king and therefore, everything that he desired he had to get. It had to happen. Why was he not able to get

Nyaradzo? Such thoughts would usually make him very agitated and violent.

The problem was that whenever King Zihwe got agitated, his agitation would not go away on its own. For him to cool down, it required that he meted out his violence onto someone else. On this particular day, the unfortunate victim was his second wife. The poor woman was beaten up so severely that everyone in the king's residence felt sorry for her. His excuse for beating her up was that she had cooked gravy that was too thin for his stew.

When Nyaradzo told her husband Chafunga of her encounter with the king that day, he was distraught. Later on, he said to her,

"My dear, do not lose sleep over what the king did. If he really wanted you, he would have forced you to marry him, and no one would have stopped that from happening. He may just be saying these things now, but in truth, he is no longer interested in you. It is well known in this area that the king despises falling for women who have already slept with other men. He believes that doing so undermines his powers and it also weakens the charms that protect him." Although Chafunga said these words, he very well knew that there was no truth in them. He just had not found a thoughtful response to appease his wife, and these words had found their way out of his mouth. The words, however, were pleasantly received and believed by Nyaradzo.

Chafunga laid on his back, facing the apex of his thatched hut, his mind restless because of what his king had said to his wife. He scratched his neck, rubbed his eyes, and tossed and turned, planning what he would do about it. This went on and on until the first rooster crowed, breaking the silence of the darkness. He began to entertain the idea of running away with his wife from Dangadema to settle near his in-laws in the Kingdom of Musita. To him, this was a perfect idea, although it would mean that he would be labeled a coward by society. Yes, he would live peacefully and comfortably with his wife there, but people would laugh at him and tease him for being the woman in his marriage. Men do not do things like that. A man comes up with plans that prove him to be brave and wise. What Chafunga was sure about was that King Zihwe was like an animal. His behavior was driven more by instinct rather than logic. A thirsty cow will only rest once it quenches its thirst by drinking water. He knew that he could not dare Zihwe into a fight. Zihwe would thoroughly beat him up, even using just one hand. Ater that, he could take his wife and kill him with no one raising even an eyebrow about it.

Chafunga was troubled and could not come up with a foolproof plan to take him out of his predicament. By the time he eventually began to feel a bit sleepy, he had made up his mind on running away with his wife to settle in Musita. He consoled himself with the words of the departed ancestors who noted that a coward does not unnecessarily attract scars on his body. All he needed to do was to plan how he was going to disappear from Dangadema without King Zihwe's knowledge.

Just as he tried to close his eyes to sleep, Chafunga heard the sound of the communication drums, and he listened carefully. He listened to the fast five beats followed by the slower five pounds.

Immediately he heard the same sound coming from a smaller drum. He carefully listened to the sound again to make sure that he had correctly decoded the message and then breathed a sigh of relief. The sound was just a notice that messengers would visit the warriors to deliver an order from the king. This was good because it was not a notice of an urgent attack or call for the warriors to go to war. This message just meant that the warriors had to be at their homes at the time that the messengers would arrive. Chafunga realized that he had to rearrange his plans for the coming day. He had planned to go out into the forest to cut some poles that he needed to use as support beams for the roof of the granary that he was building behind his two huts. Upon hearing that her husband would be spending the morning at home that day, Nyaradzo was overjoyed. Such days were rare.

Later on that morning, two messengers arrived and informed Chafunga that the king wanted all the warriors in his regiment to go and commence the building of the national granaries at Katuri Mountain. They were expected to embark on this trip after the following two days. The journey to Katuri Mountain took three days for one walking on foot from the king's palace. All the warriors were required to converge at the king's palace, where they would be given food supplies and tools that they would use during the construction. The central granary for the kingdom was still at the king's residence during that time. The two messengers went on to the next homes, delivering their message.

"So sweetheart, I suggest that you pay a visit to mother and your other folks at Musita during this period that I will be gone. I do not feel good leaving you here on your own for over two months," Chafunga said, looking into Nyaradzo's eyes.

"Going to visit mother and them is indeed a good idea, my dear husband, but trust me, nothing will happen to me even if I am here on my own. As long as my two dogs, Zvanyadza and Semai are here with me, I'll be fine. I cannot leave my groundnuts unattended for that long. I need to weed them one last time. For most of the days that you shall be gone I'll be going to sleep in aunty Mai Shamiso's kitchen, so don't even worry about me. Very soon I'll be having my own kids so that even if you go wherever and whenever you want, we won't be thinking of you." The two then broke into laughter.

Chafunga tried again to convince his wife to consider his suggestion, but Nyaradzo would have none of it. She was adamant that nothing would harm her during that time. Chafunga's mind was still not settled because of what King Zihwe had said to Nyaradzo. He realized that if he mentioned his plan of running away with her from Dangadema, she would panic again. He had managed to calm her down the night before, and therefore, this was not a good time for him to confuse her. He decided to only tell her about the plan once he got back from Katuri. Chafunga was also relieved when he remembered that King Zihwe would be going with the warriors to Katuri Mountain because he had severe control issues. Such a big project could not be undertaken in his absence. King Zihwe was also abundantly talented on matters of construction, and so he liked to be present at these sites to control and give his ideas.

On the day that Chafunga was leaving, Nyaradzo cried so much that he felt distraught. She hugged him and locked her hands around him as she cried, wetting his whole shoulder with her tears. Chafunga reminded her that he wasn't going to fight in a war where chances of dying and not returning home were high, but he was just going to take part in the building of a communal granary at a place where very few people in the kingdom knew about. He reminded her that they would be back together in just two months! Although he was saying all this to her, inside, he panicked and felt scared. He did not want to leave his new wife alone for such a long time. He was very close to breaking into tears, but he forced himself to keep calm and composed. A man should not cry in front of a woman. That is not allowed.

As they walked, every warrior had a bow on his shoulder and arrows in a quiver on his back. In his hand, he held a spear and other tools such as axes or crowbars that were to be used at the construction site. There was also another group, which traveled with them. Members of this group carried other things like maize meal and other foodstuffs. The warriors did not bring any meat, as there were plenty of animals in the forests to hunt for meat whenever they needed it. The brigade went with King Zihwe on the lead. They began their trip in broad daylight. For some time, the young goat herders followed warriors, enjoying their songs and the way they were marching. They later on returned when they realized that they were drifting too far away from their livestock and homes.

The warriors took a direction that was completely opposite to where they were destined. They kept going in that direction, marching, and singing until the sun had set. In the middle of the night, the brigade was instructed to turn around and start walking back to where they had come from. After a while, the warriors began to trot silently. They passed very close to the boundaries of their villages, with the sleeping villagers not even anticipating what was going on. Many dogs howled, causing a ripple effect among the neighboring dogs but not raising any suspicions. At this point, the troops were heading to Katuri Mountain. They kept running until dawn was breaking then they went into a small hill where they took a break. They were now very far away from the villages. Two colonels took one young warrior who had kept on struggling with his breathing and disappeared with him in the dark. When they were next seen, the young warrior was no longer with them. None of the troops asked about him because they all knew that asking such a question could trigger responses such as,

"You can come with us, and we will show you where he is."

They knew that if that happened, you would also not come back. A warrior does not ask such stupid questions.

When they got to Katuri, they hit the ground running. King Zihwe and some of his governors already had a plan on how the construction was to be carried out. The warriors were divided into smaller groups under the command of colonels who would supervise them. The project was supposed to be smoothly and speedily executed as a way to minimize the chances of the enemies getting wind of it. This meant that all the warriors were expected to work very hard. They were all aware that the punishment for being lazy or inefficient could mean that the offender may no longer make the trip home.

Chapter 3

Nyaradzo looked at the patch that she had weeded on her groundnut field and smiled as the dark green groundnut leaves rustled in the wind. Her crop looked healthy.

"If only I can get two more days of weeding before it rains again, I'll have a handsome harvest," she thought to herself as she looked at the small patch that still needed weeding and cultivation. She then rushed home and cooked her meal and one for her two dogs. After that, she went down to the river Chengura to take a bath. She was muddy and sticky from working in her field. Her aunt had once laughed at her for taking a bath every day even when her husband was away. Many people in Dangadema did not consider taking a bath regularly as necessary. The practice was most familiar to young bachelors and bachelorettes who desired to get married.

During the few days that had passed, Nyaradzo had gone back on her menstrual cycle. This had been a big disappointment to her as she had thought that her womb had finally decided to cooperate with her in producing a baby for her and her husband. She had gone for two months without going on her monthly period. Her aunt, Mai Shamiso, had told her that her situation was not peculiar to her, but it was one that was very common to those trying to get pregnant for the first time.

"You must actually be happy that this has happened now. You would not have liked it if the baby had been called by the evil ones after you had given birth to it.

You see, some notorious witches have the habit of calling to them, babies that are still in their mother's wombs. If your child is a clever for nothing one, it listens to the voices of those witches, and it answers. Once it answers, it is gone from your uterous. You must be glad that this was not your child. When yours comes, it will stay," Mai Shamiso had told her when she complained. On this day, she wanted to visit and learn from Mai Shamiso on what she could do to protect her unborn baby from listening to or obeying the witches' voices. As soon as she finished her lunch, she rushed to the river to take her bath.

Nyaradzo took off her clothes made from animal hides. She also removed the cloth that was wound around to cover her chest, leaving her completely naked. She then started bathing, scooping the cold water on to her body using her cupped palms. It was a hot afternoon, so the cold flowing water felt refreshing on her skin. She got carried away a bit and kept on enjoying the water as it ran on her skin even though she had already finished bathing.

The birds that were chirping and making various noises on the tree above her suddenly stopped. Even the soft southeasterly breeze that was blowing seemed to have suddenly stopped. Nyaradzo immediately stood still, inclining her head slightly to the side as she tried to hone her senses to pick if there was anything out of place. She could only hear the shrill of the cicadas from all directions. She felt the hair on her skin slowly rising, and she immediately had the sensation that someone or something was watching her. Her heart began pumping exceedingly fast, and she felt her blood begin to race in her body. She turned around and looked, moving her head slowly to scan the area, but she could not see anything. Her brain began to contemplate a lot of things in a short space of time. Could it be a wild animal? No, wild animals roamed in the forests that were far away from human settlements and most of the dangerous ones preferred hunting in the night!

Slowly she continued to pour water on herself again, rubbing her body and trying to get the fresh liquid on to every part of her skin. Her ears were still very alert to her surroundings. Again, she could hear the cicadas that seemed not to care about rhythm in their song. The birds around her, however, had not resumed their melodies and the sensation of being watched kept niggling her. She could not think of who or what it could be. She began to shake again, and the hair on her skin stood on edge. Her strength drained from her limbs. She could not walk to get her clothes. She thought of continuing to cool herself with the water, but at this point, she just froze like a confused antelope.

She told herself that she was just panicking. This side of the river was reserved for the women to bathe and do their laundry, and the whole village was aware of this. Even small boys knew this. Men would never trespass into this zone of the river. If someone were staring at her, it would definitely be a woman. Many women loathed her so much, but all they could do to her was to peep from a hiding place and nothing more. Even though she thought of all this, she could not reign in her growing panic of feeling that somebody's pair of eyes were planted on to her body. She looked up in the tree, but there was nothing apart from the birds and leaves. She could now hear her heart drumming in her rib cage. She turned to look behind her and came face to face with a huge man with flashing red eyes. He was totally naked. Nyaradzo put her hands on her mouth as she looked at King Zihwe in his red eyes. She could see death in his eyes. She wanted to scream, but she failed. The blood vessels on the king's hands swelled as he moved slowly towards her.

Nyaradzo's brain raced to no avail. She knew that screaming was useless at this point, as many people were still out in their fields working on their crops. The fields in this village were located quite far from the river Chengura. The mad bull in front of her could easily kill her. She could not even consider running away as she would be caught before she got anywhere. She remained standing, her hands still on her mouth as Zihwe slowly advanced closer to her. By this time, all his limbs were erect and laced with billions of swollen blood vessels. As he got closer, he looked more like a muscular buffalo bull salivating and ready for a fight. He got very close to the frozen Nyaradzo, and she removed her hands from her mouth, using them to cover her eyes. At that very moment, she felt a forceful push on her shoulders, and she landed on her back. She could not do anything except to feel her brain shut. King Zihwe did all he pleased with no one to stop or even resist him. Afterward, he took his clothes that he had left in a nearby bush and disappeared in the manner that he had appeared.

By the time Nyaradzo regained her consciousness, King Zihwe was long gone. She sat up and groaned in the process, then she slowly looked at herself and saw a pool of blood around her, and she remained seated. She thought that she had lost her mind. She remained seated, focusing her gaze at one place although she had no idea what she was looking at.

Hours went by, and she remained in situ. A group of women from the village who had come to take a bath saw her sitting in clotted blood. They cussed at her for being so filthy and not knowing the importance of cleaning or hiding her menstrual discharge. They demanded that she immediately clean it up because it was nauseating them. She did not resist because she had more significant problems to pay attention to. She bathed herself again and forced herself to limp home. She left her water container at the river and never gave it a second thought. She just wanted to get away from that horrible place. The women spat as they watched her leave. Some said her filth was like that of a pig.

When she got home, Nyaradzo locked the door behind her and just went straight to her bed. Insomnia knocked at her door and let itself in to keep her company. The following day she remained in her room without bothering to cook nor looking for something to eat. Mai Shamiso sent her kids to her to find out why she had not honored her promise to visit her. She told the kids to tell her that she would arrange for them to meet on another day. She remained in her hut, crying. She still could not believe what had actually happened to her. She kept hoping that at some point, she would eventually wake up and take a deep refreshing sigh of relief from the horrible nightmare.

What Nyaradzo and most people from Dangadema were not aware of was that, towards the end of the first month from the time that the troops from Chafunga's brigade had left for Katuri, King Zihwe had disappeared from the construction site. The warriors and the three governors who were at Katuri had not been aware of this because the construction was taking place deep in the caves where it was very dark, and they were using artificial light most of the time. They all thought that the king was amongst them all that time, and therefore, no one wanted to be caught by him resting or being a nuisance. Everybody was focused on taking care of his duties and targets. Those who had remained at home in the king's province also did not suspect that the king had returned home for a short time, except for Shupai and Takunda, his nephews. King Zihwe had actually stayed in Shupai's *gota*. Shupai organized the king's meals during this short period.

After three days without hearing a word from Nyaradzo, Mai Shamiso decided to check on her, so she went to her home. There was no sign of life except for the two dogs that were lying in the shade cast by Nyaradzo's rondavel. Mai Shamiso almost went back, but she just decided to knock on the door of the bedroom hut. She let herself in, first taking her head in, then dragging the rest of her body into the rondavel. As soon as she got accustomed to the darkness in the hut, she saw Nyaradzo lying on her straw bed. At first, she was shocked. For a fraction of a second, she thought that she might be dead. But she quickly calmed down after she saw Nyaradzo lift her head, then put it down again. Nyaradzo looked so devastated, and Mai Shamiso promptly guessed that she hadn't eaten in a long time. Mai Shamiso was so worried about the condition of her brother's daughter. It took a lot of probing and begging to get Nyaradzo to tell her aunt what had taken place three days back. The two women cried at the same time for a long while without either of them saying a thing to the other.

Later on, Mai Shamiso then said,

"This situation we have on our hands is no laughing matter at all." She went silent after saying this, her left cheek resting in her left hand. She then carried on, saying,

"Here is why I say that it is a complex issue; there is nowhere where you can report this and get a favorable result. You see, for starters, no one will believe you, or even if they do, no one will be willing to even lend you their ear the moment you mention King Zihwe. No one even saw him come back from the time that he and the troops went away. You cannot tell your husband also, because in doing so you will be waking the sleeping demons. You know that men do not like to stay with women who have been raped. I know that it will not be nice for you to be violated like this and then live with a man who will do anything and everything to get grounds for divorcing you because you are a rape victim. It should not be like that, my dear. Now from my assessment of this whole issue, I advise you to just keep mum about it. You should not repeat it to anyone, and I really mean anyone! This is your own business, and it is best if it stays just with you. Your husband has no clue that this has taken place. Even if you consider going back to our land, Musita, you know how hard it will be for you. You know how they look down upon women who have been sent back home by their husbands."

Nyaradzo felt like protesting but then decided against it. She did not have the energy to do so at this point. In fact, she considered what Mai Shamiso had said and agreed that there was a lot of wisdom in all she had said. It hurt so much, and she felt so degraded, but there was a lot of sense in what her aunt had said. She wondered how she was going to look into Chafunga's eyes and pretend that the rape had not occurred. A rapist of a king had polluted her heart and spirit. She wished that she had been initiated into witchcraft. If she had witchcraft powers, she would not have practiced it only during the nights like most witches. She would have gone for Zihwe in broad daylight, making sure that he would be aware of what would be done to him and by whom. She would castrate him using his toenails and manufacture lightning to amputate his legs, leaving him alive to have him feel the pain for the longest time!

During the three days that had passed, the thought of taking her own life had gotten very cozy with her. The idea came back to her very strong at this time. She thought committing suicide would be quite simple for her. She knew of a small but extremely poisonous green frog that was well known for killing cattle after they swallowed it by mistake while grazing green grass. She would just take that little frog and swallow it, and her problems would be instantly erased. She knew of three people back in her village in Musita who had used that frog to exit the problem-infested world. Nyaradzo found out that this thought and plan of actioning it actually brought her some well-needed relief. This she was going to do once Zihwe and his men were back from their expedition. She would die right in the king's court so that no one would be mistaken about the connection between her death and the king. Mai Shamiso had no clue what was going on in Nyaradzo's mind. She cooked *sadza* while Nyaradzo was just planning as she lay on her straw bed. Mai Shamiso was surprised when she then called her for the meal, and she accepted. Her face had brightened up. Mai Shamiso was happy that Nyaradzo had taken her advice as the best reaction to her predicament.

The days went by, and Nyaradzo got well. The troops came back home, and there was much jubilation in Dangadema. Nyaradzo welcomed her husband, Chafunga, who expressed a lot of happiness in seeing his wife. During the following days, Chafunga did not spend too much time away from his house. The two spent a great deal of time together, even going to the fields together. King Zihwe threw a banquet to celebrate the return of his troops. Chafunga took his wife to the king's court where the celebrations were held. Nyaradzo had decided not to go, but Chafunga told her that it was the law of the land for the warriors to bring their spouses to such events. King Zihwe saw Nyaradzo in the crowd but did not act as if something had taken place between the two of them. Nyaradzo feared that if she allowed her eyes to have contact with Zihwe's evil eyes, she would suddenly scream because of the deep anger and hatred that she had for that man.

The return and constant presence of Chafunga seemed to have killed Nyaradzo's idea of taking her life because she ended up procrastinating about it. She ended up going for three months without going on her monthly period. Mai Shamiso told her that the morning sickness that had been gripping her in those days meant that a seed that had been sowed in her womb was growing. All she needed to do was to ensure that she found the plugs to stuff into her unborn baby's ears to prevent it from listening to the infamous voices of the greedy night villains. Talking about the expected baby brought extremely happy emotions to the two women. Stories about expected babies always bred affection amongst women. Women instantly became very protective of a fellow pregnant woman. In that very moment of deep connection, the two women suddenly looked at each other at the same time, directly in the eyes. Mai Shamiso was the first to speak saying,

"Ee-e Nyari, tell me when was the last time you went on your period?"

She did not get an answer as Nyaradzo immediately broke into tears and started crying like an irritated baby. She cried, cursing her ancestors and their spirits for having turned their backs on her.

Mai Shamiso, feeling so devastated herself, consoled her and said,

"Listen to me daughter of my brother and listen very well. In situations such as these, you must always seek the wisdom of our departed elders. Our elders knew what they meant when they said that a paramour is never the father of a child. Chafunga must not ever know that this child that you are carrying is King Zihwe's biological child because then your whole plan will go right into a pigsty. Men have no idea when they plant their seeds into women's wombs. You will realize that Chafunga is going to accept the child, and he will actually go around the whole land beating his chest for fathering that child. On the other hand, King Zihwe should never suspect that you are carrying his child or else he will have all the reasons to command you into his palace for his fourth wife."

Mai Shamiso looked at Nyaradzo and read all the disbelief in her eyes. She knew she had to convince her some more; otherwise, the whole thing would explode right in front of her. She carried on saying,

"Do you remember the days that I came back home at Musita after I fell very ill?" Nyaradzo squinted her eyes a bit as if she was trying to search her memory. Mai Shamiso carried on,

"It was during those days that *tsikamutanda* the witch hunter came to our village after a lot of children had mysteriously died."

"Oh yes, I remember the time very well aunty," she said as she wiped her tears with the back of her hand and occasionally switching on to the other side to use her open palm.

"Good. Now I want you to carefully examine the face of my boy Simbai, ee-e that one who comes after Shamiso. I want you to carefully analyze his facial features and try to see who among our neighbors back in the village at Musita looks like him." Nyaradzo closed her eyes partially and inclined her head upwards, thinking. She then opened her eyes wide open and looked at her aunt before she cried,

"Haa aunty, he looks like Masiriri the medicine man! Oh my dear departed ones! So what is it that Masiriri was administering on to you at his house? You were definitely no longer sick." The two women let out a choreographed laugh that started at the same time, same pitch, and same tones, ending with a high five between the two.

For a moment, Nyaradzo forgot all about her problems and listened to her aunt's crazy experience. Mai Shamiso said,

"Yah, I was healed, but I needed to be certain that I was completely well, so I would go to Masiriri's home to get some medicine. I would usually go in the afternoons at the times that his wife and kids would be out working in the fields. One day, my hormones were raging and up to no good. I was feeling very amatory, and I remember wishing if I could send my waist to go for a hunt by itself. To make matters worse, your *bamukuru*, my husband was far away here in Dangadema. On that day, as Masiriri was mixing the various roots and crushing them for my medicine, I just sat right in front of him and opened my legs just a little bit. I have no clue how Masiriri saw that, but what followed next was him on top of me, and we were breathing heavily, locked onto each other. I went back to his home a couple more days and got what I wanted. Masiriri comforted and encouraged me by telling me that he did not doubt that by that time, my husband had gone through all the divorced women here in Dangadema and that therefore there was nothing really wrong if I also got my aches massaged.

"Now you are the only one, you hear me, the only one that I have told this. Everyone else just thinks that Simbai is my husband's biological son. You must, therefore, behave like a grown woman and control everything that is hidden in your chest. You just have to be gratified and happy that the seed, which was sown in you, is growing and you have a husband who loves you. Just imagine how bad it would have been had you been raped before you had gotten married."

Nyaradzo again heeded Mai Shamiso's advice and kept what was in her heart under a secure lock. Like what her aunt had said, Chafunga walked with his head very high, slamming his chest like a gorilla as a way to release some of his pride for his coming baby. He had shelved his plan of running away from Dangadema once he saw that his wife was carrying a baby inside her. During those days, King Zihwe had directed most of his attention to the construction at Katuri and other strategic places in his kingdom. He spent a lot of his time visiting those places and taking different brigades to the various sites. Even Nyaradzo was now at ease. She knew that as a married and pregnant woman, it was not usual to bump into the king. Once a woman was pregnant or had a child, she got a lot of respect from society. Even foolish men and the village idiots were very much aware of this norm. Married women were not expected to be found all over the place, especially where men gathered. Loose women were an exception. The society did not judge them harshly for that, as people knew that they would be on the hunt.

Chafunga's lack of livestock and wealth prevented him from taking Nyaradzo to her parents' home in Musita for them to monitor and take care of her during the remainder of her pregnancy as was prescribed by the law of the lands. He had to carry out tasks for other families so that they could pay him in the form of goats and other things that he needed to present to his in-laws before they would agree to look after his wife on his behalf. He was also working very hard to make himself and his wife comfortable at their new home. He only managed to get the minimum requirements by the time Nyaradzo had just gone past her seventh month of pregnancy. This is the time that he had gone to Musita for the ceremony, accompanied by his *bamukuru*, Baba Shamiso.

Chapter 4

There were two rondavels, a granary, and a chicken house at Chafunga's homestead. There was no cattle kraal, as he did not own cattle, and he had not even acquired goats yet. This was very rare for a man of his age. He had been unfortunate to lose his father at a young age, and a lot of his father's wealth had been inherited by his older siblings, particularly his eldest brother who had received almost everything of high material value. The two huts stood right in the middle of the yard, with the granary behind them. The two shelters faced westwards such that towards sunset, the sunrays would fill the rooms if the doors were open. The whole homestead looked quite neat with the beautiful decorations that Nyaradzo had made on the walls, using red soils and white ashes.

Chafunga stood looking at his homestead before he set his foot in the yard. He stared and hesitated. Voices in his mind were debating on what he had to do. One told him to just be brave and proceed into his home. Another asked him if he was really confident that he would not break down if he did that. This was his first time back at his home from the time he had come back from Musita, where he had gone to bury his wife. He had gone straight to stay with Nyaya, his elder brother when he came back from Musita. Staying with his brother had helped him absorb the shock of his wife's sudden passing. Chafunga had brought back his newborn son from Musita. The elders there had arranged and instructed that Nyaradzo's sister, Rudo was to take some time off and go with Chafunga to look after the baby. She and the baby would stay at Mai Shamiso's home and Chafunga would visit Mai Shamiso's house every day so that he would spend time with his son.

Time is not stagnant. It moves ahead all the time. As days and weeks went by, Chafunga accepted that it was not proper for him a grown man to continue to be fed and sheltered in another man's house. This realization was triggered when he heard his brother and his wife talking about him. He did not eavesdrop on them, but he just clearly overheard them. It was actually the wife, who was complaining to Nyaya saying,

"Your brother wakes up very late every day," Nyaya affirmed to what his wife said, but he never mentioned it to Chafunga. Chafunga knew that this was just an indication for him to make another plan about his abode. There was no truth in what his sister-in-law was saying because he had been taught at a very young age that it was not proper for a real man to rise from his bed after the sun had risen. He just had to leave. Nyaya and his wife pleasantly received the news of his plan to move back to his own home. They did not even attempt to stop him from leaving. They just promised to help him if he needed to borrow anything from them like farm tools.

Chafunga kept staring at his house like one deciding whether to take a deep dive into cold water from a very high point. He began to see Nyaradzo strolling and sitting in the shade that was cast by the kitchen hut. Nyaradzo appeared to be rubbing her big tummy softly. She kept smiling at him. Chafunga kept on seeing this vision until it was disturbed by his two dogs, Zvanyadza and Semai, who came running and wagging their tails happily. The dogs whipped his legs with their tails as they licked his hands, both seeming to be in serious competition for their master's attention. The dogs jumped, lifting their front legs and resting their paws on his arms and Chafunga patted them. This was when he remembered that he had left his dogs on their own, taking care of his home. He had not worried much about their food because he knew that the dogs would hunt and catch the hares that roamed in the nearby fields. He looked at where he had seen Nyaradzo, but she was no longer there. He tried and wished that he could bring back the vision, but it did not happen. Tears were already rolling on his cheeks, and he quickly wiped them, reminding himself that he was a warrior and nothing was going to harm him. He then walked into his home.

The days that followed proved to be quite difficult for Chafunga. He found out that he did not like cooking for himself anymore. Cooking was not that big of a problem compared to doing the dishes, which he hated. He would visit his friends at convenient times that would coincide with meal times. Most of the days, he would eat at Mai Shamiso's house when he went to visit his son. He made sure that he took a lot of the game meat each time he came back from hunting antelope to Mai Shamiso's.

The baby boy grew up bouncy and healthy. This bewildered many people because, during the boy's first days, he survived on goat milk. Measles came and shook him, but he survived. Many bet that he would not make it, but he proved them wrong. Nyaradzo had named him Shingai, and like his name, he became a courageous little boy. Shingai was not a crybaby, and the elderly could tell from that age that he would grow up to be a very determined person. Rudo became his mother. Many had expected that Rudo was to assume the role of her departed sister since she was the most suitable person to do so. It was prevalent for a man who had lost his wife to be given another from amongst his wife's sisters, but it did not go that way with Rudo. It was not that Chafunga had not warmed up to that idea, but when he tried to role-play "husband and wife" with Rudo, she was furious, and she cussed at him. She told him that she had her own boyfriend, whom she dearly loved, and who was wealthy. She said to him that she would never consider being married to Zihwe's little poor warrior who would never be able to provide for her, condemning her to utmost famine and toil. Rudo also warned Chafunga that if he ever tried it again, she would leave his son so that he would raise him on his own. This had calmed down Chafunga and sat him in his place.

Sixteen days after this event, Rudo's boyfriend came from Musita to visit her. The following day the two disappeared from Dangadema, and soon word circulated that Rudo had eloped. Shingai was devastated by the sudden disappearance of his mother. Mai Shamiso immediately assumed the role of caretaker for the poor boy. Usually, kids of his age would quickly forget about such things, but it took quite a long time for Shingai to adjust to the new set up. He missed his mother so much. This happened when he was one year and seven months from his birth. Chafunga felt his son's pain, but all he could do was to increase the amount of time that he spent with him. Shingai was always very happy when his father came to visit. He enjoyed playing with him. Chafunga had to find ways to vanish when the time came for him to go back to his home and leave him at Mai Shamiso's.

As the days went by, many women began to frequent Mai Shamiso's home in search of piece jobs such as harvesting crops or grinding various grains. Some just came to seek information that was readily available from many other women in the village. Mai Shamiso was quick to figure out what was driving these women to her home. As more days passed, the women moved from seeking work to volunteering their services to Mai Shamiso. Chores such as doing the dishes, sweeping on the yard and in the houses, and even working in the fields were taken off Mai Shamiso's list during that time. The special *sadza* that was made from carefully prepared maize meal and usually only eaten in king's quarters became abundant at her homestead. Shingai began to get a lot of affection from these women. They played with him and bathed him.

Amongst the women who frequented Mai Shamiso's home, was one that caught Chafunga's eye. It was unusual for girls of her age to be unmarried. She was called Marujata, daughter of Ndove. Marujata was a woman who had gone way past the marriage mile peg. She was tall and had big eyes, which boys said were as white as a cow's fresh milk. She had a narrow gap between her center top teeth, but people would rarely notice it. The only time that she exposed this opening was when she would be playing with Shingai. She had a voice that was deeper than that of most girls. During her heydays, Marujata had earned her badge of notoriety for her snootiness when resisting boys and men that would hit on her. She had been like Nyaradzo, but only that she had not been as lucky as her. Her ancestors and their spirits seemed to have sent out a bad vibe that had engulfed her.

As if they had planned it, the boys and men who used to pursue her decided at once to stop going after her. Each one of them had decided that it was enough, and the new ones did not want to add to the numbers of those that had failed to get through to her heart. Time had done what it does best. It had moved, and many of Marujata's peers got married and began to raise their kids. It did not help that word rose and spread in the whole land that Marujata was possessed by the spirit of the ancestor aunt of her clan, who was said to have died at old age without getting married. They said she had failed to build a home because she had a massive appetite for newborn babies, therefore if her aunt had gotten married, she would have eaten all her children. No man wanted to endanger his unborn children by starting a family with her.

All this had bounced off on Chafunga. He had shut his ears to it all because he had been delighted by how well Marujata and Shingai got along. To him, there was no one else who was going to be able to take care of his son in the manner that she did. When Chafunga asked Marujata to share her life and world with him, she did not waste time before agreeing, although she claimed to have done so because all she wanted was to see Shingai happy and in a home that had both parents present. Marujata's parents were not distressed by her choice to marry a man of a humble background. They told him to take as much time as he needed to raise a very modest dowry for his new wife. Mai Ndove, Marujata's mother, was relieved from the constant laughter that had filled the winds because of her eldest daughter, who had failed to find a man to marry. She thanked her sleeping ancestors who remembered her and finally answered her call for intervention. Many people who watched from a distance whispered to one another about Chafunga, saying,

"That bird has stepped right into the snare!"

Chapter 5

Shingai had made up his mind now. To him, it was all the same, whether he had stayed or run away from home. Staying at home meant certain death once his father returned. Running away into that dark night also meant that beasts of all kinds could make a feast out of him that night. His mind spun between the two options, and he finally settled on running away. He thought that running presented a very slim chance of survival. Yes, the beasts would crush his skull alive, but then he would die trying to fight them. He could not imagine taking on his father in a fight. That was unheard of. A child had to just stand still as his father did as he pleased with him. The beasts that he feared most were those that were sent out by the people of the night. These were difficult to deal with because only a few people knew what exactly they looked like and much fewer could see them. Everyone said that they could actually feel their presence when they got to a place where the beasts roamed.

Just the thought of these night beings was strong enough to send him back into the hut where he slept so that he could hide and try to gather enough courage for him to commence his journey. As for the beasts of the forests, he was not too scared of them, and he was resolute about facing them off. He had not yet seen or come across the lethal ones, but if he saw them, he would be able to recognize them, and he also knew how to escape from most of them. The wise hunters who used to venture into the vast forest, Mazivandadzoka had provided a lot of vital information about these creatures to him and the other boys as they told them stories of their expeditions. Although there were many exaggerations about these beasts, there were a lot of consistencies in their stories. So he kind of knew what to expect. The other option was to run away during the day, but then he risked being seen by one or some of the many big-mouthed villagers who would happily point to his father the direction he would have taken.

As Shingai was thinking about all this, he had packed a few essentials into his sling bag that hung by his waist and a dry hollow gourd filled with water. He had also carried his favorite weapon, his bow, and arrows. He had confidence in his efficiency with that weapon. Many boys of his age in the village would not dare him to a shooting competition. By the time he got to the age of six years, he had killed his first duiker with one arrow shot that went right in the neck.

The young boy closed his eyes and took the first steps into the thick darkness that covered the earth on that night. Even when he got accustomed to the dimness, he could barely see as he walked. He wished for the moonlight but then quickly cursed himself for thinking like a fool. He reminded himself that the wise elders would tell him that a man would first go through a lot before he surrendered to death and that only a coward would allow himself to get a thorough beating while doing nothing to retaliate. He was just going to run away from Dangadema no matter the circumstances ahead of him. He knew the path that he was going to take because it passed through the old fields where he and his friends herded their goats.

As he began to walk, his fear began to vanish because he was still in a familiar zone of the villages.

His stepmother Marujata used to send him to many different places during night times, so he was used to walking in the dark. The thought of his father's plan of killing him came back and made him sad as he was walking. What had gotten into his father that had driven him to consider such a cruel option? It must have been right that Marujata had definitely bewitched him using a powerful potion. If that was not the case, then his father had clearly misplaced his marbles. The mind can travel to many different places in a short space of time. Shingai was taken on a trip down the memory lane of his short life from as far back as he could remember staying with his father. He recalled those good days that he had spent with his two parents, Chafunga and Marujata.

These two had taken excellent care of him such that many people had actually forgotten that Shingai was not Marujata's biological mother. Marujata had loved Shingai so much the way a mother would love her own child. Things started to change for Shingai when Marujata bore her own son whom she called Svotesai. Those that whispered to Shingai had told him that Svotesai was born two years after Chafunga had married Marujata. During those days, Shingai was still a four-year-old boy. He was thrilled that he now had a baby brother who was going to play with him. Marujata also celebrated, thanking her ancestors for their great gift to her. She had said that her enemies had been shamed and that all those who laughed and teased her for being childless had been put in their rightful places. Marujata's relatives began to descend at her home and stayed for long periods. They were free to visit any time that they wanted. What bothered Shingai was that these people did not seem to notice that he was a member of the host family. They would often send him out of the room if they were spending time with little Svotesai.

Bit by bit, Shingai felt the waves of hatred stirred up by this family, drowning him. Marujata began to shout at him and to beat him up for things that she never used to care about. One day Shingai was given a brutal open palm slap on the cheek, overlapping to his ear by Mai Ndove. For a moment, he thought that his ear had been blocked or that he ruptured some part inside. He did not know why he was slapped, and he did not ask why. He just went outside the hut and sat outside in the cold. When his father came back that evening, he told him what had happened, and he confronted his wife demanding an explanation, for it was not proper for him to even consider asking his mother-in-law. That day, the man regretted his action, and he learned a lot. He was told of his feet that looked like those of a hippopotamus. She described how horrible every organ on him was before he was told how he never liked to see her people at his home. She cussed at him and would not give him a moment to respond. He could not say a word but just stare at his wife in disbelief.

The following day Shingai was again handed another three hot claps for no apparent reason by Mai Ndove, and she told him to tell his father again when he came back. Shingai was a fast learner, and therefore he never reported anything ever again concerning the hostile treatment that he received from the Ndove people, which had then become the status quo at that homestead. They would beat the broad daylight out of him for no apparent reason. If anyone from the Ndove family had thick phlegm sitting on his throat, he would look for Shingai, clear his throat, and spit it onto his face.

It was not long before Chafunga adopted his wife's hatred for Shingai. He not only embraced it, but he actually perfected and polished it, becoming more ruthless than the Ndove people. The neighbors were saddened by this development. Although most of them did not like it, there was not much that they could do except to just hang their heads in sorrow. Many said that Chafunga had been given an extreme potion brewed from some of the meanest witches and wizards in the land. Some had claimed that Marujata had prepared a concoction using her menstrual blood and served it to Chafunga with antelope liver. They said she did this so that it would harden his heart towards Shingai and make him think like her. One does not starve to death in a village. Those that were touched by Shingai's plight often made sure that they gave the boy some food every now and then.

Shingai suffered from malnutrition. He developed a swollen and tight belly, but his arms and legs had grown so thin, resembling twigs from a dead tree because of kwashiorkor. Svotesai found it normal as he grew up to physically abuse Shingai. He knew that no matter how much he would assault Shingai, Shingai would not retaliate or even try to stop him. There were times when Svotesai would take a stick from the fire with a burning ember at the end and poke Shingai's soft skin with it. Shingai would just jerk in pain but not do anything to the little boy, who would just mischievously giggle. No one would rebuke the little boy when such things occurred. Shingai wondered why his life had taken such a turn to end up with him having to live so miserably. This had, however, influenced him to learn many things that were done by grown men even though he was still a young boy. He learned how to use the bow and arrow, and he became very good with it. While herding goats, he was involved in a lot of fistfights with the older boys who did not show any mercy on him on for coming from a wicked household. They would beat him up, and he learned how to defend himself in the process, although he was not aware of the sort of training this was doing to him.

Things got very bad when Shingai turned seven years old. At this point, Marujata did not need to fabricate issues to get him beaten up. She would just punish him by sending him to Mai Ndove's home, which was quite some distance from her house. She would send him on such errands only before supper was served so that Shingai would conveniently skip the meals. Shingai did not mind being sent on errands. It was usual for children to be assigned to various chores as adults saw fit. He could sense, however, even at that age that what his stepmother did to him was purely to inflict as much hurt, physically and emotionally as possible on him. Marujata would send him in the evening to go and inquire from Svotesai's *mbuya* if her red hen had hatched. He would only realize his feelings about the message while on the way to the Ndove's. He would cry and get over it with no one seeing him. Any form of resistance to such a command would result in him getting a thorough beating from mostly his father.

Meals at home became very rare for him. He had learned to hunt the hares that were abundant in the old fields where he grazed goats with the other boys. He knew how to preserve hare meat by drying it on fire. He would eat the dried meat and various wild fruits from mother earth's big orchard without anyone from his home knowing. When he shot and killed his first duiker, he felt very proud of himself, and he was very confident that he would earn some new respect at home for being able to provide good meat for the family at such an age. No one thanked him for it. The whole carcass was given to Marujata's young brother, who was on one of his frequent visits, to take it back with him to the Ndove's. Shingai heard Marujata say,

"The poor duiker was probably dead or about to die when he shot it, but you must eat the meat with no worries."

Shingai had learned his lesson very well. He realized that anything that he would hunt from that time on was his and that it was much better for him to give it to those neighbors who often offered him food than to waste the game by bringing it into his own home.

Shingai's father had become his real enemy. He had become the cannibalistic pig that could just wake up and decide to eat its piglets. When he looked into his eyes, all he could see was blood. He could not establish the source of this bizarre hatred. No one had volunteered to explain to him why his father hated him to that extent. Where had all this come from?

What Shingai did not know was that in life some people volunteer to look for things that are hidden or things that when revealed, will not in any way improve their livelihood or even benefit them. When these people find such items or information, they broadcast it into the air so that their colleagues in the rumor industry can catch the waves, analyze them, and then broadcast them further until the airwaves are saturated with the information. Some of these people had invested their time into looking at Shingai as he was growing up and they had claimed to not see any of his physical features that resembled those of his father, Chafunga. This observation had spread throughout the village and further into other communities of Dangadema with many people asserting that Chafunga's seed had been so weak that Nyaradzo's seed had overpowered it. But still, some had claimed to know it all. Those had argued that Shingai looked nothing like any of Nyaradzo's people from Musita. If this was so, what then did it mean?

The likely answer to all this came from Mai Ndove. Mai Ndove was a close friend of King Zihwe's second wife. She used to do a lot of chores for her in return for various goods. The friendship was mostly based on Mai Ndove's desire for access to unique products from the queen and her fascination with associating with the famous. Being associated with the queen made her feel special among other women. One day she got the shock of her life when she saw a boy who was eating *sadza* in the queen's house. She almost called out,

"What are you doing here, Shingi?" She quickly held back her tongue when she realized that the boy was a bit older than Shingai. It was not long before the song was being sung in the whole kingdom of Dangadema that Shingai was King Zihwe's son. These words were not spoken in public, but they occupied all the airwaves for a long time.

On receiving the word, Marujata did not waste any time. She told Chafunga to find time to take a closer look at the facial features of the king's young son with his second wife and compare them with those of his son Shingai. When he discovered what his wife meant, his eyes became like those of a mad cobra because of fury. For many days he could not sleep properly or even eat regular meals. He got angry when he could not come up with a reason why Nyaradzo had not told him the truth about the boy. He concluded that the king and his late wife were having a secret affair. The two had planned to make a big fool out of him. What Nyaradzo had told him about the king making advances at her and that she did not trust the cruel king was all meant to blind him further on their secret romance. Chafunga remembered the time that he had advised her to take some time to visit with her parents in Musita, but she had declined. This made him believe that all that and his brigade being the first to be sent on the construction mission at Katuri was part of the grand scheme for the two secret lovers to have some time to themselves! The man was filled with rage, but he contained it within him. He took his hunting weapons and went into the Mazivandadzoka. He came back, but the lump that had developed in his throat because of suppressed anger was still swollen and growing bigger. The ancestors had smiled at Shingai from above, for when Chafunga came back, the boy had literally not crossed his path. Had he done so, Chafunga's sharp ax would have landed with sheer force on the poor boy's head.

The smile of Shingai's departed elders had not ended there. King Zihwe summoned Chafunga's brigade to go and complete the construction of one of his palaces, the one that was close to Katuri Mountain. Chafunga went with his anger simmering. In his mind, all the people he met and those who saw him were laughing uncontrollably at him for having been made a fool and raising someone else's son thinking he was taking care of his own! There was nothing that he could do to Zihwe, but there was plenty he could do to Shingai for him to remove the scar in his heart. Killing the boy would surely cleanse his soul. He had a plan. Once he came back to his village, he would go into Mazivandadzoka to hunt. He would begin his trip in broad daylight so that many people would see him go. After three days he would then slip back into the village during the thick of the night. He would take Shingai from his *gota*, telling him that he would be going with him into the forest to teach him how to hunt bigger game. The two would then slip back into the giant forest. On getting deep into the woods, he would just strike him with one blow of his club, tie him on to a big rock, and throw him into one of the many crocodile-infested pools in that forest. He was confident that *Ngozi*, the avenging spirit would not be able to go after him. His own ancestors would not allow such gross stupidity of their son raising another living man's son. They would protect him jealously. The *Ngozi* would just go and terrorize Zihwe because he had failed to take care of his actions and responsibilities.

As the warriors were building at the king's palace, a friend of Chafunga got injured after the logs supporting one of the houses that were being constructed accidentally fell. He was ordered to go back to his village to recover from there. When the warrior got back to his home, he told his father, VaChipadza about Chafunga's anger over discovering that Shingai was not his son. He said to him that the issue was troubling Chafunga so much that most nights when he fell asleep, he would speak out incoherent sentences. The one thing that would continuously come out from his talk had something to do with a murder.

Chafunga had not revealed his plan to anybody, but the woke could see that winds carrying potent evil were circulating over him. VaChipadza as a sage whose hair had grayed a long time back quickly knew what was happening and what Chafunga was planning to do. He knew that in such instances, it was never the fault of a child. A child does not apply or convince its parents to conceive it, therefore, for one to spill a child's blood was something that Mother Nature did not take lightly. Such actions were known to make rain frown upon the land or for winds to bring swarms of locusts to the area where they would destroy anything green that they can find. VaChipadza considered all this in his mind. He planned in his memory to get Shingai to disappear urgently from his village and the Kingdom of Dangadema. He did not even share the idea with his son, who had informed him of Chafunga's pending iniquity. He decided that it was better for Shingai to be killed and eaten by the wild beasts of the forests than for him to lose his life at the hands of one of the citizens of Dangadema.

On the morning of the day that Shingai was to run away, VaChipadza had planned to meet him while he was on his way to graze the goats. He managed to see him before the other young goat herders had joined him. The wise old man began by making the boy laugh at his jokes. He asked him many questions about goat herding before he got into his serious issue. He asked Shingai if he remembered the days that he used to go with his father when they visited his grandparents in Musita. He then got into his issue saying,

"Now listen here, my grandchild. Because of what you have gone through in your life so far, you are no longer just a boy, but you have now qualified yourself to be a man. The whole kingdom knows of your plight. Your life has become like that of an ox that is flogged as it pulls a load. Like I've said, all this has helped to make you stronger and to know many things that most of your playmates cannot even imagine." The old man went quiet as he took out his ground tobacco and put some in the center of his open left palm. He then pinched the tobacco dust using his right thumb and middle finger to push the tobacco into his nostrils, inhaling it three times. He ended up rubbing the tip of his nose with his left palm. Shingai cast a long stare at the old man wondering what he was going on about. He threw his eye on the goats and saw that they had not yet begun to wander away from him, so he decided to wait and hear what VaChipadza had to say.

VaChipadza then carried on saying,

"Now I need you to open your ears and store everything that I am telling you. I do not mean those flaps that are hanging on your head but your inner ears. I do not have the time to explain all that I know about your life but please my son, take these words that I am going to tell you as lifesavers and do not whisper them to any other living soul. If you do not do what I'm going to instruct you now, then you must be sure that your life on earth will come to an immediate end soon. So here is what you must do, when you are sure that everybody has gone to bed tonight, you must rise and take up your bow and arrows, and fill your water gourd, then carefully disappear from your father's home. After you do this you need to walk like you have never walked before such that by the time you feel the first sunrays hitting on your back, you'll have crossed that river which borders Dangadema and Musita. You know the river that I'm talking about, right?"

"Yes, sir. I remember that river," Shingai responded, still not having the slightest idea as to what the old man was talking about.

"If you walk like a man on a mission, you should reach your grandparents' homestead in Musita by the time the sun sets. When you get there, you must just tell them that you are not coming back to Dangadema. If you do this, you will start to lead a new and happy life where your mother's people will give you genuine love and care. They will probably ask you why you haven't gone to your aunt Mai Shamiso's home, but you must just tell them that you were instructed by an old man to go to them because you are in a situation where you can only find true peace if you are in the land that ate your umbilical cord. Do you hear me, son?"

Shingai's face remained calm, as he still had not grasped what VaChipadza was trying to say to him. To him, this talk was full of confusing riddles and was too clogged in secrecy for his young mind to understand. When he crafted a question in his memory to respectfully ask the old man for more understanding, he was stopped before he even started.

"I know that all that I have said does not make much sense to you at the moment, but one day you will understand. Now you must be brave and keep calm because what I am about to tell you will be heavy to receive for your ears because you are still too young to comprehend the words. I am just going to tell you because there is no other way and you have proven to me that you are a smart and strong boy. Your father, Chafunga, has developed an evil plan for you. No one knows the reason why, but it has come to my attention that he is planning to kill you. Shingi, you know more than anyone else that you are not wanted at your home at all, therefore, please my son, when the whole village has rested tonight, get on the road and just go. I have a lot of confidence that you will make it. May the eyes of your departed ancestors light your pathway for all of your days."

VaChipadza stood and started walking away from Shingai without even turning his head to look back. Shingai remained standing where he was with his mouth half open. He could not comprehend how he was feeling. He stood for a long time dumbfounded by what he had just heard. He did not know what to do or think. When his companions caught up with him, they were in jovial moods and enjoying the echoes of their voices that filled the valley, oblivious to what he was going through. He quickly told them that he wasn't feeling too well and that he was not going to join them in their daily games. He watched his goats while sitting on top of an anthill and his head resting peacefully in his two palms. The other boys could see that he was in deep thought, but his face did not betray any of the worries that were within him. VaChipadza had said many things to him, but only one thing had captured and ran away with his mind. His pending murder at the hands of his father had been set aside as something fictitious and way out of his imagination. The prospect of him going to stay with his grandmother forever had filled his whole life ahead of him with so much hope and light that he felt like a prince. He saw all the misfortunes that had befallen him vanish before him with a blink of an eye.

Why hadn't he thought of this before? His happy mind took him back to the few times that he had stayed in Musita with his grandparents. He had gone there three times. The first time he was still very young. The second time he had gone there after his grandparents had asked Chafunga to allow him to visit them. The third time was when his father had taken him to show him where his mother was buried. By this time he was a bit older and could comprehend a lot of things that were going on. Chafunga had also started to show hatred towards him, beating him up at the slightest excuse. Chafunga had then left him in Musita for a whole month, then he went back to fetch him.

What brought the happy feeling when he thought of Musita was that all the time that he had gone there, he had lived like a prince. He was given anything that he wanted. All the people that were close to his grandparents' home, including the neighbors from the many homesteads, liked him a lot. His life there was a huge contrast of how he lived at his father's house, where he suffered more than the slaves that were captured during the wars. Shingai found himself feeling very fond of VaChipadza. He even imagined hunting down an eland bull and dropping it at the old man's feet just to express his gratitude for opening his eyes. He could not just leave everything to fate and allow his father to slaughter him like a goat. No, he would not do that. The sun became lazy on this day, and it seemed to stay on one spot. During the afternoon, everything seemed so easy for him. He knew the way to Musita. The path was clear and straightforward.

Shingai suddenly remembered where he was. His mind went blank, and fear gripped him when he realized that he had left the last villages behind him, and he was now in the fields at the edge of the giant forest. This was a scary place. Grown men tried as much as they could to avoid passing through it after dusk. It was said that all the witches from the Kingdom of Dangadema held their regular meetings in this area at night. Some hunters also claimed to have seen the towering ghosts who resembled humans in many ways except for their size and that their whole bodies emitted flames all the time. They said, at times these ghosts fought each other, and when they did, no one could pass through to the other side. This area also marked the edges of the notorious Mazivandadzoka forest.

Shingai felt his hair stand on the edge, but he continued walking. The sensation that a hundred pairs of eyes of witches and their night pets pinned on him grew stronger as he walked. Many people were believed to be witches in his village. People that he knew and who had seemed innocuous in their daily lives were said to turn very lethal when the sun had gone under to rejuvenate itself. If some of these villagers were looking at him now, then they would surely tell his father the direction he was taking on his flight. This worried him. Some tree stumps appeared as if they were moving towards him, but when he looked at them directly, they would stop. It was quite difficult for him to tell apart a tree stump from a ghost or goblin. Those who claimed to know said that goblins could quickly change into tree stumps or small boulders as a way of hiding themselves for the ordinary human eye if they did not mean to inflict harm on that person.

As he became more and more afraid, he began to regret his decision. He wondered how he had let himself be tricked by the devious old VaChipadza. A part of him began to think that the old man had actually set him up because he was one of the wizards of the village and he was waiting to pounce on him in that darkness. He cursed himself for a long time and only stopped when he realized that he had passed the baleful acres. Even his hair had relaxed. Maybe on this day, the belligerent giant ghosts had taken their fights elsewhere. Perhaps the witches had already gone into the villages to commence their witching acts before the sun rose. His eyes were now on the lookout for the wild beasts even though he was walking on a footpath that was used by people who went up and down between the two kingdoms. He was aware that some dangerous predators would now and then step out of Mazivandadzoka to hunt for the small animals that stayed near human settlements. The predators would also at rare times go for the docile domestic animals, breaking into cattle kraals and goat pens to prey on livestock.

As the eastern horizon began to turn reddish, Shingai thought he saw some animals or something ahead of him moving towards him. He immediately stood still and became like one of the stumps that surrounded him while his heart beat with the rhythm of a war drum. He then heard what sounded like voices, but at that very same time, the tones, and the blurred images of the creatures just vanished. Shingai remained standing, not knowing what to do although his brain was racing all over the place. He thought his time had finally come to meet the witches. Nothing happened, his solitude seemed to continue, so he decided to bypass the area where the evil messengers had vanished. He walked slowly and carefully towards his right side, not making any sound that would give him away. For a moment, he thought that the witches or their servants might not have seen him. He scratched his nose with his little finger as he walked so that his luck would not leave him.

There was tall and dry savanna grass in this area, so Shingai was well concealed. It was getting lighter and lighter very fast, and this increased his hope of escaping the witches. He knew the one thing that witches feared the most, which was to be seen in their nakedness under daylight. If they had seen him at this hour, then they would have probably hidden from him and would soon be rushing into their homes in the cover of darkness. Shingai had heard stories of witches who had been caught naked at cattle kraals after they had lost track of time during their work only to realize that the sun had risen before they had taken cover. This was also said to happen when they tried to bewitch people who had their own particular protection from the charms they would have found in distant kingdoms.

If these were wild animals, then they were going to have a banquet after killing him. His thoughts were frozen when suddenly a group of warriors sprang from the grass and surrounded him, some bellowing like bulls and others whistling loudly, their eyes wide open. Their sharp spears were pointed at him. Shingai was not able to see much more for he just swooned and fell to the ground.

He regained his consciousness, and for a little while, he was confused as to where he was but the sight of the nine warriors sitting around a fire quickly brought him back to what had happened. He was horrified. The warriors laughed at him when they saw how shocked he was. One of the warriors then asked him,

"And what on earth do you think you are doing out here so far away from the village and walking in total darkness son of Chafunga? Has some irresponsible spirit gotten into you?"

Shingai kept quiet, as he could not come up with an intelligent answer to the question. VaChipadza had not advised him on what to do or say if this had happened.

"Oh, so you have suddenly become deaf too?" another warrior asked, much to the entertainment of his crew, who laughed heartily at the jibes. Shingai felt a little irritation from being laughed at by the warriors. He wanted to tell them to stop giggling like hyenas, but he was wise enough to keep those words locked in his mouth. VaChipadza had said to him that he was now a grown-up who could do almost all that adults could do, and therefore, he had to come up with a fast and intelligent response to the warriors. He then told them that he had gone hunting and had not realized that he had gone too far from the village. The hyenas burst into another irritating laugh.

The warriors were wearing black pigments on their entire right sides up to the necks, leaving the right sides of the face untouched. The left side of the face was painted with white ashes from the cheekbone down to the neck. They were members of Chafunga's brigade. To Shingai, this meant that his father was also on his way home or had already reached his home during the night when he had started walking towards Musita. The warriors did not seem to pay attention to what he had told them for their leader just said to him,

"Young man, let's get back on the road home."

Shingai then tried to convince them to let him be on his own since he knew how to get back home on his own, but they told him that they were not stupid parents who would leave a young boy such as him on the boundary of a dangerous forest. They said that they would not take the risk of being blamed for his loss of life by the beasts of the woods. They were responsible parents. Shingai did not even entertain the thought of running from the warriors. They would catch him before he would have taken even three steps. He realized that he had to just resign his fate to his father's cruel hands. He had heard elders saying that death was every human being's way of departing the earth to join those that resided in the winds, and each person had their own time. When death called, no one could hide from it but just obey the voice. His time had come.

The trip back home was quite stressful for Shingai. VaChipadza had told him that his father Chafunga was planning to kill him, but he had not mentioned how he was going to be killed. He had not disclosed that information. To fill in the void of how he was going to die, he began to think about the animals that he had killed and those like cows that had been slaughtered in his presence. This only escalated his stress levels. His father kept a sharp slithering machete that was tucked between the purlins and the grass thatch of his bedroom. For the greater part of the trip back home, he just imagined his father crushing his skull with powerful blows using the sharp machete. The warriors seemed not to have noticed that Shingai was running away from home when they saw him. They seemed to have believed his hunting mission story. They were busy talking about other things while he was suffering many deaths by different methods in his mind. The group rested at the time that the sun was hitting on their fontanels (around midday). They roasted fresh impala game after one of them had shot the antelope, as it was drinking water.

The warriors and Shingai got to the first homesteads when the sun was on its way down, but it was still hot. After passing by a few homes, they got to one where there was a beer party. The warriors did not waste time. They turned and mingled with the other men from the villages. One of them turned to Shingai and said,

"Hey kid, now run straight home before it gets dark. Your father should be home already because he and his crew were ahead of us. As soon as you see him, tell him that Hasha said, 'I'll be by your doorstep around midday without fail' do you understand?" Shingai responded,

"I do understand my father. I will tell him." He immediately started walking towards his home. He did not look back until he had walked for about six hundred meters. He could not believe what had just happened. He walked on with his mouth wide open. One of his top eyelids began to twitch ceaselessly, a sign of good fortune. He was amazed. The elders claimed that the ancestors do not bless a man more than twice, but here his ancestors had definitely given him another chance. Once he got to an area where he could no longer see the huts where the warriors had joined the beer party, he turned from the footpath into the bush and ran towards the forest. He ran towards Musita. The fear of the ghosts and wild animals had left him at this moment. All he wanted to do was to get as far away from the villages as he could in the shortest time that he could. He kept running until the sun had gone down. The mountain that he was using to maintain his bearing could no longer be seen clearly, but he kept running towards Musita. No one followed him, or if they had tried, they would have used the footpath and therefore would not have seen him.

As the darkness grew thicker, the fear that he had suspended came back to haunt him. By now the village was a long way back in the east. He stopped to carefully listen to the sounds. He could not hear even the dogs barking, so he knew he was safer from the people. The witches and their ghosts had no business deep in this part of the forest. There were, however, emperors and chiefs of areas such as these, being the lions, and other forest predators. If anybody had followed him this far, then they would need to go through these killers before they got to him. Fatigue also set in on him, but he thought that if he tried to rest, his father would get to him, and the sharp machete would obey his force and split his head into countless pieces. This forced him to keep walking. He could see the stars and Milky Way galaxy up in the sky, and this helped him maintain his direction. He would drink water from his gourd, as he got thirsty from the exhausting walk.

When he crossed a small stream, he refilled his water vessel and carried on his journey. As he walked on, he felt the weight of his feet getting heavier. Walking became a bit difficult because of the rocky terrain that he was passing through. He had never set his foot in this area before. He sat down at the bottom of a big granite boulder to take a rest. He leaned on the stone and began to smile. He immediately fell asleep.

A cool breeze blew on to Shingai's face, and he woke up, not knowing how long he had slept. It was still very dark, and the bright star that rises before dawn had not risen yet. He just yawned, stretched, and in no time, he began to walk. He was no longer walking too fast because he was waiting for the light from the break of dawn to try to give him an idea of where he was. Shingai knew that he was walking on the southern edge of Mazivandadzoka forest, but he needed to see how far off he still was from Musita.

When one is waiting for the sun to come out, the sun gets lazy and slower. Shingai kept on checking in the eastern horizon, but it was all just thick darkness. He kept walking, knowing that it would eventually rise. True, even if it gets lazy and moves slowly, it will definitely get to a point where it ascents and shines, The eastern horizon began to show the reddish color that quickly turned to bright red-orange. The birds started to call each other from many trees. When the guinea fowls cried, making high-pitched noises, the sun had finally risen. The sun rose in a different direction from where Shingai expected. This was strange. He noticed that he was in a valley surrounded by small hills. He could not see the landmark that he was looking for. He thought of climbing on top of one of the knolls to locate the mountain that he was looking for, but he still could not see it. This did not scare him. The footpath was close by. The sun had just risen in a different direction, but that did not matter. He would just walk in the direction he knew Musita to be.

The pleasant heat from the sun coupled with the weariness of regular walking made Shingai feel very tired and sleepy. He slept under shade and woke up later to proceed with the walking. He could not use the sun to try to figure out where he was as it was now afternoon. Given the strange direction from which the sun had risen, he just walked randomly, sometimes avoiding the thick bushes and going in the direction that he believed the footpath was located. He started to walk very fast again as the sun was going westwards. By this time he still had not indeed confirmed his bearings. He had expected to have crossed Mukukurajecha River by this time, and this was beginning to worry him a bit. People traveling from Dangadema to Musita would cross this river as they were getting into Musita. Shingai had walked a very long distance, and he should have reached Musita by the time the sun would be setting.

His gut had begun complaining of lack of food, but he told himself that he would eat dinner with his grandmother that evening, so he kept walking fast. The sun went down, and the boy began to really get worried. Had he been lost? No, he did not want to think like that. Walking in the bush was very different from walking on the footpath. The distance would be longer for one walking in the forest. He began to run, but he quickly quit after he tripped on a tree root that ran on top of the soil. A random thought came to his mind as he was walking. He thought that he might be in the area where the witches of Musita met during the night, and these witches were causing him to be confused so that he would not get to his grandmother's home. This thought did not disturb him as much as that of what he would do if he had actually been lost in Mazivandadzoka. When he thought of this, he stood still and listened. There was no familiar sound that he could hear. He looked for a place to sleep, but he could not sleep. He was now terrified. He began to cry and cuss himself for having been lost. He was hungry, but he could not think of eating. He decided that he was going to take care of that once the sun had risen.

The morning came, and Shingai was surprised when he woke up. He did not know how and when he had finally slept. He was happy that he woke up alive. When he looked around him, he realized that many leafy trees surrounded him; therefore, he could not tell his current bearing. He climbed one of the trees, and all he could see was just more and more of the same trees in all directions. He decided to just keep walking in any direction hoping that he would find his way out of the maze that he had gotten into. When he saw fresh elephant dung, he realized that he had gone quite deep into the big forest, which even the bravest warriors would think twice before stepping into it. The hunters would only venture into this forest in groups and would have their dogs to help them track their way back to their villages. The stories of strange happenings in this forest began to flood his mind. He remembered some hunters talking about how a lot of people would lose their sense of direction once they stepped onto some sacred parts of the forest. Many were said to have mysteriously strayed from the hunting groups and were never to be seen again.

To Shingai, all this meant that if his ancestors had frowned on him, he would end up being a cuisine for the wild animals. Tears started rolling down his cheeks as he wandered. As he walked, he saw a duiker and instinctively shot it dead with his arrow. The aim was so sharp that the arrow tore the blood and air vessels on the neck of the small antelope. He made a fire by rubbing some sticks together, and he roasted some of the meat. He dried most of the steak and left the boney meat for the scavengers. When his meat was dried, he put it in his sling bag and began to just walk in no particular direction.

The sun went down and rose, and it set again before Shingai saw any sign of human life. At this point, he was beginning to think that being killed by his father would have been better than wandering alone in a dangerous forest. Being killed by his father would have been fast and less stressful than this slow death of fatigue and anxiety, only to then be killed by wild animals. Now his biggest problem was that he did not have the slightest clue as to which direction home was even if he had chosen to go back. He would refill his water gourd each time he got to an area where he found water. He would quickly move away from that place for he knew that many animals would go there towards sunset for a drink.

Chapter 6

Days came and went with Shingai just walking undirected in a forest he was not familiar with. He passed through many different terrains. One day he came across a savanna plain and saw mountains that were very far away. He quickly decided to walk in the direction of the mountains. He wanted to climb to the pinnacle of the highest one so that he could scan the area beyond the hills properly. He thought that he would probably see a piece of land that was familiar to him or some village where people lived. He thought he might even see some civilization that he could go to and begin a new life there. He walked fast, but he only got to the foot of the first mountain on the second day. He quickly scaled it, and when he reached the top, he saw more mountains ahead, but they were not very steep, so he climbed again. He kept hiking up and down, but the mountain range seemed to just carry on and on.

After some days the mountains became more difficult for him to hike. They were getting steeper, and they had many big caves in them. The area became too scary for him although he was now used to walking alone in the forest. One day he was given a big scare by a troop of baboons, and he ran like he had never done before. He kept running even when he realized that it was just baboons like the ones he used to chase from the fields when the primates came to steal crops back at home.

Everywhere he looked, he could just see mountains and more mountains. He was no longer in a hurry to get anywhere because it seemed like he was going nowhere. He was prepared to face any danger, and he did not really care anymore. Walking was now just a way of averting boredom and to hunt the little animals for fresh meat every now and then. He had lost three of his arrows in those mountains, trying to shoot rock rabbits that basked in the sun just before sunset.

One day, as he was about to lie down to sleep on top of a granite boulder, he saw a bonfire at the foot of one of the mountains. He ran towards it as if his life depended on it. The fire was quite some distance away, but he kept running, keeping his focus on the distant flames. He got to a place where it was very steep, and so he needed to descend slowly and carefully. He was frustrated when he eventually climbed down because he could no longer see the fire. It was as if the blaze had disappeared. He climbed back to a point where he had last seen the flames, and it appeared again. He descended again, still being very careful and not wanting to lose the direction of the fire, but once he got down to the foot of the mountain, the flames would disappear. He kept repeating the process with no luck. He thought that if it were a ghost, then it would mean he was now nearer to where people lived. He was not afraid of it. He knew that he was very far away from his home, and no ghost would come for him this far from his village in Dangadema. Ghosts had their rules. They did not attack people that they did not know. Shingai decided to find a place to sleep so that he would try to see where the fire was burning the following morning.

He was up with the birds the following morning, looking for the mysterious fire. He searched and searched again and only found the dead charcoals when the sun was right above his head. He quickly realized what had happened. A group of hunters had extracted some honey from a big tree. The area was full of green leaves that had been burnt to pacify the bees with the smoke. There were also honeycombs full of bee larvae that were scattered all over the place. He carefully inspected the site, not wanting to lure the remaining bees. He could not tell much more about the hunters from the remaining evidence. The area had tall, dry grass, so he could not track the path that the hunters had taken from there nor tell how many they were. He decided to sleep at this place so that he could take the little bit of the honey that the hunters had left. He could only do this at night when the bees would get passive.

The hunters did not come back. The days kept on going, and Shingai became a resident of the forest. Taking a bath became so rare to him, and the only time that he did so was when he crossed the streams. His finger and toenails grew very long and were like talons of old eagles. He would brush his teeth using sticks from *muchakata* trees as and when he would come across the trees. He had learned not to shoot his arrows unless he were sure he would find them after the shots. He did not want to risk losing his arrows in the forest where he could not find the iron ore to make new arrows.

The season began to change. The trees started to shed their leaves, and it became windy for many days. During those days, Shingai caught a cold, and his belly ran for several days. He knew that the harvest season had come to an end in the villages and therefore, soon the rains would follow. He did not worry too much about the coming storms because he was in an area with lots of caves in the mountains. He would get good shelter in these caves.

Months went by as Shingai kept wandering in the forest. He faced a horde of dangers. There was a time when he spent three days in a tree with a lion waiting for him at the bottom. When he saw that the lion was waiting for him, he knew that it was an old one for if it were still active, it would have left him and gone hunting for other animals. Trouble had begun when he was about to fill his water gourd at a pool. Living in the forest had seen him become tough. He could now run very fast. When he saw the lion, he had not waited to look it in its eyes and hope it was going to get shy. He had heard some people say that lions were timid animals and that if one looked at it right into its eyes, it would turn and walk away. However, the lion would, later on, try to sneak and pounce on the person, making a meal out of them. This was not a time to experiment. Shingai just went for the nearest big tree, and in no time he was up on the top branches. The lion followed him. It trotted for a little bit and then just walked and stood under the tree.

Shingai took out a rope that was made from fibers of tree bucks from his sling bag, and tied himself to a sturdy branch in a way that would prevent him from falling down the tree even if he were to get carried away and sleep. On the third day, the lion gave up and left the tree, and it went back in the direction of the pool sneaking up on other animals that had gone for their evening drink. Shingai could see all this from the tree. He was careful not to make any movements that could have alerted the other animals about the lion or to get the lion to come back to continue his wait for him. As soon as the sables and the lion disappeared, Shingai quickly climbed down the tree and ran in the opposite direction.

The rains came and brought along with them rain troubles. One day he was caught in a hailstorm that left his head aching. He saw hailstones that were bigger than all he had seen before. Some were as big as his clenched fist. The storm ended as soon as he got to the mouth of a cave. He fought off big snakes and some brutal creatures in some of the caves when these occupants tried to defend their territories. He knew which animals to displace and which to run from. The streams and rivers became flooded, and it became difficult to cross them. On many days, making fire became difficult as the sticks were wet from the rain and they could not readily catch fire. The mosquitos and other stinging insects also came and made sure that they had their share of him. They bit him and sucked liters of his blood. At some point, he spent many days in a little cave because he was very ill. As soon as he got a bit better, he carried on walking to where he did not know.

Shingai was no longer afraid of living alone in the forest, but his desire to get human companionship never faded. What he was sure about was that he was now very far away from kingdoms that he knew of such as Dangadema, Musita, Chifumi, Chiutsi, Manjeka, Dotarehwe and others that were close to Dangadema. When he was back in his village, he remembered that some people used to talk about the existence of other kingdoms that were very far away from Dangadema where even the languages that were spoken there were strange. Shingai could not even contemplate what it could be like to have people talk in a style that he would not understand. He kept on thinking and being hopeful that one day he would get to a place where people lived, and these people would show him the direction to Musita, where he would go and live happily with his grandmother.

The rains appeared to have taken a long break. The grass and tree leaves had developed a robust and healthy green color, much to the pleasure of the herbivores. Shingai remembered with some nostalgia of his goat herding days. Back in the villages, the well-nourished beasts around this time of the year would bring smiles to those who owned livestock. In the forest where he was traversing, he would bump into a lot of wild animals every now and again, as pools of water were now found everywhere. The animals did not need to trek to distant water holes.

Shingai kept on walking towards nowhere in particular in the big forest. One day as he was walking when and the sun was about to set, he saw thick clouds of smoke rising. He felt his heart beating a little faster. He was a bit surprised that he did not impulsively run towards the smoke and he wondered why this had been so. He was a bit troubled when he realized that the smoke resembled the type that is produced when people would be clearing lands for new fields and they would burn logs and tree stumps, generating a lot of thick smoke in the process. This process was done way before the rains, so who would be doing this in the middle of the rainy season? Shingai thought to himself as he walked slowly and carefully in the direction of the smoke. As he drew closer, he saw a village with a lot of grass-thatched rondavels burning. The roofs on many of these huts had already collapsed into the circular enclosures. Worried and confused dogs were barking and running around in the several homes of the village. Shingai drew closer to the burning homes, but he could not see any people.

His conscience whispered to him, "Shingi, there is nothing for you here, turn around and walk away from this village very fast." Before he obeyed the little voice, he saw grievously mutilated dead bodies lying on the yard of one of the homes nearest to him. The corpses seemed to be mostly of men. There were many flies on the swelling bodies. He scanned the other houses, and he saw more corpses. In some of the homes, the vultures had already landed, and the dogs were struggling to keep them away from their dead masters. Shingai felt nauseous, and immediately, he threw up violently. His knees felt weak, and he could not stand, so he began to crawl backward. As soon as he regained some strength, he got up and started running away from the village and its horrible sight.

But what had happened? He did not know. In his whole life, he had never experienced war, but he had heard that wars could destroy villages or kingdoms in such a manner. This must have been an act of war. People fought, or a wicked army had just raided and killed the men who may have resisted capture. Could this have been the tribe of cannibals that was said to live alone somewhere in the forests and who actually cooked and ate human flesh? He had heard about the notorious cannibals who were different from the witches. It was said that the witches ate raw human meat but only after extracting it magically from the graves soon after the burial of a dead person. The cannibals actually hunted and killed other people to cook their meat. The rondavels that Shingai had seen burning were built differently from the huts that he had seen in the villages and kingdoms he had been to before. He could not even ascertain which direction the savaging army had taken from the burning settlement. He just kept on running far away from that village. He only started walking when he had covered a significant distance. On this day, insomnia visited him very early and kept him company throughout the night. He kept on checking around him, expecting to see or hear something unusual in the air. He did not see nor hear anything except for his heart, which kept on pounding loudly, so much that he thought it would give out his hiding place.

At dawn, he carried on his journey by running away for his dear life to an unknown destination. He wanted to go as far away as he could from the war-devastated village. His body soon signaled that he was no longer feeling too well. After three days of walking, his health had deteriorated a lot more. He felt like his intestines were being tied into knots. Up in the sky, rain clouds began to gather. The area that he was walking in was not mountainous anymore, and therefore, he had no caves to hide if the rains then came.

As if to punish him for thinking about that, the rain did not delay. It poured down heavily on him. He could not even contemplate hiding under a tree. He had been told that lightning usually laid its eggs on lone trees in the valleys or in open spaces. The lightning would then regularly come back to hatch the eggs by striking such trees. It could also assault if a human or an animal got close to its nests on those trees or bushes. Lightning is short tempered and therefore should not be tested. The rain stopped for a while, and Shingai noticed that there were more trees further down into the valley from where he was walking. He walked in that direction to get away from the open areas that were infested with potential lightning nests. As he got closer, he could hear the sound of flowing water. When he got to the denser trees further down the valley, he saw a very big, wide, and flooded river. He had never seen a river so majestic in all his life. He began to walk along the banks of this mighty river in the direction of the flow of the water. The rain came back falling mercilessly on him. Shingai began to stroll as his illness prevented him from maintaining a fast pace.

As he was walking, he would eat some of his dried meat, not because of hunger, but he had learned early in his life that an ill person needed to eat food to help him recover much quicker. He needed the energy to carry on. His head would ache, and when it was done, it would pass on the pain to the eyes. The eyes would feel like they were being pressed into the sockets by big thumbs, and when the eyes were done, they would send the pain back to the head or to the stomach. The cycle of the pain would go on and on. The hippos and crocodiles that saw him walk on the edge of the river must have felt sorry for him because he would get very close to them as he walked, but they would not do anything to him. The rain stopped again for a few more days, and Shingai felt a little bit better. He was able to kindle some fire so that he could get warm and he even managed to get some decent sleep.

As he was falling asleep, he went into a trance and saw a woman who had a very familiar face. He thought it was his mother, but then he had never seen her when she was alive so he could not be sure that it was her. The woman had long, dark, and braided hair.

She emitted a faint light, which made her glow, and the area around her also glowed from that light. She smiled at him and then she said,

"My name is Muthlomo, we are with you Shingai."

After saying these words, she smiled again at Shingai, and then she vanished in the manner that she had appeared. Shingai had dreamt of this person during the days that he was in Dangadema, but her image and the memory of having met her in his dreams would always disappear as soon as he woke up. An encounter with her would usually signal the occurrence of an event that would impact him significantly. The problem was that he would only see the connection between the two in the dreams, so it never made sense to him.

Before long, he was rudely awakened from his sleep by falling rain. He rose and began walking down along the banks of the big river. His illness came back with increased vigor. His eyes were very sore and could no longer see clearly. He hit his head on a tree, which was in front of him, and he fell into the muddy water on the ground. He lay facing the sky. The cloth that he was wearing was now reduced to just strings hanging on his loins. He was so filthy that lice were fighting for space on his head and on all his hidden areas. Shingai felt that he had tried to hang on to life by a thread for a long time, but now was the time to let go. He no longer had the reason to keep holding on. He felt that his life had ended there. To him, his ancestors had seen that it was now time for him to pay them a visit. Slowly he felt his energy dissipating. He closed his eyes and went quiet with his mouth wide open.

Chapter 7

When the regiment and its prisoners of war got near Dzivarenjuzi, the colonels decided to camp for some rest. From this point, they intended to move fast to get to the confluence of the two big rivers, Nyanjuzi, and Manyoka where they would cross to get to their land, the Kingdom of Magocha. It was best for them to pass at the confluence during that time of the year because it was shallower than most places along the two rivers. The rain that had fallen during the few days had hit the group hard, and they had nowhere to hide except to just keep walking in the showers. The rain stopped at night and the morning sky was sunny. They were able to kindle some fires to cook and warm themselves up. The children and a few elders amongst the captured were struggling with hunger by that time.

Colonel Magodo strayed from the camp and walked towards the river. Nature called, and the warrior had to answer, far away from the crowd. The sun had risen, and daylight had filled the earth. There was not a single cloud in the sky; unlike the previous days when rain clouds had seemed to be a permanent feature hanging onto the sky. Even the prevailing southeasterly winds also seemed to have taken a break on that morning. As soon as the colonel squatted to answer to the call of nature, he took out his ground tobacco and began to inhale it from his open palm, possibly to kill the smell of methane that was escaping from his gut.

While in that position and mesmerized by the relief, Magodo cast his eyes on the restless waters on the

Manyoka River, and he listened to the gushing sound that was very familiar to him. The river was heavily flooded. The various objects that were carried by the raging waters fascinated him. Sometimes it would be big logs while other times it would be whole trees being swept away. Sometimes dead carcasses of mostly wild animals would also flow by. Magodo thought that the crocodiles must have been feasting during those days. Then his mind wandered. He saw him and the other colonels standing tall before King Rubonga. He saw the king congratulating and praising them for their successful raid on Chemhindo, the little kingdom of the forest. While still rooted in his daydreaming, his eyes took him to the southern bank of the river, the side where he was squatting, and they rested on something that shocked him.

He was looking at the body of a boy that was near him. He felt embarrassed, having been seen by a child relieving himself. Carefully he pruned some leaves from a nearby bush so that he could wipe his behind, not wanting to alert the boy. He then sprang up and landed near the still body intending to frighten the boy, but the boy did not move an inch. His first thought was that the young boy was one of those who had followed their captured parents. But after another quick look, he realized that this was not so. The boy was very different from the boys of Chemhindo and all the other kingdoms that he had been to. His body had no tattoos and marks other than just little scars. He was still shocked by the sight of this strange boy. Magodo moved closer and realized that the boy was breathing faintly.

What could he do? He thought of just leaving the boy right there, but this troubled his conscience. A man could not leave a young boy to die without doing all he can to save his life. He knew he was under the watchful eyes of the ancestors and their superiors. Why was he the one to see the boy in that state? He was not just in a natural area. He was too close to a very sanctified area, the Dzivarenjuzi pool. The Pool of Mermaids was known for its supernatural mysteries. Many people were said to have perished in the enigmatic pool after having answered to the call of mermaids. Such disappearances of people into pools like the Pool of Mermaids were usually known to happen to those who would have been haughty to their ancestors or disobedient to their instructions. However, some people were said to have been followed by vast wealth after having been sprayed with water, or if sand was thrown on them by the mystic creatures while passing by the sacred pools.

Magodo sought deep into his soul and confirmed to himself that he had not done anything that would have angered or provoked his ancestors for them to want to punish him. He had no outstanding beer ritual for them; it was all right on that end. The pool was still a reasonable distance from where he was at that moment. Also, there was still a significant distance between him and the general boundaries of the sacred place that one had to be wary of before indulging in any sort of activities, especially relieving themselves. He quickly corrected himself. Boundaries were for mere mortals to obey. There was nothing that would stop mermaids from leaving the pools to take a swim up or down the river, minding their own business. However, he still needed to be very cautious of what he had to do with the situation that was at hand.

Magodo remembered a dream that had persistently visited him in his prime life. In his trance, he would find himself swimming in ponds full of semi-solid human waste. Although the fecal paste would be cumbersome, he would always manage to swim and pull himself out of it. Knowing that the ancestors often talked to the living through dreams, Magodo was troubled for a long time, and so he ended up going to consult the dream interpreters. He asked a total of seven interpreters. It was not advised for one to seek the interpretation of just one or two oneirocritics. Of the seven that he consulted, five had told him the same thing. They had said to him that it was a good thing for one to dream of human waste for it signified a lot of wealth that would flow into the house of the dreamer. Messages conveyed by the spirit mediums and oneirocritics were usually cryptic. Very often, they would not say when the said wealth would be accessible to the dreamer or how and what format the wealth would come in. The dreamer would then just have to look out for it. Magodo was a patient man. He had left it to whenever the wealth would show up.

Looking at Shingai as he lay out cold, waiting to die, Magodo told himself that the mermaids had thrown the young boy in front of him from the deepest of depths of the pools, where the mermaids lived in their kingdoms. He told himself that they had given him the boy so that the boy would give him all the wealth he needed. Once he thought of this, Magodo did not waste time debating in his mind what to do with Shingai. He carried him and quickly went back to the camp with him. When he got to the station, he immediately summoned his fellow colonels and explained to them what his ancestors had done for him.

A debate ensued, and voices were raised. The opinion was divided with some urging Magodo to take the boy with him while others were warned him that he was about to invite the wrath of avenging spirits into his home by bringing the strange boy with him, even just by laying his little finger on him. Many people who were listening to the debate sided with the group that claimed Magodo was making a big mistake in taking Shingai home with him, especially when they heard the mysterious boy utter words in a language which none of them had ever heard before. By this time, Shingai's mouth was just frothing, and his limbs were jerking. This started when Magodo placed him near a fire. Magodo was not moved by the warnings. He gnashed his teeth and resisted. He then told them firmly that if there was anybody who could stop him from taking the boy with him, it would only be the elders and the other higher authorities in their home Kingdom of Magocha and not anybody from within his regiment. The other colonels saw that they could not convince him to do otherwise, so they left him to do as he pleased.

One warrior who was sympathetic to the strange boy and Magodo then said,

"Colonel Magodo, your boy seems to be suffering from a severe malarial fever. Allow me to help him."

"Please do what you can do to make him better!" Magodo responded, taking off his eyes from Shingai and optimistically looking at the kind warrior. The warrior pulled out and broke off a clean stem segment of the long joint-stemmed grass. He opened Shingai's mouth and then used the stem to tickle his tonsils. Instantly, Shingai vomited a large amount of bile-filled fluid, some of it exiting through the hidden hole on his rear. The curious people who had gathered were briefly fascinated, and they immediately moved backward, each one crying "oooh!" as if it was choreographed.

Shingai opened his eyes, and he was stunned to see a lot of eyes looking at him. He looked back at these people, moving his eyes quickly to take in as much information in the shortest space of time. He realized that he had never seen people like them in his whole life, and he had not even heard a description that slightly matched them. He could not even decipher a single word that was spoken by these people. Being a boy who had been taught manners back in his village, he tried to politely ask after their health. The people looked at each other and began to speak in their language, which sounded like mumbles to him. Their bodies were inscribed with many different tattoos. Most of these people had long and thick black hair. He began to tremble as his shock was dissipating. He could see that there were many warriors amongst those people.

Magodo took him to a pond and gave him a bath. Shingai could not do or say anything. He had no energy to run away even if he wanted. He began to seek in his mind, where he was and how he had gotten to be in a place like that. After the quick bath, Magodo put him back near the fire. He was given a thin brown porridge, and he quickly ate it all. The eyes of the prying crowd were still pinned on him, but this did not interfere with his eating at all. Soon after he finished, he began to feel sleepy again. He tried to fight the sleep without success, and as he started to close his eyes, he saw the mysterious woman, Muthlomo amongst the curious crowd. Muthlomo smiled at him, and she began to move backward and away from the group. At that time, her appearance was similar to that of those strange people, with some tatoos also. Shingai tried to call her, but he could not find the strength to do it. As Muthlomo disappeared, Shingai closed his eyes.

When he woke up, a man gave him a liquid that was mostly water but with some plant roots and herbs that he did not know. He just drank it. The fluid induced another round of vomiting, but soon after that, he began to feel much better. The people tried to talk to him again, but they still could not understand each other. Magodo looked at Shingai right into his eyes, and Shingai reciprocated the look. They read into each other's soul, and they clicked. Shingai convinced himself that it was not going to be a problem for him to stay with these people. It was possible that these people were planning to kill him or to make him live as one of their slaves. He concluded that there was no problem in them taking him with them. As much as he tried to think back, the memory of where he had come from did not come back to him. He could not tell why he had gotten into the situation that he was now in.

Chapter 8

The highest decision-making body in the Kingdom of Magocha, after the king was made up of eleven men who were known as The Council of The Wise Eleven. There were eleven districts in Magocha, and a Governor headed each one of these. Each area was expected to independently elect a man whom the citizens unanimously agreed to be full of wisdom and of a distinctive character to represent them before the king's court as their Governor in the council.

The long departed forefathers of the land had demarcated the kingdom into the eleven districts and established that the eleven heads of these districts form The Council of The Wise Eleven to assist the king in running the affairs of Magocha. They had deliberately chosen an odd number for the governors as a way to ensure that they would always be a majority on verdicts of critical issues concerning the kingdom. The eleven Governors would vote, and the decision that had the support of six or more Governors would be recommended to the king. Although most of the times the recommendations made by the Governors would influence the king's decision, the king had veto powers. He could override the decisions of the council and just do as he pleased without anyone trying to convince him otherwise. The king was mighty and feared.

The king's home was in an enclosure built of granite stone bricks. Inside the high wall, were two guesthouses that were occupied by two governors that would be on duty. The eleven governors were on a duty roaster that would see two of them staying close to the king for two months at every shift. It was important for these governors to help the king with decision making when matters that needed urgent attention arose and could not wait for the whole council to be summoned by the king.

Most of the court and government proceedings were held under the shade of a giant and evergreen tree, with the king's throne always under the shade and close to the massive tree trunk. The seats of the governors and that of the king formed a sort of blunt crescent. There were six seats on one side of the throne and five on the other. Those invited to events would sit on the other flank, facing the king and his governors. This place was always kept very clean, with four warriors guarding it all the time. None of the visitors were allowed to bring their weapons into the king's court except for these guards and the governors. They would leave their arms with a guard before they started descending the long stairway with short stairs that led to the court.

Although Shingai no longer knew where he had come from or what sort of people he had lived with before, he could tell that the court at the king of Magocha's palace was very well organized and pleasant to look at. He and Magodo took seats in the middle of the front row. King Rubonga wore a headgear made out of guinea fowl feathers. The crown also had smaller patches of black and white feathers from smaller birds. It also had three sharp porcupine spines pointing upwards, seen from the front central part of the crown. A thick belt made from the skin of a leopard's tail held the feathers and the barbs together. The king's upper torso was covered with a soft leopard hide, which complemented his headwear, although there were more spots on the headwear.

Behind the king, were two vicious and beefy looking warriors. Shingai thought they were scary to look at. He thought he could see blood dripping from their eyes. The warriors seemed to be very alert. Shingai looked around and saw that most of the people who were present at the court had tight faces. He wondered why this was so and ended up assuming that there must have been a funeral of a famous individual in the area. King Rubonga was a well-built man who had gone past his middle age. He had muscular arms, and he too wore a mean face. He was a man of few words during court times. His governors did most of the talking, asking questions and interjecting speakers every now and then. On the first day, Shingai did not even hear the king's voice.

Colonel Magodo was asked to share his story with the gathering, and he began to talk. Shingai did not understand a word of what was being spoken, but he could see that the people were talking about him. Magodo explained how his ancestors had smiled on him and allowed the natives of the underwater world of Manyoka River to give him a special boy. The governors asked the colonel a lot of questions. When they were all satisfied with their queries, they ordered the colonel and his family to go back to their home and to return to the king's court after three days. The Council of The Wise Eleven needed some time to analyze and digest the matter, which they said looked simple but had the potential of having inherent dangers that could be harmful to the kingdom.

Colonel Magodo was a father of six, and of the six children, four were girls. His eldest son had left his *gota* and was, therefore, living with his wife. His other son Kurauone shared his *gota* with Shingai. Kurauone was older than Shingai by a good three years. When he spoke, Shingai could not understand a single word, but he could tell that he was a good-hearted boy. Mai Magodo did not complain to her husband about bringing a strange boy into her home. She had been scared of the unknown, but her husband had assured her that all was going to be well. Together they communicated to the rest of the family members that Shingai was to be well treated and respected as any other member of their family.

When the three days had passed, Colonel Magodo and his family returned to King Rubonga's court. The family was asked if they had all agreed to take Shingai into their home, and they confirmed that they were all in agreement. They cited many other families who were staying with strangers from other lands and the prisoners of war who were working for some families without any problems. Three of the eleven governors kept shaking their heads in apparent disapproval as the Magodo family was giving their testimony. The other eight did not show much concern. Some of them actually seemed curious as to how it was going to pan out if they allowed Magodo to keep the strange boy who did not have a single tattoo on him like a newly born baby.

One of the governors who was known as Governor Gondo stood up and respectfully clapped his hands twice before saying,

"My fellow citizens of Magocha, I want you to know that the matter we have here is not bad nor complicated at all. If we look amongst ourselves, you will realize that most of us are living with complete strangers in our homes who help us with various chores. We all know that the wisdom of our elders has not left us. They used to say that, 'He who brings a skunk into his home exposes his own family to its pungent smell.' If Colonel Magodo has by bringing that strange young boy into his home, invited the wrath of some unknown spirits, then surely those spirits will deal with him and his family as they please. The avenging spirit is intelligent. It follows him that would have awakened it. When it finds him, it tracks his bloodline and makes sure that his family's stay on this earth is cut short. If the good colonel's ancestors gave him this boy, then who are we to deny him from keeping his boy? We may even find ourselves upsetting our ancestors as we try to disrupt their plans.

"Let us remember that from up there, they have a much better view of what is going on down here. What we could actually ask is for Magodo to update The Council regularly on the boy's developments as he grows. Magodo should also keep the eyes in his mind open for him not to miss anything crucial that we might need to know on these developments. We will wait until the boy can speak our language and then he will tell us exactly where he comes from. We, therefore, say to you Magodo, take care of this child but bear in mind that this boy is very different from us. His umbilical cord is not buried in our lands, and therefore his ancestors are not here. Let this be crystal clear to you colonel."

People clapped their hands in agreement as Gondo sat down. King Rubonga nodded his head with his eyes fixated on Shingai then he congratulated Colonel Magodo on the task that he and his fellow colonels had succeeded at when they raided the little forest kingdom, Chemhindo. The court session was dismissed. Some people rose to congratulate Magodo on being blessed by the revered river people as they proceeded to their homes.

Chapter 9

Shingai began by learning the names of many people, starting with those of Magodo's close family members, then those of his neighbors and eventually those of the influential leaders of the Kingdom of Magocha. After some time, he could understand some words of the language that was spoken by the people of Magocha, but he was not quick to let people know of his progress. People would talk about him in his presence, and he would pretend to not understand them. He enjoyed this because he got to know what many people thought of him without them being aware that he could understand them.

During his early days in Magocha, many people feared him, and others even hated him. Some speculated that he was a child born by the evil spirits who were sent to destroy the whole kingdom of Magocha. Some claimed that he was a son of the mighty witches and wizards from far away who had dumped him so that whoever would take him to their home would invite a lot of bad luck and bad vibes into their home. When he met kids of his age on the footpaths, they would turn to walk far off the path to avoid being in the same space with him. Pointing at him was equaled to pointing to a grave. There was a story that did the rounds of a boy who had his fingers bent backward and remained like that after he pointed at Shingai. There were also claims that his shadow actually started some wildfires after he walked through dried grass.

It so happened that before Shingai could speak the language of the land, two of Magodo's daughters got married to one man at the same time. The man was a prince, one of the sons of the king of Magondo. The prince happily paid a huge dowry price for the two girls. He voluntary gave five-fold what Magodo had asked for. He brought a big herd of cattle and sheep, and he also brought various precious stones with him. He brought beautiful leather skins from rare wild animals such that Mai Magodo was one of the most elegantly dressed women in her village in those days. The word about this marriage was told in all the districts of Magocha and even further. It did not take long before people began to claim that Magodo's fortune was a result of Shingai's presence in his home. Many began to whisper,

"The boy has now begun his work."

In no time, Shingai had transformed from being the son of the dreadful winds to be one from the supreme ancestors. Suddenly people began to like him. People wore broad smiles when they met him. When they met him on the paths, they found ways to have him shake their hands. Some older people even went the extra mile to hold his palm with both their hands when they greeted him, an action that was reserved for highly respected people. All this was done in an attempt to rub off some of his powers on to themselves. Both the young and the old idolized Shingai.

Mr. Kanisiyo, a neighbor of Colonel Magodo, had his leg amputated at the knee after having been attacked by a crocodile as he was walking along the banks of Manyoka River near Dzivarenjuzi, the Pool of Mermaids. It was said that the man had had many sleepless nights of constant nagging from his wife as she urged him to be like other men who knew how to attract fortune. VaKanisiyo was fortunate in that his dogs were able to pick his scent when a search party was sent out to look for him. His grandchildren were able to take him to a medical practitioner, who was able to apply a concoction of herbs, which fortunately prevented infection and further deterioration of the wound on time. Although he was successfully healed, he ended up having to walk with the support of a wooden crutch.

Shingai grew and began to fluently speak the language of the Magocha people. He began to learn a lot about the kingdom. It happened one day, as Magodo was tilling in his field that he hit a rock crust with his digging tool and a fragment of the rock shot up violently. It was immediately followed by a gust of water shooting upwards. The water kept oozing from the ground ceaselessly. Magodo thought the water would stop, but it just carried on and on. Shingai told him that he had heard of places where rainfall was erratic all year round and that in one of those places, some intelligent people would harvest the water and use it to irrigate their crops to attain good harvests. He said Magodo could try to do the same to his plants from the supernatural water source that was in his field. By doing this, he could obtain an early harvest much to the indignation of his neighbors. Magodo did not waste time. Together with Shingi, they cleverly channeled the water into his fields.

The miracle of a field that had healthy crops before the rains had fallen and at a time when most vegetation was still brown and dusty was quickly spread throughout Magocha and even beyond that kingdom. People heard all about it and for many to just hear about it was undoubtedly insufficient. Their eyes needed to witness the miracle for them to believe it. They traveled from far and wide to see the field. This was not received well by everybody. Some were jealous, and they spoke about Magodo's blatant witchcraft and how he was not even ashamed of evil deeds being witnessed in broad daylight! They claimed that his use of charms meant that the side effects would have a severe repercussion on their own yields when harvest time came. They believed this because the powers that watched over them from above did not approve of a man using charms to get an unfair advantage over others. They all would be punished for not stopping him! Magodo's relatives would ask for Shingai to visit them even for brief moments, but he would not allow such a thing. Shingai would always be at his home.

Magodo's newfound joy, however, did not to stay with him for too long. One day, two warriors paid him a visit and left with Shingai, for the king had summoned the boy. Magodo tried to prepare himself to accompany his son to the king's court, but the warriors told him that it was not necessary for him to do so. Shingai looked at the old colonel in the eyes, and he found himself tearing uncontrollably.

"You do not need to cry nor be despair, my son. You will soon be back home. King Rubonga is a good man. There is definitely something that he probably just wants to hear from you personally, and after that, you will find yourself on your way home," the colonel had said. These words did not console Shingai, and he could feel it deep down in his heart that something was not right. He thought that if there were nothing serious, then the king would not have summoned him. The king was not a young boy, so what is it that he wanted from him a mere inferior subject in the land of Magocha who was even a foreigner? Magodo treated him so well such that he was beginning to feel so much at home with his family. He was starting to feel as if he was staying with his real and loving parents. Shingai wondered why he felt like he was being taken away from his home to never come back yet the warrior messengers had only said the king just wanted to see him. His heart told him that something was not right.

When they got to the king's enclosure, Shingai was told that he would be staying with King Rubonga's first wife. Rubonga had five queens and his house was in the center, circled by four big rondavels belonging to each of the four younger queens. The senior queen was known as Mai Tongai. Her huts were the closest to the king's house. Most of her children were grown except for the young Prince Masimba who was about Shingai's age. The other queens had sons and daughters who were all younger than Shingai. Mai Tongai took Shingai in with open arms, and before long he and Masimba became very close.

Living in a royal residence was a new experience for Shingai. There were no set chores for them as they were of royal blood. They were, however, taught many lessons by several warriors who went to them to conduct the lessons. At first, Shingai was scared of most of the people in the royal family, and he did not trust them. This gradually changed as the days went by. He became more comfortable, and he began to enjoy the high life. The privileges were excellent. He had never been around so much good food in his life. Every single thing he could imagine eating was found in the king's residence. They would only eat freshly killed animals.

They were fortunate enough to choose the type of meat they wanted to eat. There were teams of specially trained hunters who knew how to hunt specific animals and who would target the right ages for premium meats. The king was quite selective when it came to game meat. He loved the tender hogs with good fat cover.

During the mornings and evenings when the king was around the palace, Shingai and Prince Masimba would go to him to ask after his wellbeing. The king did not have much to say to the boys. He did not say much to Shingai and one time he called him and said,

"I am not interested in precious stones or cattle, for I have more than enough already. What I only want is to consolidate my power throughout this entire region. I want all the kings to pay tribute and kneel before me. You hear me?"

Shingai was astounded by the words but could only say,

"Everything has fallen into my ear, My Lord."

He did not know what this meant, but he could not ask. His answer had actually meant that he had heard all the words that the king had said, but what he had to do about them, he had no idea. He could not comprehend it, and this was not his business. Rubonga was aware of what was going on. In his mind, he believed he was not talking to Shingai but to whatever or whoever was in him. Although he did not show it, those that knew Rubonga claimed that he was a very jealousy man. Many believed that he was not interested in Shingai. He had not shown interest in him from the time that he had presided over the court that sat to determine whether it was prudent to let Shingai stay in Magocha or not.

Rubonga had a gift of concealing what was at the bottom of his heart. He could have a seemingly good relationship with somebody, laughing with him, and doing good things for him while at the same time plotting to kill that very same person. For this reason, Rubonga did not allow anybody to look into his eyes. Soon after his coronation, he had decreed that no one in the kingdom was allowed to look directly into the king's eyes. He did not want people to evaluate his soul. What attracted him to Shingai was what he heard Magodo say about the young boy during the first court session. Magodo had mentioned that Shingai was a special boy sent to him by the spirits, and who was going to attract blessings into his house if he was allowed to live with him. From that day, Rubonga cast his ear open so that he could catch and assess all that was happening to Shingai and to the old colonel. By the time that news of the water that miraculously gushed out ceaselessly in Magodo's field reached him, he had long decided that Shingai had to come and live close to his court. This happened when Shingai had turned ten years of age.

A fox feasting on its prey will immediately stop eating it if a lion approaches and roars. The fox will watch bitterly from a distance, salivating. All he could do was hope that the lion would somehow stop eating and leave its kill. The lion can eat the whole carcass with the fox just looking helplessly without being able to fight for its food. This is what King Rubonga did to Colonel Magodo. From the time that Rubonga took Shingai to stay with him, Magodo did not get a chance to speak to Shingai even to ask after his health. He waited for many days thinking that the king would return his son to him, but this did not happen.

It was against the laws of the kingdom for ordinary people, especially the grown-ups, to talk to the royal children. Magodo was not about to break this law. He and Shingai would just look at each other from a distance during the big gatherings that took place in the grounds of the royal residence. They could not talk to each other nor shake hands. The first time that Shingai had seen Magodo during one of the gatherings, he begun to run happily towards him, but he was suddenly gripped by one of the king's guards, whose hand went all the way around his triceps, pinching him on his biceps. Magodo quickly realized that he was not supposed to even ask to see Shingai. He was a wise soldier. In moments when their eyes would meet, the colonel would just nod slowly, and Shingai would put his right hand on his chest and keep it there for a little while to show his respect and appreciation for all that Magodo had done for him. This gesture was also an indication that he missed the man who had become his loving father. This gave Magodo a sense of contentment about Shingai's wellbeing, but it also built some resentment towards his king.

Chapter 10

When Shingai and Masimba reached the age of thirteen years, they were given some freedom to go out and walk into the villages by themselves. They were now regarded as relatively mature boys, and after another two years, they would be joining other boys of their age from the various districts of The Kingdom of Magocha for training and initiation into manhood. This brought a lot of excitement to the pair. The boys would go hunting with their bows and arrows in the woods, and they would also visit random places exploring their land. They would be well-dressed in their soft leather skins. The royal family members were the only ones in Magocha who were allowed to wear garments made from leopard hides. Shingai was not allowed to wear leopard hides, as he was not pure Royalty. He wore cheetah hides. The coats of these two animals look very much alike, but there is a difference in the size and pattern of the black spots. Cheetah hides were worn by close relatives of the royals such as offspring of the girl children of the Mupingamhuru family.

There were four skillful tanners whose job was only to prepare the skins to dress the royal family. They would tenderize and sometimes dye the skins using liquids from chosen tree barks to make different dazzling shades of the coats. These processes would produce beautiful and soft leather garments. The four men would instruct the hunters to hunt leopards and cheetahs of particular ages, depending on whose clothes they needed to make. There were other tanners in the villages that would make garments for the other regular. The wealthy and decorated members of the land could afford well-prepared leather garments as long as they were not from the skins of the animals reserved for the Royals. The quality of the leather worn by one gave away the man and his family's net worth. The lazy and less fortunate were known for wearing goatskins and brittle skins from other domesticated animals.

If the ordinary people walking on a footpath met Prince Masimba or other close members of the royal family on that same path, they were mandated to quickly move out of the way and kneel. It did not matter whether it was a man or a woman. Everybody had to do it. They would shove out of the way, kneel, and face down until the royals passed and were at some respectable distance away from them. A person carrying a heavy load would do the same. This was expected even from the elderly.

During the early days of their freedom, two warriors would follow and watch Shingai and Masimba from a close distance, but after some months, they began to let them roam on their own. The boys would only be assigned warriors from the king's guards if they wanted to explore other kingdoms outside Magocha. But the boys had no intentions of going too far out of their kingdom, for they were aware of the lurking menace from the enemies of their kingdom.

One day Prince Masimba told Shingai about an issue that left his head spinning. He told him as they were roaming in the woods.

"Hey Shingi, what is your take on my father's insatiable desire for wives?"

Shingai made a nervous laugh showing that he was being drawn into a topic that gave him discomfort. He then answered,

"And where did you learn that irresponsible behavior of talking about your father's heart desires? It is not your place as a child to even talk about that. Don't you know that when it comes to such matters, we children should choose to be blind and deaf about it?"

"A-ah my friend, don't you realize that we are the ones that are left embarrassed by such issues? It is being said as we are speaking, that father wants to take a sixth wife, and yet his youngest wife has just had her first baby. Don't you see that this is causing him to make a big fool out of himself? A man of such authority doing that nonsense."

Shingai could not find an answer to the questions. These issues had never bothered him at all. He did not even want to talk about it. It was too uncomfortable for him, and he would have preferred talking about the hot girls in the kingdom! But he quickly managed to come up with a question so that it would not seem as if he lacked concern for what was bothering his mate. He asked,

"But who is this woman that he is said to want to take in, where is she from, do we know her, and Masimba, who told you about all of these things that I have no knowledge about, nor have I heard about?"

"Ummnn, this one, that Madhlira's daughter who is the same age as us, what is her name by the way? Ummnn a-ah the name keeps, it's,"

Shingai quickly interjected,

"Aren't you trying to say Ndakaziva -?"

"Yes, that's her. Ndaka can you handle?" Masimba lit up.

Shingai laughed and told Masimba that he was bluffing. He said that it could not be true and he kept asking him who had told him such a lie. After a while, Masimba explained to him that he had overheard their mother Mai Tongai and Mai Simbai, the king's third wife talking to each other. In their talk, the women had mentioned that there seemed to be a hindrance to the king's plan because Madhlira had already received some precious stones and a cow as part of the dowry for Ndakaziva from a man who lived in the Kingdom of Machera. This, they had said, happened when Ndakaziva was still a very young child.

"Ummnn, yeah there is quite an issue here. But Ndaka is still too young to be married. This cannot be possible." Shingai said as he shook his head in disbelief.

"Mum and *mainini* Mai Simbai were saying that she is still a baby who is on her mother's breast, but they can't do anything about it because you know, when father is determined to do something, nobody can stop him. They were saying that they would try to ask *bamunini* Vandirai to try and knock some sense into his brother's head."

Getting a solution from Vandirai was not guaranteed. He was a secretive and unpredictable man. He rarely involved himself in the Mupingamhuru family matters. Lord Vandirai was King Rubonga's young brother. The two shared the same father, but they had different mothers. Rubonga's queens had contemplated getting his sisters to intervene, but they had hit a stone wall on that route. None of the king's sisters was bold enough to talk to him about such matters. Even if one of them had mustered the courage to engage him, the king would have just offered her a deaf ear. When it came to women who caught the king's eye, no one could either criticize nor talk him out of it. This was something that he alone would begin and finish.

The matter of the king's intention to marry Ndakaziva remained on Shingai's mind for a long time. When he looked at the king's queens, he thought they looked quite beautiful and loveable except for Mai Chipo, Rubonga's fourth wife. Many had wondered what exactly Rubonga had seen in her. Shingai was troubled. He pondered where the king's insatiable desire for wives came from and if it was ever going to stop. It also bothered him a lot that it seemed Rubonga took wives for the sole reason for them to bear him children because he did not have time to spend with them. If he were genuinely going to take the young Ndakaziva to be his sixth wife, it would then mean life would have ended for the poor girl right away. To Shingai, all of this was just pure wickedness. To him, this was like the case of the inconsiderate snake that would bite and kill animals that it would not eat. Just thinking about it gave him goosebumps. He felt as if Rubonga was camped in his mind and that he would punish him just for entertaining such thoughts. But what would he lose by erasing all these thoughts? This is what he was going to do. He would pin his lips together with a thorn. If he did this, then it would not be possible for him to be judged for a case that he would have nothing to do with.

A month passed from the time that Shingai had heard about the king's intention to marry Ndakaziva without anything proving it to be a matter of fact. After that month had passed, word began to circulate in the winds that Ndakaziva had eloped and gone to the Kingdom of Machera to live with the man who had paid dowry for her when she was still a little girl. By that time it was common knowledge in Magocha that the king had intended to take Ndakaziva as his wife. The king's wives, especially the younger ones, were happy and relieved because Ndakaziva had run away from the madness of it all. Even Masimba had said the scourge of that embarrassment had passed them by the wayside. Rubonga did not show any emotion that gave away how he truly felt about it. No one could tell nor ask him about such.

What happened after the days that followed left many people dumbfounded. On one of the weekdays that was reserved for resting and not doing any intense labor in Magocha, Madhlira, his young brother, and two other men arrived at the king's courtyard. With them was a young girl who seemed to be aged between six or seven years. They spoke briefly to two guards who were on duty that day. The guards then took the little girl and went in the direction of the queens' residents. They went straight to Mai Tongai's big hut, and each knelt on one knee before the first queen. One of them then spoke.

"We have brought this girl to you. The king says you must look after his new wife."

The young girl was timid. She was shaking all over, and her eyes had turned red from crying for a long time. Mai Tongai quickly spoke in disbelief.

"What is it that you boys are trying to say? I do not understand. Tell me what exactly you are saying?"

The guard replied,

"This girl has been given to the king to be his wife by Madhlira. The king says that she should live in your house in the meantime and that you should look after her. He also said that he will speak with you about it when he comes back."

Mai Tongai opened her mouth, trying to say something but the words could not roll off her tongue. She kept on staring at the guards with her mouth open. As she was about to say something, the other guard beat her to it.

"Mother, allow us to go back to our posts. We do not know anything more about this than what we have told you. His Highness said that he would come and speak with you about it. I'm sure you will get the full details from him." The warriors stood up and went back to their posts. By that time Madhlira and his team had already left. Mai Tongai stood with her hands resting on her waist, and she called her fellow queens to come and witness something that was definitely out their world.

The queens went to her, and she told them about it. All the women looked at the little girl at the same time, some full of disdain. Some cursed and some snorted while some expressed fake sympathy. They all could not believe what was happening. Even wives number four and number five who used to continually fight each other over the king found their vigor and anger lost on that day. The little girl began to cry uncontrollably with her head inclined on her side. The other young royal kids had now approached and made an oval around her. Mai Tongai then asked the little girl,

"My daughter, what is your name?"

"My name is Mukai. I want to go back to my mother now!" The little girl spoke, punctuating her response with sobs. As soon as she answered, she burst into a louder cry. The women became genuinely touched. One of them shed a tear and wiped it before anyone had realized it.

Mai Tongai consoled Mukai and told her that she would certainly go back to her mother, but she had to eat some food and to gain some strength. She asked her to follow her into her kitchen. Mukai tried to resist, but eventually, she followed her. The eyes of the king's wives and children were pinned onto her back as she walked into the big thatched kitchen.

King Rubonga had married all his other wives when they were matured and were ready to take on the roles of wifehood. What he had done this time was new. His queens were greatly troubled and wondered what it was that had gotten into their king to partake in an act as despicable as that. But none of them could say anything about this issue to the king. They knew that the king could thoroughly beat up any one of them without fearing or suffering any consequences for it. If he had not been crowned king, Rubonga would have been sat continuously before the council courts in the villages for wife beating.

It was only Mai Tongai who could sit down to talk to him about many issues and sometimes to even restrain him from doing certain things. Also, as that was, she had her limits. She was not concerned about him taking more and more wives. She was no longer as jealousy as she had been when Rubonga had taken his second wife because she was now regarded as a mother to everyone in the kingdom, including the other queens. Mai Tongai could sense it deep down that there was certainly something that had prompted her husband to do what he had done. She even thought that this was Rubonga's way of covering up the embarrassment that had ensued when he failed to marry Ndakaziva. But even if it had been that, Ndakaziva was also still a child, and she was still far from reaching the age at which she would be ready to become a wife.

So what could have driven him to do this? Could it have been from the new medicine man that had come to practice in Magocha and had become a favorite with the king? If it was him then definitely his ancestral spirits were perennially sleepy if they could come up with such lame prescription for whatever the intended result was. Mukai was a cute little girl, but this did not mean much. Some women who were once cute little girls had turned into ugly grown women. How could a whole mature man even look at such a young girl like that? Not Rubonga. No! She was going to unearth it in some way. She was not in a hurry to get answers anyway.

Deep down, Shingai was troubled. He thought he remembered hearing it being said by the elders, that such actions could invite serious trouble for a whole kingdom. It was claimed that it could cause the senior residents of the spirit world to renege on their duty of providing rain and good harvests. They could also send their armies to bring famine and diseases to that particular kingdom. Shingai wondered why the ancestral spirits of Magocha seemed to condone such stupid behavior. How could Mukai's mother have agreed to marry her off when she was still such a little child? All these questions and concerns just kept doing rounds in his mind. The mind is difficult to harness and control. He knew how to keep his mouth shut, and he reminded himself that this was not meant to bother him since there was just nothing he could do to stop it without losing his own life. Even if Prince Masimba was going to try to make him talk about it, he was just going to find a way of changing the subject. Fortunately for him, Masimba did not talk about it again.

King Rubonga returned from his travels and gathered his family and told them formally that Mukai had come to stay with them. She was going to be *mainini* to everyone in the palace because she was like a young sister to the queens. He warned everyone to not make life difficult for Mukai in any way if they valued their peaceful stay in the king's home. He ended by asking if any one of them had a problem with that arrangement. None indicated that they had an issue with it, so the case was closed just like that. The days spun, and Mukai began to get accustomed to living at the king's home. Before too long, the royal family had forgotten that Mukai was the king's wife because she was treated just like the other children living in the king's home. The king's children addressed her as "*Mainini* Mukai," but the queens just called her by her name only. Rubonga did not talk to her at all. This strengthened the belief of the queens and many other people in the kingdom that the king had only taken Mukai for some ritual purpose. They believed that this was definitely a prescription by Gezi the *n'anga*. What they could not certainly put their finger on was what the medicine man's order was for. They could not even imagine what would happen in the end.

Chapter 11

When Shingai and Masimba reached their sixteenth year from birth, they prepared to go to the Boys Initiation School like many other sixteen-year-olds in the Kingdom of Magocha. There, they would be taught how to be real men. The Initiation process was emotionally stressful to many parents in the kingdom, especially the mothers. The boys would be trained to survive under inhumane conditions. So hard was the training that each year, there would be several boys who would not make it back to their homes. Many women that had sons turning sixteen would cry openly as the days for the training approached. A lot of men also felt the pain, but they would not show it. Turbulence in a man's heart should remain hidden there for him to deal with.

The mothers would prepare a lot of food for their boys to eat during their journey. The venue was far away from the villages of Magocha. It would take them five days of walking from the King's courtyard to reach the place, taking only a few breaks along the way. The boys would stay there for a whole year before returning to their homes. All the sixteen-year-old boys would first gather at the King's outer court for the King to address them and give them words of encouragement. The group would then leave the King's court during the day, led by some of the elderly instructors on their way to the Pengapenga Mountains, where the training would take place.

At the school, the boys would learn a lot of life skills. They would be equipped with skills that one needed to survive on their own even in the wild, like swimming, hunting, wrestling, boxing, and using tools and weapons such as spears, bows, and arrows. They were taught how to fight in wars as teams and how no man should be left behind at the mercy of the enemy on the battlefields. Bravery was stressed all the time during the course. A warrior was supposed to be so brave that it was forbidden for him to return to base or home with an injury on his back inflicted by a weapon of an enemy. Such an injury could only result from a coward running away from his foe. Even on a tactical retreat during battle did not warrant a warrior exposing his back to the enemy.

Different instructors taught different skills. Some instructors taught the boys how to identify and extract unique roots, herbs, tree bucks, and the like, for use as medicine to cure ailments that did not need *n'anga* or specialist medicine people that prescribed medications only after consulting those from the spirit world. Some instructors taught about societal norms and values.

"It is only a foolish man who lays his hand on his wife or who is even seen getting into an altercation with a woman in public." A teacher would be heard talking to a group of boys. By the time that the boys would return to their villages in the districts, they would be capable of living totally on their own, and even if they were to take wives soon after the course, they could run their families just like other grown-up men in Magocha. Above all, it was a must for each of the boys to be able to go to battle if enemies of Magocha came to attack, or if the King decided to attack another kingdom.

The assessment of the boys on the initiation course was used to assign the graduates to various jobs in the state. Being drafted into the army was the most envied state duty by the graduates. After the warriors had been drafted into the various regiments, came those that were assigned to hunt for the King and his governors, and the guards to be placed at strategic sites throughout the eleven districts of Magocha. Those that survived the training but did not meet the grade for these top priority duties were assigned to work in the fields of the soldiers that would have gone to war or who were on the King's other assignments. The boys that made this group were also tasked to smash and carry granite rocks that were used to build the walls and houses at the King's residences and shrines in Magocha. Being a member of this group brought a lot of shame to the boys and their families. They would not walk with their heads high in public. The hot girls despised them so much that the boys would usually marry mostly desperate spinsters and single mothers in their villages. This piled pressure on the boys when they went for training to try to attain the highest grades. However, each year, there would always be a group that failed to achieve the top grades needed to escape coming back home as a member of that notorious group of shame.

By the time that Shingai and Masimba reached the age of fifteen years, they had long started to secretly take some of the lessons that they would learn at the initiation school in the Pengapenga Mountains. This tradition was practiced in the royal family to avoid the embarrassment of having the King's sons performing below the expected standard during the training. When the boys got to Pengapenga, they were all treated as equals. Royalty or nobility was not recognized for the duration of the course. It did not matter whether the boy was from the royal house or if he was a son of a member of the District Governor; they were treated like any other boy on training. This was one of the laws that were strictly observed from generation to generation in Magocha. Shingai did not find the training very challenging because many of the lessons that he was given; he had been through before when he roamed on his own in the big forests when he was still nine years of age. He had also taught Prince Masimba some of the skills during their play times when they were still young boys. Even though they had done all this, no one was certain as to how the classes would go that year. The instructors would leave the villages for a long time to carefully design the training course at Pengapenga. Each year they would bring out something new, but one thing was always sure; the boys would find the training very tough!

The drums pounded in the eleven districts of Magocha, and the boys began to assemble at different points in those districts on the first day. On the second day, the groups began to march towards the King's region. In all the villages throughout the kingdom, the mothers were crying holding their bosoms as if something would miraculously snip this period out of their lives without anyone noticing. The somberness that engulfed the villages was as if many funerals were going on at the same time in the whole of Magocha. The boys walked without looking sideways or backward. Their chests were pushed forwards. If one did not walk like that, they would be regarded as weak by the other boys, and this could trigger teasing for the duration of the training ahead. Cattle and goat herding days had equipped the boys with such knowledge. As they walked, they sang war songs, finding their thick voices, and sounding very brave and determined. One of the songs that they sang went like,

"Amai nababa
musandicheme
kana ndafa
nehondo!

Ndini ndakazvida
Kugwira nyika
yaMambo
Rubonga!
..."

The song was to tell the parents not to worry if their boys would not come back from the war because they had chosen to give their lives away while protecting their country, led by King Rubonga.

Mai Tongai did not appear anxious when her boys left for the King's court where the other boys had gathered. She had packed a lot of food for the journey for Prince Masimba and Shingai. She just stood by the door of her kitchen, leaning on her shoulder on one end of the granite doorframe. The King's main court was inside the granite enclosure. As the boys were entering the main entrance, they were asked to leave their bows and arrows with the warriors who guarded that entrance. They proceeded to the court and sat on the floor as they waited for the King to address them.

As they waited for the King, one of the instructors went to them and started rearranging the way they were sitting. He ordered the boys not to sit next to someone that came from the same village as them or to even sit next to their relative. When they were done with reshuffling, the teacher then exclaimed,

"The person who is sitting in front of you, on your side and behind you is now your relative and friend. He is also your enemy. You must always be aware of this!" The teacher then sat down without soliciting a response from the boys. One of the King's wise Governors who was known as the mouth of the Council stood up and addressed the boys. His name was Chitsere. He was a tall man, and his height made him look a bit slim. Even though he looked slim, one could tell that he was fit. The flesh on his bones was as tough as that of a very old rooster with long talons. Chitsere told the boys how to behave when the King was addressing them. After he finished his address, he went to tell the King that he could come and talk to the boys.

Low drumbeats began to fill the air with *mbira* and shackles joining the instrumental music. The music carried on, and soon, some of the King's wise governors started to walk into the court to take their places. Chitsere returned and also took his seat. After him came the Governor who was the King's most consistent companion during court sessions, VaGondo. VaGondo was a man who the elders described as having suckled adequate milk from his mother when he was still a little baby. This was because of his obesity. The children spoke of him as the man who was pregnant with twins. He had a clean baldhead with just a little bit of hair near his ears. Many people feared him, not because he was vicious, but because he always had the King's ear. If he thought of anything and told the King, he would just agree with him. VaGondo took his seat, which was almost double the size of all the other stools for members of The Council of The Wise Eleven.

Suddenly the music died, and at that same time, eight mean-looking warriors sprung into the arena screaming, whistling, and making strange war cries that the boys had never heard before. They came in from the direction that the wise elders had come from. The warriors quickly took their positions., Several boys were unnerved by the action of the warriors. They just marveled at the showcase. A deep and modulated voice was heard bellowing in the dead silence that ensued soon after the warriors had taken their positions. The roaring sound recited praises to King Rubonga. Shingai had never seen such a display nor heard a voice that thick from the time that he had lived in Magocha. He and the other boys could only imagine the size of the giant who had the lion's roar. The wise governors and the generals stood up when they heard the voice. Chitsere turned to the boys and lifted his hand and the boys quickly rose and stood attentively.

The giant kept on thundering, and as he drew nearer to the arena, the voice grew louder. The boys could feel the vibrations from his voice going through into their rib cages and exciting their pulses. What surprised the boys was that, when they eventually saw the man who was heaping praises on the King, something did not add up. The size of the voice and the size of the man did not match. Although he was not a midget, the man was small compared to the average man in Magocha. The little man carried on bellowing about the grandeur of King Rubonga.

"He is here, the King of kings
The beast of the wild forests

A real lion is in our presence, men of Magocha!

If you try him, your soul will quickly find its way into the Kingdom of The Dark Spirits

Him who even the trees fear!

He is here the mighty son of Mupingamhuru

Him who can swallow the hot coals of mupani timber!

He is here, husband to us all!

The warriors whistled, and the boys joined. Drumbeats pounded so loudly that the sound echoed in the chests of all the men present. War cries were barked, and King Rubonga stepped into the arena. All the noise instantly died. VaGondo and his big fat belly was the first to kneel on one knee facing the ground. The wise governors and the generals followed suit. The wave followed the hierarchy like dominos till the boys sitting in the last row fell on their knees. Only the King's guards were allowed to carry weapons in the arena when the King was present.

These warriors remained standing like stone statues with only their chameleon eyes inspecting all the motions. King Rubonga, elegantly dressed in delicate leopard skins strolled looking at all the men. He carried a short gold and copper coated spear with a shining blade. He sat on his throne, and one of his security details clapped three times loudly. All the men lifted their heads while still kneeling and looked at the King, avoiding direct eye contact with him. Rubonga then slowly nodded a few times. As he did this, VaGondo took his seat, and this triggered the hierarchy wave to flow once again as the men began to sit.

VaGondo looked at all the men, then turned his head to the King and said,

"Oh men of Magocha, let us salute the king!"

He began to clap his hands in a way that emitted a deep sound. This was a sign of respect. The throng did the same with some men whistling, and VaGondo shouted some praises to the King's Lion totem. The King responded by just nodding once. Chitsere stood and said,

"My lord, we have come with your youthful warriors who will be going for training this year. They are now ready to be shaped so that they can be counted amongst the real men of Magocha. All of them are prepared to work for you until they join the inhabitants of the spirit world. They said that they cannot possibly go to such an undertaking without packing some of your wise words into their hearts. For if they do so, it will only spell disaster for them. Whatever they are going to learn for the whole year cannot be as powerful as two words from you, the great lion. They want you to take the first giant step for them so that the rest of the journey will be easy for them ..."

Shingai wondered when the boys had sat down and come up with such a proposal. He ended up thinking that this had been planned when the boys were still in their various villages in the districts. Having stayed with the Royals, he could have missed such programs! He thought to himself. At that time Prince Masimba had been made to sit amongst boys that he did not know. Boys that he did not realize also surrounded him. He and Masimba had been stripped of their royal dresses and were wearing garbs made from cowhides like most of the other boys. Only a few of the boys were wearing skins from other wild animals like elands and sables. In this group, only those that knew the

Royals very well could identify them after looking at them. They looked like the other boys without the glamour of their royal garb.

King Rubonga stood up, and after wild clapping of hands, he began to address the boys.

"A kingdom is, because of its people. For a country to be known as excellent, it is because of the excellence of its people. For a kingdom to be known as strong, it is because of the strength of the men in that kingdom. The Kingdom of Magocha is known far and wide as great and strong. All this is because of the greatness of the people and the strength of the men of Magocha. Year in and year out, we lose warriors due to various reasons, including death and retirement at old age. Every year we produce other warriors with vigor and determination when the duty to stand by and defend Magocha calls. Now we have put under our feet, some little kingdoms such as Chemhindo, Machera, Matangi, Magondo, and others from the east. This is not enough! We want to conquer territories that are south of those two rivers, Nyanjuzi and Manyoka, but before we do that, we must first bring the Western Kingdoms under our yoke.

"All this awaits you, the young and hot blood of Magocha. Therefore, if there are some amongst you who are planning to go to Pengapenga to put up a dismal performance during your course of studies, they will definitely live to tell others that which hinders the dog from laughing while it is able to grin. I believe in you. I seriously do. I want all of you to come back well as men made of iron. All the wealth of the Western kingdoms awaits you and you only." Rubonga went on to say a lot of other things with the boys listening attentively. As soon as he finished his speech, the bellowing little man was heard again, thundering as the King left the arena the way he had come in.

In no time, the boys had assembled into five broad groups. The boys were to orderly march behind their group leaders as they headed to Pengapenga. The groups began to move quickly, taking different routes as they left the King's district. Their bows and arrows were left with the guards at the palace gates. Many of the boys showed some excitement as they marched, although deep down, they were crippled with anxiety and fear of what awaited them ahead. They had been mixed up, and there were rare instances where boys from the same village found themselves in the same group.

The five groups gathered at the site where they had been told they would be camping for the night. It was now very dark, and they were a long way from the villages. They were already past the boundary of the human settlements of the last district of Magocha towards the Pengapenga Mountains, and they were deep into the wild forest that stretched beyond the Pengapenga range.

One of the instructors spoke in a loud voice asking all the boys to find a place that they could cleverly hide their prepared meals. A place they would remember. He said he needed to take the boys to some place and that they would only eat when they came back. They were given very little time to do this, as they needed to follow the leading instructor in each group. The instructors started walking, and immediately, the boys were in tow. They walked for a long time, and many began to wonder if they were going back to their meals at all. The snakes in their stomachs were complaining ceaselessly, wanting to be fed. Shingai thought he was used to going for long periods without taking any food, but he soon realized that it had been a long time since he had gone hungry.

The boys followed the teachers, maintaining their pace. In the east, the horizon grew brighter, and the sun rose with the caravans still on the move. They got to a place where they were told to rest for a little bit. One chubby boy asked about their prepared meals, and he was answered with a supersonic open hand clap on the face by one of the teachers. The boys went silent with shock. The warm sunrays found their way through the leaves of the trees on to the boys' skins and quickly sent them napping.

Before long, a cry was heard instructing them to get back on the move. They got to a river and crossed it, but no one licked a drop of the water that looked so cool and refreshing because no one had instructed them to do so. After they passed that river, they saw many ripe wild fruits, but they did not touch them. There were teachers ahead, teachers mingling in the groups, and teachers walking behind the boys. All that the boys could do was just to salivate as their eyes gathered the fruits and enjoyed them without causing any problems. Only that all this had to start and end in their eyes!

By the third day, seven boys had fainted, only to regain consciousness after cold water had been splashed on them. They continued walking and when they got to another river, this time they were allowed to drink the water. Some boys had to drown themselves a bit so that they could swallow a lot of water quickly. They were then given a short time to find some fruits to eat in the nearby bushes. A drum was to be beaten to signal the boys to return to camp. There was commotion as the boys ran in all directions scurrying for food. There were very few wild fruit trees in this part of the forest. By the time that the drum summoned them back to camp, the boys went back disappointed, only to be pleasantly surprised to find that the teachers had killed two kudu bulls and had finished skinning them. The boys devoured so much meat on that day. None of them knew when they would be allowed to have their next meal, so they had to make sure that they ate enough to carry them for a long time.

The groups eventually got to the Pengapenga Mountains late on the following day. This was now the fifth day from the time they had left King Rubonga's village. They found that some senior teachers had been stationed there much earlier in the year. One of the head teachers happened to be King Rubonga's young brother, Lord Vandirai. Shingai had never met him before, but he had heard about him. Lord Vandirai was one year younger than Rubonga. One could see similar facial features on both men, but they were not identical. Vandirai had devoted himself to be an instructor of the boys ever since he got injured during one of the wars. This decision made many elders of Magocha happy as they felt that his military ingenuity would not go to waste. Their boys would benefit a lot from the knowledge that he would pass on to them. Every year Lord Vandirai would be stationed at Pengapenga conducting and monitoring the training of the boys.

The trainees would stay in temporary shelters made from poles, mud, and grass. The teachers lived in well-constructed houses. Vandirai had a slight limp on his right leg, and thick blood vessels ran down his strong arms. He wore a tense atmosphere around him, and it was rare to see him smiling, unlike the other teachers. It was not a secret that the other teachers feared him. It was said that if he stared at a boy without saying anything, that boy would feel like he was not dressed or he would have fouled his bottom garments. The boys were surprised at how quickly Lord Vandirai memorized their names in the short space of time that they had been at the training camp. He only needed to hear a boy's name once, and he would not forget it. When he saw Prince Masimba, he spoke to him for a long time asking him about the people at the palace. This was the only time that the boys saw him smiling for a little bit.

The first three days lapsed with the boys whipping each other using fresh sticks from the bushes. When they started this activity, they were giving each other light lashes, but then it got more intense when some felt that they had received tougher beatings from their partners. When their turn came, they would lash harder at the other. Two boys would be pushed to the center of a circle and asked to thrash each other while the rest of the boys would be cheering. Those that were caught not cheering were thrown into the ring next to fight. This made the cheering wild and loud. By the second day of thrashing, many of the boys had lost their voices. The teachers appeared to not notice it. None of the boys received any beating from the instructors during this period despite the imminent threats they shouted at the boys. Those that showed signs of wanting to cry received the worst threats. The boys could not understand the meaning of the exercise.

At the end of the third day, they had stripes of open cuts all over their bodies.

More and more lessons were conducted. Shingai and Masimba performed well. The first two months were all about physical and mental exercises. It involved running up mountains and crossing flooded rivers. They were made to carry massive rocks for some distances and then take them back. They were taught techniques of how to climb different trees. When it came to running the marathon, they would run to a mountain in the distance, and when they reached the summit, they would get a particular type of pebble from an instructor who would have gone there earlier than the boys. They would then run to another mountaintop to surrender the stone to another instructor there. If a boy lost the pebble along the way, they had to go back to the first mountain to get another one and complete the full course. Failure to do that would result in the boy getting thoroughly beaten by the teachers. Losing the pebbles was considered a case of pure carelessness and hence meant increasing chances of one attaining lower grades at the end of the training course. The boys knew this, and they made sure they did not lose their pebbles.

Lessons on hunting and living in the wild were the scariest and most painful. It involved the boys learning how to track animals that could harm or even make meals out of them. Hunting lions was done in groups of fours. Many boys were injured, and some lost their lives during hunting expeditions for lions and buffalos.

That year, only sixteen boys lost their lives during the course. Of the sixteen, buffalos had killed eight boys that were hunting the ill-tempered beasts. One buffalo gored three boys to death while the fourth boy survived because he had taken refuge in a tree. The survivor did not meet the top two grades of the course when training ended. The instructors had asked him how he had managed to keep himself alive and unhurt when the others had perished. He told them how he had seen all that had happened while sitting on top a tree branch. The teachers told him that if he had not left his mates to fight the bull on their own, they possibly would have overpowered it and his boys would have also lived!

The other five boys had died later on from injuries that resulted from fighting the buffalos. One of the boys had his belly torn after he was caught by a buffalo's horn and swung into the air. The boy saw his strewn insides out in the open before he breathed his last. It took several spear-blows on the right spots to take down a grown buffalo. The hunters would stab the beast with spears then jump into nearby trees where they would continue the assault. Some aces would use an ax to acrobatically strike a blow on the buffalo's neck, just behind the horns to cut through the spinal cord and paralyze the beast before finishing it off by cutting its throat with a dagger. Such a skill was said to only be for those that would be possessed by a hunter's spirit.

The other boys had died when they were crossing flooded rivers, and crocodiles preyed them on. What pained the boys was that, of their colleagues who had perished, some had died not because they were cowards or careless, but they had died in the process of trying to save their pals from danger.

The boys learned many other skills such as warfare, building houses, leather crafting, iron ore smelting, and making tools such as hoes, arrowheads, spears, hand axes, daggers, and many others. Some of the lessons were totally new to some boys, but others had already learned them from their relatives. A student who had a relative that specialized in hunting would learn quite a lot about hunting from that relative from his boyhood days. That boy would be a step ahead during the hunting lessons at Pengapenga. The boys were also taught social skills, such as living in harmony with their families. They were trained on what a man was expected to do at home and how he was expected to look after his wife and children, complementing the skills that the women brought into the household.

By the time the year had elapsed, they had learned quite a lot. Lord Vandirai assembled the boys and their teachers and told the boys that all they had learned was only the beginning for them to start living like grown men. He implored them to keep on sharpening their skills and to develop peculiar skills for themselves, which would differentiate them from the others when they joined the skilled men in their districts. He told them that all the men they saw in the villages had taught themselves new skills on their own after leaving the training school.

"Is it not a fact that if I were to ask you to fight right now, you would all try to use the skills that we taught you here? Now it is prudent that every one of you be able to fight in their special way. You know about the wrestling and boxing contests that you shall have in the villages. It is now up to you to do as you please with what you have learned."

Lord Vandirai then went on to announce to the gathering that he would be taking a break from teaching the boys the following year because he needed to slow down and live at his home.

On the day that they left the Pengapenga camp, the boys now had new spears, bows, and arrows. They were feeling proud of graduating into real men. Shingai had taken to heart the instruction that he had to go and find new ways of fighting and sharpening his skills when he got back to the palace. He had a faint memory of some fighting skills that he had seen somewhere although he had no idea where that could have been. He had not seen anyone being taught those skills at Pengapenga or even back in Magocha. This would give him a starting point.

The boys got back to their homes. There were tears of joy in many homes in Magocha as the families received the young men back home, but there were also tears of sadness for the few families whose sons, the insatiable earth at Pengapenga had swallowed.

Chapter 12

Three months after the boys returned from Pengapenga to their districts in Magocha, a welcome back ceremony was held at the King's court. The youth in the kingdom looked forward to that day each year. The boys would be smartly dressed in various animal skins. They did this because on this day many girls attended the ceremony and the after party. The girls would also put a great deal of effort to look good, dressing in fine animal skins and applying powders made from the dust of some unique rocks on to their faces. They would wear beautiful jewelry and bracelets specially made from seeds and grass and some from wood.

The day began with a late breakfast for all the guests. Cows were slaughtered on the day, and the King's hunters brought in a lot of game to increase the variety of relishes prepared for the day. Skilled women made a wide range of brews using ground millet and sorghum grains. Some of the beer required several days to mature while others only needed to ferment overnight. Whatever the time it took for the fermentation, the beers had to be ready for the imbibers on the day of the ceremony. Some men with weak bowels would be seen offloading in public because of the generous alcohol content in the beers. If such incidences were not witnessed on that day, the brewers would feel sad. It showed that their product would have lacked potency.

Singing and dancing would follow. The musicians and poets would proudly demonstrate their skills. On days like this, Chitsere would be like one possessed by a dancing spirit. He would curve his spine as if it were the tail of a chameleon. When he did his *ngororombe* dance, people would stand around the arena in order to get a good view of him. Even King Rubonga, who was known for hiding his emotions when in public would be seen smiling and clapping his hands when Chitsere stepped on the dance floor.

When the shadows began to grow tall eastwards, the older citizens would move to a different arena where they would join the entertainment of the King and his wise governors through more song and dance as well as other displays that they enjoyed watching. This is when the boys and girls would mix and mingle. They would also put up some displays, where mostly boys needed to show off their skills, especially those that were not blessed with sweet tongues. A lot of the boys and girls chose their future spouses at this event.

On the day of the ceremony, Shingai saw a stunning girl. He thought he had never seen such beauty and doubted if he would ever see anyone more gorgeous than her in his life on earth. The girl looked like she was about five or four years his junior. She was elegantly dressed. Shingai had had affairs with a few other girls before in Magocha, but none had attracted his eyes the way this girl did. His heart began to thud as he stared at her. The girl was having a chat with Princess Kundai, one of King Rubonga's daughters with his second wife. She had long, dark black hair and beautiful tattoos on her forehead. She wore a short skirt made from beautiful impala skin. Her chest was covered with a piece of a garment made from skillfully prepared leopard skin with shiny fur.

She wore a smile throughout her entire conversation with Kundai. When she inclined her head on one side, Shingai found himself also tilting his head on that side. Kundai kept on talking, and the girl just kept listening and smiling. He could not take his eyes off her. He kept admiring all that he saw on her. He was a bit surprised that the girl did not take her eyes off Kundai to look around at the other people around her.

It seemed that she was used to being stared at by men and boys. They would look at her with amazement as they walked by. But why were the boys not approaching the two girls for a chat? It was common knowledge that on this special day in Magocha, boys and girls would socialize freely, talking about anything they desired without fear of crossing sacred cultural lines. Even the girls that had overly protective brothers had nothing to fear because they did not owe anyone an explanation for whatever they did or whoever they talked to on that day. A decree had been made by the previous kings of the land and solidified by King Rubonga himself to protect them. No citizen desired to break this law and risk being reported to Rubonga. As Shingai kept daydreaming with his eyes fixed on the girl, he suddenly felt a pair of soft hands covering his eyes, and he immediately knew who it was.

Shingai turned around, feeling a little bit embarrassed, and at the same time, he felt a flush of irritation run through his nerves for the unexpected interruption.

"Really? Are you just going to act like you have forgotten about me because of today's freedom, my darling? Tendai jokingly quizzed Shingai. He looked at his girlfriend and smiled, but the smile quickly went away.

"What is on your mind that is making you act like you have lent your brains to somebody? Tendai asked again without waiting for the answer to her first question.

Shingai noticed that Tendai was wearing a beautiful garment made from a zebra hide. She was looking quite good with the makeup and ornaments that she was wearing but he acted as if he hadn't noticed it all.

"So who hunted that zebra you are wearing?"

Tendai looked at him for a moment as if she was composing her answer.

"Seriously Shingi, why are you so nasty to me like this? What is wrong is with you today?" Tendai was surprised, and she started getting annoyed by him.

"So am I not allowed to ask you such questions?" Shingai responded as he lifted his head, suddenly trying to locate Prince Masimba in the lively crowd. He did not want the prince to see the mysterious and beautiful girl before he got the chance to try to seek her heart. Masimba was not slow. He had broken many hearts in the kingdom by declaring his love to many girls, even those he did not like at all. Shingai was determined not to let the prince do anything that would cause any sort of pain to the beautiful girl. The two boys had made a pact that respected the other's prey. They referred to their girls as birds. The treaty banned one of them from going after the same girl that the other was interested in. Even if the girl would have refused to go out with one of them, she became a no-go territory for the other boy. Rejection of one boy by a girl was rejection for both boys.

"Does your question really deserve my answer Shingi?" Tendai asked as she could see that he was absent. This was a surprise to her. Shingai was not like that. Shingai was a good listener, and he would always listen to everything that she said, even the silly things. What could have caused this unexpected behavior? Tendai thought deeply. Shingai saw Masimba charming a group of girls, making them laugh. The Prince of Magocha was going on and on while the girls would laugh in a chorus, now and then, ending each sequence with the clapping sound of a high five. Shingai's heart settled down. He then turned to spy on Kundai and his mysterious girl, but the two were no longer where he had seen them. He searched with his eyes everywhere, but he could not locate them. The sun had picked up pace as it headed into the western horizon, and many girls were now heading to the various paths that led to their different homes from the King's courts.

Tendai's mouth had fit into her nose by this time. She was miffed. Embarrassment and guilt began to settle on Shingai. He began to regret what he had done to her. His mind and heart were still torn in two. He was supposed to walk with Tendai and leave her near her home. He knew that by the time that he would get to Tendai's house it would be already dusk, meaning that he would not be able to see the other girl or even know where she would have gone to. He was not ready to go hunting for the girl he did not know in the night! These were not things done at night.

"Aa-a, I'm now going to my mother's house. I would be foolish to think that I have your attention today." Tendai spoke mostly to herself, mumbling the words but Shingai heard every word. He then apologized and blamed the stupid behavior on the little bit of alcohol that he had taken earlier on. He claimed that the alcohol must have been quite active, causing his head to spin. They started walking towards Tendai's home. They did not talk much on this day because Shingai did not have much to say. Tendai was walking in front on the narrow path as he followed behind. His mind was still glued on to the girl he had seen that afternoon. His heart was yearning for her. At one point, his mind was a bit conflicted because of what he had done to Tendai.

Tendai was a beautiful girl with a beautiful soul. Her parents and relatives had begun to believe that Shingai was the man who was going to drive a herd of cattle to their home as *roora.* Shingai looked at Tendai from behind and decided that even though she looked very beautiful and voluptuous, she was no way in the league of the girl he had seen that day. The zebra-skin garment sat very well on her. As she walked in front of Shingai, her rear looked as big as that of a real zebra. Shingai then remembered that he was the one who had actually hunted the zebra for that very striped hide for her and he had asked her to wear that particular garment to the ceremony. He felt as if sharp thorns were piercing through his heart. He was filled with shame. Why was he putting somebody's daughter through such pain? The human heart is stubborn and rebellious. It is difficult to confine it to a cage. It was said by the wise elders, that the human heart germinates wherever it pleases like a tree in the wild, and it cannot be stopped. Shingai's heart was running in the dark and following another heart that did not even know of his existence. Was his soul going to find a home in the new girl's heart, or was it all infatuation. If he were to follow his heart, would it not leave, running again after being subjected to pain if it was rejected? If he saw the mysterious girl again, was he going to proclaim, his feelings for her? What if the girl said, "No" to him, how would he then get back to Tendai when he had started acting the fool in her presence?

They got close to Tendai's home, and Shingai brightened up as he planned to go straight to Kundai to ask her about the girl she was talking to. They hugged, and Tendai kept holding on to him and looking deep into his eyes. Shingai felt sorry because Tendai seemed to have read all that was in his chest. He could feel her heart beating fast, and he could see her eyes loading the tears. Shingai started to free himself from her embrace bit by bit and said,

"Let me run back home now, it is late. Let us see each other again on, ummnn, you'll see me when I come." As soon as he finished saying those words, he ran without looking back as he headed back to the palace. On that day, Tendai noticed that Shingai had not addressed her as "darling."

When Shingai got back to the King's court, he found Prince Masimba and many warriors waiting for him.

"There he is, can we get on the road now?" He heard a senior warrior call out an order. Masimba quickly explained to Shingai that Rubonga had ordered a group of warriors, headed by the two of them to make a trip to the Kingdom of Magondo to collect the King's tribute. The turn had come for Magondo to show her allegiance and subordination to the King of Magocha by paying their annual tribute to him. This was an obligation for all the kingdoms that had fallen into the hands of the mighty Magocha had to observe, lest they were met with an untold assault for defiance. Magondo was the envy of many kingdoms for its abundance in reserves of precious gemstones. Sometime back, two governors had been sent by Rubonga to collect tribute on his behalf, and they had hidden a part of the treasure. The poor men had not known that Rubonga had sent moles ahead of them and the moles were present when the cache was dispatched. Rubonga had executed the two men, and from that time, he did not trust anyone receiving and ferrying his treasure except for his sons Masimba and Shingai or himself.

It was said that Rubonga's eldest son Tongai, had been a big letdown to him because of his feminine mannerisms and that he was weak. Tongai did not like to hear about physical fighting and even war tales. He resented wearing royal clothing, which made him different from the rest of the citizens of Magocha. The village grapevines claimed that Tongai's mother had saved him by instructing him to leave Magocha and build his own home amongst her brothers in the Kingdom of Matangi because he was at risk of being eliminated mercilessly by his own father. Tongai had not even bothered going to the initiation school at the Pengapenga Mountains with boys of his age as he had already permanently left for Matangi. Masimba had proved from an early age that he had the spine of a man. This had made Rubonga happy, and he had started to groom Prince Masimba as the next leader of Magocha after him. He had started this even before he had gone to Pengapenga. Rubonga liked it when Prince Masimba represented him on different missions.

When Shingai heard about the unexpected journey to Magondo, he was distraught, but he did not show it. He quickly thought of a plan.

"I just need to quickly get something from Kundai, and we will be on our way in no time!"

Masimba let out a short laugh then said,

"Sorry, my brother. Kundai went to visit *vatete*, and she will only be back after two days. We have to go now before the Cobra lifts his behind from his throne. Just grab your weapons quickly and let's get moving."

Shingai got on the road with a big lump sitting on his throat. His heart hungered for more information about the mysterious girl he had seen that afternoon talking to Kundai. A trip to Magondo meant too much time away from Magocha. It would take almost a full month of walking. The trip back would take much longer because the warriors would be carrying heavy loads of loot. For much of the time that he was on this journey, Shingai was just thinking of and imagining stuff about the girl, wondering if he was ever going to see her again. He wondered if he would ever see a girl with such beauty. Even his dreams featured the mysterious girl. Some days he would just see the girl's face smiling at him. No matter what Shingai would say to the girl in his dreams, she would not answer but just beam at him. He had to have her. There were times that the girl would transfigure into Tendai, and Shingai would wake up disappointed.

The clarity of dreams deteriorates when the dreamer wakes up. It further deteriorates with time. Soon the girl's beauty began to fade, and Shingai started to wonder if she had been that beautiful after all. She was becoming more of a myth. He had only seen her once, and this began to make him doubt his judgment. When he thought of Tendai, she was real. He knew a lot about her, and he was familiar with her voice. Shingai became happier. He realized that he adored Tendai. He decided that when he would be back in Magocha, he would go to see Tendai and put back his truant heart into its haven.

The mission to Magondo was carried out successfully without any incident. King Makanda of Magondo had received the messengers well. He had welcomed Masimba and Shingai to live in his palace for the few days that he prepared King Rubonga's tribute. He handed the jewels directly to Prince Masimba, and the squadron got back on the road to home happily. When Masimba saw that Shingai was now a bit calmer and more collected than he had been on the trip to Magondo, he put his hand on his shoulder and said,

"Shingi my brother, you need to sort out whatever issues that are going on in your head quickly. If you keep your brain preoccupied like how you have been on this trip, then you must be prepared to get hurt or killed by the enemy."

Shingai just nodded. He realized that he had acted like a young boy who had just fallen in love for the first time and had thrown caution down a cliff. He of all people should have known not to behave like that. Whatever he was going through or what was on his mind should have never been for anyone to see! A smart person's weak points should be cleverly concealed for him to minimize his vulnerability.

In the thick of the night, the squadron arrived at the King's home. The two boys went straight to bed, leaving the other warriors in the main arena waiting for daylight so that they would present the tribute to the King. The morning came, and the King went to meet his messengers. They showed him what they had brought with Masimba leading in detailing how their mission had gone. The governors that were present clapped their hands in a way to express appreciation and respect for the job well done. They had to praise the prince. It was an unproclaimed law for people around the King to clap their hands to praise the prince even for the slightest achievement. The people dispersed from the arena and Rubonga beckoned Shingai and said to him,

"Young man, you still remember the words that I said to you when you first came to live with me, right?"

"I remember the words, My Lord."

"Good. I just want to let you know that there is nothing that I do nor a word that rolls off my tongue, that is insignificant. The Western Kingdoms are now waiting for me. You know I speak to the one who is in you, right?"

Shingai found his tongue stuck onto the roof of his mouth. Rubonga looked at him and gave an enigmatic smile. Although Shingai's head was lowered and his eyes slightly lowered to avoid looking directly into the King's eyes, he saw the smile, and it reminded him of the look on some corpses' faces that he had seen just before they were buried. He felt a frosty spasm throughout his whole body.

"You may go now."

The King spoke with his evil smile still on. Shingai stood and left without saying a word.

Shingai had planned to see Kundai that morning, but after the King's words, he decided to put that on hold to give him some time to try to make sense of what Rubonga had said to him. He sat in the shade near his cottage and began to try to process it all. He took himself back to the time that he had first arrived to live at the King's palace, how he had gotten there, and why this had happened. Rubonga had spoken to him the way one speaks to a spirit medium. How was he going to achieve it? If whomever it were that the King spoke to happened to fail to meet his request, would it not mean death to the spirit medium? But a spirit could not be killed, it is only the mortal host that could be killed in an instant! He would be the one to get killed, although he did not believe that some spiritual force was operating from within him. What was this that was about to dampen his life now that was getting better and better? Could it be that the time had come for him to run away? But running away from what and to where? How would he successfully run away from Rubonga with his warriors that could successfully track human scent as if they were dogs? He was bothered. Magocha had become the perfect home for him. He enjoyed the lifestyle he had adapted there. He lived like a prince, and many people were very fond of him. They revered him because they believed him to be a son of the water royals.

His thoughts were interrupted by what he saw at the queens' rondavels. Princess Kundai and the other princesses were talking to Prince Masimba. Among them was Shingai's mysterious girl! Shingai stood up without knowing why he rose. His insides began to vibrate. Masimba had beaten him to it. The girl still looked gorgeous, and in his eyes, she seemed to have become even more beautiful. She was just smiling when everybody was competing for a chance to talk. The group then started walking towards him. His heartbeat began to thump faster and faster, and he began to sweat. For a split second, he contemplated running into the woods. He thought of going into his cottage, but still, he could not do it. He did not know what to do.

The mind can process many thoughts in a short space of time. At that moment, Shingai's mind took him to the Pengapenga Mountains. Then it took him to Magondo. From Magondo, it brought him back to the palace and flew with him to Tendai's home, where he left Tendai crying. The thoughts brought him back to that moment and queried him on how he was going to react when Masimba would introduce his new girl to him. He contemplated whether he was going to salute her as his new sister-in-law or if he was going to greet her by the name that she would be introduced as. Even though thoughts can move at supersonic speeds, time always catches up. Time caught up, and the group got to where he was standing.

Masimba was quick to joke with him.

"My brother Shingi, so you thought it very important to sit and enjoy this shade by yourself as you daydream about your girl Tendai, without even enquiring about the health of all my mothers when you've been away from them for over a month?"

Shingai could not find an answer. He felt as if Masimba's sarcasm was unnecessary, so much that in his mind, he landed a heavy blow on Masimba's left jaw. He felt embarrassed, and before he got over it, Princess Kundai took over from Masimba, and with fake sorrow she said,

"Oh, guys, please do not say that to him. Do you know that Tendai came to me a day or two after you left for your Magondo mission, and she cried a lot saying that she did not know what had gotten into you Shingi? She wanted to see you then. Even if you see her now, she is so worried and heart-broken you will even feel sorry for her."

Shingai opened his mouth to say something, but words refused to leave his tongue. He looked at the beautiful girl and saw her smiling as she stood behind the group that was teasing him. When Masimba cleared his throat to talk again, Shingai knew that the time for introductions had finally come. He knew that Masimba would take some time to remind him of their solemn oath. He prepared to have his heart pierced by a red-hot arrowhead.

"Shuvai, this is the Shingi. He is my partner to the grave."

Shingai blushed.

"Shingi, this is Shuvai. She is my sister, daughter of my uncle Vandirai, you know him from Pengapenga, right?"

A cool breeze suddenly blew onto Shingai, and he felt his blood tickling every part of his flesh. For a moment, his heart was at peace. He wanted to lift Masimba and kiss him. He realized that he still had an opportunity to exchange his heart with Shuvai's. Suddenly he realized that Shuvai donned leopard skin garments and even on the day that he had first seen her, a part of her garment was of leopard skin! He wondered how he had missed something so obvious for anyone in the kingdom to see! Masimba carried on,

"Shuvai has been staying with her mother's kin in the Kingdom of Mawisire. She is now back in Magocha because *bamunini* Vandirai is also back home from his abode in the Pengapenga Mountains. I'm sure you remember him mentioning that he had become tired of training the boys and that he needed to take a break from it."

"How do you do my brother?"

Shuvai asked, putting her hands together lightly and at the same time doing a mild genuflection. Kundai and the other princesses laughed.

"Oh please Shuvai, why are you overly nice to him like that? We just call him Shingi, and there is nothing wrong with that."

Shingai quickly responded,

"I am very well. I am just a warrior that makes sure that My Lords here are safe all the time, so please do not trouble yourself by heaping all that respect on me. I am the one that should show respect to you, Your Highness. How do you do?"

The whole group laughed. Shingai found it hard to address a girl that he had fallen head over heels for as his sister. No. It couldn't be like that. This was a challenge that he had not expected. He realized that it was not going to be easy for him even if he had found a chance to tell Shuvai how much he had fallen in love with her from the moment his eyes had first seen her. It was true that he was not biologically related to the royals of Magocha, but these people had taken him in as one of theirs. It was the elders from the King's district that had advised Rubonga to not allow Shingai to wear leopard skin like the royals because he was not of royal blood. They implored the King to observe that with much care. They knew that familiarity breeds contempt. They said that they did not wish to see a situation where an outsider would manipulate his way to the throne. This would, unfortunately, result in the outsider sitting firmly on the throne. No one amongst the royals openly talked about it, but they all knew that Shingai was not royalty.

Masimba took Shingai on the side and asked him, "What did Mhungu want from you?"

Mhungu was Rubonga's nickname that many people in the kingdom knew about except the King himself. People did not understand Rubonga, and many were scared of him. He was merciless when it came to punishing those that would have crossed him or those that he would have perceived as wanting to undermine his authority. Many people had been executed at his command even for minor and unverified issues. One old man had likened him to a cobra, and from that time the name Mhungu stuck onto him. Shingai deliberately skipped some words in his response, saying

"He was begging me to make sure that I always have my eyes on you so that I can help wade off attacks that might come from the numerous foes that are growing with the expansion of the authority of the king…"

The two boys laughed and carried on their conversation, but on different subjects.

Shuvai did not contribute to the jokes, but she smiled and laughed at what was said. Shingai kept telling himself that he had found his real love, someone that he was going to be with for the remainder of his earthly life. By all means, he had to find ways of stealing Shuvai's heart. Shuvai was still young, but she was very much aware of sexual relationships. Shingai made up his mind that he was going to assume python tactics if he was to win her heart. The python patiently takes time to attract its prey. The prey is hypnotized when it concentrates its gaze on the python's shiny skin that gives the illusion of fascinating movements. The animal then suddenly finds itself under the tight grip of the gigantic reptile, unable to escape. Shingai had to do just that. He was going to do anything that would make Shuvai see and believe that there was no other like him. He had to do all this with haste.

Chapter 13

As the days went by, Shingai continued to see his girl Tendai, but the fire had already dwindled. It was not as it used to be before he met Shuvai. Tendai could sense that something was not right, but she had no idea what it was that was killing the flame. What puzzled her was that even though many girls would throw themselves at Shingai whenever they got half the chance, there was none that he seemed to be going out with within Magocha. So what could have caused his lack of interest in her? Tendai was deeply troubled. She tried to find out from the royals that she spoke to, but still, they could not give her any helpful information.

There were times when Tendai would ask Shingai when he was going to take her away from her parents' home, and this would infuriate Shingai. She ended up not asking anything that related to them getting married in the future. Worry grew within Tendai. She began afraid of being made to wait until the dogs could cook their own meals before she got married. It did not help that her aunt had started to continually push for her to get married at what she termed "the right age." One day she decided to gauge how much love Shingai still had for her. She took a belt made of giraffe hide that Shingai had given her as *nduma* during the days that their love was still burning. She gave it back to him, saying that she did not want to keep wasting her time on somebody who had no sense of urgency or even a plan to start his own family and multiply the seeds of fertility that he had been blessed with. Shingai was pleasantly surprised by the sudden turn of events. He had struggled to come up with ways of asking for the *nduma* back, and here she was just bringing it of her own accord!

"You see Tendai, I've always known that you are very sensible at all times. I was really finding it difficult to communicate this to you. Where I come from, deep under the silt in the sacred pools, we are not allowed to marry the women of this world of yours. If I were to do that, this kingdom and many that surround it would not be habitable by any other mortal being."

By the time Shingai finished saying these words, Tendai's cheeks were already soaked with tears. She broke into a sprint towards her home. Shingai just stood watching her go and mixed emotions engulfed him. He was happy that he was finally free, however, he was also sad and remorseful for causing pain to an innocent girl. If he thought he could control his heart, maybe he would have stayed with her.

He waited for his heart to find a place where it wanted to settle.

Shingai decided to use the abundantly free time that he suddenly found to be a man of the woods. He would train his fighting skills further. The people that lived in the king's village rarely saw him in those days. He would only let Prince Masimba know what he was up to. Masimba had also begun to practice at his favorite spots in the woods. Sometimes they would go together for drills with the troops from various regiments of the Magocha army.

During that period they went to war with the kingdom of Machera, a nation which was near Magocha. The people of Machera had refused to pay tribute to Rubonga, and he had retaliated by sending his warriors to invade and raid it. It did not take much for the Magocha troops to defeat Machera. They humiliated the Machera king by making him lie on his belly in front of his people and other captured warriors. They warned the people of Machera that if they let their king continue in his foolishness, they would not hesitate to come and pulverize the whole kingdom. The Machera warriors ended up having to carry the tribute to Rubonga.

The Magocha army had a significant number of skilled personnel, but all, including the generals, took and followed orders from Shingai and Prince Masimba. These boys had developed new methods of fighting different wars that had not been employed by the Magocha warriors. Masimba was a brilliant war strategist who could predict how the war would end, so he would engineer strategies to win the battles. Many believed that he would get that information from Shingai, who they thought would have enlightened him in secret to present to the rest of the warriors. They said Shingai was able to do that because those that lived in the winds would inform him beforehand. This made Rubonga happy on the one hand but worried on the other. He worried because it reminded him of the words of advice that he had gotten from a *n'anga* who lived on the banks of a big lake called Doperakondo.

The *n'anga* told him that if he were not careful, a foreigner was to bring down the throne of Mupingamhuru. When he had taken Shingai into his home, he had forgotten all about that *n'anga*'s oracle. All he had become interested in was Shingai's said good fortune that was believed to accompany him wherever he was. Rubonga quickly brushed the oracle aside because he was now looking to begin his invasion of the Western Kingdoms. Shingai was to become instrumental in the success of the mission with his military intellect and special favor from the spirits. Only after he had completed the annexure of these kingdoms would Rubonga then find ways of eliminating Shingai before he would get too close to the throne.

"Whoever receives an oracle, has been given time to alter destiny. The words of the *n'anga* were a mere warning and a sign for me to be on the lookout. I am a smart man, and nothing shall catch me unaware."

Rubonga thought to himself.

From the time that Shingai stopped seeing Tendai, Shuvai went back to stay with her uncles in Mawisire and Shingai was troubled. He cleverly asked a lot of questions about her to Masimba, Kundai, and the other princesses in the hope of learning when Shuvai would be getting back to Magocha. The information he received was not forthcoming. The Royals could not tell him much, and he could see that they were reluctant to talk to him about Shuvai. They told him that their *bamunini*, Shuvai's father, practiced witchcraft and he was one of the most feared wizards in all of Magocha. They said his late mother had passed on the witchcraft crown to him. They also told him that he hated King Rubonga with a passion.

"*Bamunini* Vandirai is not a good person," they told him.

This was not in sync with what Shingai had come to know of Vandirai from the time that he first met him at the Pengapenga Mountains up to recent times. He knew that the citizens of Magocha highly regarded Lord

Vandirai as a man of virtue. When he mentioned this to Masimba and the other royal children, they dismissed it, suggesting that many people did not really know what took place inside the palace walls and that Lord Vandirai was a man full of deceit. They said that it was their father who really knew what kind of person *bamunini* Vandirai was because he had grown up with him.

"Have you ever asked yourself how it is that a man like him lives without a wife? How can a grown, nobleman like him remain unmarried for this long, his wife having died ages ago?"

Shingai could not answer. Masimba carried on saying,

"Word in the winds says that he beds his only daughter Shuvai. It is said that this is the reason he does not want to remarry. Even Shuvai also, they say, is notorious for being a princess of darkness. She also does not sleep at night because she will be busy at work bewitching folks while they sleep. So you see when we smile at her when she comes here, is not because we like her, no! We would just be trying to play nice so that she may spare us from being her meal!"

Masimba ended by laughing.

"So do you believe all of that?" Shingai asked Masimba, getting a little bit annoyed but keeping his cool. Masimba laughed again and said,

"Well, that Shuvai is a witch? I do not believe it. But the father, ummnn! That one, yeah, I have no grain of doubt that he does all he is said to do. Have you seen that he never smiles at anybody? Back in the day before you came to stay with us, he used to smile a little bit, and he used to like me a lot, but it all changed. Father then told us to always be on high alert because *bamunini* Vandirai wants to stage a coup on him. He said that each time he looks at us; all he sees are the hurdles that are preventing him from laying his hands on the throne."

Shingai exhaled loudly and said,

"Ummn, this is mind-blowing! I just needed to know, and I guess I'm now wiser."

"Yes, I am telling you this because I need you to be alert too. Now listen, you are not to repeat any of what we told you here to any other living person, okay?"

This is what the Royals had been told by Rubonga. It was only meant for the close family members to hear and know. If commoners heard such words, they could speak carelessly about it and enemies could then feast on such information, and use it to their advantage.

For many days Shingai tried to digest all the strange words he had heard about Lord Vandirai and his daughter. It made sense to him that Vandirai indeed disliked the king. He was the king's brother, but he rarely visited the palace to see and talk to his older brother. The few days that he did visit Rubonga, the two would only speak briefly, and then he would leave. It explained the fidgeting that Rubonga would do each time Vandirai was in his presence. So the king gets nervous because he fears that Vandirai could give him one blow of his sharp ax before ascending to his throne! Vandirai was bad. Shingai needed to be extra careful around him. The fact that he loved his daughter was not an excuse for complacency. He could tell that Vandirai truly envied Rubonga. This was written all over his face. That stone cold face was a result of his desire to dispose of Rubonga from his throne!

The thought that he did not want to entertain was that Vandirai was defiling the land by bedding his own daughter. No, not Shuvai! How could she do such a thing with that beautiful smile? Never! Shuvai needed to be rescued from her evil father. The child needed to be freed. So all the boys and men that desired Shuvai could not make a move on her because they feared the wrath of Vandirai? All those people that had seemed to respect Vandirai were not really doing it out of respect for him, but because they were all afraid of his wizardry? Shingai needed an excellent plan to be Shuvai's savior. It was difficult for a boy to love a girl but not like her parents. Something had to be done. These thoughts whirled in Shingai's head.

Chapter 14

Shingai became a refined archer. He became well known in the kingdom for his sharpshooting skills. The young and old spoke about his expertise with such admiration. They said he could shoot three arrows in succession in a short space of time with such speed that the last of the three arrows would be released before the first one hit the target, less than a stone throw away. The arrows would hit the same target at almost the same spot. It was also said that he could shoot down two doves flying side by side. On several occasions, he had shot and killed two impalas drinking water side by side with one arrow. No one in Magocha would dare him to compete on archery.

Shingai had perfected his shooting skills so much that when Magocha went to battle, he would lead the warriors, spot up to ten leaders from the enemy's side and take them out with his arrows before they were able to take cover. The enemy would be left with no integral commanders to take orders from, and this would cause mayhem amongst them. The Magocha troops would then rush in to finish off the rest the enemy soldiers that would be as confused as a group of antelopes driven into nets by mass hunters. When he went to battle, Shingai would also carry a short spear that he would use for stabbing close range enemies. He would have a dagger secured on his waist with leather belts that also fastened the spear and quiver to his back. The bow would be slipped and hung on the shoulder if there were no signs of an imminent attack.

Shingai was happy to be a warrior, and he became a soldier feared by many. His military prowess did not stop him from engaging in further training activities. He competed against himself. By that time he had turned nineteen years of age. During those days he developed a strange sensation. As he was training in the woods, he began to feel as if somebody or something was continually looking at him. He tried to stealthily find out who or what it was, but he did not see a thing. He thought that the only person who could be hovering around him without getting caught would be the slick Vandirai. Lord Vandirai was a skilled elderly warrior, but what would he be stalking him? When they met, they greeted each other civilly with Vandirai showing no signs of ill feelings towards him. Shingai tried to enquire from the people that lived near the king's residence if any of them had an idea about who it could be that was following him, but none could provide him with a clue. All of them just told him unapologetically that it was a crime for the king's subjects to talk about private royal affairs and that he was the one who was supposed to know because he lived with the royal family.

One day, Shingai saw something that made his heart skip a couple of beats. As he was walking in the woods to one of his training spots, whistling a melody, he suddenly felt that he was being watched again. He briefly stopped whistling, but he quickly resumed because he did not want to show that he was aware of a pair of eyes staring at him. His first instinct was to shoot two arrows in the direction of the trailing creature, but what if he would kill an innocent person in the process? Killing a person outside the battlefields, especially not in self-defense would definitely invite the wrath of avenging spirits. It was a bad idea to just shoot in the dark, so he discarded the idea. A real man does not kill a person he cannot see. A warrior does not do that. Such killing was for murderers and cowards. Shingai thought to himself,

"If it is Vandirai who was following him, then the old prince had shoved his head into the mouth of a yawning hippopotamus!"

Shingai was determined. He was going to sprint in the direction of the mysterious creature. Vandirai was way older than him, and although he was artful, Shingai needed to show him that which stopped the dog from laughing when it can grin. He ran like a speed demon into the shrubs where he believed Vandirai was hiding and rammed into a huge man before he fell to the ground. It was not bumping into the big man that threw him off-balance. He fell because of the man that he had bumped into. He had rammed into Gotora!

Since the time that Shingai had arrived in Magocha, he had heard of and seen the gigantic man that was known as Gotora. Gotora was an extraordinary man who stayed on his own and was rarely seen in public. No one knew much about him except the many labels that the Magocha society had attached to him. His two front teeth were big and stained from bad oral hygiene. He had creepy reddish eyes, which would make anyone that looked into them find themselves teary-eyed. He dressed in garments that were made from baboon and monkey skins. None of the other people used hides from these animals to make clothes. Gotora was said to be a skilled herbalist, and he was well known for his ability to identify and dig up useful medicinal herbs and roots. He was not a fortuneteller or *n'anga*, but he would only assist those that were brave enough to approach him for help on health matters.

Shingai remained on the floor with his back on the ground, looking directly into Gotora's eyes. He was now trembling visibly. At that moment, he felt annoyed, and he cussed at himself for being a weak warrior that showed fear in front of another man! How could it be like this? But Gotora was not just any other man. Shingai had not heard any tales about Gotora being a fighter, but nobody that he knew would have picked a fight with him or even dared him to one. He was notorious and feared for his witchcraft. He was known far and wide for his high position on the witches and wizards' hierarchy. As Shingai delved into the visions that emanated from the society about the big hermit, he concluded that Gotora and Vandirai had joined hands to crush his head and chew him live with their bare teeth. The whispers in the winds claimed that wherever Gotora was, he would have pieces of dried human meat in his sling bag for his occasional snack.

Shingai had known about Gotora's personality during his early days in Magocha. Gotora's only hut, which was his home, was buried in the woods near a river, far away from human settlements. The giant hermit would never walk in the footpaths that other people walked on. He preferred to walk in the woods even when he made trips to his patients' homes. When kids made noise at night or were just being annoyances, the grown-ups would tell them that such behavior could invite big Gotora to come and take them away with him. This was be enough to pacify the kids until the following morning. Pregnant women were warned not to look at him and also to avoid thinking about him because if they did so, their pregnancies could mysteriously disappear. It was said that when he gravely craved for human meat, he would call children from their mothers' wombs and when he did that, the fetus would answer his calls and go to him. While many people feared him, many still went to consult him for medical prescriptions. On that day, Shingai had come face to face with the feared wizard in broad daylight, and in no time, it seemed to be getting dark. This was weird.

It was Gotora that broke the silence,

"Are you a rhinoceros that goes about charging at every bush in the forest?"

Shingai did not answer. Gotora's voice sounded like one who was speaking from a cave. He did not wait for an answer from Shingai. He just walked away without looking back.

Shingai walked home, mollified.

"Could it have been Gotora who had been following me all this time? But what would he be trying to find out from me? Could it be that he had been assigned to trail me by Vandirai? What would be the meaning of all this because Vandirai honestly has no reason to consider me his enemy? If Vandirai is looking for somebody to kill, then he should be trying to kill Prince Masimba and not me! I am just a foreigner in this land living with King Rubonga. Maybe Vandirai wants to clear me out first because he regards me as Masimba's protector; hence, my elimination would leave his real target Masimba without protection."

The questions kept multiplying in his head with no answers forthcoming. Shingai concluded that the quickest way for him to get those answers was by asking

Gotora the questions. He was now convinced that he had been the one following him over several days. Shingai had also noticed that when he bumped into Gotora, the big man had not shown any distaste towards him. There was something that he wanted to say, or that he was up to. Shingai needed to know what it was.

Chapter 15

Some days after Gotora and Shingai'sencounter, Shuvai came back to Magocha. She had further matured, and in Shingai's eyes, she had become more beautiful. Shingai saw her at her father's home. Vandirai's home was about an hour's walk from the king's palace. Although only two people lived at that home, there were four neatly built rondavels of different sizes in the yard. Lord Vandirai usually stayed there alone because Shuvai regularly lived with her uncles in Mawisire. Shingai had gone to Vandirai's home to spy on the veteran warrior. He told himself that if he were to protect himself vigilantly from his enemies, he needed to be familiar with the enemy's strength and weaknesses. During one of his spying missions, he had used the tactics of a leopard hunter to see Shuvai. He had to study her movements without alerting her. For a couple of days, he had to follow her from a distance as she went to fetch water by the springs. This was one of the few occasions that she would leave her father's home. When he became familiar with her routine, he decided to fake a "bumping into her" as she went to fetch water. Shuvai appeared a bit startled when she saw him.

"Hey, hello, Shuvai. How come you no longer come to visit us at the palace?"

Shuvai smiled before she spoke, making Shingai feel like his heart had just melted. He felt his heart beating faster and faster such that for a moment, he was tempted to look down at his chest to see if the vibrations were not visible. He could not hide the amusement that was printed all over his face.

"Oh, hi, how are you my brother, Shingi, right?" Shuvai asked, her smile still full.

"Ah, come on Shuvai, your brother is Masimba. I am just a foreigner in your family. But seriously how is it that you have been back in Magocha for all these days, but you have not come to see your kinfolk at the palace? What is going on?"

"I will come to see them one of these days, I promise."

Shuvai answered and quickly went on to ask who had told him that she had been back in Magocha for that long. Shingai did not answer her but instead asked if he could walk with her to the springs. She agreed, and they walked together.

"You know that people who dress in leopard skin are not allowed to go the springs or rivers to fetch water because they have people who do that for them, right?"

Shuvai laughed a little, shaking her head before she answered.

"Well, this is one of the reasons why children of royal blood often choose to leave their marital homes to go back to stay with their parents. They fail to do the simplest household chores in their marital homes. My father consistently tells me that being of royal blood is not an excuse for not learning to do things by yourself."

After talking for a few moments, Shingai could not think of what more to talk about. This was strange to him. He always had something to say when he was with beautiful girls, but now he did not know what to say to keep the conversation going. The more he thought about it, the more the wise words ran out of his head.

He suppressed his frustration and quickly bade her farewell, telling her that he had something to attend to at the palace. Shuvai pleaded with him to not tell the other royals at the castle that he had seen her!

Shingai was very happy as he went home for just being able to talk with Shuvai, but something bothered him. Shuvai's request for him to not let the other royals know about their meeting was a confirmation that the hatred between Rubonga's family and that of Lord Vandirai was more deep-rooted than it had seemed to him. His mind raced. Even if Shuvai was to love him back, how would the relationship be taken by the Rubonga family, considering that they took her as one of their sworn enemies? If he was to marry her later on, what kind of father-in-law would Vandirai be to him? Prince Masimba and the other royal children would regard him as a sell out; a *svukukuviri* the two-headed snake!

Shingai had grown up in the king's house and was treated as a royal by many people in Magocha and beyond. His heart yearned for Shuvai. This he was very sure of. He also began to realize that from the time that Vandirai had relocated back to his home from Pengapenga, Rubonga had suspiciously doubled his security details. Rubonga was getting temperamental, and in the process, he began to fire his guards for the slightest of offenses but mostly for suspicions of allegiance to his enemies. A select group of warriors known as the "Ears and Eyes" of the king was broadcast into the whole kingdom of Magocha. These people were instructed to gather as much information on what was being said about the king and his family so that they could report back to the king. The group was expected to sniff-out the enemies of the king well before they could plan an attack. More members of the Ears and Eyes were deployed after *n'anga* Gezi's oracle that there was a surge in the number of people who were after the king's head.

On one of those days, Rubonga called Shingai, and the two talked about many issues. This had never happened before. The talk was not about the king expressing his usual desire to conquer the Western Kingdoms. He was asking about the identities of the enemies that had been revealed to Gezi by the spirits. Shingai expressed his lack of knowledge for the mysterious enemies, but he promised to throw his nose into the whole kingdom till he smelt who they were. Rubonga then went on to ask Shingai what he thought about him. Shingai had not expected this kind of questioning. He chose his words carefully and told the king that he was delighted and grateful for what he had done for him such that if he were to hear anyone bad-mouthing the king, he was prepared to lose his life in battle with such a person. Rubonga seemed to have believed him because he smiled and said to him,

"You must grow eyes on your occipital, and you must be very careful for there is a green snake in the grass that is known as Lord Vandirai. I want you to study him carefully and establish what he is planning to do. I know that he is up to something stinking. He is my young brother, I grew up with him, and I know him. You see, this special task that I am assigning you to can only be carried out by you. The other people in the kingdom are discouraged from involving themselves in matters between royals. This is where you come in, do you understand?"

Shingai concurred and promised to do everything in his capacity to keep his king safe from his enemies.

"Now I warn you once more, that you should be very alert as you go about this business because Vandirai has dog instincts, okay?"

"Everything is in my ear, Your Majesty!" Shingai replied, and the king dismissed him.

Unbeknown to Shingai, Rubonga had already assigned some of his "Ears and Eyes" to follow and watch all his movements. Rubonga had assigned these people at different times; therefore, they were not aware of each other's activities. With each day passing Rubonga's paranoia kept growing. He believed that his throne was in grave danger. His entourage also kept increasing, guarding him wherever he went. The king no longer went for walks on his own as he used to do, and this came as a blessing to the queens as they found their husband spending more time at home close to them. VaGondo assumed most of the king's duties, and he would report everything back to him. During those same days, Prince Masimba became unusually quiet and reserved. He became afraid of going out on his own. A bad vibe was rising with the winds at the palace.

Sometimes what is terrible for the serpent is good for the bird. Shingai had found an excellent excuse to see Shuvai freely. He spent a significant amount of time visiting her, and he would even slack on his official duties. When some members of the Ears and Eyes reported that he was regularly seen talking to Vandirai's daughter, the king was happy because he believed Shingai was doing his job very well and that he was soon to report some good news to him.

Shuvai would look at Shingai with her eyes full of love and affection, but when he asked to share her heart with him, she would tell him that she had no interest in boys at all. She told him not to even entertain the idea of him and her being romantically involved. One day Vandirai saw the two of them talking, and he gave Shingai a long stare as Shuvai respectfully walked away from him. Vandirai kept looking at him without saying a thing. The look had spoken to Shingai in a language that he quite understood. It had warned him to stay away from the veteran warrior's daughter if he knew what was good for him, but Shingai had also spoken back with his own look of respectful defiance, telling Lord Vandirai to get used to him seeing his daughter. Vandirai then followed his daughter, taking about four steps with his eyes still fixed on Shingai.

The following day early in the morning, Shuvai looked for Shingai and found him.

"My friend, that little incident yesterday when father caught me talking to you has caused some trouble for me. There is a lot that is going on between *bamukuru* Rubonga and my father that you do not know. Right now I have to go back to stay with my uncles again so I will see you when I come back. Please do not put your plans of looking for your soul mate on hold, thinking that my heart will one day feel for you. You are just somebody with a beautiful soul who is nice to talk to. But as for me, no one can take care of my heart."

Just as Shingai was about to respond, Shuvai carried on saying,

"Let me rush off now. The old man is already waiting for me, my friend."

She ran, leaving Shingai frozen with his mouth wide open.

Shingai thought that she was only playing, but later on, he heard people talking about Vandirai's relocation to his in-laws in Mawisire. The king's governors and other high ranking warriors laughed heartily at Vandirai's decision to leave his own royal status and land to go and live amongst the ordinary people in Mawisire even though his wife was long deceased. The king joined in the mockery of his brother, and Shingai could see that Rubonga became more relieved and relaxed. The love he had for Shuvai had superseded all of his other emotions. He felt angry that Shuvai had been made to leave Magocha because of jealous issues between two grown men. At that moment, he felt hatred for both Rubonga and Vandirai. If it weren't for the two antagonistic brothers, Shuvai would not have gone back to her uncles. She would still have been in Magocha, melting his heart with her smile!

King Rubonga revived his plans to invade the Western Kingdoms. Shingai prepared to go with the other warriors for the initial assault. He decided to use the time before the departure to the west to go into the woods to practice his arrow shot. He took his weapons and trotted to his training spot. Just as he got into the woods, he instinctively picked the sensation of being watched, that had become too familiar to him. He had learned his lesson well, and on that day, he did not charge carelessly like a rhinoceros. He walked in the direction he thought the pair of eyes that were staring at him was hidden.

He saw Gotora staring at him, and he looked directly into his eyes. He decided to speak first this time.

"How are you, sir? I want to know why it is that you are always following me?"

Gotora responded in his rumbling voice.

"Following you, when and where? Do you know what you are talking about?"

Shingai realized that he could not reason with the big man. He could see through Gotora's reddish eyes that he needed to say something to him, but he probably could not find a way of saying it. As he was trying to find a way to politely get him to talk, Gotora then spoke saying,

"If you make your bow string from the hide of a buffalo and use a *munyamagundere* stick to make your bow, you will be surprised at the strength of your shot."

Gotora finished up his short and unsolicited advice as he walked away. Shingai stood still trying to figure out what had made Gotora tell him about bows and arrows. Many people in Magocha knew Shingai as the most skilled archer. What did Gotora know about bows and arrows that made him speak about it authoritatively? He wondered. However, Gotora had just explained to him what would happen if he made his weapon from the hide of a buffalo and a *munyamagundere* stick. Shingai decided to look for straight branches of a *munyamagundere* shrub, and he got several sticks. He chose not to practice that day but to make a bow the way Gotora had suggested. He was curious, and he wanted to find out quickly. He had strings of various sizes made out of buffalo skin that he kept in his *gota*, so it would not take him long to find out!

Shingai was wowed by the power of his new bow. He tested his shots on a tree trunk, and he found that it was difficult to retrieve his arrows from the tree. He found himself smiling on his own in the woods. From that time, even when he knew that Gotora was watching him while he practiced, he did not mind. He turned around to look, and Gotora acknowledged by just nodding his head and then going on his way. Shingai was happy, and each time he saw Gotora, he began to greet him with sincere respect. He was also pleased that his weapon was different from those of other warriors because it was not waxed with mysterious charms through rituals he did not know about. Many warriors had their arms endowed on them with relics by healers and *n'anga* to make them invincible in battle. Many of them got disappointed when very often, the weapons lost power in the heat of battle, leaving their holders vulnerable to their enemies. Gotora had not even touched Shingai's weapon. He had just told him how to make it better!

Slowly Shingai and Gotora began to get along and talk a lot more. They would generally meet in the woods or near Gotora's home at the banks of the river. Gotora began to tell Shingai many things, especially about warfare. Shingai was amazed by how much Gotora knew about him. One day Gotora asked him where he came from and he tried to tell him the tale of him being a son of the mermaids and that he was not supposed to talk about it. Gotora laughed his heart out. This was the first time Shingai saw him laugh like that and he never saw him it again. Gotora then said,

"Young man, I am different from all those other people out there. Everyone in this kingdom believed your fake story but not me. I knew that it was a lie from the first time that you set foot in Magocha so don't try it on me."

Shingai was embarrassed that he had been exposed. He felt foolish and for a moment, regretted why he had lied. But this is what everyone in the kingdom knew and believed, making it the safest narrative to anyone that wanted to know about him. It was the story that had kept him alive and made him live with the Royals. Since he no longer knew where he came from, in his mind, he was starting to believe in his legend. He then confessed to Gotora that he had lost his memory of where he was from and that he was not sure how Magodo found him. Gotora did not look surprised when Shingai told him that. He just told him that he was also a foreigner in Magocha. Shingai had known that he was a foreigner because when people spoke about Gotora, no one claimed to know where he had come from, and no one dared to ask him about that.

Shingai asked him why he had chosen to teach him and why he had selected him particularly from among all the young men in Magocha.

"You are very different from the other boys Shingi. It is not that you are a foreigner in this land like me, but there is something special about you."

With these words, the discussion ended. On another day, they spoke about other events that took place a long time back in Magocha before Shingai's arrival. Shingai began to get a new perspective of Magocha and the dynamics of the politics of that kingdom.

Chapter 16

Rubonga's warriors were gathered in their battalions looking menacing and ready to spill blood like caged buffalos. They sang songs, chanted war cries, and bellowed like bulls spoiling for a fight. Their arrows, spears, and other weapons had been sharpened, ready for battle. Some had taken their weapons and performed rituals in their sacred family shrines to improve efficiency. Each warrior carried two or three weapons that he felt most comfortable to use in battle. There were the archers and those who carried spears. There were the athletes that used daggers and clubs and these soldiers specialized in running after and capturing retreating enemies.

Geographically Mazimbe was the closest to Magocha amongst the Western Kingdoms. The generals had planned to attack this kingdom first because it made sense for them to systematically attack and capture the nearest territories before moving into the interior. Rubonga had instructed the generals to bring the King of Mazimbe to him alive. He had warned them that failure to do so was as good as them not coming back to Magocha. At that time, the generals were standing before The Council of The Wise Eleven to bid farewell to His Majesty, King Rubonga. Shingai and Prince Masimba were amongst the commanders that were about to go for the raid.

Shingai stepped forward and posed a question to the commanders.

"I would like to know something from you sirs. How much do we know about this kingdom that we are going to attack and also how much do we know about its neighbors?"

Before the generals could respond, Chitsere spoke quickly from his seat.

"Are you getting frightened of going to war Shingi?"

This drew laughter from the confident generals. The laughter was laced with an arrogance that seemed to have invoked a sense of renewed bravery in the top military men.

"If you hear anybody claiming that they are not scared of going to war, it is usually a lie because those that are not scared are usually killed early in battle. A person that is scared has a motive to preserve his life, and therefore, he is very cautious during wartime."

Shingai calmly answered Chitsere, who had not expected Shingai's response, but he just went on and told him authoritatively, that there was no need to change the working formula, and that when they would go into battle, Shingai's only job was to identify and take out the commanders with his arrows before the enemy knew what had hit them. Most of the men at the court affirmed by nodding their heads. However, some seemed to wonder why Shingai had asked such an obvious question. They did not expect any serious resistance from the Mazimbe army.

Rubonga was also curious. He wanted to know why Shingai was asking the questions about how the war was to be executed as if it was different from others that they had fought and won. Shingai moved closer to the King, knelt on one knee, and whispered in his ear. The governors and the generals looked at each other, and all went silent. They were dying to know what

Shingai was relaying to the King. The King massaged his goatee, looked at his men and said,

"Tell your warriors to go back home and wait until we call them."

The generals immediately went to address their troops, but they were confused. The wise governors mumbled angrily at what had just happened. Chitsere whispered into VaGondo's ear, and the fat man first cleared his throat before he asked his fellow governors to meet at the King's court the following morning for an urgent matter.

The following day at sunrise, The Council of The Wise Eleven convened their meeting. They grumbled and mumbled about their power that was being stripped down by Shingai. They said that if it had been Prince Masimba that was usurping their power and influence to the King, they would not have minded. They resolved that the King needed to be informed of the trouble that he was blissfully creating for himself. Everyone among the wise governors agreed that the boy had trespassed way too deep into their territory. When Rubonga eventually joined the meeting, Chitsere did not waste time. He stood up and put his hands together, interlocking his fingers on both his palms and spoke before the King.

"Your Highness, we have gathered here together, we, your highly esteemed wise governors but before we convey the resolutions of the discussion that we've just had, we want you to know that all of our great minds combined are not even half as wise as yours. We misfire, we lose our direction, and we stagger when we walk, but with just the mere awareness of your presence as our guide, we fear nothing. We bounce about here and there, but we do so with the full knowledge that our tails are firmly pivoted on you.

"Allow us, oh King of the Beasts, to just waffle, but please give us direction if we are lost. We have agreed that it is wiser for us to voice our concerns so that you are aware of what is going on in our minds, rather than for us to conceal our views from you because we may then find ourselves regretting having been aware but keeping it to ourselves. Your Majesty, we have come to you because we are distraught in our hearts and minds by the power that is now frothing over that boy, Shingi. You must remember, oh Great One that we look at issues with eyes that are sometimes blind or see only as far as our noses. Please restrain us with much lenience so that we stay in your preferred paths.

"If this were Prince Masimba's doing, a-ah, we wouldn't have been worried at all. But we really fear that the other boy may have smeared his body with burnt oils from python fat and this may be giving him the ability to leech Masimba's royal blood, or even yours Your Highness, into his! I am sure you know how a python uses its shiny decorated skin to hypnotize an unsuspecting antelope. The antelope will only realize what is going on when it is crushing under the python's powerful grip.

"My King, please bear in mind that this boy is not only a stranger in your home but in Magocha too and all the other kingdoms that surround us. We are not saying that you must not listen to him or consider what he has told you, but we are saying that you must carefully pay heed to what he says and take time to use your wisdom in determining your plan of action. You may not also know that he has of late become a very close associate of the King of the wizards and witches of Magocha. As we said, at the beginning, our father …

He began to clap respectfully.

"Please forgive us for treading on your grounds without permission. Our direction comes from you. It is our elders who said that a baby that does not cry for attention may end up dying in its crib. We thank you."

Chitsere sat down, full of false humility as the other governors made groaning sounds in support and approval of what he had said. Even though Rubonga could sense the flattery in Chitsere's speeches, he always fell for it. He liked to be praised. He rested his cheek on his right hand and seemed to be in deep thought. He too made a sound without opening his mouth in agreement to the Council's concerns and said,

"A-ah Governor Chitsere, are you not known as The Council of The Wise Eleven? Your first and foremost responsibility is to be the spring of wisdom that the King drinks from. Is it not true that if I wanted stooges to agree with everything I say and do, I would have simply appointed even tree stumps to sit in your Council and nobody would have stopped me? You must never hide what you feel at the bottom of your hearts, my fellow leaders. This is your kingdom, and I am merely the head.

"Anyway, I have heard and considered your concerns. However, I am way ahead of you on this matter that you have brought forward. Unfortunately, I cannot disclose the matrix of the game that I am playing because it may weaken my plans. What you have said is true and wise. You have made me conscious of certain issues that I was no longer paying full attention to. Prince Masimba is the most exposed and vulnerable entity to machinations of sly foreigners. He should always be aware that he is standing on a pedestal."

The King and his men carried on discussing the issue about Shingai. The governors were happy and relieved to know that they were still favored by the King's ear.

Meanwhile, Shingai and Masimba did not know or even suspect what the discussion between the King and his top men was about. They just got on the road with two of their helpers and headed to the Western Kingdoms. They had planned to go on an espionage expedition so that they could learn as much as possible about the kingdoms that they were to wage war on.

That night, King Rubonga failed to sleep properly. He had plans involving Shingai that he needed to execute, but his men had raised issues that had unsettled him. Shingai was taking more princely roles than the heir apparent to the Mupingamhuru throne. Rubonga was conflicted. Shingai had become very wise and intuitive. All that he did proved that he was a thoughtful young man. Rubonga had taken Shingai to stay in his home because he wanted the blessings that seemed to follow him wherever he went and much more. Everything that was happening to Shingai seemed to be going very well with what he had in mind. Shingai had become a renowned warrior, and the King was quite confident that he would conquer the Western Kingdoms. This would make Rubonga more powerful, and this was his sole goal!

What troubled him was what would happen to Shingai after all the victories. How was he going to strip him of the powers that were piling up on him? How would he reduce him to an ordinary subject in his kingdom? If those kingdoms that he would have defeated would then hear that Shingai was no longer in his army or that he would have been demoted to a nobody in the top echelons of power in Magocha, would they not then plan to rebel against his dominion over them? All this would leave him vulnerable.

The fact that Shingai was spending time with Gotora did not worry him at all for he knew that Gotora did not stray into issues that did not concern him. He was not, in any way, a threat to the Mupingamhuru throne. It was the fact that Shingai was trying to get intimately involved with Shuvai that worried him. The Ears and Eyes of the King had informed him that Vandirai was totally against Shuvai dating somebody who lived with the king. But Lord Vandirai was not somebody that Rubonga could trust. Vandirai was the green snake that took refuge in the grass and was difficult to track. When he just thought of Vandirai, his bowels became unsettled. What consoled him on his thoughts was that Vandirai did not have a son who could be interested in taking over the Mupingamhuru throne and that the injury he had suffered on his right leg had weakened his fighting stamina. He was no longer a primary threat to his kingdom like he had been in his earlier days. Vandirai could no longer take him up on a one on one fight. Even though he was now weakened, Rubonga knew he couldn't afford to slack on his guard. His brother was a crippled man who had many skills of getting himself around.

After three months, Shingai and Masimba returned to Magocha from where they had gone to spy. They reported to the king and his wise men how their trip to the west had gone. They had disguised themselves as ordinary young men who were traders selling axes and other tools made of iron. They went from place to place in the different kingdoms looking for iron ore that they needed to make the tools to trade for other goods with the residents in those areas. By doing this, they acquired a lot of livestock and salt. They had not spoken much to the citizens of those lands. Some people had looked at them with suspicion, but after staying in those areas for a long time, many began to take them as harmless traders that were just using their trade to create wealth. Their ears and eyes had done a lot of the information capturing. They had noticed that the banks of the Mhathlehuru River had been lined up with warriors on the eastern front stretching for a long distance. Amongst the warriors were drummers and kudu horn blowers ready to warn other warriors at the slightest sign of an invading army.

The boys explained that there must have been a senior member of the Magocha government that had tipped the kings of the Western Kingdoms about the imminent invasion by King Rubonga. They had not established the identity of the renegade official. Seven kings, including three from the more prominent kingdoms of Magweza, Zibere, and Mazimbe had made a pact and joined their armed forces to fight off Rubonga when he chose to invade them.

All the governors looked uneasy because of Shingai and Masimba's account of their trip to the Western Kingdoms. Each of the governors seemed shocked and puzzled by the report. Rubonga did not show it, but he felt as if his heart was on hot charcoals. He was burning inside. One of his leading men had turned into a rotten egg. The boys took turns to narrate other things that they had seen and learned about the western territories. Masimba ended the narration saying,

"Even though the enemy is ready for us, my king, their plan is very porous. We drafted several ways of how we can attack them and take advantage of their poor positioning, but we cannot say it now lest our friend is probably listening to expose us again."

Before Prince Masimba took his seat, Chitsere was up and simmering with anger, he addressed his fellow governors.

"Men of Magocha! The words that Prince Masimba and Shingi bring are a curse to us. A snake has entered into our house and disappeared! The maggot that these boys are talking about is right here in our midst. None of the common people in Magocha have access to such confidential information on the King's plans of attack. The mole is right here as we speak. Let us not try to hide behind our index fingers! If the culprit is wise, he should just be man enough and confess right here and now because if we then expose him using other means, gentlemen-"

Chitsere took a deep breath as his eyes went from one governor to the next. Each time he looked at one, that governor would quickly move his eyes away from him.

"Honestly if we catch you, we shall kill you and everything that you own, even your hens and their chicks. Just confess now my brother, whoever you are. You know that our king may even give you a light sentence. He may just sentence you only to death and your family may be asked to just leave Magocha!"

Chitsere snorted as he sat down.

For some moments, the wise men seemed to have all at once lost their wisdom. One by one, they stood and consented to Chitsere's words. None of them had anyone that they suspected to be the traitor. As all this was happening, Rubonga was stone-faced just moving his eyes to look at each of his governors. In the end, all the men just sat quietly, waiting for the king's word. The King thanked his sons for what they had done and their wisdom in executing all that they had done. He asked The Council of The Wise Eleven to return to their districts and wait for him to summon them. Rubonga wanted to take some time to speak with his sons so that they could plan what to do next. When they had gone, he asked the boys who their suspects were. Shingai and Masimba told him that they had also failed to even come up with a suspect among the king's top men. Rubonga had also hit a stone wall on that. The three of them agreed to give themselves time to come up with a way to smoke the suspect out from the leaders of the districts. The boys thought there was no wisdom in going to war before they had weeded out the traitor.

Rubonga had not disclosed his suspicions, but in his mind, he was convinced that this had everything to do with Vandirai. Vandirai was his archenemy. He knew Vandirai in and out. Vandirai had been a prick in his soft flesh ever since Rubonga inherited the Mupingamhuru throne after their father had passed on. The King needed to act fast to weaken his enemies. Vandirai had a habit of disappearing and going under the radar for long periods, and therefore he could have been plotting with the enemies of Magocha to overthrow Rubonga. The best way to deal with a cunning enemy like Vandirai was to quickly send him to join the departed spirits. An enemy that moved underground like a mole was the most dangerous one. He was tricky to trace, and he could strike unexpectedly with the speed of lightning. Rubonga thought long and hard of a plan in his mind.

On the days that followed, additional warriors beefed up his security. Even the food that was prepared by his wives had to be sampled by a chosen warrior. The warrior would be monitored for some time to make sure that the food was void of poison, then the king would eat the food.

On the days that Shingai and Prince Masimba came back from the Western kingdoms, Shuvai and her father also returned to Magocha. Shingai was overjoyed by the presence of Shuvai in the territory. Conditions had changed, making it difficult for the two to regularly meet, but where the heart desires to be, a man will create the means to be there. Lord Vandirai had instructed Shuvai not to see or talk to Shingai because they did not know who he was and what he was about, but his words seemed to have bounced off a granite rock.

After many days of Shingai reciting poems and doing everything to prove that he was the man, Shuvai agreed to be his girl. Their romance set the whole kingdom on fire. Even though the two saw each other in hideous places, people became aware of their passion and spoke about it in great detail. At night the walls develop ears, and so that which was said in the homes was laid bare in public throughout the kingdom of Magocha. There were some who at first, bad-mouthed their union, but they then ended up cheering them on.

People said a lot about Shingai and Shuvai. Some claimed that Shuvai was going to be taken to the sacred pools to be introduced to the mermaids and other underwater creatures, while some claimed that she had already turned into a mermaid. Others claimed to have known way back that Shuvai's extraordinary beauty was one of those that lived deep underneath the silt of the sacred pools. Some said that Shingai had been sent by the elders of the spirit world to play a unifying role between King Rubonga and his young brother Lord Vandirai. Those in the royal family believed that Shingai was just not aware of the level of witchcraft practiced by Vandirai and his daughter and that it was not going to take very long for him to regret his stupid decision. They were all waiting for that day to arrive.

Rubonga was troubled by it all. On the one hand, he admired and enjoyed what Shingai was doing for him, but on the other, it worried him sick. He could not think of what to do with Shingai. In those days, Shingai had become a happy man who whistled a melody as he walked around. He felt like he was sitting on top of the world because Shuvai had completely stolen his heart. For many days Vandirai was infuriated by his daughter's affair with Shingai, but there was something that always restrained him from upsetting his daughter who had matured into a young woman without her mother. On the days that he would lose it and complain angrily about whatever she would have done, she only needed to hang her head on the side, and he would immediately stop. When Shuvai became aware of this, she did not like it, and she told her father to just keep the trust that he had in her since her childhood days.

Shingai shared his secret with Shuvai, telling her that he could no longer remember where he was really from. But that he had a deep feeling that he had lived in some land far away from Magocha. He told her that he had conveniently let the people of Magocha carry on with their belief that he was a son of those that lived deep under the sacred pools of Manyoka River. He asked her to not whisper it to any other person as this could jeopardize his whole existence in Magocha. She assured him that there was not a single soul in the kingdom that she could talk to about such information. They laughed when they spoke of people who claimed to know everything every time.

People had a habit of filling any void of information about anything they did not discern with suspicions and pure lies without any shame. This taught Shingai not to trust a lot of what he heard from people, especially if it was not something he had actually witnessed. Even as it were, there were many other things that he had heard and believed from such people, sometimes helping to spread the false narratives, only to be left with a rotten egg in his face after the truth had been revealed.

Shingai told Shuvai the bizarre word that was doing rounds amongst the royals about the purportedly incestuous affair between her and her father. She did not seem surprised when she heard it. She only smiled at him and asked,

"And what did you say about that?"

Shingai told her that he had not once believed it, not because it was just an unbelievable theory, but from since the first time that he had seen her, he was undoubtedly convinced that there was nothing she could do that could be associated with evil even if she tried.

"After that day when I first saw you, I thought to myself that you were not capable of sweating and that even if you stepped into muddy water, the water would instantly turn clear just because of your beauty!"

They laughed again.

"They are mad those people at *bamukuru* Rubonga's home."

Shuvai said, cracking her ribs from laughter.

Chapter 17

With time Shingai and Gotora became really close. Shingai disclosed a lot of information about his life and the developments in the kingdom to Gotora, but Gotora did not speak much about himself. He talked a lot about Shingai's fighting prowess. He also told Shingai about some significant events and stories that had taken place in Magocha a long time before Shingai and Masimba were even born. He told him stories that the people of Magocha had made sure did not reach his ears or those of Rubonga and his royals. Shingai began to get answers to issues that had many loose ends on how the people of Magocha behaved when confronted by certain circumstances.

He was baffled by what he learned about the history of the Magocha royal family. He realized that many people in the kingdom had mastered deception and were able to pretend that things were going well, even though deep down in their hearts, the opposite was true. Shingai began to distrust many people because of what he heard from Gotora.

The story that got his head going in circles was the brief history of the family and throne of Mupingamhuru. Gotora claimed to have witnessed most of the events that he talked about, but he also confessed that he had learned a lot from his ability to send his ear around without people being aware of it. One day the two swam to a little island that was on one of the big rivers. The island was a no-go area for most people. Hippos would graze there and for one to get to the island, they had to be skilled swimmers that could maneuver past the crocodiles. Gotora would often go there to get some special herbs that he could only find on that island. They sat on a dead tree trunk that had fallen a long time back, and Gotora took his ground tobacco out of his sling bag and inhaled it.

"So young man, you have decided to be an in-law of the royals?"

Shingi figured the question was rhetoric. By now he knew that if Gotora spoke like that, he was about to talk for a long time, so he just chuckled.

The big man began to make marks on the ground, using his wooden staff as if he was trying to write or draw something. He then cleared his throat and began to speak.

"The acrimony between your fathers-in-law, King Rubonga and his young brother Lord Vandirai developed a long time ago. I knew Vunganai Mupingamhuru, you know him, right?"

"Yeah, just hearing from other people that he was father to King Rubonga, yes that is what I know."

"Yes, that is him indeed. Now that man was an outstanding and wise leader. He led his people with great wisdom and love, not these rulers that we see today. The whole kingdom had great respect for him, and even other neighboring domains regarded him as a king with integrity. King Vunganai had two wives. The first queen who happened to be Lord Vandirai's mother was also a good woman who did not aspire to have a lot in life other than just loving her husband and their children. This woman bore the king four daughters before she gave birth to Vandirai.

"Because of pressure from the kingdom elders and his own desire to have someone that would inherit the throne and grow his name further after his time with the mortals was done, he took a second wife who incidentally bore him a son out of her first pregnancy. The son was Rubonga. This made the second queen very haughty, and she began to openly tease the first queen for her stupid ovaries. Teasing and taunting other people was a habit she had picked from the time that she was still a little girl. However, having a first-born son, which the king had wished for so much, for a very long time had severely inflated that habit. Funny enough, the next time that the first queen got pregnant, She bore Vandirai. She thanked her ancestral spirits for having answered her plea and silencing her enemies. Her enemy was indeed silenced, but not for very long. The second queen began to train Rubonga to be hard-hearted, telling him that if he did not keep his eyes open, Vandirai would take over the throne after their father.

"Even though Rubonga's mother was training him to be wicked and cunning, her son and Vandirai grew up together playing and loving each other as close brothers do. For most activities that they were involved in, there was a latent competition. As the boys grew older with time, the teachings that emanated from each of the two houses began to manifest for the public to see. Rubonga became known for being wicked and rough. He had no respect for anyone while Vandirai was respectful, kind, and wise. Vandirai was also short-tempered, but he learned how to suppress the weakness. He took his time to personally know many people in the kingdom, and even those that were influential in the surrounding territories. The first queen had another son, while the second queen had three more sons and two daughters. Rubonga's young brothers from his mother did not get the same teaching that he had received from their mother. She had heaped cruelty, mischief, and fraudulence on him. The rivalry remained between the two senior brothers.

"The Council of The Wise Eleven that worked with King Vunganai at that time were charmed by Vandirai's character so much that they even advised the king to appoint Vandirai for anointment as king after he was gone. The king had agreed with them because Vandirai was wise and a good war strategist, among other qualities. Rubonga was also good at fighting, but there were a lot of unrefined traits in him that would hinder him from becoming a good king. When the waves of this arrangement sailed in the wind and landed before Rubonga and his mother, they were not pleased. There was still plenty of time for them to scheme some evil plans because the king was still very strong and fit to lead while the boys were still too naive to run the kingdom. Rubonga's mother visited all the *n'anga* that she knew. Where she could not go, she would sent her brothers to consult on her behalf about the future of the Mupingamhuru throne and to seek for spells that could harm or prevent Vandirai from ascending to that throne. Of all the herbs and medicine that were applied to injure Vandirai, none seemed to have worked; instead, he kept growing stronger and wiser.

"Now it happened one year, when the boys Vandirai and Rubonga had grown into young men that a very fine-looking girl came to Magocha. The girl had come from Mawisire to look for her brother, who had been taken captive by one of King Vunganai's warriors. Sometime during the year that had ended, Magocha and Mawisire had gone to war, and Mawisire had lost. In those days, the prisoners of war would work for the warriors that would have captured them. A warrior could use his own discretion to set free a prisoner of war that would be working for him if he were satisfied with the work he would have done. Now, these days, the king owns all the prisoners of war! Anyway, the girl from Mawisire brought jewelry to buy her brother's freedom. She found where her brother was slaving, and after a short discussion with the warrior master, they agreed that the brother was to be freed once he had harvested the crop that he was working on. By the way, the girl was called Maruva. Maruva asked to stay at the master warrior's home so that she could assist her brother with the harvest, as she was also familiar with the crop that her brother was growing. This, she had said, would allow her to take her brother home earlier because the more the hands on the task, the faster it would take to complete.

"In no time, the whole Mupingamhuru district became aware of a girl that had the beauty of a bouquet of flowers just like her name, Maruva, that had come to stay in that district. News about this girl reached many boys, among them Rubonga and Vandirai. It did not require an announcement for the race to win the heart of Maruva to begin. The boys did what they could, each trying to prove that they had the most erect mane. Vandirai charmed and won the girl's heart, and many people that were watching from the sidelines were happy for him. They did not like Rubonga. Rubonga was bitter and very angry, and so he hated Vandirai even more. It was only after his mother had consoled him and explained to him the power of patience in that game, that he cooled off a bit. She told him to be like a *chapungu* the bateleur eagle that plans to catch its meal from high up in the sky. It plots and makes precise calculations of the speed and angles at which to attack its prey. When it does this, it becomes almost impossible for it to miss the victim. He had to be a *chapungu*. Rubonga planned to make his revenge so powerful in a way that its shockwaves would go beyond the borders of the Magocha kingdom.

"At the time that Rubonga was trying to win Maruva's heart, he already had another girl that he really loved, but when Maruva decided to give her heart to Vandirai, Rubonga suddenly lost interest in girls for a while. So, he did not go back to the girl that loved him. After some time, his girl also lost patience and got married to another man of a Gumbo totem. Vandirai married Maruva, and the two were soon blessed with a baby boy. Maruva bore him another son and then a girl. In those days, Rubonga was seen less and less in public, and people did not know what he was up to. Some began to say that he had realized that he was not suitable to inherit the throne after his father and that he was, therefore, preparing to take a lesser role in the running of affairs in the kingdom. He was no longer as cruel as he used to be. While Vandirai's daughter was still on her mother's breast, the king of Bengwa invaded Magocha to fight King Vunganai, and a destructive war ensued. There was animosity between these two kingdoms, but nobody had expected that it would escalate to such a bloody war! The last time that they had gone to war was when Rubonga Mupingamhuru, Vunganai's father was still king.

"A lot of blood from the people of Magocha was spilled. What shocked many people was the way the enemy managed to get to the core of Magocha's power. King Vunganai and his four sons were all killed in this war. Rubonga and Vandirai fought bravely, but it did not help much. Many of the Magocha warriors ran to find refuge in the mountains the moment they became aware that their king had been killed. Word got to Vandirai that Rubonga had been captured by the Bengwa army and that they had taken him with them, claiming that they had apprehended the person who was meant to be the next King Mupingamhuru to lead Magocha. Vandirai was torn, and he quickly put together a contingent of eight brave warriors to go on a mission to free Rubonga and bring him back home. The warriors he took were skilled in surprise attacks, and they were prepared to die while executing their mission. The members of the squad camouflaged themselves by applying colored mud, blood, and other pigments onto their faces and the rest of their bodies. Many people did not know about that plan because they had scurried to the mountains.

"Vandirai's squad caught up with Rubonga's captors deep in the woods. The captors had sat Rubonga in the middle, and twenty-three warriors surrounded him. At first, the squad would wait for a warrior to leave the bonfire to relieve himself and they would latch on to him, slit his throat with sharp daggers before he was able to make any sound. They said the enemy only began to suspect that something was not right when five of them had disappeared into the woods. The enemy then began to walk in groups of fives or fours, but now arrows that seemed to mysteriously hit them from were taking them out one by one. The archers tried to be as precise as possible, targeting the captors' necks without missing. Those that were shot just fell down without making much noise. One of the archers missed his target and bruised a warrior on the shoulder, and the injured warrior raised alarm with his wild cry. Fierce fighting ensued until the remaining Bengwa warriors fled. It is said that some of them believed that ghosts were helping the Magocha warriors attacking them. By that time three of Vandirai's warriors had been killed, leaving only six of them including Vandirai.

"In this struggle, Rubonga was left alone bound on both legs and hands by a rope made from buffalo skin. Vandirai realized it and stealthily moved to where Rubonga was. When he tried to cut off the cord, he was stabbed on his thigh by a Bengwa warrior who was hiding. The dagger sliced through Vandirai's leg to his calf, breaking some vital tendons and ligaments. It is said that if one of Vandirai's warriors who was alert had not crushed the sly warrior's head with a machete, Vandirai would have died at that spot.

"Vandirai stood up, but he could not walk. His warriors made a stretcher bed using freshly cut wooden poles, and they began the journey back home to Magocha. No one is said to have followed them. I think that the survivors ran most of their way back to Bengwa, constantly checking over their shoulders. At this point, five of Vandirai's men were left. With Rubonga and him, the number became seven. Vandirai's health began to deteriorate because of his injury. He had lost a lot of blood, and the bleeding had not entirely stopped. The squad needed to get back to Magocha quickly so that he could be attended to by a medicine man.

"It is said that as they were walking back home, Rubonga disappeared into the woods alone for some time and came back to join the squad later on. He is said to have then asked the five warriors to quickly hunt for a duiker or even a hare for them to have something to eat before they got home. The warriors did as the Prince had instructed them without questioning. Rubonga remained behind watching over Vandirai. Vandirai was now breathing lightly and not looking too good. The warriors quickly returned and roasted the baby duiker they had killed. Soon after, they were back on the road, walking very fast. By the time they were getting into the village, Vandirai was sweating profusely. They took him straight to a medicine man. By this time, he had lost consciousness, and many had already declared him dead.

"Yes, a person dies, but if his ancestors have not yet prepared a place for his soul in the winds, they decline him from joining them. Time passed with Vandirai still holed up in some cave where nobody but the medicine man knew. The medicine man with the help of his assistant had taken Vandirai to the sacred caves so that if anybody was planning to bewitch him, they would not dare set their foot there. Even Maruva and her children had no clue about his whereabouts and health. They had left it up to the ancestors. Whatever they were going to decide, the mortals had no say.

"Rubonga soon declared himself the new king, claiming that it was not proper for Magocha to carry on with a power vacuum, as that would leave it much more vulnerable to attack. 'The kingdom must pick itself up and grow a strong army to bounce off any threats from its enemies.' Rubonga had ordered The Council of The Wise Eleven to rush with his coronation and install him as King of Magocha. Soon after the inauguration, The Council was restructured. Five of the old governors were fired and replaced with Rubonga's handpicked ones. The winds began to fill up with words about the significant number of internal enemies that were freely roaming in the kingdom and that needed to be flushed out. The enemies were to be picked up and disciplined in various brutal ways. Many of the said enemies were exiled from Magocha while some were sentenced to death. Rubonga began to rule the kingdom with a heavy hand, and he made sure that people always feared him.

"As Rubonga was busy strengthening his grip on power, word went around that Vandirai had survived but that he was probably not going to be able to ever walk again. Vandirai came back, and he was told all that had taken place while he was away. His brother did not pay him visits, nor come to thank him for saving his life. Rubonga did not show any joy or gratitude for Vandirai's survival.

"The medicine man that had worked on Vandirai was found dead. Somebody struck him several times on the head with a wooden pole until he died. Before long, one of Rubonga's warriors began to lose his mind. His family members began to die mysteriously, and the poor warrior would be seen engaging in a conversation with an invisible person. The invisible person would sometimes command him to climb a tree and let him fall to the ground from a high point. Sometimes he would be told to laugh out very loud and immediately stop to do something else like crying or kicking rocks with his bare feet. The invisible person refused to be asked for forgiveness. Those that saw what was happening felt sorry for the warrior. One day he was asked to extract honey from a hollow tree trunk without pacifying the bees first. The bees stung the warrior all over his body. The warrior confessed to having killed the medicine man, but he would not tell why or who it was that had instructed him to commit the crime. This baffled many people. They spoke about it in the comfort of their homes but as the elders used to say, 'At night, walls develop ears and mouths.' Some of us heard a lot.

"No one knows what really happened, but it is said that before the medicine man was murdered, he had told some elders that someone had put venom of a deadly snake onto Vandirai's open wound. When people analyzed the narrations that had been given by the squad that went to rescue Rubonga, many concluded that Rubonga had put the poison in Vandirai's wound when he sent the warriors to hunt and he was left alone with Vandirai. It is said that the snake poison is what caused Vandirai's healing to take very long. Prince Vandirai was supposed to die, but the herbs that the medicine man gave him must have been from very far away places because they neutralized the snake venom and it failed to kill Vandirai.

"When Vandirai heard about this theory, he was slow to believe it. He knew that Rubonga was highly antagonistic to him but not to the extent of planning to kill him. One can doubt, but once a seed of accusation has been sown into one's mind, it finds a place where it is stored. If the seed of conspiracy is exposed to the right conditions, it germinates and grows. The accusation is regularly taken out and set up in various scenarios to establish if it is congruent with the scenes. The delay by Rubonga to visit him when he returned from the sacred caves was congruent with the theory that his brother wished him dead! He realized that he had to be very cautious or else his life could quickly end.

"Word that came from Bengwa claimed that it was actually Rubonga who had betrayed Magocha by organizing with the Bengwa army to attack Magocha without them expecting it. They said he wanted King Vunganai and all his sons except for him alone to perish in that attack. He wanted Vandirai to be killed so that he would be crowned king without any hindrance. They said that those that had captured Rubonga had done so thinking that he was Vandirai because they believed that he was the heir apparent to the throne of Magocha. They needed their king to personally kill him on Bengwa soil. Vandirai had fought and beaten all the Bengwa warriors that had tried to apprehend him. Vandirai's survival in the battle had put Rubonga's plan into disarray. He could not disclose his identity to the warriors that had captured him because only a few people, even from the Bengwa army, knew about the plan.

"The days spun over, and Rubonga married his first wife. They had their first-born; a son and Rubonga named him Tongai for he was now the ruler of Magocha. You have not met him yet Shingi, the one that went to build his home among his mother's kinsfolk. People whispered in their homes that Tongai had not lived up to his name but instead had been a disgrace to his father because it was difficult for many to see his masculinity. His body structure had a lot of feminine features. Rubonga had other daughters, and later on, he had your friend, Masimba. He then went on to take other wives. He would love a woman and marry her, but as soon as she gave him a child, he lost interest in her, and he would take another wife! Vandirai eventually healed after a very long time. He went on to have other sons and daughters, and then he had Shuvai as the last born."

Shingai opened both his ears and eyes wider as if he needed his eyes to help him hear what he was being told. Shuvai was his life, and anything that he could learn about her was vital. He quickly interjected Gotora.

"So where are his other children? I know that Shuvai's mother passed on but what about these other children that you are talking about because I have never seen or even heard about them. Where are they?"

Gotora was slightly irritated by the question that broke his monologue. He looked at Shingai with a taut face and quizzed him,

"And how did she die? The mother?"

"A-aa, I don't know but-"

"But listen to me and only ask questions when I'm done telling you what I want to tell you, you hear me?"

"Yes, sir. Please break it down for me, I'm listening."

Gotora looked at him with his red eyes for a little longer till Shingai was a bit uncomfortable, then he carried on.

"What happened then was that Rubonga did not stop monitoring all that was going on with Vandirai during this period. Vandirai's healing caused a lot of discomfort to him. He got a bit of relief knowing that although

Vandirai had healed, the injury on his leg had weakened him, and thus, he could not use his leg fully. The limping prevented him from running and involving himself in physical fights like he could do before. Rubonga told himself that he needed to be on high alert all the time lest he is caught off guard. Vandirai had sons, and if he trained them to be as artful as he was, then they could pose a real threat to his throne.

"One day, when you get a chance, you must ask your Shuvai about what I am going to tell you now. You must not ask her these days because she might hate you and never want to see or talk to you again just because of her grief. The trapped sadness that is sitting on her throat is like the one that her father has. This is because of the pain that resulted from what I am about to tell you now, therefore if you sincerely love and care for her, please young man, do not mention these words to her or even let her know that you know about it. She will tell you about it when she is ready, so give her time. You should wait until she gets to the point of regarding you as a part of her life that she cannot do without, then you can ask her about it, and she will tell you.

"Anyway, so what happened is this, on one night it was so dark that one walking outside actually felt the weight of the darkness dragging him backward. Many people were lost in dreamland and Shuvai suddenly had severe diarrhea from having overeaten cooked fresh corn. She could not hold it, so she woke her older sisters up and asked them to go with her outside so that she could relieve herself. The sisters refused because they did not want to be disturbed from their peaceful sleep. Shuvai was only a four-year-old girl then, and she was terrified. She realized that if she kept standing in the hut, her insides could blow up and fill the whole rondavel with diarrhea, so her urge to relieve herself overtook her fears for a moment, and she ran outside and squatted near the bushes just outside the yard.

"At that moment, it is said the dogs from the nearby homes began to howl like wolves, passing on the howls from one homestead to the other as if it was something planned. Shuvai was not bothered by the noise, as much as her bowels that felt like they needed to expel everything inside, including all her internal organs. The fear returned to her when she was done and looking for leaves to wipe herself. As she was about to reach for some broad leaves, she saw moving flames, and she froze. She thought the night people that she always heard being talked about had come to clap her with their open palms. She thought of screaming, but at that moment, her voice seemed to have abandoned her. In no time Shuvai saw flames engulfing the huts and the granary. She saw five or six men going around the burning buildings. She could see them because of the light from the angry flames that quickly began to consume the dry grass thatch on the premises.

"Next, she heard people panicking and wailing from the burning huts. She could not do anything. She thought of screaming again, but fear still got the best of her. The men were wearing masks on their faces so she could not tell who they were. To her, it looked like there were more men at the boy's hut than at the other rondavels. Shuvai claims that she saw one boy getting out of the rondavels in flames but as soon as he got out he was hit by a club on the head and he fell to the ground. One of the men who were waiting outside rolled him and threw him back into the burning hut.

After that, no one else came out of the burning huts. The roofs of the burning huts collapsed inside the walls from the pitch, and when this happened, the men quickly ran and vanished into the bush. Shuvai stood there paralyzed, just watching the fire with tears rolling down her cheeks. The neighbors began to arrive one by one with each one of them shouting for others to come and help. Some got green tree branches, but they could not get too close to the menacing flames to extinguish them.

"The sun rose with smoke still rising from the hot embers of the burning logs. Shuvai did not go to where the people were standing because she was not sure which of them were good or evil people. She kept hiding under a bush. Some men who were walking around the yard trying to establish what could have happened found her. The young girl broke into a cry that left many women sniffling. Towards midday, some men were able to get into the walls that were left standing. They discovered that people had been burnt to death in three huts and that they had tried to escape through the doors of the huts, where they had fallen on top of each other. This bewildered the people, and it seemed as if someone had deliberately burnt the rondavels with the intention to kill the people inside. In the boys' room, there were three bodies burnt, which meant that all the three sons of Vandirai had perished in the fire. In the girls' room, there were also three burnt bodies indicating that only little Shuvai had survived the arson. In the main bedroom, there was one body. The people asked Shuvai where her father was, and she told them that he had gone hunting before sunset on the previous day.

"The people were baffled by how Shuvai escaped the fire unhurt when everybody else had not survived. Shuvai could no longer answer anyone because she was sobbing again. This made the people fill in the gaps of the narrative with what they suspected and created the building blocks to the whole story of the demise of Vandirai's family. Some said that little kids have prophetic powers and therefore Shuvai had known what was going to happen, so she had left before the fires began. Some said that the spirits of the waters possessed her and so any fire could not burn her. Still, others said that it was her, the little strange and naughty girl that had done everything, setting the huts on fire and magically shutting the doors so that no one could open them because she was the body that hosted evil.

"King Rubonga and his delegation arrived later expressing a lot of sadness at what had happened. Some of the governors from The Council of The Wise Eleven suggested that a *n'anga* be quickly summoned to identify the villains and bring them to book. Rubonga opposed and rejected the idea claiming that this was a clear act of war. Because it was an act of war, there was no danger of avenging spirits waking up. He also said that the onlookers had done a thoughtless thing by walking all over Vandirai's yard as it now became difficult for trackers to identify the footprints of the people involved. Rubonga said that the people that he knew were capable of committing such an act were the Bengwa warriors. The Bengwa warriors were still bitter at Vandirai for spoiling their plan when they had captured Rubonga during the battle that took his father's life! He said he had known about their hatred for Vandirai from listening to them when they discussed during the short time that he was in their captivity. Many people found Rubonga's version plausible, but the gray heads knew exactly what had taken place. They just shook their heads slowly in sorrow.

"Had it not been that Shuvai was still alive, Vandirai would have taken his own life. The man loved his family so much, and this event hurt him to the bone marrow. He cried like a baby, and even Rubonga showed some sympathy for his loss. Without a family, a grown man loses his gravity. After he buried his family, Vandirai took Shuvai and went with her to Mawisire were the two stayed for a long time with his in-laws. When he came back, he volunteered to spend his time teaching the boys at the initiation school in the Pengapenga Mountains. Rubonga agreed to the proposal and gave him free rein over it. From that time, people did not see much of Lord Vandirai in Magocha or know about how Shuvai grew up. In his mind, Rubonga felt very safe. He emerged strong. There was no longer anybody that could challenge the legitimacy of his reign.

"Rubonga tried to resuscitate his affair with his boyhood sweetheart, but he could not marry her as she was already married to Madhlira of the Gumbo totem. The girl is the one that became Ndaka and young Mukai's mother. You probably realize now that the reason why Rubonga wanted to marry Ndaka and then ended up taking Mukai was just out of his desire for their mother. He was acting like the eagle, which when it misses its prey, it picks the dirt or twigs near the target. Rubonga became more hard-hearted, with not even one person able to restrict him. Even his sister's eldest son, Musavengana had received many gifts from him in exchange for forfeiting his role in the family as one who could not be restricted from cautioning even the most respectable members of the family.

"Over the past few years, you have shown a lot of wisdom and possession of mysterious powers and ever since Vandirai retired from his positionas head teacher at Pengapenga, we have noticed that the king is no longer comfortable. He seems to be deeply troubled. In days like these, Rubonga acts like a wounded buffalo that destroys anything that appears to be threatening its survival! This is the reason why I saw it fit to teach you to be more skillful in your fighting and keeping yourself away from danger. You have a lot of enemies that you are not aware of. Now, from all that I have told you, do you have any questions for me?"

By the time that he asked this question, Gotora was already stretching and yawning.

Shingai slowly shook his head. The sun was setting, so they proceeded on their journey back to their homes. Gotora was close to his, so before long he was at his hut. Shingai went back to the palace with his mind heavily distressed. He had heard a lot on that day that seemed to provide answers and clues to many questions that he had. But at the same time, many questions also arose from the same information. All these problems seemed to rest on him. How was he going to react when he would see the various people that he now had new information on? He knew Gotora as one who always told the truth, and also as one person that knew the lives and behaviors of the people of Magocha. He seemed to have information about everything that took place in the whole Kingdom of Magocha.

So Vandirai was not an evil person, after all, no, he was just bitter about what had been done to him by his brother. But could it also be true that he wanted to overthrow his brother from the throne like what the Royals believed? As for him, he should not have anything to fear about because he had nothing to do with what the Royals did, right? So what did Vandirai think of him? If he was going to become his son-in-law, wouldn't that be reason enough for Rubonga to kill him? And how much of all this did Masimba know? Masimba loved his father and had a lot of respect for him. He praised the king for most of what he did except for his indulgence in women. However, Masimba was in a way not different from his father in that regard. Although he was still a single young man, he loved to have many girls at the same time. Could it be that Masimba knew all that was going on and if he became aware now that he knew what took place, would he tell his father? The questions multiplied in his head.

Shingai thought of how much pain Shuvai had suffered in her life, and he felt hurt just by the thought of it. So this is what caused her dislike for her relatives, although she would conceal her feelings towards them very well, especially when she was with them. Probably for the ones that did not know her, they probably thought she had no idea of how her mother and her siblings had been killed.

Shingai went for a couple of days resting at home, claiming to be suffering from an aching head. He did this so that he could use the time to think through everything and reset his mind. He had learned from experience that a smart person does not make decisions when they are emotionally charged, on either extreme.

He needed to act as if he knew nothing about what had happened in the past to avoid mudding settled waters.

Chapter 18

"So sweetheart, when did your head stop aching?"

Shuvai asked, putting her hand on Shingai's neck and rubbing it.

"This morning. I woke up feeling much better. And who told you about my aching head?"

"A-ah, come on Shingi, you think a person with somebody as special as you in their life would let them suffer and not do anything about it? Kundai told me. I came and saw all my mothers, but I could not gather enough courage to come to your *gota*. Well, I would have come, but then they told me that you were now taking your meals well."

Shuvai inclined her head on one side with her gaze focused directly into Shingai's eyes. The two sat facing each other on top of a boulder. Shuvai was smiling at Shingai just the way he liked. She would incline her head on one side and keep staring into his eyes. She would then hold her cheeks in her hands and still look straight into his eyes and then say,

"Sometimes I just can't stop marveling at the fact that you are all mine! Those that sent you out of the sacred pools were definitely sent by my ancestors. Ummnn, boy I love you so much!"

Shingai would smile back, pulling up his upper lip to the side and put his hand on his chest without making any effort to suppress his pride. They were deeply in love. They spent a lot of time together, and each time they would complain about how time seemed to sprint only when they were together.

On days like this, Shingai would walk Shuvai and get very close to her home, then when he would bid her farewell, she would also walk him back. They would end up just standing at the halfway mark as they laughed at themselves. On one such day, Shuvai told him that she really needed to rush back to prepare supper for her father. They hugged and looked at each other and then remained locked in this position for a little while longer, and while they were in that position, Shingai thought he saw Shuvai's ears stretch a little bit like what a dog would do. In a split of a second Shuvai pushed Shingai on the chest and she fell back on to the grass. An arrow whizzed and hit the tree that was between where the two were standing with such a strong force, making pieces of the tree buck to splinter in different directions.

"What happened Shingi?"

She was shocked and breathing fast. Shingai had already loaded his arrow and looking in the direction that the arrow had come from and not saying a word. When he could not see anybody, he began to check all around with his face taut.

"Shingi I asked you, what is it that has just happened here? This arrow; who shot it? Are they aiming at us? I'm scared Shingi."

Shingai only answered when he was confident that they were out of danger for that moment.

"Well I don't really know, I think you sort of instinctively pushed me back- but you eh-h, you seem to have fallen backward also, what happened? There is no animal close by for us to think that maybe some hunter missed and his arrow strayed towards us, but even if that is what happened then the hunter would have come to retract his arrow and apologize. Hunters are trained not to release their weapons unless their targets are not in the direction of humans."

Shuvai began to shiver and shake, saying that she was petrified. Shingai retrieved the arrow from the tree and planned to investigate who it was that had shot it. He quickly walked Shuvai back to her home, not willing to put her in any more danger. He stopped just when he got to the edge of her yard. She asked him to quickly run back home and to place an eye on his occipital as he walked back. He watched her walk into one of the huts before he trotted home. The arrow that he had retrieved belonged to some warrior. This meant that he now had an apparent enemy that was after his life. There was a warrior who was hunting him. No warrior would be hunting a girl like Shuvai to the point of trying to shoot at her! But who could it have been that was stalking him? What is this that wanted to complicate his life, only now that it seemed to be going so perfect? Who could it have been that was not scared of spilling the blood of the one from the feared underwater dwellers?

He remembered that he needed to act wisely for him to catch his enemy before the enemy got to him first. He was no longer afraid of killing the enemy because this had become a war thing. He who is killed when fighting in a war is prohibited by his ancestors from returning to haunt his killer in the form of an avenging spirit. For him to protect his sweetheart, he was to avoid meeting her in obscured places, and he had to make sure that she would be home before sunset.

Rubonga called Masimba and Shingai, and the boys quickly went to him. After asking each other about their health, the king then went straight into his issue.

"Boys, the issue of the deviant who whispered our plans to the enemies has been bothering me since you informed me about it. I have tried to establish from my Ears and Eyes, but nothing solid has come from them yet. I think it is about time that we just consult a *n'anga* to assist us in revealing him. Why should we die of thirst while walking in a flowing stream? Gezi will just point to us the villain, and then it will be upon us to deal with him. I don't know, what do you boys say about it?"

Shingai responded first,

"I am not so sure, what do you think about it, Masimba?"

He did not want to speak his mind out because he didn't know who his enemy was at that point, but he had not exonerated the prince and the king from the list of suspects.

"Ummnn, but father, why did it take you this long before you decided on engaging the spirit medium Gezi? What would the wise elders recommend in such cases? You always tell us that it is not all issues that should be thrown to *n'anga*. What has shifted your stance now? But your wise governors are usually reliable in sniffing out those involved in actions that may put the security of the kingdom at risk. Why don't you give them a bit more time, Your Highness?"

"Well, our elders used to say that *n'anga* are mostly good at tracing issues following family bloodlines than what happens out there unless the spirit mediums are intervening for something that involves multitudes of clans. Sometimes our traitor may also have consulted his own *n'anga*, and his *n'anga* could have cast charms on him that would make him invisible to our *n'anga*, and in such a case we may not be able to stop him, meaning he will continue to erode us from the base."

The king went on to say that he had been told some years back that when this time came, he needed to attack the Western Kingdoms so that they would be under him because failure to do so, meant that those kingdoms would plan to destroy Magocha. He said because of this, time was not on his side. The sellout was supposed to be apprehended before they went to war with these kingdoms. The boys nodded. Rubonga did not give them time to keep discussing the issue because he said that The Council of The Wise Eleven was meeting the following day to discuss the engagement of the *n'anga*. The boys saluted and left.

Rubonga instructed one of his warrior guards to signal the drummers to summon the governors to court. Shingai badly wanted to stay for the meeting because he wanted to look at each of these influential and feared men in their faces so that he might decipher who amongst them was trying to eliminate him. From amongst Rubonga's wise men, none was still able to shoot an arrow with the strength of the one that had shot at him and Shuvai. He was confident that the warrior was acting under the instruction of one the governors or a higher authority like King Rubonga or Prince Masimba. Shingai was not permitted to be present when the king and his wise men debated. Even Masimba, the heir apparent to the Magocha throne, was not permitted. It was only meant for the king and his governors. Rubonga had however recently ordered that two of his giant guards be present wherever he was because of the dark shadow of the enemy that was hovering above his throne those days. Shingai decided that he would make sure to greet each of the members of the Council after their meeting so that he could carry on his investigation.

The drums were beaten, and soon other drumbeats could be heard from the nearby hills surrounding the king's residence. The drumbeats were carried further by the other drummers, and before long the coded sounds had been relayed right to the homes of the governors in each district. The governors that stayed too far from the king's palace had been asked to occupy their residences in the king's home in those days. The governors got on the road and headed straight to the palace.

During those days, many could see that the king was troubled, and that he had a lot going on in his mind. He would focus his eyes on something, and he would remain staring at it until he got disturbed by one of his wives, bringing him some snacks like dried meat or roasted and salted peanuts. One could easily mistake him for a carved wooden statue when he sat on his chair and did not move. The musicians would take turns to play soft *mbira* tunes to serenade him, but the melodies seemed to be reaching a man that no longer had his outer and inner ears. He no longer showed appreciation for the music like he used to. What was eating his mind and soul seemed to have been locked deep down his heart.

Shingai had noticed that the king had changed in many ways. As big of an introvert as he was, there were a few moments when he had openly expressed his happiness. There were days when he would make time to play with his younger kids, asking them silly questions and laughing his lungs out with them. There were days when, after having imbibed some brew, he would dance to the sounds of *mbira* and drums in front of his family. Those were the days that his family would see him smile and his wives would also be pleased, for when such things happened, they knew that one of them would be taken by the king to sleep in his bedroom that very night.

There were days when the king would move around inspecting work carried out in his home and in many other places in his district. On such days he would be seen interacting with his subjects and demonstrating his knowledge on the various tasks that they would be working on. Now, such visits had become scarce, and he hardly knew what was going on in the kingdom. The king was no longer comfortable with his life. Even his body seemed to be giving in. His eyes appeared to be falling deeper into the sockets of his skull. His hair was graying fast on the sides because of stress. He was getting more and more paranoid. Shingai thought that this might have been payback that was being inflicted upon him by the spirits for the many sins that he had committed over the years. His mind, body, and spirit were being consumed all at once. Shingai considered the life of the king for a moment and concluded that it was not for him.

The governors began to arrive one by one, joining VaGondo and other governors that had been staying at the palace. When they were all present, the musicians moved further away and kept playing their instruments on a low tone. They moved away so that they could not hear what was being discussed. Shingai found time to go and greet the governors before they began their deliberations. When they saw him, they all looked at him in a way that people look at one that would have soiled himself and smeared the dirt all over his body. When he greeted them by respectfully clapping his hands and asking how they were doing, only a few of them responded, including Chitsere and VaGondo. These two paid some attention to him, speaking a few kind words accompanied with smiles.

While all this was taking place, he got to look into each one of them in the face, but he could not come up with a likely suspect because they had all shown him attitudes that emitted smoke of hatred towards him. This took him by surprise. In a short space of time, the number of his enemies had multiplied. All he knew was that among these men, was one that desired to see him and the king dead. How was he going to find out who this person was, especially since they had all shown him disdain? He could not complete his analysis because he had to move away to permit the governors to carry on with their meeting. They needed time to freely discuss some issues before the king joined them. As he left, he felt stupid and cursed himself for having gone to greet them without Masimba. If he had gone with him, he could have observed them better. He felt the twenty-two eyes piercing his back as he walked away from them.

The meeting began, and Rubonga put his issue before his men.

"Wise men of Magocha, we do not want to waste time on this issue. Up to now, our man is still scratching his nose with his pinky finger in the hope that we will forget about it and move on, but that is not possible. We gave him ample time to confess, and if he were a clever man, he would have given himself up, but no, he still thinks we are playing hide and seek with him like little children. Now what we are going to do is give him one last chance to confess right here, but if he decides to stay underwater, well, then we will find those that can fish him out of that water. I am ready to summon Gezi the *n'anga* to come and throw his dry bones on the ground and point to us the culprit so that you will all know what we do to such miscreants. Now get on with it quickly!"

His eyes had turned red, and his forehead showed the kind of anger that could make him eat raw flesh.

Feeling irritated by all this, Chitsere quickly stood up and hurled out a mocking laughter that pained and annoyed the other governors who had become very uneasy by this time. All eyes were on him as he began to speak.

"Honorable wise governors allow me to salute the Lion that is sitting amongst us, him that is husband to us all! Men of Magocha, this son of Mupingamhuru that we have here is such a true blessing to us from the great ancestors of this land who now dwell in the spirit world. Your Majesty, you have just taken all my words. You know it has been really frustrating my heart that you gave the sellout that much time to confess, but he has decided to sit here quietly and arrogantly like a cat, even after you have given him more time to make his confession. I said to myself, 'But why does the king not just take the *n'anga* route?' not knowing that is what was on your mind! I think we should not even continue to waste your time by asking the person to confess when it is clear that it is not going to happen. Let your wish be executed now. Perhaps you should already send your boys to get Gezi, eh, I believe he is your preferred choice for this job, right? My mouth may be speaking faster than my thoughts. Please summon the *n'anga* of your choice so that you quickly find your resolution to this. I may also be blocking some of my colleagues that may have better ways of outing the enemy of the kingdom. My fellow wise men, let us do what we always do when we have such issues. Those that believe we should allow a *n'anga* to tell us who the person we are looking for is, show by raising a hand!"

By the time he finished talking, his hand was already up.

It was clear that the rest of the men did not want the issue to be resolved by a *n'anga*, but they feared victimization and suspicion of them being the perpetrators or having the knowledge of who was behind the heinous act. All the men began to look at each other, and slowly, hands began to rise. Rubonga had stood up from his throne and was walking in front of the men assessing the behavior of each of his men. Grown men began to shake uncontrollably except for VaGondo and Chitsere.

"Why is everybody shaking and acting strange?"

Rubonga thundered, but no one answered him. He was scared, thinking that all his men were in the process of rebelling against him. He quickly sent one of his guards to tell Gezi that he was wanted at the king's court the following day. He was to come prepared to do his work there. He dismissed his men and went into his house. By that time, the wise governors were no longer talking to each other.

On the next day, Gezi arrived at the king's palace with a black hairdo. The hairpiece was made from feathers of a black hen and lined with 6 porcupine spikes on the front band. His ears had hugely pierced holes that had rings made from knitted green grass. The grass earrings were connected on each side to a piece of a carved twig that went through the center of the tip of his nose. He wore a skirt that was made from black and white pieces of cloth. The pieces of cloth ran from the waistband to just above his knees. On top of this were three tails, one of a baboon, the other of a hippo, and the third one of a hyena. He was horrific to look at. When he walked into the king's yard, the little kids ran and hid behind their mothers.

In front of him walked a man playing *mbira* and another shaking a pair of rattles. Behind him was a drummer. All these people were eerily dressed, especially the drummer. He had a stuffed monkey strapped on to him. Everybody in the palace yard stopped what they were doing to look at Gezi. Gezi and his team went around the king's home twice without saying anything to anyone. Suddenly Gezi broke into a powerful sprint heading towards the king's court were the king and his men were seated. He jumped over some of the governors, and the king's warriors drew their weapons ready to strike. Even Rubonga was startled for a bit, but he quickly settled down. Gezi raised his palms to the level of his shoulders and continued to run, this time speaking in a language that no one could understand. He then ran out of the gate and headed northwards to a small hill.

The drummer then translated what Gezi had said to the king and his governors, saying,

"*Sekuru* has refused to practice the divination by throwing dry bones in the home of a high standing royal. He said people should move far away from the king's residence because there is an evil spirit that is trying very hard to gain access into the palace. Therefore, all the people that are involved in today's case must follow *sekuru* Gezi where he has gone. The king and his men were soon on their feet, trekking northwards. Shingai and Masimba were asked to tag along. They found Gezi sitting on a flat rocky area with his legs folded in the same manner, with his knees pointing outwards. The group was stopped from getting to where Gezi was when they were still about one hundred and fifty meters away. The drummer was the only one who walked all the way and sat by Gezi's side. Gezi then shouted, saying.

"Sir, you the son of those from deep under the sacred pools, please may you go back home because *sekuru* will not be able to execute his work if you are in his presence!"

Rubonga looked at Shingai and used his head to tell him to excuse himself. Shingai quickly got it and went back home. His heart was burning with the desire to know who the enemy of Magocha was. After he left, the group was asked to move closer to Gezi.

Gezi began with a bellow, then he threw his bones into the air and let them land on the rocky ground. He then talked to the bones in a strange language that only the drummer and the bones could understand. The drummer would then translate what was being said to the whole group.

The drummer said that *sekuru* could see that many issues were troubling King Rubonga in his palace and throughout his land. He noted that the *sekuru* was also aware that although the king had many pressing issues, there was one, in particular, that was giving him sleepless nights. The *n'anga* could not go through all these issues. So, Rubonga had to pick one that was the gravest of them all.

"Amongst my governors *sekuru*, right there. My governors!"

Rubonga spoke not so sure whether he was answering Gezi's question or whether he was helping Gezi to get to the person faster. Gezi cast his bones again then he began to whisper to them before shouting at them and then he said that some of the governors needed to resign from their positions. Rubonga spoke again.

"But *sekuru*, can such a treasonous offense be closed by just retiring people? Oh, and so more of them are involved in this?"

Gezi shot up in an instant and began to cuss at the king's men.

"Sons of witches! Are you not ashamed of yourselves? Why do you do these things? Where do you think you are going to get another king who has a heart for you like him? I asked you, why do you do this?"

Chitsere clapped his hands respectfully and for attention, and then spoke.

"We are deeply sorry, oh, *sekuru*. Accept our apologies, grandfather. The wicked person has refused to confess on his own, so we implore you, the one that can see all over from the spirit world, to show your respectable grandchild the maggot that has mutated from being one of his wise men to being one that trades the kingdom secrets and plans to the enemies. We are truly sorry *sek-*"

"Can you just shut up! You, clever for nothing thief that has finished all the people's chickens in the villages. What *pworry pworry* nonsense are you going on about? You think I am not aware of the king's concern? I said, why do you people do it? Don't you know that crime committed by one of you is a crime committed by all of you, huh? Don't you know it? You should have apprehended your man way before it reached the king's ears. What is wrong with you kids of today?"

The *n'anga* went on complaining while all the men were sweating with fear, all their faces staring at the ground. None of them wanted to have eye contact with Gezi. Gezi turned to Rubonga and said,

"And you a little boy, don't you know that such cases are not divined in the home of the great kings of this land? Now if your person had been revealed to you in the royal courtyard, would you not have spilled blood right there in Mupingamhuru's home? Anyway, my work here is done. What you do afterwards with your person is entirely up to you. *Sekuru* is done. Your sellout is Revesai!"

All the men lifted their heads up to look at Revesai. They were relieved but shocked. Revesai stood up and froze with his mouth wide open. At the same time, Gezi's drum started beating, followed by the rattles and *mbira*. Gezi led his team away without looking back. Rubonga looked at Revesai and fixed his eyes on him. Some of the governors were now a bit relaxed, but deep in their hearts, they were also shocked and wondered how Revesai of all the governors had committed such a crime.

Revesai looked at his king with anxiety and thought to himself,

"This is just a nightmare, and I will soon wake up from this bad dream."

But unfortunately for him, he did not wake up. His mouth remained open like that of a live bream taken out of water. Chitsere broke the tense silence that had gripped the whole court.

"So this is the calm dog that the elders claimed to have the sharpest bite! Who would have thought you could pull such a feat? Ummnn, wise men of Magocha, I no longer have anything to say. This is just crazy if you ask me."

Rubonga kept looking at Revesai and Revesai did not take his eyes away from the king's. When he finally tried to mumble some words, a warrior gave him a mighty blow that stretched from the back of his ear and his occipital and grounded him in that same moment. By the time he opened his eyes, he had already been bound all over. Even at this time, he had not come to terms with what had happened. He still believed it was unreal.

Revesai was thrown into a dungeon and left there for two days without being given any food. Even if he had been given something to eat, he could not bring himself to swallow it. His mind was overwhelmed by what had happened to him. What is it that he had done to anger his ancestors to the point that they had left him on his own without even warning him about it. And what was it that Gezi's *sekuru* had seen in him that he chose to blame him for something that he was completely unaware of? Revesai took a journey down memory lane and convinced himself that he had been somebody that had served his kings loyally throughout their reign. What was it that had really taken place that caused him alone to be singled out as the enemy's informant? How was the king going to kill him?

The man was distraught. He wished to kill himself in that very dungeon. The problem was that there was nothing in that jail that he could use to kill himself! The cell was built of big granite boulders that were skillfully cut into bricks with smooth surfaces. One could not scale the walls without using a ladder. It was on top of a hill that was always guarded by armed warriors. The prisoners would be taken out once per day just to relieve themselves and then taken back in.

After the two days had lapsed, the drumbeat for summoning the older residents in the king's district was heard, and the people gathered at the king's court. Revesai's family had been rounded and brought to the king from his community. The ten governors were still staying near the king's home, waiting for Revesai's judgment. The people were told to go and gather around the tree of smoke. The tree of smoke was a place where people that had committed severe crimes in Magocha would be tried. The people of Magocha wore heavy faces on that day. The Governor that everybody in the kingdom respected for his uprightness had been found guilty of rebelling against King Rubonga. This had baffled them, and most of them knew that Rubonga was going to pass a harsh judgment. Many women were sniffling and shedding continuous tears. The men could be seen continually swallowing saliva as a way to suppress the lumps that had grown on their throats from grief. As all this was happening, warriors were sharpening the machetes they intended to use to chop up Governor Revesai. His grave had been dug already, but it was much bigger than those that other people were buried in.

The ten governors joined the waiting crowd, and all sat down, with many faces looking on the ground. The music began playing as an indication that the king was approaching. The singers sang a sad tune that intensified the people's sadness. Governor Revesai's family members were bound in ropes and as they wailed sorrowfully. The little kids were not bound, but all they could do was just hug their mother, confused as to why she was crying ceaselessly on that day. The king arrived, and everybody went dead silent. The only sound that could be heard was that of the women sniffling as they continued to cry. Some men were also overcome by emotion and were seen dropping tears, but when this happened, many of them sniffed their tobacco to put themselves under control. A man should not be seen crying in public. It is a sign of great weakness.

VaGondo went down on one knee and saluted the king by clapping his hands on behalf of the crowd. The king responded in a deep voice full of fury. Chitsere stood and told everyone what had happened. He warned the people not to even contemplate doing what Revesai had done because the wages of such stupidity were clearly death as they were going to witness. He ended by saying,

"Your Royal Highness, please be at ease now that you have caught the pest that has been eluding you for many days and you are now going to do as you please with it. Citizens of Magocha, you may now look at the treatment that is given to those that try the king, the Lion himself sitting over there."

Chitsere sat down, and the old grannies stood up, most of them with the aid of walking sticks and ululated. They doddered slowly and knelt before Rubonga and pleaded with him for clemency. The leading granny spoke for the group.

"Son of Mupingamhuru, this is the job that your father left for you, to take care of all of us children of

Magocha. If one does not err, then they are made of rock. You are a father to us all, we make mistakes, but we have nowhere else to seek refuge but to you. Please kindly forgive this one son of yours, dear father. The ground shall be full from blood one of these days, but we implore you, please let it not be by this man standing before you today. Look at those little kids that he has, oh great Lion. We know that deep down somewhere in your heart is a spot where you can bury your hurt and fury and then find another way to discipline your child that does not involve the spilling of his blood. The elders indeed said that a bird does not change the way it cries but look, Your Majesty, is this thing that he has done the way he normally cries? We know very well that you are always proud of him. Is it not that on a day such as this one, if he had been sitting with his colleagues over there, you would have specifically asked him for his wisdom on how to handle this issue? We are your children, our dear father. Please hear us!"

The grannies went back to where they were seated and ululated one more time before they settled down.

Rubonga stared at one place and remained that way for a long time such that people lifted their heads to quietly look at him. Shingai and Masimba exchanged whispers then Masimba stood and walked towards his father. Before he had gone far, his father had lifted his right hand, ordering him to stop. He went back to where he had been sitting. What the grannies had said to Rubonga had sunk into his head. It made a lot of sense, but as he considered it some more, he thought he would appear weak, and his subjects would no longer fear him thereby opening himself up to disrespect from his subjects, the people of Magocha. This would weaken his grip on power. He was quiet for a long time. Even Revesai's wife stopped crying and looked at the king. Governor Revesai did not make any movement. He just sat quietly bound with strong ropes.

Rubonga sent for his daughter Kundai to be called from the palace. She quickly came and spoke to her father. No one in the crowd could hear what the two talked about. Rubonga asked Kundai what she thought should be done to a man who had put the lives of many warriors and that of the king in grave danger. Kundai was quick to answer. She did not even debate it in her mind.

"A-a my father, would you let loose a man who is planning to kill you? It is obvious that if this person had succeeded in his plan, he would have just caused your death without any scruples and if you by any chance let him go, he may plan for another attack that you may not be able to smell before your demise."

Rubonga thanked his daughter and asked her to go back home. People kept staring at the king holding their hearts in their hands, wishing for the king to show mercy on his governor.

The king then stood and addressed the gathering.

"My grandmothers, I thank you for your wise words. You are very correct that what Governor Revesai has done is not congruent with his character. Indeed, it is not him who did that. The person that we are disciplining here is the one that possesses him. If a person has done what he did, he is like the seed of a wicked weed, if you do not take it out, it will suffocate all your good plants, and you will be left wishing and saying, 'If only I had known.' Now, this is what we do to people who invite evil into their hearts and give it space to do as it pleases. Boys, get on with it now!"

With those words, Rubonga sat down on his throne. The warriors began by throwing Revesai's chickens into the pit. The chickens were tied on their feet to prevent them from flying out of the hole. After the chickens, they threw his three dogs in. The barking dogs and the chickens that were trying to fly out of the pit caused a lot of noise. The noise also picked up as the people saw what was going to happen next, and they also began to cry. The women were wailing loudly and uncontrollably by that time. Revesai's wife was thrown into the pit falling in headlong, followed by his eldest son. The son tried to fight back, but he was given one blow of the machete on the head and then kicked into the pit by one of the warriors. The little kids did not resist and felt better following where their mother had gone. Revesai was the last to be thrown into the pit, and the warriors quickly began to cover the hole with soil.

Some of the warriors menacingly instructed the people to stop making noise in the presence of the king, warning them that if they kept crying, they could also be thrown into the pit with no second thoughts. The people instantly stopped the crying and sat quietly. None of them was prepared to forgo their life on that day. The pit was filled up, and the sounds of the Revesai family crying died in the people's ears, but in the minds and hearts of many, the sounds continued for many days after.

Many people suffered from insomnia during the days that followed because of the killing of Revesai and his family. The massacre had been too horrific, and it could not be easily erased from their minds. Shingai kept on seeing Revesai's little kids clinging on to their wailing mother, and he would also envision Revesai's eldest son trying to free himself so that he could fight back the people that were destroying his family. Shingai had known the boy from their time at the Pengapenga Mountains. He was a joyful guy who never meant trouble for anybody. He had succeeded in his training and had come out as one of the top warriors. Shingai was extremely troubled. Yes, Revesai had committed a severe offense of dining with the enemy. What he had done had the potential to get many more people killed by the enemy. But for his wife and kids to be killed for something that they had neither played a part in nor had any knowledge of, was nothing but pure cruelty. It was not good. With that being said, there was nothing that he could do about it, and even if there was something that he could do, what use was it now that Revesai and his family had become maggots?

Shingai told Shuvai all that had taken place, and she just shook her head. She said that she was embarrassed to have a close relative that was as cruel as King Rubonga. After some silence, Shingai remarked,

"But why did Revesai do what he did? With all that he knew about his king, he shouldn't have even contemplated it at all."

Shuvai just laughed with her head looking away from Shingai. She asked where his friend the big hermit Gotora had been during those days. Shingai realized that she was not keen on discussing the Revesai killing, and he asked her.

"How come you do not seem to want to hear or talk about the killing of Governor Revesai, why Shuvai?"

She put her palms on Shingai's jaws and looked at him straight in his eyes and said,

"My darling Shingi, am I done talking to and about you? I don't have anything that I live for other than just coming to see you and talk to you. That's it. Only that!"

She smiled at him the way she knew would make him melt. He forgot about all the sad issues for that moment. She kissed him on the forehead, then on his nose and she let go of his jaws. Shingai laughed and said,

"You should just keep my jaws in your hands forever."

They smiled at each other again then hugged as they talked about other matters. They spoke about the giraffe skin that Shuvai was wearing that day. She liked the giraffe skin a lot and wore it regularly. Her chest was covered with her leopard skin bra. He asked her why she always wore some part of her royal garb when she did not like the way her *bamukuru* Rubonga ran the kingdom.

"It does not mean that if one has fools and mad people for relatives, they should cut out the relationship, no. They will forever be my relatives, and I will always be a royal child of Mupingamhuru."

Shingai then asked her if it was old Vandirai that had killed the giraffe to prepare the skin for her garment. She laughed and said,

"It was actually me that killed the giraffe!"

The two burst into laughter, and then Shuvai carried on.

"My father got hurt a long time ago, but he recovered. He can do almost everything. He actually does things better than most men and anyway, hunting of animals requires a set of skills that do not necessarily involve running and many physical activities, but having knowledge about the animal being hunted."

Shingai remembered those words being stressed by Lord Vandirai at Pengapenga, and then he said,

"Truly, you are a child of your father. Those words that you spoke, he also taught us during a hunting class."

They laughed again and then talked some more about their affection for each other.

The killing of Revesai kept occupying Shingai's thoughts, but he had no one to talk about it with so that he could try to clear his mind of the memories. He thought of talking about it with Prince Masimba, but he then decided against it realizing that it could cause some unnecessary trouble for him. He could no longer trust Masimba completely in those days. Masimba had become a bit cold and unpredictable. He was spending more and more time talking about issues with the king. He had no qualms about them talking to each other for he admired father-son companions. What he was sure of was that the two were not happy and comfortable with him seeing their *bamunini* Vandirai's daughter. He then thought of paying his old friend Gotora the giant hermit a visit. He knew he could tell him some truth.

When he saw him, he requested for them to swim to the little island where they could freely talk about issues without the risk of eavesdroppers. They did that, and he then asked Gotora what he thought about the killing of Governor Revesai and his family. Gotora told him that what he needed to know first was that Gezi was a big trickster. He said Gezi was a fake *n'anga* and as a result, Revesai may have suffered injustice by being accused of a crime he had not committed, and the real villain may have been left to roam freely. What Gotora knew was that Revesai had refused to take a bribe from Gezi during the first days that Gezi had come to Magocha. Very few people knew about that incident. The second issue was that Shingai was supposed to be aware that life was not fair but full of cruelty, and therefore, he had to be alert all the time for him to stay safe. Gotora then asked Shingai if he knew about the two men that were tailing him those days. Shingai said that he knew there were people following him, but he did not know their faces or names and how many they were yet.

"I do not know those people myself, but even if I knew them, I would not tell you. What I know is that there is a person or people that want to slay you soon so if you are a smart man you had better grow a pair of eyes on your back."

Shingai thanked Gotora and promised him that he was going to be alert and take care of himself. He said the person that was following him moved like a snake that was capable of disappearing without leaving tracks in the grass. Gotora told him that if he used his mind smartly, he would soon catch the man that was after his life. Shingai went back home with more questions than answers. He promised himself that he was going to entrap his enemies in no time.

Chapter 19

Rubonga called Shingai and Masimba and signaled his guards to give his children and him space to talk. After the boys had asked after his health, they talked about various developments in the kingdom.

"Boys, now that our enemy is just humus deep under the ground, why don't we get on the tracks of our plan to raid the Western Kingdoms now?"

The three were in agreement that it was an excellent time to carry out the invasion. Shingai added,

"I believe it would still be prudent for you not to disclose the plans to your governors and some of your generals since we are not very certain that Revesai was snitching alone or if it was a group effort. It is my thinking that you could call one of your special brigades to come for a special task. The message shall not be broadcast via the drummers, but you can send individual messengers to visit each one of the warriors of that particular brigade and deliver your message. When we go, we must not take the route that the enemy thinks we will take. The enemy has lined up troops along the banks of the Mhathlehuru River; therefore, we should go south first, avoiding the Bengwa and keeping on the south. Then we attack from Maringa. We can also attack Magweza at the same time. E-eh Masimba, do you remember the path that goes past the bottom of that big lake, - e-eh what is it, yes, Doperakondo. This means we do not need to have many warriors to go with us. I think your *makondohwe* brigade is specially cut for such a mission. Your Highness, if you just send the word out to summon this brigade no one would even suspect that we are going to invade the Western Kingdoms."

"I agree with what you have suggested Shingi. But what I am thinking is that, if we are planning to take a small number of troops, then it is better for us to take the middle route, that way we should be able to force the remnants of the troops left in Maringa and Magweza to retreat eastwards. This way, they will not get a chance to warn the bigger armies that are waiting for us along the Mhathlehuru River. Also, remember that there are not many warriors left in Zibere, and if we smartly execute our plan, we will be done before many people realize what is going on."

Rubonga listened as the boys knitted the plan together, and he was pleased. They gave him satisfactory answers when he asked or had concerns as they planned. He realized that the boys were getting better and better at war strategies, than his members of The Council of The Wise Eleven who at this time were ten in number. He finally agreed that it was wise to not tell his governors about the mission at hand. He knew that his governors would grumble about him trusting a mere foreigner of the land more than his chosen men, but at that point, he just did not care how they were going to feel. To him, the seed that he had sown when people were sleeping was about to bear fruits. He was now at the point where he would happily harvest. Because of Shingai, his mission had been made very simple. The boys requested two days to finalize their plans, and the time was granted to them. The messengers were already on their way throughout the districts delivering the highly confidential message to the *makondohwe* brigade!

Shingai ran to tell Shuvai about the new developments. She was saddened when she heard about it because she did not like wars. She said a war could suddenly snatch from her the man that was going to be her future husband. She kept urging him to take good care of himself and to avoid playing the brave warrior all the time.

"You must always remember that the coward bears no scars, you hear me?"

She said this wearing a stern look. Shingai told her that he would do as she had asked him, more so because he also could not even tamper with the idea of leaving his sweetheart on earth all by herself. They hugged for a long time and listened to each other's heartbeat. They bade each other good-bye when the sun was still high up, and Shingai promised to see her before he embarked on his journey after the following two days, and he quickly walked home.

As he was walking, he felt his hair tingle, and he sharpened his ears. He quickly knew that someone or something was following him. He kept walking and quickened his pace. He knew that it was his guy and so he walked quicker in the direction of a small castle kopje that was nearby and began to climb it. His trailer kept following and also increasing his pace. He turned to check his back, and from the corner of his eye, he saw the man hiding behind the trunk of a huge tree. The man had an arrow sitting on his bow, ready to shoot. Shingai began to move faster, walking around the big boulders on the kopje as he went up. He did this to disturb the man from taking a good aim at him. Shingai was heading to a place on the kopje that had a deep cliff on one side. He had already planned how he wanted to trap his guy. When he got to the spot he wanted, he went behind a huge boulder and slid into a narrow crack on that rock. The man in pursuit followed carefully and stealthily. He hesitated when he got to where Shingai had disappeared because the path was very narrow and could only fit one person at a time. The cliff ahead meant that any wrong step might mean him falling over and landing on the thick bristle bushes that were way down below. No one would be able to find him because no man could access the bottom of that cliff other than by falling down to his death.

As he moved carefully, the man was suddenly gripped on the throat by Shingai's strong hand, and in that instant, he disarmed him. Shingai went for the man's arm and twisted it hard with one hand while the other held on to a small branch of a shrub so that he could maintain balance for the two of them to avoid falling off the cliff. He knew the man's face, but he did not know his name. The man was a much older warrior than he was, but he was still fit for battle. Shingai twisted his arm hard and furiously he asked him,

"Who are you and who sent you? Why are you following me? Tell me before I shove you off the cliff now! TALK!"

Shingai was breathing heavily. The man quickly gripped Shingai's hand in an attempt to push him over the cliff so that they would both fall in. He was determined.

Shingai could not let go of the branch that he was holding on to. They remained locked in the same position, the warrior refusing to talk and Shingai not able to push him over the cliff. Shingai wanted to know who had sent the man, so he was not too keen to kill him at that point. He quickly let go of the hand that was twisting his foe and went for his throat again. He got a firmer grip this time, but still, the warrior did not let go of his hand. Shingai pressed hard on the warrior's trachea, and his eyes opened wide. He wriggled about, but Shingai kept his grip on the throat tight. Slowly he began to let Shingai's hand go. Shingai realized that the warrior could die before he confessed and so he wrapped his right leg onto the trunk of the shrub. He was then able to twist the warrior's arm and keep the other hand on his throat, adjusting the grip to allow him to breathe and talk. He shouted again at the warrior, asking him to speak and promising to let him live if he mentioned who it was that had sent him.

The warrior gasped for breath. Shingai then clenched his fists and landed several blows on to the warrior's head and floored him but still keeping him close to the wall of the boulder. He sat on his chest and put both his hands on his throat.

"Now talk! Who sent you? Tell me"

The warrior just smiled, exposing his bloodied teeth from his crashed jaws.

"You must know that what you and your Rubonga are doing, burying people alive shall soon come to an end!"

The warrior then started laughing. Shingai beat him some more and then he rose, wanting to scare him again by threatening to shove him over the cliff. When he tried to lift him, he saw that the warrior's belly was full of blood and a dagger had been planted in his gut. Shingai had not noticed that the warrior had stabbed himself as while he sat on his chest. The warrior had failed to stab him because he had not been able to move his hand freely and, so he decided to take his own life.

Shingai was startled, and before he could fully digest what had just taken place, the warrior rolled himself and went down the cliff. Shingai saw him crash his head on to a rocky surface, splitting his skull into two before he disappeared into the bristle bushes below. He kept on staring and wondering how a strong man could easily allow himself to lose his life just to keep another man safe. How did one develop such loyalty? The warrior had gone with his secret. He had not told him who his boss was and why he wanted him dead. All that Shingai could do was to just take the warrior's bow and arrows and go home.

He decided that it was not prudent for him to tell many people about the incident because it could then make his enemy wiser. His enemy must have been somebody quite close to him. The wisdom of the elders claimed that it is usually those close or related to a person that have reasons to bewitch him. Shingai did not have any relatives in Magocha, but the closest he had for relatives were the Royals. His suspects were Rubonga and his son Masimba. These are the two people that had the power to command warriors, and the warriors feared them. A warrior could sacrifice to die at the hands of somebody else but not before these two. But before the warrior died, he had said,

"You must know that what you and your Rubonga are doing, burying people alive shall soon come to an end!"

These words stayed on his mind. Could it then be that Rubonga had coached the warrior on what to say if he had been caught so that he would not be implicated on the crime?

The other person that was high on his list of suspects was Vandirai. Vandirai did not approve of his affair with Shuvai so he could have sent the warrior to follow him when he was with Shuvai or after when he was alone on his way home. Vandirai may not have trusted Rubonga's warriors, but at the same time, the warriors had great respect for him from the time that he had trained most of them at Pengapenga. He could easily find one loyal warrior to do his dirty work for him. All this nagged and disturbed his peaceful sleep at night. He just convinced himself more not to share his secret with anybody yet. Shingai just needed to look out for the person who was going to be looking for the missing soldier, and he would know where to begin.

Chapter 20

The journey to the West began in the early hours of the morning before the first rooster had crowed. The brigade walked southwards of Magocha towards the Nyanjuzi River, as Rubonga, Shingai, and Masimba led the troops. There was not even one governor or army general amongst the warriors. VaGondo was left in charge of the kingdom, but he too was not told the truth of where the king was heading to and for what purpose. Rubonga had said to him that he was going to the little forest kingdom, Chemhindo, to collect his tribute and to assess the fields that he wanted to farm on in the coming season. Even the warriors that he had taken with him believed that was the purpose of the mission. They were surprised when they took a turn and were being led towards Bengwa but still walking southwards of that kingdom. None of them asked what was going on or why they had changed course because the king himself was leading the brigade. Some silently requested to know, but they found their own answers in their minds. The king could not be asked about such things. All a warrior does is to simply obey the command of his king.

Shingai and Masimba would regularly inspect the troops to check if they were still strong enough and to see if any showed signs of fear or lack of interest in what was going on. They would do this so that if they found any amongst the group, they would reassign or punish them. Such soldiers would be a bad influence on the rest. All the troops were fit for that mission. The warriors just followed quietly those that knew the way.

On that trip, the brigade avoided traveling during the daytime. They walked in the cover of darkness at night because they did not want to be seen by anybody.

They walked deep in the forests and only kindled fires during the day when they were resting. They had been divided into two groups. One group would sleep in the morning while the other stayed up on guard and did the cooking. The other group would take over when the sun would be hitting on their fontanels up to dusk when the whole team would start walking. Where the king slept, the warriors would create a room of four human walls. The warriors would face outwards of the quadrilateral, and the king would sleep at the center. The guards were not permitted to turn their heads back to look at the king. Doing so would spell death to the lawbreaker because this would be a clear sign of an intention to rebel against the king. Such a person was said to be no different from the enemy that they would be guarding against. When he woke up, Rubonga would clap his hands twice, and one side of the wall would move to open like a gate. This would happen at the times that the king would need to relieve himself. As soon as he would have moved out, his regular security team would take over and go with him.

It took the group many days to voyage because they used a longer route to get to where they were going. Their course was much longer since they could not take the path that was between Lake Doperakondo and the southern mountain range for fear of being seen by the fishermen. They had to go further south, avoiding the mountain range. They were now cautious as they were in the area that they wanted to attack. They knew that there would be a lot of Watchmen in the mountains. Masimba and Shingai knew this from the time they had spent in that area as spies. They changed course, still in the forests heading westwards but kingdoms like Maringe, Magweza, and other little villages were now to their north. The troops had so far achieved what they wanted. No one had seen them, and now they just needed to capture the two kings of Maringe and Magweza in no more than four days. This was meant to shock and throw the remaining kingdoms into pandemonium such that when the Magocha troops would come back to attack, it would be simple to defeat them and bring them under the reign of King Rubonga.

Masimba and Shingai briefed the rest of the warriors on the plan. Masimba and his troops were to attack the warriors that had been left guarding Maringe while Shingai and his team would do the same to Magweza. Rubonga specified that he was going to join Shingai's group. Shingai spoke last as he gave the Warriors a pep talk.

"Defenders of Magocha, our time has come now. We have not come here to play games. Our enemy is not sophisticated at all because the warriors that have been left guarding these kingdoms are inexperienced. Their generals and the experienced fighters are stationed along the banks of Mhathlehuru River waiting for us to attack from the east. So the warriors that we shall meet are still young boys, but you must be cautious that young fighters can be powerful and fast such that if anyone of you blinks, your bones will rot here. Even though we say they are not sophisticated, we should be aware that their strength is within their unity. These people are so united that when they have been instructed to do something, they would rather die in the process of honoring that command than to deviate from it. We must do everything with haste. Remember, the main purpose of our mission is to just destabilize their strategy. If we plant disunity and distrust within them, then we will know that more than half of our overall task would be done. We are not here to raid and look for jewelry or the like but just to capture the two kings so that we take them with us back to Magocha. We will get more instructions ahead. Does anybody have any questions?"

No one had a question, so Rubonga, Masimba, and Shingai sat down to further plan the attacks and to decide where they were to meet after the job would have been done. They agreed to use the same route as they had used to getting there because it was safer than going through the shorter eastern route that was beleaguered with enemy warriors. They just needed to be quick in executing their strategy in four days or under. If they left it up to the fifth day, then they could also be forced to fight the bigger armies that would by then be aware of the enemy in their territory. They did not have enough warriors for that type of combat.

"Masimba, you still remember where the watchmen of Maringe camps, right?"

"Do not worry about me, my brother. I remember it very well," Masimba responded confidently.

"That is awesome. So we are good to go because once we eliminate the criers in these areas, we will have slowed down their communication, and we will be able to execute our mission with little resistance and disturbances."

Rubonga was quiet as the boys discussed and planned, but one could tell that he was amazed by their intelligence. He reminisced his former days when at about his boys' ages, his troops would just force themselves into the enemy camps, and winning was based on the physical strength of the warriors and not by careful planning of attacks and retreats. Rubonga and Shingai's group left first because their target was further than Masimba's.

Both groups were meant to arrive in the areas that they would be fighting during the night although the attacks were to be carried out during the day. The warriors had applied pigments on to their skins made from ashes, animal blood, berries, and many leaves to create excellent camouflage for that area. Although Shingai and Masimba knew where the watchmen in these kingdoms operated from, they did not know how to get to the exact places. They had to learn this quick. These watchmen had to be eliminated in the early hours of the morning. It was quite tricky to get access to the watchmen of Maringe. There were three homes built on the mountaintop. The watchman on duty would climb higher up the mountain to see and further better. The other off-duty warriors would rest at their homes on that mountain. The dogs at these homes made it difficult for anyone that wanted to approach incognito. The other side of the hill was mostly cliffs, and so it was inaccessible.

Masimba thought fast. He sent some warriors to hunt for a small animal quickly and to also bring him a very poisonous snake. This did not take too long for them because they were in a rocky thicket. They brought him two hares and a black mamba. Masimba then took the mamba's head and minced it on a rock. He then applied the paste from the minced snake head on to the dressed carcasses of the two hares. He and his troops then waited until it got dark. They waited until it was almost dawn, then they began to ascend to the top of the mountain. One of the warriors hiked higher and got close to the homes. The dogs started to bark and charge at him. He threw the hares in front of the dogs, but the mutts did not even look at the meat. The warrior ran down the mountain with the dogs in hot pursuit. They shredded one of his calves and his bums before they left him further down and they trotted back to the homes.

The warrior squirmed, but he did not cry out loud. He only stopped running when he got to where Masimba and his crew were. His behind was now bleeding continuously. Masimba ordered him to follow the track they had taken back to where they had camped so that he could nurse the bites and prevent himself from contracting rabies. They all knew that some dog bites resulted in the victims developing the dreaded virus that would make them chew on things and sometimes led to deaths. The warrior knew the herbs that he needed to use.

Lights were lit in the rondavels and men were seen coming out. The men whistled, and their dogs barked as they ran towards them. Soon the men went back into their huts, and the lamps were blown out. Prince Masimba stood still, thinking deeply. His plan had failed. He then spoke in a low voice,

"Men, we now just have to go up stealthily and quickly shoot all the dogs dead. As soon as those men come out of the huts, we should just take them out with our spears. I'll be heading straight for the watchman on duty who is sitting on the mountaintop before he beats his drum or blows his kudu horn, so let us be off. We need to do this quickly!"

Masimba led his crew as they drew closer to the huts. Their daggers were drawn. The dogs did not bark or make a sound, making the warriors briefly stop for they then anticipated a surprise attack from them. They carefully drew closer to the homes and then realized what had happened. All the dogs had died. When they had returned from chasing the warrior, they had eaten the poisoned hares, and the venom had killed them right away. The warriors smiled in the darkness. Masimba went up intending to slit the throat of the night watchmen. He found the man sleeping peacefully near some burning charcoals. He woke him up just so that he could take one last look at the world around him before Masimba sent his sharp dagger right into his heart. The watchman did not make a sound or movement, but he just took his last breath with his eyes wide open. The other warriors waited outside the huts to take out anyone who came out. Things went well. The squad went back to join the rest of the troops as they waited to carry out their attack on the enemy at sunrise.

During those days, there was only one watchman in Magweza because the kingdom was expecting an enemy that would approach them from the eastern front. Their army generals had not expected an enemy that would attack them from the West, as the terrain was full of mountains that were extremely difficult to hike. Shingai did not have difficulty in bringing down the watchman who had just stood on the giant rock and from there; he could scan over a vast area eastwards of Magweza. As somebody that was looking eastwards in the morning, the sun had filled his eyes so he could not clearly see what was in front of him. With his back to the east, Shingai could see the watchman clearly. The watchman seemed to be enjoying the warmth of the morning sun for he did not even appear to have felt pain when Shingai's arrow landed on his throat. He was standing quite close to the edge of the rock where the cliff began. The arrow went in through the trachea and came out at the back of his neck, just below his occipital. He slowly and quietly fell down the cliff but landed with a crash where Shingai and his crew were standing. Shingai pulled out his arrow and cleaned the blood on it by piercing it into the soil.

The raid was simple. The Warriors stormed into the villages and caught their enemy unsuspecting. They slaughtered all the enemy warriors that tried to fight back. The clever ones quickly fled to take refuge in the mountains, and they survived. Rubonga did not even raise a weapon. He just followed his troops walking, between walls of his security team. He just wanted to get to the residence of the King of Magweza.

Shingai arrived at the king's residence before Rubonga and his team. The king of Magweza's guards put up a brave fight and managed to kill some of the Magocha warriors, but they were eventually defeated. They threw their weapons on the ground, and they lay on their bellies. King Mutambanemoto came out of his house and sat on a chair in the middle of the yard. There was crying and sniffling throughout the whole palace. Strangely the king did not show any emotion. He was an elderly man who had many children and grandchildren as well as some great-grandchildren. He sat, staring at the Magocha warriors as they approached him. By now, he did not have even one of his guards standing.

Shingai moved closer to him, and some of his warriors began to bind the old king, but he stopped them. King Mutambanemoto turned to and fixed his eyes on him. Shingai did not know what to do. He had not considered what he would do if this had happened. When he was in Magweza on his espionage expedition, he had not been able to see this king. He had only heard that he was an old man, but in his mind, he had not perceived his actual age. He looked at him and felt sorry. The king then said to him,

"Son of Zihwe, what have we done to you that you come here to raid us? Where did you find these people that you are with? They are not your people these ones."

Shingai was confused, and he asked himself,

"What is it that this old man is saying?"

The name Zihwe sounded like one that he had heard before, but he could not put the name, place, and face together. He could not remember where he had heard it. His head began to spin, and he felt dizzy. He could not respond to what the old king had said. His fellow warriors could also not make sense of what had been muttered by the king. One of them then said,

"Hmmnn, this old man is clever for nothing. He just wants us to think that an ancestral spirit has possessed him. This is nonsense. Let me just clap him hard once, and you'll see him behaving like a normal old man!"

The other warriors laughed, but Shingai could not.

At that moment, Rubonga and his team arrived at King Mutambanemoto's residence. Shingai felt a bit relieved and said to Rubonga,

"My lord, you may now finish your work. I am not too well at the moment. I am dizzy and would like to sit down for a few moments."

He went and sat down in the shade to cool down. Rubonga instructed his warriors to search for precious stones and other goodies. They found a little bit, and he thought that there must have been some more kept in secret storage that they hadn't revealed. Rubonga then asked old Mutambanemoto, where he stored his valuable treasures, but the old man remained quiet. The Magocha warriors were surprised by the search for precious stones because they had been told that the purpose of the raid on that trip was to capture the two kings and return with them to Magocha. These questions were reeling in their heads, and the answers were also answered in their heads!

"Old man, if there is one teaching from my mother that I remember and hold dear to this day, is respect for the elderly. Now your silence when I am asking you important questions seems to be your way of asking for a thorough beating from me. Don't test my patience!"

Rubonga spoke while looking into the old man's eyes. At that time Shingai's dizziness had left him, and he had returned to where the others were gathered. Then old Mutambanemoto retorted to Rubonga.

"Your greediness is going to be your downfall. Even if you kill all the kings and the people of these kingdoms, you should also know that your time of breathing air on the land of the living is quickly running out. All you people here must write my words in your hearts. Your king is going to die because of greed. How many big rooms and granaries do you now have, but still, you just won't stop raiding other kingdoms? Do you think that your ancestors are the sole rulers of the spirit world? That is the trouble with people who boast of power based on stolen crowns."

The old king ended by snorting aloud. Rubonga madly sprung up and drew his short spear and pointed at him.

"What did you just say? Do you know what I can do to you? Now I'm going to take you with me so that you can experience how painful a slow death is, you hear me?"

He ended up pointing his spear close to the old king's chest. Rubonga's troops were all quiet and tense. Mutambanemoto's warriors remained flat on the ground, and the old man did not change his demeanor. He kept staring at Rubonga.

What happened after Rubonga's words took everyone by surprise. The old man suddenly snatched the spear that was pointed at his chest and immediately pointed it at Rubonga's chest. Rubonga's heart missed a couple of beats from fear and disbelief. His cobra eyes shot out and would not blink.

"I am not the one who is going to be responsible for ending your life. You are going to have a much more horrible death than I will have."

Soon after those words, the old man then acted as if he was going to hand back his spear to Rubonga, turning the blade back towards himself and then without any warning, he stabbed himself into his gut with Rubonga's spear. Blood gushed out, and the old man took three deep breaths then went silent. All the people opened their mouths and froze. Shingai pinched himself to check if he had not seen visions. The old king had killed himself! Rubonga broke the silence that had ensued.

"Let us go back home!"

He began walking right away, and his security details only took their positions after he had made several steps without them on guard.

Loud wailing began immediately at King Mutambanemoto's residence as the mourning for the old king and other slain warriors burst out. The Magocha troops could not carry their deceased mates to give them decent burial because King Rubonga needed to get back to his home quickly. They got to where they were supposed to meet with Masimba's team and found the team waiting for them already. Maringe had not been difficult for Masimba and his team to put under because there were very few warriors that had stayed behind. The king of Maringe had gone to Mazimbe where the other western kings had gathered in anticipation of the Magocha attack from the eastern front. Masimba and his team had just collected some treasure tokens from the king's houses. When Shingai heard Masimba talking about precious stones he was convinced that the father and son had planned the search for jewels to be carried out at the same time as the attacks and capture of the two kings. For a moment, he believed that Masimba was slowly getting as greedy as his father.

Shingai narrated to him how their mission had turned out. Masimba could see that his father had endured a lot of bruises in his heart because of what had happened in Magweza. He also decided not to ask him about it as he could see that it was still fresh in his mind. Asking him could have pained him more and the irritation by it all could have led Rubonga to snap at him. He did not want this to happen, mainly because they were amongst many of their junior subjects. Shingai suggested to Masimba that it was no longer prudent for King Rubonga to join them when they went out for wars because he had smart children who could command the fights well on his behalf. Masimba agreed, and the troops began their journey back to Magocha.

After one day's travel, the troops found a place to camp for the night and prepare the evening meals. On the journey back, they could freely travel during the day, as they were no longer planning on taking anyone by surprise. Rubonga refused to eat that evening. No one was talking to him, and he seemed to prefer it that way. Shingai and Masimba would just ask after his health at the appropriate times and would quickly move away after he had responded. They respected whatever battles were being fought in his mind. In the morning, Shingai began to hit his forehead with the inside of his palm. He continued to do this for some time. When the troops were about to start walking Shingai then said,

"My instinct is telling me that we should not use the same route that we used on our way here. We should use the other route to go around that mountain. I don't know what it is, but I just have this feeling."

They had camped at the foot of a big mountain. Masimba smiled and said,

"There you go again, Shingi. You want us to go back using the long route? You of all people here know that the path that you want us to take is infested with sharp rocks and it is difficult to walk through. There is nothing that can harm us if we use the other route. We are warriors, and both man and beast run away from us.

Let us get on the road, the minds of most men here are now on their women back home."

Some of the warriors laughed and agreed with Masimba. Shingai also laughed and then said,

"Those that want to go with Prince Masimba, please join him and those that want to go with me on the more difficult path, let us get on."

All the warriors indicated that they wanted to go with Masimba. They were surprised when King Rubonga interjected saying that he would go with Shingai. Only then did they realize that for a moment they had forgotten that there was an important man amongst them. Rubonga's personal security team had no choice to make. They just had to join Shingai and the king. Masimba teased his father,

"Are you also getting weak in the knees like Shingi, my king?"

"We will meet ahead. Let us go!"

Rubonga answered without entertaining the joke, and the troops marched in two different groups.

On the following day, Shingai and his crew arrived where they were supposed to meet with Masimba's crew, but they were not there. Three warriors inspected the area to check if the other team might have been there much earlier, but there was no sign of them having been there. They decided to prepare a meal as they waited for them. Shingai and another warrior from Rubonga's security men stepped out to hunt for the game to be roasted. They returned at the time that Masimba and his crew were also arriving. Rubonga's security guards began to laugh at their mates, but they quickly transformed their laughs to worried faces when they noticed that their mates were wearing long faces.

They stood quietly, waiting to hear the source of sadness that had clothed them. Masimba narrated to Rubonga and his men what had happened.

He said that his team had gotten to a lake where they stopped to drink some water. They had not been aware of a herd of buffalos that was also drinking up the lake on the same side that they were. They heard roaring lions that had probably caught a buffalo or two. The warriors had instinctively risen to check what was going on and suddenly stampeding buffalos engulfed them, flattening everything on their path. Many of the warriors had survived by running into the water. One of them had then fallen prey to a crocodile. Another four warriors had been trampled to death by the charging beasts. Many were injured with others suffering fractured limbs. Masimba was one of those that had not been seriously injured. They had then dug graves to bury the dead warriors. Carrying the critically injured ones is what had taken them long before they got to the meeting place. Shingai and Rubonga's guards consoled their colleagues by somberly shaking their hands.

"When a person has gone to war, there can only be two possible outcomes. He can die in battle or get back home alive. Let us go back home."

Rubonga spoke without displaying any emotion on what had happened.

At home, the warriors were happily received by their families, but there were also those that had received depressing news of the loss of their loved ones. They grumbled to their ancestors, but in the end, they left it to those same ancestors, for only they knew why they had chosen to take their children at that particular time. King Rubonga seemed a bit relieved to be home. His wives welcomed him, and later on, he spent a great deal of time talking to his daughter Kundai. He quickly sent word to summon his governors to his palace so that he could share with them his army's adventures of the West. He ended up sitting down with VaGondo to get a briefing of what had taken place during his absence from Magocha. Shingai did not waste time as he quickly went to see his girl. Shuvai was happy to see him. They embraced tightly for a long time without saying anything to one another. Shingai lifted her up and swung her around once before he let her stand, and they further tightened their grip on each other for a little longer.

"My heart would beat so loud at some moments I thought it would burst whenever I thought of you. I was getting scared and worried that you would just make me a widow even before taking me to your yard."

Shuvai said this hanging her head on the side and smiling as she looked at him. Shingai smiled back and began to boast about his trip to the Western Kingdoms. He made himself look like a wise and brave young warrior that had successfully maneuvered a challenging feat. Shuvai listened attentively, changing her facial expressions according to what was being said by her man. Although he was telling mostly truths about what had happened, here and now he would inflate that truth to glorify himself more. When he spoke about what King Mutambanemoto of Magweza had said to Rubonga, Shuvai's ears stretched like those of an antelope disturbed from grazing by slight noises in the grass. She asked him to repeat the old king's words. She wanted to hear the part where the king had said,

"… That is the trouble with people who boast of power based on stolen crowns."

Shingai heard the sounds of the words that King Mutambanemoto had spoken, but he had not made sense of them. Even Shuvai's interest in the words did not ring a bell in his mind to link them with what Gotora had said, that Rubonga had ascended to the Mupingamhuru throne by cunning means, sidelining Vandirai in the process. He had not even noticed that this was what had shaken Rubonga. The words were spoken in the presence of his warriors. It only became clear to him when Shuvai said,

"So this is what has taken happiness and pride from *bamukuru*! So why were you saying you are not sure what it is that is bothering him when it is all clear? King Mutambanemoto's suicide was just a minor occurrence to *bamukuru*. The issues of 'Stolen crowns' and 'imminent death' are that which is eroding his heart and mind. I know him. He is my father. Anyway, let us talk about something else. This has nothing to do with us."

"Ummnn girl, you are too smart. How did you manage to figure that out when I, the eye and ear witness could not? What could-"

"A-ah Shingi, can we focus on us now? I haven't seen you in ages, and I just want to talk about you only, a-ah, you!"

Shingai picked that she was no longer interested in talking about Rubonga's predicament as it obviously reminded her of how her family had perished. In a split of a moment, he remembered the story that Gotora had told him about how her family had suffered a painful death, and he felt the pain as if he had been there when it happened. He felt sorry for his girl. She really did not want to talk about it. She then broke the short silence with a question that Shingai had not expected.

"By the way, when are you going to take me? What is our plan? Where are we going to build our home, dear father of my future child?"

Shingai acted as if he had not heard her question.

"Hmmnn … I beg your pardon, what did you just say? Oh, a-ah that is quite simple."

He smiled and began cursing himself in his mind. How come he had not thought of such matters before? He did not have a single word to answer Shuvai's question because he had never even thought about it previously.

"I did not say that it is anything difficult, my husband. I just want to know when and where?"

She smiled as she said that. She subtly enjoyed seeing Shingai getting embarrassed. She had seen that he had not thought about it at all. He tried to turn it on her.

"But what did you have on mind, my sweetheart?"

"A-ah guys, seriously, I do not want to bypass what you have on mind. You must always remember that when you eventually take me you are going to assume the role of my father and so what we are talking about right now is something that is planned and organized by the father in our home, so over to you, father!"

They both burst into laughter, and Shingai confessed that he had not thought beyond them just being lovebirds.

"Oh, I see you, Shingi. You want to do to me what you did to Tendai, right? At some point, another prettier girl will just come and steal you from me, and you'll leave me looking all stupid and heartbroken. This is what you are planning right Shingi?"

Shingai felt uncomfortable, and for a moment, words to clear himself hid from his tongue.

"Don't even think like that sweetheart. I went into your heart and welded myself to its walls. I am in your system, and it is now impossible for me to get out. Not even death will manage to force me out of there. My eyes now only know one definition of beauty, and that definition is you. When I look at other girls, I just feel like I am looking at boys. You have probably cooked the household gecko for me even before we are married. I suspect you mixed it with the chicken that you cooked for me when your father was away that day. I have never eaten chicken that tastes so good like that in my whole life! Just thinking about it makes me hungry already. You can't tell me that it was just the normal chicken people cook in their homes!"

The two burst into laughter once more. Shingai kept on stressing that there was not going to be any other girl in his life except for her. Shuvai looked at him in his face and said,

"Time is evidence that does not lie. If it was about where we've been, we would say 'It was like that, then it became like this. But as for tomorrow, no one can be certain. We just have to be faithful."

Chapter 21

There was no grain of doubt in Vandirai's mind that his daughter and the boy from the sacred pools were madly attached to each other, but he had not had a discussion about it with his daughter. Shuvai had not even tried to introduce that subject to her father. Such affairs were not among those that a father and daughter could sit down and talk about. They were reserved for mothers and the father's sisters. Shuvai's mother was dead, and she did not have anyone that she could confide in on such issues in Magocha. Her surviving vatete at that time was under Rubonga's armpit, and Vandirai had told her not to ever share too much information about her life with his sister because she would not hide anything from Rubonga.

It was only through Shuvai's uncles in Mawisire that she became aware of her father's resentment of her affair with someone close to Rubonga. She had just laughed it off, and her uncles did not even stress her about it. They did not like to see her sad. They knew that she was a wise girl who could not be enticed by vanity. Even her father was confident that he had brought her up well and had stressed well to her that she needed to grow eyes in her heart, her mind, and on her face. There had been times that she had demonstrated more wisdom than many girls of her age. Growing up without a mother had strengthened and matured her heart. Vandirai was also aware that evil had grown and mutated in Rubonga's blood and that once he had made up his mind that he hated somebody, he would not rest until that person had been buried in the earth. He knew from what had happened before that Rubonga would seek to harm Shuvai not because he thought she could be of any danger to him and his throne but just to inflict pain on his archenemy.

As soon as Shuvai got back to her father's home, she quickly told him what was said to have happened in the Western Kingdoms.

"Shumba, have you heard what happened where *bamukuru* Rubonga and his troops had gone?"

Vandirai immediately knew that Shuvai was addressing him by his totem so that he would not focus on what could annoy him but on something else. He knew that Shingai had told her, and she did not want him to think about their love affair. Being addressed by the totem name by his daughter always softened him up even though he knew why she did this.

"No my daughter, no one has told me anything. Is there anyone in this kingdom who would tell me about your father's adventures and live to the see the sun setting before they are put under the soil? What do they say happened?"

Shuvai narrated what she Shingai had told her. Her father listened intently looking into the burning fire. He then spoke after she had finished, saying that things had taken a complicated twist. They then talked about other things, Vandirai reiterating many of the issues that they had spoken of and planned about in the past. He ended up by saying that the time had come again that the two of them went back to stay with her uncles in Mawisire because it was highly likely that the people of the west were going to come to Magocha to launch an attack to avenge the death of one of their kings. Shuvai had not expected this turn of events. She thought they were going to be in Magocha for over a whole year. Going to stay with her uncles meant leaving Shingai behind. Shingai could not leave Rubonga at that time because Rubonga would hunt down him until he found him. She was deeply saddened. Vandirai told her that they had to vanish from Magocha without anyone knowing about it. The words that King Mutambanemoto had said shortly before he died meant that Rubonga would target killing Vandirai, as a preemptive strike on someone who he thought had the motive and capacity to kill him.

Early the following morning before Shuvai had left the house, her father gave her a cold look and made a subtle threat.

"I know you are about to hop like a hare to offload our plans of running away to Rubonga's people."

Shuvai said she was not that foolish, and she promised him that she was not going to tell anyone about it. Vandirai knew that despite the promises she had pledged to keep, she was going to bid farewell to Shingai. When she saw Shingai, she did not quickly tell him about the horrible news. He immediately noticed that there was something that was bothering her. He tried to think of what it could be before he asked her, but he failed. He tried to think back if he had said or done something that had offended her the previous day, but he could not come up with anything. He ended up just asking.

"My love, what is wrong with you today? Who has stolen your happiness?"

Shuvai said that it was nothing and he should not worry, but he kept on inquiring. Shuvai thought of something to make him stop questioning her.

"I know that you gave me a treated hide of a lioness that I keep amongst my most valued belongings and I have noticed that you do not take off that beaded necklace that I made for you. But what else can we do to strengthen our bond such that it may only be broken if one of us has been taken up by those of the spirit world? That is what would make me jubilant. What can we do Shingi?"

Shingai looked into her eyes for some time. She managed to force out a smile, but as he looked deeper, he could see that she was really hurting inside.

"There is nothing that will ever be able to take your place in my heart Shuvai. This will not happen."

Shingai went on to assure her that his heart had settled on her and her only. He then told her his plan. He suggested that they have similar permanent tattoos on their waists, just above the hipbones. He volunteered to get cut first. Shuvai used the tip of his sharp arrow to cut three short vertical parallel lines. He ground his teeth to numb and hide the pain. A man does not flinch because of pain in the presence of a woman. A man is brave.

Shuvai's turn came, and Shingai struggled to get himself to cut her smooth skin. Her skin was too beautiful for him to stain with cuts and also just to inflict pain on her was beyond his imagination. He asked her to be brave and not to cry as it was going to take a short time. He was pleasantly surprised when she did not show any sign of pain from the cutting. She was as still as a rock when the arrow cut on her skin. He took her numbness to have been caused by whatever it was that had been bothering her since that morning. This worried him again. She said that she was happy and satisfied with the oath that they had taken. She also warned him that if he was going to be reckless and forget the promise, her ancestors would take leave from their spiritual habitat to come down and deal with him severely. She became a bit relaxed after this, and they kissed and cuddled.

Later on, Shuvai told him her story.

"Shingi my dear, what you saw in me this morning is true. My heart has been pricked all over by thorns, and they are still pinned on to it. I am so hurt because father told me we are going back to Mawisire to live with my uncles again. He says what you people went and did in the west is likely going to invite a vicious attack on Magocha with those people avenging the death of their elderly king. When such attacks happen, it is mostly innocent people that suffer the most. For young girls like us, we risk being captured and parceled out as gifts to appease their elders for their loss-"

Shingai sprang to his feet from the log that they were sitting on and stood with hands akimbo.

"What did you just say?"

Shuvai had never seen his face frowned like that before. If it had been any other day, she would have commented on his sculptured body that melted the knees of many girls who saw him but on that day she could not. The sun was scorching hot that day and Shingai was wearing a short leather skirt made from a cheetah hide, exposing his muscles and erect body.

"Are you telling the truth Shuvai? Huh? Why don't you just say 'No?' Actually, we should just elope, and everything will be sorted before you know it. If it means running away from this kingdom with you to another, I'm prepared to do it right now. Shuvai, please don't be like this, my friend. You just came back a few months ago and now, a-ah, no!"

Tears quickly filled Shuvai's eyes and began to drop as she wept. She did not make an effort to wipe them off when she started responding to his suggestion.

"It is not that easy Shingi. I also thought about all that you are saying when father told me about his plan, but it is not easy my love-"

She could not finish her words as she was now weeping bitterly. Shingai was not easily moved. He was still shocked and angry.

"So when do you return to Magocha?"

Shuvai said she did not know, but she knew that they would be coming back at some point. Her tears kept on spilling out, and Shingai felt his own tears forming in his eyes. His emotions quickly switched, and he began to feel sorry for her. He pulled her from where she sat and drew her close to him, then patted her back. Her tears fell on his bare back as she breathed and sobbed on his neck.

The human mind is strange. At such times one would think that the two would just be thinking about their sorry situation but Shingai's mind for a moment beat his chest and made him proud and boastful that a girl as beautiful as Shuvai had actually shed tears for him! He felt that he was the man! His gorgeous girl believed so much in him, and whenever she was in danger or confused, she would find solace in him. He was her pivot and her force of gravity. He then found the strength to comfort and calm her down, telling her that they would find a way out of their unfortunate situation. They just needed to apply themselves to finding a smart solution to stop their dependency on other people altogether.

Shingai knew that time would lapse and they would put the sad episode behind them. He also knew that the people of the west were not too militant to plan an organized an invasion into Magocha just to avenge the death of King Mutambanemoto. They would be prepared to defend themselves when intruders attacked. To him, this meant that he and Shuvai would be back together before too many days had passed. This would give him the much-needed time to put his plans into order. He would plan how he would marry Shuvai, when he would do that, and where they would live. Although he was living comfortably in Magocha, by now he knew that some people loathed him and would celebrate to see him meet his demise. He was not too concerned about these people because he could protect and defend himself well. The complicated part would come when he would have taken Shuvai. Rubonga would probably evict him from Magocha, or he could even plan to kill her. At that time he was one of Rubonga's most trusted commanding warriors. He could not just vanish from the kingdom like that. Yes, Colonel Magodo had rescued him or brought him to Magocha and treated him like his own son, but Rubonga had also given him a privileged life as one of the royals. Rubonga regarded him as a son, and so he respected him for that.

Eventually, Shuvai stopped crying and explained further to Shingai how difficult it was for her to suddenly disobey her father. Soothed with compassion, Shingai then spoke some words that he had never spoken before.

"Rubonga is one spoilt big baby who needs a thorough whipping to get him to his right senses!"

Shuvai was shocked to hear him say that, but she did not comment about it. He also sought in his mind, the source of such stupid bravery, but his emotions cheered him on. For Shuvai, he could do anything. They passionately hugged when it was time for them to part. Shuvai promised to see him for the few more days that remained before she would be on her way to Mawisire. She implored him not to share the information of her pending departure to anyone in the kingdom because she had promised her father that no one would know about it. Shingai laughed.

"I do not allow issues about my family to escape the confines of the walls of my home."

They kissed, and Shuvai went on her way as Shingai headed to the palace.

When she got home, she almost collapsed when she heard what her father said to her. Vandirai had anticipated that she was going to see and tell her boyfriend all about their plans to temporarily exile themselves from Magocha, so he just let her go to see him but as soon as she was back, he told her that they were leaving that very night. He said they needed to travel at night to get as far away from Rubonga as they could. He suspected that Rubonga would send a gang of assassins after them. He knew about the killers that his brother employed to do his dirty work. He told Shuvai that their lives were in grave danger and that she had to take every word that he had spoken to her seriously.

She was distraught, but there was nothing that she could do except to just lament in the dark. Her father was telling the truth. She knew he deeply loved her and that he did not want anything nasty to happen to her. Most of what he did was to protect her from the fangs of life. She knew that Shingai would be devastated when he would discover that she had left without saying bye to him, but there was nothing she could do about it. He just had to understand that she had to go. The two packed their garments and other light essentials to carry with them, and they got on the road. Shuvai had quickly prepared a meal just before they left, but they had not sat down to eat. They would only stop to eat when they had covered a considerable distance.

What happened after two days convinced Shingai that Vandirai knew what he was doing and indeed had the instincts of a dog. From that time, he began to respect and admire Vandirai. Even though he did not like him, he concluded that Vandirai's real enemy was Rubonga. He also began to lose the love and trust that he had for his king. Meetings were held, and the wise ten were briefed on the attacks of the Western Kingdoms. The governors were shocked. None of the ten had had any suspicions that the group could have gone to launch an attack on the Western Kingdoms! They were told that the war with those people had not ended and that they would be informed about the next move when the time was right. The governors were terrified. They could tell that although the traitor Revesai had been eliminated, the king still believed that he was not the only conspirator. Except for Chitsere and VaGondo, the other eight governors looked worried. Rubonga introduced the new governor who had been chosen by the people of Revesai's district to fill the gap that the governor's death had created. At the end of the meeting, Masimba and Shingai greeted the governors. Some of them avoided shaking Shingai's hands except for Chitsere, VaGondo, and the newly installed governor.

Chitsere asked for Shingai's ear and took him to the side.

"Look, my son, some time ago I sincerely despised you, because I didn't understand you. I thought you had been sent to this kingdom to bewitch and trick our king, but now I realize how lost I was. His Highness is indeed blessed to have a person like you. His ancestors are obviously shepherding him well. Keep up the good work, but at the same time the eyes on your occipital must never blink, for there are many who are not pleased with your wisdom and influence on the king, you hear me?"

Shingai was thrilled to hear these words from Chitsere. It was clear that most of the governors loathed him and so Chitsere's words of belief in him had made him happy. He thanked him for his kind words, and he headed to his *gota.*

The meeting ended after dusk so he could not go to see Shuvai. The following morning, after having his breakfast, Shingai went to see his girl. He went round Shuvai's home making a coded whistle to get her attention, but she did not come out of the rondavels. Vandirai's home was secluded from many people. Shingai went to his nearest neighbors and asked if they had seen Shuvai and they told him that they had not seen anyone at her father's home even on the previous day. Shingai was disturbed because Shuvai had promised that they would see each other for a few more days before her and her father left for Mawisire. So where was she? He decided he was going to do other things and then go back later when Shuvai would be back at her home.

He was horrified by what he saw when he went back to Vandirai's home later. He almost bumped into some bulky armed men who were approaching Vandirai's home stealthily. He was puzzled by what he saw. The men were walking carefully like a lioness preparing to pounce on an unsuspecting prey. Was everything okay? His mind sped, and in no time, he was up a tree hoping from one tree to another like a monkey. He got to a tree that was near the yard without the burly men noticing him. He set his arrow and drew his bow. He waited to see the man who would lay his hand on Shuvai or her father, and he was going to end his life right there. He would take out the six men without them having a clue of where the arrows would be coming from. The men then forced open a door of one of the rondavels, and one of them trembled as he looked inside. Shingai's bow was ready to send the obedient arrow towards the target. He was about to let the arrow go when he heard one of the mercenaries speak out loud.

"There is no one in here!"

They went to Vandirai's bedroom and did the same, but there was no one in that room. Shingai was prepared to shoot, but he knew that if Vandirai were in one of the rondavels, he would defend himself to death. This would give him time to strategically direct his aim from that tree to the mercenary who would pose the greatest danger to Shuvai. The men then assigned one of them to inform the king that his birds had flown from the kingdom much earlier than he had anticipated.

Shingai remained in the tree long after the men had gone, just analyzing what had happened. He tried to make sense of what had happened.

Shingai concluded that Vandirai and Shuvai had definitely left Magocha. They had done a smart thing by running away. Rubonga had become an evil man. He could now see that even his own life was in grave danger. He was alone in all this, and he had to be extra smart; otherwise, he would bid the world farewell before he was ready. The mercenaries made it clear that they had been ordered by the king to finish off the father and daughter in one attack. Could it have been the king that had sent the assassin who had killed himself at the cliff? But that assassin had said both Rubonga and him were his enemies. So who could it have been? Governor Chitsere had warned him about many people that were after his life in the kingdom. Shingai concluded that he had come to the Kingdom of Magocha on his own and hence he was alone in all that was happening. He was his own keeper.

He thought of old Mutambanemoto saying something about him being a son of some name that he could not recall. The dizziness that had engulfed him had been so severe that he had not heard all of the old king's words. His mind had completely shut down. He thought of asking some of the warriors who were with him at the time, but he quickly decided against it. It could cause the people to speculate what they had no clue about. It was best to let people believe that the old king's words were being influenced by dementia. Only Rubonga and he knew that although the words had come out of King Mutambanemoto's mouth, someone had spoken them from the spirit world!

When he had defeated the assassin who had been tracking him, Shingai recruited some boys to spy for him. Many boys idolized him in the kingdom. He had cautiously selected those that had open eyes but that nobody would suspect to be information gatherers for the semi-royal commanding warrior of Magocha. He told them that he was planning to recruit them to be part of the spies for the kingdom. This job required people who had stable hearts and minds, those that had ears which could hear things being said from far away, and those that had eyes that could see where they were not looking. The boys were expected to learn about a person's behavior and movements without them knowing that someone would be studying them. Shingai told each one of them that an enemy who no one had information about had entered into Magocha; therefore all the information that they would gather was meant for him only as he would know how, and what to do with it without compromising the security of the kingdom.

The boys did not know each other. Each was recruited and instructed separately. They were delighted by their assignment and would tell Shingai a lot of information, and he would assess and weigh the information. He learned about people that were said to be thieves, witches and wizards, murderers, and general lawbreakers. He also learned about men that were said to have *mubobobo*. From what he heard, there was nothing that had shown evidence as to who his real enemy was. Rubonga had been one of his chief suspects, but because of the critical tasks that the king would assign him on, coupled with his growing paranoia, he actually wanted Shingai to be protected so that his own protection would be guaranteed. He concluded by believing that there was somebody else that wished to end his life, but he still had no clue who it was.

Chapter 22

The days went by, but Lord Vandirai and Shuvai did not return to Magocha. Shingai thought of taking a trip to Mawisire in search for his girl, but time did not permit him to do that. Rubonga was sitting on him. The tasks that he was assigned to left him with no time to be away from the king for more than two days. Rubonga knew that he wanted to visit Shuvai in Mawisire, but he feared that if Shingai went there, there was a high possibility that Shuvai could tell him about things that had happened in the past. This had the potential of causing a rift between him and Shingai to the extent that Shingai could rebel against him. What he was not aware of was that Gotora had already told him all about it. Rubonga then decided to send Prince Masimba and Shingai to go for another attack on the Western Kingdoms. This he did to keep Shingai from overthinking about Shuvai.

The boys went back with their troops and fought well. They returned, and people celebrated them. They had been away for over two months so Shingai was confident that Shuvai would be back in Magocha when they got back, but it wasn't so. He was genuinely concerned in his heart. When some girls that lived in the king's district saw that the young man was now alone, they began to throw themselves in his way, but he did not notice them. He could tell what they wanted, but he was just oblivious to their actions. Prince Masimba used to host parties that were attended by many girls and boys from the king's district and other nearby districts. At the parties, there would be plenty of roast meat prepared by the boys who attended the parties. There would be plenty of beer too. Shingai would go to some of the parties, but he would not stay long. He wasn't as flamboyant and wild as the others.

At one of the parties, Masimba said to Shingai, "Did we not once tell you how wicked your girl and her father are? Now, look at yourself. How can you be called a real man if you can't even flirt with all these girls? Just look at how beautiful some of them are. Tell me, do you really think that my sister, wherever she is, is still waiting just for you? Remember the hare that fooled the lion by telling him that his paw was holding onto a root and not to his leg. When the lion let go of the hare's leg, the hare immediately escaped. You, my friend, may be holding on to the root while the hare has long escaped. Open your eyes!"

Shingai laughed.

"Can you stop it my brother, the workload that we have these days requires a lot of focus. If I do what you are asking me to then, I'll risk messing up His Highness' plans, and it will not be a pleasant situation for me if that happens."

This he had said, but Masimba's words had disturbed him. He felt like somebody had slapped him in the face. What if it was true that Shuvai was seeing and playing with other boys wherever she was? Yes, they had a binding oath, but he who has traveled, has gone out of sight. What is too distant for the eye to see the ear should hear, but he had not heard from or about Shuvai. What if she had planned not to return to Magocha, how were they going to see each other again? And how was he going to be a perfect husband who could run his own family affairs if he had a wife that said, "Yes" to everything that her father wanted? Shuvai obeyed her father too much as if he was the one that would marry her. The belief in the rumor that Vandirai had an incestuous affair with his daughter visited him at that time, but it was pushed out of his mind by other thoughts. Shuvai's relatives who truly loved her were those from her mother's side, so it was possible that she could live amongst them for the rest of her life. If she and her father would come back to Magocha, what sort of life would they live when their *bamukuru* Rubonga was still alive?

These and many other questions disturbed Shingai on this day when he was in his *gota* and on many other days that followed. It made him have a self-introspection of where his own life was headed. Yes, he was living quite well in Magocha despite the people who wanted him dead, but what would a high life amount to? King Rubonga had made it clear to him that the reason he had taken him from Colonel Magodo was to help him conquer and bring the Western Kingdoms under Magocha. This is what was happening in those days, and one day, it was going to come to an end. Now once it had come to an end, his usefulness to the king would also end and what would happen after this? Shingai saw that Rubonga could kill him or if he was lucky, could exile him from Magocha. He was still in his youthful days, but youth is only a phase that does not last. One day he would outgrow his youthfulness, and what would then happen to him? Was he ever going to build his own home and start a family? Who would he begin the family with when the one that he had chosen had vanished from his life? He was deeply concerned.

A voice in his mind said,

"If only Rubonga were not there, then Shuvai would have been right here with you. Rubonga must be killed definitely."

He laughed when he thought of this and then another voice, still in his head responded,

"Now see why they say the mind cannot be contained, it knows no boundaries of what to think and what not to think about. What is this nonsense about killing the king?"

He then decided that if Shuvai would not be back in Magocha in the following two months, he would begin to look at the other girls whose beauty he was starting to see again. Slowly he would plan to detach himself from Rubonga so that he could do as his mind pleased and not to live at the mercy of another man.

The wars with the Western Kingdoms were escalated. Shingai and Masimba got to the point of competing on bringing tribute from the defeated kings. The armies were divided into two groups, one headed by Shingai and the other by the Prince of Magocha. One of the days when they were going for a raid, Shingai asked Masimba to lead his group taking the route that passed through the southern region of the Bengwa. He was going to take the northern course. Masimba perceived what was on Shingai's mind, so he agreed. He did not tell the king because he also wanted to know what it was that his *bamunini* Vandirai was planning. Shingai wished to pass through Mawisire and look for Shuvai. He needed to find her and confirm with her what the plan was.

When they were planning this, the two months that Shingai had set for himself had long passed, and there still was no word from Shuvai. On the day that the troops left Magocha for the west, Shingai told the senior warriors in his group where he was to meet them after three days. Before long, he had disappeared from his group. Nobody saw him leave, and nobody knew where he had gone. What he knew was that members of the Ears and Eyes of the king would report about his disappearance for two or three days but eventually returning to his troops. He also knew that Rubonga would not ask him about it, but that he would lose his temper on his men for failing to track their target and gathering all the information on what he was up to. The members of the Ears and Eyes of the king were many, but most did not know each other. For them to not report what would have happened was a big misdemeanor. One of them might make a report on something and if others did not, the members would be individually dealt with. For Shingai, what mattered was that he had found time to learn about what was going on with Shuvai.

It did not take long for him to find Shuvai's uncles' home. He just asked a few people, and they showed him the way until somebody pointed to him the exact compound. He spied from a distance, but he did not see Shuvai. He looked at the men who were moving about in the yard, but none of them was Lord Vandirai. He gathered some courage and decided to approach the two men that had now moved to the cattle kraal and were milking a cow. Two young boys were with the men. The older man was about Rubonga's age, and the other one was younger but way older than Shingai. Shingai could see that he was already married and had children. He shook their hands, and they half-whispered some greeting words. The men looked at him and waited for him to speak first. He asked how they were doing, as well as how the weather was treating them and their lands. They politely responded, telling him that from the look of things, the heavens seemed to not have any complaints against them. They then waited for him to say more, and he began to feel awkward. He had just approached them, but all the words that he had coached himself to say had flown away in different directions. As he stuttered trying to arrange new words, the younger man then spoke.

"Brother, have you recognized this young man?"

The older man squinted his left eye slightly and looked intently at Shingai before he slowly shook his head and said,

"No, I have tried to look at his countenance, but I can't match it to somebody I have seen before."

"A-ah, *mukoma*, this is the little boy who is planning to take our wife! Look at him."

"Oh, is it? Damn, please hand me my spear, I want to teach him a lesson that he will never forget!"

The two men laughed, and the younger one began the greeting process again, this time much more relaxed and cheerful.

"Hello, Shingi my son."

Shingai blushed as he greeted them again. He was surprised at how these men knew a lot about him when he had never seen them before.

"We are your uncles, brothers to Shuvai's late mother. Shuvai does not keep her mouth shut when she talks about you. We saw you once when we came to visit our brother-in-law, your *tezvara*, Vandirai."

Shingai had not known about the visit that the men had had to Magocha.

When he asked how Shuvai was and how he could see her, her uncles looked surprised. One of them asked him,

"But seriously, how is it that you are asking us how your wife is doing and her whereabouts, instead of you telling us about all that?"

Shingai was taken aback by the question. He could see that the two men were not joking with him. He told them that Vandirai and Shuvai had left Magocha for Mawisire a long time back. They said that Vandirai had taken his daughter and had said he was going to farm in a new area where nobody knew of yet.

"From the way that our niece adores you, we were so certain that she had at least told you where they were going to farm."

Shingai's mind wandered about, and he was distressed. The two men told him that the lives of the father and daughter had become so endangered for them to live freely because King Rubonga sought to have their lives shortened. He then told them the incident of the deadly assassins that were sent by Rubonga to kill Lord Vandirai and Shuvai. They both shook their heads in despair, staring into the ground. The two men then reconfirmed to him that they did not have the slightest clue as to where Vandirai and Shuvai had gone to hide. They reassured him that he was going to see his girl again and that his future father-in-law was a smart man and that only a few men knew the depth of his wisdom.

"There is definitely something that he is up to, and he must be setting up his snares at strategic points. With everything that he does, you must know that protecting his daughter is his number one priority."

Shingai bade his uncles farewell. He refused to get into their home because he did not want to be seen by people who might then tell Rubonga about it. They understood his intentions, and they also bade him farewell. They did not even walk him for a short distance. They just watched him walk away from the kraal before they carried on with their chores. They watched him for a while, but he did not look back. Before long, he had disappeared beyond a hill that was to the south of their home.

He got to where he was supposed to meet his troops before them. The forces were surprised to hear the whistle of the parrot that they communicated with each other when it was time for roll call. At first, they thought they had heard the actual little parrots whistling up in the trees, but then they saw him sitting on top of a big granite boulder. Shingai asked the senior colonel what his plans were like. The colonel told him, and he was happy with the plan. They were going to camp only after they had passed a territory that had a thicket of bushes littered on the route that they had taken. They carried on with their trip, and their mission was successful. They were met with little resistance wherever they went. They collected Rubonga's tribute and went back to Magocha. Masimba and his woodpecker brigade arrived back in Magocha after six days. They had also conquered their enemy. Even though Rubonga was depressed continuously in those days, he was quite pleased by what the boys had done.

Chapter 23

Months spun into seasons and seasons turned into a year, but not a word was heard from Vandirai or his daughter. Nobody knew where they were. This pleased Rubonga because he believed that as long as Vandirai was far away from him, his throne and his family were safe. Although he had waited for a long time for the return of his girl, Shingai's heart was slowly losing the faith. The military raids on the Western Kingdoms had managed to keep off his thoughts and heartaches of missing Shuvai. The Magocha army had carried out victorious strikes, and the citizens of those kingdoms had surrendered to Magocha. They had agreed to be under Rubonga's rule, but there was something sinister about those people. They seemed to be planning a revolt against Rubonga. The king had picked up this vibe and made sure that Shingai and Prince Masimba made frequent trips to assess the situation.

As Shingai went about his business in the kingdom, he got the sensation of being followed again, but this time, the person who was following him was maintaining a considerable distance between them. He suspected that it could only be Rubonga's people stalking him. When they stopped following him, he would know that Rubonga was happy with what he would be doing in those days. To King Rubonga, a living Shingai was more precious than a dead one. Shingai's boys did not stop spying for him, but they did not tell him who it was that could have been planning to kill him in Magocha. In those days, Shingai also started to see the beauty in other girls although when he would compare them to Shuvai, he would find many impurities in them.

Tendai saw an opportunity to rekindle the flame between them, but he pushed her off when he thought that he was likely to hurt her again in the future. He kept on imagining what would happen if Shuvai were to suddenly come back to Magocha. He saw it becoming a reality, and he stopped himself before he went too far. When he took a quick secret trip to Mawisire to check if Shuvai had been back, her uncles would tell him that only Vandirai had briefly visited to let them know that all was well with Shuvai and himself. They said he had not divulged out adequate information on what he was up to. They said they had a lot of faith in their brother-in-law. This had raised his hope in Shuvai coming back to Magocha.

When ancestors yawn, the demons can find an opportunity to strike. Shingai's ancestors must have yawned for too long and left him vulnerable to demons. One day he cussed at his ancestors, wishing that they had been visible on that day so that he could sever his ties with them in broad daylight. King Rubonga was in good spirits during these days, and so his whole family gathered together in the family court just to spend time with each other. Shingai and Masimba were sitting with the little boys telling them tales from the various wars and battles that they had fought. Such days had become rare in the royal family, and so the young kids and their mothers were also in a happy mood. While this was going on, two warriors approached the family court and knelt in courtesy. They greeted the gathering by clapping their hands in respect to the king and his family. Masimba went closer to them and took over the clapping, extending it to the king. He explained that the clapping was a show of subordination by the warriors to the king. Rubonga responded by lightly stroking the arm of his chair. The warriors then whispered to Prince Masimba, stretching their necks to get their heads closer but keeping their bodies as far away from him as possible. Warriors should not get too close to royals. It is disrespectful to do that. Masimba then spoke so that the whole family could hear.

"Great Lion! Your guards here are saying that there are some messengers to you from *bamunini* Vandirai."

Rubonga's ears moved, but the rest of his face remained calm and unmoved. To Shingai, the name "Vandirai" was now sounding as if it was the same as "Shuvai!" His heart gave one big beat, and he thought everybody had heard it pound.

"Where are those people?"

Rubonga asked. He seemed reluctant to have anybody telling him what the messengers had to say. He wanted to hear from them what the message was before anybody in his family heard it. He needed to hastily hear from the messengers.

"They are outside the security wall, Your Highness."

One of the guards answered.

"Run and bring them here now!"

Rubonga roared, and the whole family went quiet. He knew that everyone who entered the security stone wall would be disarmed at the gates, making it unlikely for anybody that would have come through to carry out a random attack on him and his family.

The whole royal family went silent and just looked at the king and the two messengers that were walking towards the family court. When they heard the name "Vandirai," they all knew that it must have been something big. As the messengers got closer, the king rose and went to meet them a bit further from the family so that they would not hear what was being discussed. Shingai became restless. He wished he could throw his ears between the king and his *tezvara's* emissaries. The messengers greeted the king by kneeling and facing the ground as they clapped their hands. One of them then spoke a few words to the king, still facing the ground. Rubonga laughed out loud that all the family heard him. He went back to his chair and sat down then he instructed that the messengers be given stools to sit and share their message as it was meant for the whole family to hear and discuss.

Shingai was astonished. His curiosity grew, and he could not sit still. His mind told him that Lord Vandirai was asking to be allowed to come back and live in Magocha and that he wanted to live in peace and harmony with his brother the king. This would mean that Shuvai would be coming back to live in Magocha for good. This would be the best news he would have heard in a long while.

The emissaries were asked to convey their message to the entire family. The whole family, including the children, threw their ears and eyes at the emissaries. The man who appeared to be the spokesperson began to talk.

"Your Highness, the mighty Lion and all you exalted blood of the mighty Mupingamhuru gathered here. We have very few words for you. We have been sent by your *bamunini,* Lord Vandirai. He says that, had it not been for his leg that is currently giving him sleepless nights from pain, he would have come to deliver this message in person. Your uncle is asking his brother, King Rubonga of Magocha to permit him to come back to his home. He said he did not depart from Magocha in a manner that is expected of reasonable men. He went without informing his brother, as if there was some mischief he had done and had to ran away from. But that was just pure stupidity for a whole grown man."

The women made sounds that despised Vandirai and implying that he was indeed a stupid man. Some snorted, not out of anger but just disdain for their *bamunini.*

"Your *bamunini* is asking for his brother to be merciful with him and to choose for him, a young family that should build their home near his home so that they would constantly check on him as he shall then be living on his own. He said that his wish now is for him to come back to live among his people so that if anything is to happen to him, it will happen while he is in his home kingdom where the bones of his departed fathers are buried."

"Oh, shame!"

One of the women remarked, shaking her head and dragging the words as if she was sincerely touched by Vandirai's plight.

Masimba was listening with his mouth wide open. Shingai thought that Vandirai had finally come to his senses and warmed up to the fact that Shingai was going to be his official son-in-law and that is why Lord Vandirai needed someone to stay with. He would need somebody to assist him with household chores! The messenger then went on with his message.

"Lord Vandirai also asked us to deliver two heifers that we have left outside the wall to hand them to you great Lion for-"

"So *bamunini* Vandirai thinks he can bribe father with just two little calves! Has he forgotten how big father's herd is? Why didn't he just stop at asking for forgiveness with his words only? A-h, he has gotten really delusional lately, right?"

Masimba interjected and drew a burst of hysterical laughter from the other royals. Even the king laughed and then said,

"Can you let him finish what he has to say and then if you have questions, you can then ask after that."

Rubonga wore a smile that Shingai did not quite like. Shingai began to get a series of butterflies, and he began to sweat. He felt that he was the only one that had not found anything worth laughing at, about what the messengers had said so far. The family obeyed the king's instruction, and once more everyone went quiet, looking at the messengers and urging the one that was speaking to carry on.

"The cattle are part of Shuvai's dowry. Some of the dowry goods were given to her uncles in Mawisire as the people who looked after her for the longest time. If you are in agreement with your young brother's request to come back, Your Highness, the other part will then be brought home. This is just a token to you the fathers of Shuvai, to take as an acknowledgment that your daughter was married in a well-dignified manner and so by accepting the gift, your daughter shall receive your blessings. Shuvai is now married to a man who lives in Mawisire."

The sensational laughter that gripped the royal family on this day was the first and the last that was witnessed in Rubonga's palace. The women shed tears from too much laughing, and the girls rolled on the ground uncontrollably. Shingai could not find anywhere to bury his face. Dizziness engulfed him, and he closed his eyes as he held his head in his hands, going dead silent. Kundai was reminding everybody how she had unequivocally warned Shingai to stay away from the wicked Shuvai, but then he thought that she was just a good for nothing, nosey girl. She spoke of how she had equated Shuvai to those chilies that looked dazzling and delicious, but when one ate them, they could burn off the skin lining in the mouth. Shingai seemed not to hear all this. Masimba tried to calm and stop the family from laughing, but his efforts were futile. The laughter was more directed to humiliate Shingai further. Rubonga had to intervene and asked everybody to show some respect to Shingai. Masimba thought of consoling him, but he stopped in his tracks as he sensed that it was not the best time for him to attempt that.

When everybody was quiet, the king then consulted his family,

"So what do you think of this message?"

The women said they did not want anything to do with such a treacherous wizard. They noted that Vandirai was draining happiness from their husband because of his jealousy and plans to overthrow the rightful King of Magocha using bizarre means. The king then asked Masimba what he thought about it.

"That one is totally for you, my fathers. It is for you, my king and *bamunini* Vandirai to deal with. Whatever you should decide is what shall guide us. As someone who has confessed and asked for forgiveness, I would say you could consider his request and make sure that you assign people to keep an eye on him. If he should then display the slightest evidence of his deceitful tendencies, then you will hastily take action."

Shingai was still facing downwards with his hands supporting his head. Little kids had surrounded him, filled with curiosity as to what was going on with him.

The king then spoke after taking a bit of time as if he was thinking about his responses carefully.

"I did not send my brother into exile, and therefore, I do not know why he is even asking to come back. The home is his and like he said, here in Magocha is where our departed fathers from many generations ago sleep, so who am I to stop him from coming home? Yes, I was not amused by the way he left without informing me. He could have just told me like he used to. About his daughter getting married, a-ah, that is excellent. He has given me something, and I appreciate it. Kundai and your sisters, you should take after your sister and also make us proud by getting married in such a good way."

Kundai pulled her bottom lip down in jest and then broke into a burst of loud but quick ending laughter. Rubonga carried on saying.

"Go and tell Vandirai that all his words are good. We shall see him when he returns. Travel well!"

King Rubonga had taken Masimba's advice, not because he was sympathetic to Vandirai's plight nor because he was just an understanding man, no. If Vandirai stayed closer with somebody assigned to watch over him all the time, Rubonga would be more relaxed because he would then be able to keep him on the radar at all times. Shuvai's marriage was a bonus for him. It had infuriated Shingai so much that he would not be interested in hearing about Vandirai and his daughter, and in the tug of war between Rubonga and Vandirai; Shingai was definitely going to pull in Rubonga's direction. This was going to be interesting to see as it unfolded. Rubonga was once again happier. It was true that from that moment, Shingai hated Vandirai as much as he despised his ancestors. His dizziness slackened, and Rubonga saw it and said,

"Shingi, you are a man. Do you remember when I told you that Vandirai is a snake that moves on its belly on the ground? Look at what he has done to you today. You can go and take a rest."

Shingai went straight to his *gota* and closed the door behind him. Masimba wanted to follow him, but once again, his conscience advised him to slow it down and leave Shingai to deal with himself for some time. Kundai could not stop herself from laughing. She did not let out the sound of her laughter, but her eyes got red from shedding tears of hilarity. She told herself that this was an excellent example of the wages of not listening to other people's advice!

For three days, Shingai could not swallow his food. What he had heard had drained out all the energy from his body. He could not make sense of it all. It still felt like he had been slapped in the face. His heart had been split into two, and he was standing in between the two pieces. On one side, he cussed and blamed himself for not being able to have read something that had been so clear to him for a long time. So had his mind slept like a dry log in front of Shuvai for him to be turned into such a big fool?

On the other hand, he blamed everything on the viper-headed Vandirai. Vandirai was one of the biggest schemers he had ever known, but still, Shuvai was now a grown-up, and she could not have been forced into marriage by anybody. She could have just run away. If she had run away to him, they could have easily escaped together from Magocha. This disturbed him a lot. He thought of all that he had been told by Gotora and took it all to be lies. The story was not congruent with what Vandirai and his daughter had done to him. The two could not have been victims but pure schemers who could have burnt their own home.

It could be that Gotora was also a lair or that he could have been working with Vandirai to deceive him all along. He was no longer supposed to rely on the old cannibal. These two people had almost managed to sever ties between him and the person that genuinely loved and believed in him, King Rubonga. He planned to ask for forgiveness from Rubonga for not having taken his advice about Lord Vandirai. This is what he was going to do. He had to make it his number one priority, to achieve all that his king wanted him to do so that his enemies would be shamed and put down. These new thoughts calmed his mind and insulated him from the embarrassment that he had brought upon himself, and at the same time, it began to turn him into a cruel young man.

Rubonga was sitting on top of the world when he listened to Shingai's confession. He had won another major battle. Both of the people that he did not trust and feared had thrown themselves into his hands at the same time! Nobody could stop him now. His ancestors had planned and executed everything for him. He could now let Shingai survive, but as for Vandirai, he had to ingeniously arrange his demise. The close relationship that was about to be built between Vandirai and Shingai had been razed to the ground, so he did not worry much about Shingai. Rubonga then told his family to stop teasing Shingai because of Shuvai but to actually help him get over her by organizing a new girl for him. Later on, Masimba just advised him to put Shuvai behind him so that he could move on with his life.

Chapter 24

"*Mukoma,* I saw something that shocked me in the middle of the night. I could not even shut my eyelids for the whole night just waiting to tell you about it."

This was one of the young men that Shingai had recruited to spy for him. He panted as he spoke. Shingai had just stepped out of the palace enclosure straight from his *gota* early in the morning on that day.

"So these people did not see me because-"

"Ho-o ho, young man, can you stop and breathe, yes calm down and breathe. What people? What exactly are you trying to say?"

The young man calmed down and explained, still filled with excitement.

"So a few days ago I had gone into the forest to hunt for some game then, I remembered that I had forgotten to take grain to my grandfather. My mother had asked me to do that before I left for the forest, so I immediately turned around to go back and run the errand. As I was coming back to the village, I used the path that passes by the foot of the Chineninga Kopje. As I was walking past that sacred kopje, I heard low voices coming from the foot of the hill, and instinctively, I decided to investigate who it could be conversing at such a place and time! They were walking near the big rocks, and they stopped just behind the rock that I was hiding from because one of them needed to empty his bladder.

"Thanks to the full moon that graces the sky these days, I was able to see that the three men were warriors because of the weapons that they were carrying. At first, I thought they were members of our army on a secret mission, but I soon learned that they were not when one of them said, 'But the man is a high ranked official in Rubonga's inner circle team, and so he knows all that Rubonga is planning.' They said that they wanted to meet with him quickly so that they would return to their land before anybody had seen them. I did not hear more about their contact person because they had said they would camp just above the foot of the hill for them to meet with their man. One of the men asked his colleagues if it was not wiser for them to camp much higher on the hill where it was more obscured, and the other answered that it did not matter because the people of Magocha revered the kopje and where terrified to get too close to it because it was a sacred shrine. He said that if the people of Magocha took it lightly and wandered into the hill they could just disappear and never to be found, but they were strangers in this kingdom and so the wise spirits would not punish them because the divine laws of this kingdom did not bind them.

"I was tempted to draw closer to them, but then I thought I could alarm them if I made a silly mistake and they would leave without us getting to know what it is that they wanted to do in Magocha. I also feared that they could even kill me right there, taking the information with me into the soil. I then remembered your words that if I were to come across any suspicious information, I should hastily get it to you."

Shingai kept looking at the young man's eyes and then excitedly asked,

"Are you telling the truth Chidhure?"

Chidhure swore by his long-departed grandparents that he was telling the truth. Shingai thought about it for a while and asked many other questions, repeating some of them several times. He believed Chidhure's narration.

It was true that the people of Magocha were terrified at the sight or thought of Chineninga hill. The dead kings and some high standing royals of Magocha were buried in a secret cave that was on that hill. Cattle and other domestic livestock were forbidden from treading or even grazing near that hill. For the intruders to know about all this information was evidence enough to show that they had an informant from within the kingdom. Shingai knew that if he saw these men, he would probably know where they were from. He thought of going to injure them so that they could not run away and thereby giving him the chance to interrogate them and find out all the information he needed. He dropped the thought when he realized that if he was to injure and question them, the real enemy of Magocha, who happened to be their informant could slip away from them. He then took Chidhure with him, and he went to see for himself, approaching the spot carefully. It was easy for him to do, as he was good at tracking and hiding.

In no time they were at a point where they had a good view. They saw that there was one warrior on guard. The other two might have been taking a nap. Shingai could tell from the dressing of the warrior on guard that he was from the Western Kingdoms, the Kingdom of Mazimbe to be precise. They quickly moved away from their spot, taking the path that they had walked on their way to the foot of Chineninga and headed back to the palace.

When they got to the palace, Shingai left Chidhure waiting for him outside the main enclosure as he went inside. He was delighted that he had found something that would make Rubonga happy. This was going to endear him to the king again. He would earn more respect, as the king would be certainly proud of him for his outstanding skills. With the foolproof plan that he had, the enemy of the state was soon going to be exposed to all the citizens of Magocha. He called Masimba so that he could present his exclusive news to him and the king in one sitting. Rubonga was furious when he heard the news. He was about to send for his troops to go and finish off the enemies at once, but Shingai stopped him. He shared his plan of capturing the intruders and their informant at the same time. They would release the warriors after torturing them so that they would take a message to those that had sent them to not even contemplate such a foolish mission again. The enemy, together with Revesai, had opened the valves and evil spirits had flooded Magocha.

Shingai's plan was for him to go back to the spot where he could see the intruders and anybody who would approach them. This would allow him to see who they were going to talk to, and after that, he would quickly aim for the four men's calves with his arrows. This would stop them from escaping, and they would all be apprehended with little effort. Masimba, two of the king's guards, and Chidhure would accompany him on the ambush. Chidhure could not be left out of the plan because leaving him could compromise the whole scheme as he could share the information with somebody who may then warn the enemies. Rubonga said the idea was good, but he would not stay behind and miss out on the revelation of his two-faced adversary. The team took out their weapons and Shingai led them. They had to whisper whenever they needed to communicate amongst themselves.

When they arrived at their spot, the sun was on its way to its resting place, but it was still bright for the eye to see quite far. Two of the intruders were talking to each other and not showing any sign of alertness to a potential enemy attack. Shingai and his team laid low and kept their eyes on the unsuspecting intruders. Before long, the team was all shocked by what they saw. They did not have to wait till nighttime. They looked at each other with open mouths as if they were in a choir and getting ready to start singing at once. VaGondo was seen holding a short hoe, stopping to dig for herbs as he walked towards the enemies. The intruders saw him and at first attempted to hide from him, but then they stopped and held their mouths as they began to control their laughter. Rubonga tried to whisper, but his voice was audible to those around him saying,

"So Gondo is the rodent that has been biting me right inside my house!"

He closed his short statement with a loud snort and a spit onto the ground. VaGondo stopped to dig under a little shrub. There third intruder had now joined the other two watching VaGondo. They did not draw their weapons to aim at him. VaGondo was only armed with the carving chiseled-hoe that he used for digging his herbs. His belly stuck out in the open, and his neck was soaked from sweat, for it had been scorching hot on that day.

Rubonga and his team were bewildered by what Shingai did in a split of a second. When the intruders laughed again, the king and his team heard arrows whizz just over Masimba's head, as he lay low on the ground. At that same moment, the three intruders had fallen down with arrows pierced in their calves. They were confused and crying while lying on the ground. It took some time for Rubonga and his team to see what had taken place. VaGondo had thrown his hands in the air, looking back and front trying to locate where voices of grown men crying were coming from. The old man shook like a chicken suspecting that the time for it to meet the knife had come.

When the intruders were laughing facing VaGondo, behind him was Chitsere. Chitsere had drawn his arrow and intended to sink it into VaGondo's neck from behind. Shingai had suddenly developed a chameleon's eye and had quickly figured out what was taking place. VaGondo was going about his business, digging for roots, and collecting herbs. It was Chitsere who had come to meet the intruders from Mazimbe, and when he saw VaGondo in his path. Chitsere had weighed his options and had decided to eliminate VaGondo instead of letting the senior governor seeing the intruders talking to him. VaGondo would certainly report to Rubonga. Shingai wanted these men alive. Masimba went to help with the binding of the intruders in leather ropes. From the time that they were bounded in codes to the time that the team arrived at the dungeons, Chitsere did not stop cussing at King Rubonga.

Some of the offensive words were targeted at Shingai, but most were directed at the king himself. He did this because he knew that his life had come to an end. From some of the cussing, Shingai had heard

Chitsere mentioning that Rubonga had stolen the crown from Vandirai. He remembered hearing the same words from Gotora, but he quickly dismissed them assuring himself that Gotora, Vandirai, and Chitsere were masters of deception, possibly working in cahoots to undermine King Rubonga.

Rubonga suddenly hit Chitsere on the occipital with his knobkerrie, and Chitsere collapsed. He instructed his guards to cover his mouth so that he would not make more noise when he woke up. Rubonga wanted to take time to consider a fitting punishment for Chitsere. VaGondo was delighted that Shingai had saved his life, but the shock he got from that incident was etched in his heart. He did not have the slightest idea of what was happening. When he was back in his *gota*, Shingai retraced the events of the day and began to fit in some pieces of the puzzle of what was going on in the kingdom. It became clear that it was Chitsere who was trying to eliminate him from Magocha and not the king, as he had believed. Every time he met Shingai, he spoke to him politely. This was a way of deflecting from being suspected amongst the traitors. Shingai smiled and felt proud of what he did. He had succeeded in revealing his king's dangerous adversary.

The intruders were asked to name who it was that they were working with, in the kingdom to get information on the secrets of Magocha. At first, they refused to cooperate by keeping quiet, but when they were handed to some senior warriors, they confessed that they were only working with Chitsere. They said they had met him twice in the season that had ended. They were mainly looking for information about when Rubonga would be planning to raid them so that they would prepare. They claimed that the western kings were hoping that in the event of defeating Magocha, they would install Chitsere as their vessel king in Magocha even though they were aware that he was not of royal blood. The intruders had only managed to give out this information after the senior warriors had subjected them to torture. The warriors had roasted some hard and dry seeds and then forced the hot seeds into the mouths' of the spies. After that, the warriors then took thorns and forced the sharp ends into the space between the fingernails and the skin of the prisoners' fingers, making them scream at the top of their voices.

When they were asked again, the prisoners ended up volunteering even more information than what they had been asked. The interrogation ended with a thorough beating of the enemies. They had deep cuts and were bleeding all over their bodies. The prisoners screamed and wriggled when they were thrown onto a colony of stinging ants. The people who were watching ended up feeling sorry for them. They were then freed and told to go back to where they had come from and inform their superiors what was in store for them if they dared to attempt such stupidity again. All this took place while Chitsere was locked up in a dungeon breathing as much as he could, knowing that he had finally reached his horizon.

The drums were beaten, and the grown-ups, mostly from the king's district headed for the king's court. When the people were gathered, VaGondo rose and narrated to them the events of the previous few days leading to the apprehension of the spies and the traitor Governor Chitsere. Many in the crowd were stunned by the news. Some mumbled loudly about how Gezi had blamed Governor Revesai for something that Chitsere had done, but VaGondo refuted the allegation, claiming that it had been discovered that the two had been working together on destabilizing the foundation of the kingdom. Although many had not believed the explanation, none of them publicly protested. VaGondo ended by letting the people know that the king had already planned on how to discipline Chitsere. It was clear that the judgment for such a crime was death. They just did not know what the chosen method of the execution would be.

Shingai was happy that his enemy who had been elusive had finally been caught and was about to be slain. He wanted to see how it was going to be done. He also wanted to whisper in Chitsere's ear telling him that he was the one who tried to kill him and that he was the one who was responsible for the death of his missing assassin. The marriage of Shuvai to another man had hardened his heart. He never used to like seeing people getting killed except during war times but this time he even wanted to have a hand in the spilling of Chitsere's blood!

A huge pile of dry mupani wood was made. Chitsere was to be placed on top of the heaped wood and fire would be lit from the bottom of the altar. The fire would burn and consume the wood and Chitsere together until they were both reduced to a heap of ashes. His relatives would be left with nothing but his ashes to bury. A group of mean looking warriors dragged the disgraced Governor Chitsere and set him high on the pile of wood, arms and legs bound by strong ropes. On this day none of the people who gathered at the tree of smoke tried to beg for clemency on behalf of Chitsere. However, some elders were overheard lamenting and predicting that the heavens were not going to release its precious tears in Magocha because of the amount of blood that was being carelessly spilled during those days. When Shingai tried to move closer to the altar, he felt his head begin to spin slowly. The dizziness that frequently visited him decided to snooze him at that moment. He turned around and saw Muthlomo beckoning him from behind the crowd. Her face looked disgruntled. He remembered that he wanted to ask her about how she and her people had let Shuvai fool him as they had done if they were concerned about him at all.

Whenever Muthlomo disappeared from Shingai, he would completely forget about her. She would visit him in his dreams at times. When he would see her, his questions and concerns would return to him, but something would prevent him from asking. He held his head with one hand and went to Muthlomo. Those who saw him assumed that he was talking to himself, but they could not hear what he was saying. Masimba saw him walking towards his *gota* and did not stop him because he could see that he was not feeling well. Shingai kept on asking Muthlomo about Shuvai so that he would not forget about it as they walked towards his *gota.* As soon as they got into his room, Muthlomo spoke.

"Do not let your heart rejoice for what is not in your system. Cruelty is not for you."

She disappeared immediately after saying those words, and he instantly fell asleep.

When he eventually woke up, Chitsere was only a heap of ashes. Prince Masimba tried to explain to him how it had happened, how horrified the people were, and how sorrowful the whole event had been. Although Masimba explained it clearly, it did not stick in Shingai's mind. He was more worried about what it was that caused him to miss out on such important events. He could not explain it. Rubonga even asked him to explain his absence and all he could say was that he had had a splitting headache, and so had gone to rest in his *gota.*

On the following day, the kingdom woke up to worrying and sad news of the murder of Mangundu, one of the most trusted senior members of Rubonga's security team. He was found dead on the banks of the river on the side that was reserved for men to bath. A group of boys that had gone to take a bath before sunset discovered him. Mangundu had disappeared two days back and had missed Chitsere's execution. His wife thought that he had gone hunting because she had been cranky and nagging him to do something about the family's craving for fresh game meat. What shocked the people was that there was sufficient evidence that Mangundu had been murdered. It looked like he had been shot in the chest with the arrow piercing right through to his heart. After the shot, the killer must have made an opening with his dagger on the middle of Mangundu's gut and cut off Mangundu's wrists then planted them in his belly through the opening he had made. The people of Magocha had not seen such a sight before. Those that spoke in the open claimed that it was an act of witchcraft that had never been witnessed before and must have been new in the kingdom. Those that whispered in dark spaces contended that it was the avenging spirits that had come to punish the people that gladly oiled Rubonga's cruelty first before it would consume the king himself in the end.

Of the five *n'anga* summoned to consult on the death of Mangundu, three had just stuttered and shaken their heads without saying anything. They, later on, said they were not getting revelations because those that spoke through them were hiding from them what had actually happened to the deceased warrior. One *n'anga* claimed that the people of the west had now started their assault on Magocha and therefore the king and his armies had to be alert. Gezi apportioned the blame of the murder on Mangundu's relatives who stayed in Magondo. He said that if the deceased's relatives in Magocha prepared a special brew to offer to their ancestors, it would be revealed to them why the culprit had committed the act. Rubonga and his esteemed council that at that time had ten members took Gezi's oracle as the most probable explanation. They doubted that the attack came from the west because those people had not yet received the information about their foiled mission. The intruders were still limping on their way home. If Mangundu had been shot and killed by the arrow and then left to rot like that, there would have been a slight chance that it could have been retaliation from the people of the west. Mangundu's murder screamed ritual killing. This was a plain family issue.

Chapter 25

A few days after the gruesome murder of Mangundu, Lord Vandirai returned to Magocha and went to see his brother King Rubonga. He was now walking with the aid of a walking stick, showing that he was in pain from his infirm leg. Shingai had expected to see the whole royal family shouting at, and teasing Vandirai when he arrived at the palace, but he was surprised when they courteously greeted him. Mai Tongai led the queens as they went and sat on the ground before they politely asked after Vandirai's health. They talked about other things and even managed to joke with him, accusing him of not being their caring husband he used to be. They left later on and went to their rondavels.

The children also went and greeted him respectfully, the girls bending one knee as they shook his hand. Shingai did not go to greet him. He just gave him an eyeful that did not attempt to conceal his disdain for him. Vandirai, in return, acted as if he had not seen that he was present. Rubonga spoke with his brother for a short time, and then he called two of his guards. Before long, the young couple that had been chosen to build their home near Vandirai's came and left with the veteran warrior. After four days had passed, Shingai went to check if it was true that Shuvai had not returned with Vandirai to Magocha.

Shingai now loathed Vandirai with a passion, but he realized that he had not erased his desire for Shuvai from his heart. He felt like something was not right about the whole situation. When he realized that

Vandirai had awakened his memories of Shuvai, when the two of them had set the world on fire, he sat on one boulder where they used to sit for long periods just talking. He put his hand on his waist and rubbed it, searching for their contractual tattoo. As he felt the small bumps of the tiny scars, he wondered what Shuvai thought of when she felt her tattoo and what it symbolized. He also wondered what she told her husband if he inquired what the symbols meant. He snorted when he realized that it was getting dark while he was busy thinking about things that were already in the distant past. The memory of food eaten many days ago does not satsify present hunger.

On the following day, Shingai walked towards Tendai's home. From a short distance, he saw Tendai sweeping the yard at her mother's house. He kept staring at her in admiration then he began to walk closer so that he could call her to him. After he had taken a few steps, he heard a voice behind him.

"E-eh, hello sir!"

He turned his head quickly and saw Tambudzai, Tendai's younger sister.

"Hey! Hello, my dear. Wow! You have really grown in the last few days, and you are getting more and more beautiful! You seem to have absorbed your sister's beauty into yourself." Shingai said, as the two of them slapped each other's palms, making a clapping sound. Tambudzai blushed and looked down. She took down the gourd that she was balancing on her head and she then asked,

"Is everything well? How is it that royalty has found it worthy to set foot on our grounds this afternoon?"

Shingai was a bit embarrassed by the question, but he answered it and added a laugh.

"Oh come on my dear, what royalty are you talking about? Can a man not freely visit his family anymore?"

"A-ah *bamukuru* Shingi just stop. With the way you humiliated and hurt my sister, you shouldn't even be stepping on the soil in this area. We heard it all that karma served you a really cold dish when someone took your Shuvai."

Tambudzai ended with a laugh that was filled with mockery.

Shingai had anticipated the mentioning of the Shuvai issue, but he still felt annoyed when Tambudzai teased him about it. He suppressed the irritation and put on a smile as he told her that he had put it all behind him. He said that was the reason he had decided to go back to the person who truly cared for him and not the whirlwind that he had chased. Tambudzai made a short melodic laugh, one that was not caused by reflex but one that meant to say, "You've got jokes." She then retorted,

"Oh, dear, this is funny. Are you for real *bamukuru*, or you are just here to be your haughty self again?"

Shingai became focused.

"I am not joking *mainini*. This time I am ready to plan my future with Tendai. You just found me when I was about to call her to come to me so that we could talk."

Tambudzai looked at Shingai in his eyes and shook her head, and then she said,

"You hurt my mother's child badly. The fact that she can still walk like this today is only because our ancestors fought fearlessly in her corner. Tendai had really believed that her life had ended when you were taken by Shuvai."

Shingai inclined his head to one side and was touched. Tambudzai went on to say,

"Anyway, I know very well that you are dishonest when you say you still love my sister because if it were so, you would have known what happened to her after you dumped her. You are probably the only person in Magocha that does not know it. Anyway, would you royals know what goes on with us your subjects? We truly live different lives."

Shingai was totally lost. He could not think of what could have happened to Tendai.

"Can you not speak in riddles *mainini*? What are you trying to say?"

Tambudzai responded with a question.

"When you looked at Tendai, what did you see?"

Shingai looked up and saw that Tendai had stopped sweeping. She was standing with one hand on her waist and the other holding the broom looking directly at Shingai and her sister. He felt like raising his hand to beckon her, but instinct stopped him. He looked at her intently again and said to Tambudzai,

"All I can see is that my girl is still as beautiful as she was before. In fact, she seems to have become more beautiful, and she has developed more pronounced curves from the last time I saw her."

He looked at Tambudzai and grinned foolishly.

Tambudzai shook her head again and threw her hands in the air and said

"Ya-a, men! I do not know how you people were created or wired. Tendai is now four months pregnant. A young man who lives very close to our home married her and so each time she misses us, she just walks over to our home. But did you not hear about it? A big ceremony was thrown for her. Even Princess Kundai knows about it. Your coming here like Tendai's lover can cause unnecessary misunderstandings between her husband and her. Please do not be a home wrecker. If you have any respect for my sister, then please find your tracks back to the palace immediately. You see, the problem is that Tendai's husband knows very well that you and his wife were once a hot couple in the kingdom, so it would not be nice if he even imagines that the extinguished flame between the two of you can be rekindled once more."

Shingai returned home carrying a sad heart. He wondered why Kundai had not told him about such a significant development. He was relieved that only Tambudzai and Tendai had seen him near Tendai's home because if other people had seen him, they would not have believed that he was not aware that Tendai was now a married woman! Women were not given much respect from the time they were toddlers, and even when they became young adults. But the moment they got married, this all changed. The woman became esteemed and revered. Her pots, cooking utensils, livestock, and many other possessions became sacred. Careless handling of these possessions by other people could invite the wrath of avenging spirits. It was known that the avenging spirits of a mother could not be appeased by any price. If they went after anybody, it would just be disaster after disaster until the victim perished.

Shingai did not ever want to look like someone who had no regard for those expectations and observations. If he had known about Tendai's marriage, he wouldn't have even gone in that direction. As he was thinking about it, he realized that some dark fortune had attached itself firmly to his tail. For with Tendai, he had been that cow that never knew the importance of its tail until that day when the tail was cut off, and it was no longer able to shoo off the flies that brought harmful germs to it. Perhaps if he had not left Tendai, he would have left his *gota* already. Maybe the baby that was growing in Tendai's womb would have been his. When he got home, he thought of asking Kundai why she had not told him about Tendai's marriage, but he then ignored it. He made himself feel better by remembering his favorite saying that; "If only" is a fool's way of wasting time.

When Shingai entered into the enclosure, he saw King Rubonga pacing up and down near the family court. One of his hands wrapped his chest while he held his chin with the thump of the other hand, and the rest of the fingers stroking his neck. He kept on pacing up and down. Shingai looked at him for some moments. He now knew that if the king was acting like that, there was something that was bothering his mind. Most of his guards were stationed at their designated posts, but three of them were kneeling in alertness, with one knee on the ground, answering questions that the king asked as he continued to pace. Shingai noticed that Masimba was not with the king. He did not like to approach the king without Masimba when the king was in such a mood. He thought twice and ended up proceeding towards the court where the king was still pacing up and down.

As soon as Rubonga saw him, he quickly asked,

"Shingi, what is going on in this kingdom? Hmmn?

Shingai was perplexed and could not find an appropriate answer to the question. He opened his mouth for some time, but not a word rolled off his tongue. Rubonga did not wait for him to find an answer. He shot another question.

"And where is your friend Masimba now?"

Shingai said that he did not know. Rubonga then spoke again, his voice betraying the panic that had gripped him.

"Now you boys are busy walking around without knowing the whereabouts of each other when our security has developed wide gaps like this. What do you base your carelessness on? I told you long back that I am not comfortable with you not knowing where your other is."

Rubonga went on talking, but Shingai still did not know what he was talking about or what was causing him to speak like that. Shingai felt relieved when he saw Masimba walk into the enclosure, whistling happily.

When Prince Masimba saw his father and Shingai, he stopped whistling and started walking quickly towards them. Rubonga did not respond to Masimba's "Good evening, Shumba." He just said,

"Now that the two of you are here. I want a quick explanation of what it is that is going on in this kingdom."

Immediately after saying those words, he got into his house, leaving the boys puzzled. Masimba then asked,

"What is the Cobra trying to say?"

"I thought you were going to fill me in on it. I have no idea what the king is talking about. I got here just some minutes moments before you."

Shingai answered him. The boys concurrently looked at the three warriors that were still kneeling before them, and Shingai asked them.

"Gentlemen, what is the Cobra talking about, what question are we supposed to provide an answer to?"

If it had been any other day, the warriors would have laughed first and answered later. But on this day they kept quiet, each of them looking at the other and hoping they would speak or answer first. Shingai could tell that there must have been a big issue. One of the warriors then spoke.

"A-ah, My Lords, we are so sorry to let you know that your senior guard Mutoweshindi is no more."

Shingai and Masimba responded in a chorus,

"What?"

Mutoweshindi was the guard who deputized Mangundu in the king's security department. Soon after the burial of Mangundu, the king had ordered Mutoweshindi to take up the vacant position of Security Chief without delay. When a person falls ill for a long time, and he eventually passes on, his people get sad, but they get consolation from saying that he would have at least rested from the agony. This is not what had happened to Mutoweshindi. He was a fit man who was also very loyal to his king. He was one who would not tolerate anybody who would say anything he considered negative about Rubonga. King Rubonga trusted him with his life. He was the man that he would task with the execution of those that would have been sentenced to death. He only needed to hear the words from Rubonga, and he would not have second thoughts about killing anybody for him. Many people had seen him walking strong in the few days that had passed, and so when they heard about his passing, they found it hard to believe. Rubonga was not really touched by the death of his warrior, no. He was more worried about the way his two highest ranking guards had died in a baffling manner.

The same person had similarly murdered the two men. The killer had also dismembered the victim's palms and planted them into the victim's belly, leaving the fingers sticking out. Mutoweshindi also had his bottom lip cut-off. It looked like he was killed in the middle of the night as he was returning to his home from the king's palace. Many people strongly believed the theory of the avenging spirits that had been provoked by Rubonga by his spilling of blood unreasonably in the kingdom. Shingai and Masimba were dumbfounded. They were disturbed by the deaths and how somebody had successfully killed the king's top security men. They remained silent for some time then asked the guards the same questions over and over again. The kneeling warriors also could not answer most of those questions. Their responses showed that only those that were present at the time and scene of the murder had the answers.

A while later, Rubonga came out of his house and asked the warriors to give his sons and him some time alone. The three remained seated on their chairs, trying to analyze the case that was before them. Masimba suggested that they come up with a list of potential suspects who could commit such gruesome killings then decide how to entrap them. They came up with a long list, but they could not explain what the motive could have been for those people to kill the king's top guards.

Lord Vandirai was one of the prime suspects, but he had his alibis. The couple that lived near him had not seen him leave his home on that day. Even if he had sneaked out of his compound, the condition of his infirm leg could not permit him to kill a man of such strength as Mutoweshindi. It seemed that the killer spoke to the victims before he murdered them so that they would know who would have killed them. The three could only agree to keep watching the developments and being vigilant. Something was going to give, and they would nail their suspect. Rubonga thought that it could have been that the two guards were related but had kept it a secret. Therefore the murders had nothing to do with the affairs of the Magocha kingdom but a family ritual that had come to haunt the victims' lives.

In the days that followed, Shingai began to hear the narrative that the two deceased warriors were indeed related. His sixth sense suggested to him that this was just propaganda. He had thought that Chitsere had taken his propaganda skills with him to the altar and had been burnt with it to ashes. Now that Chitsere had died, who could have inherited his ability to pump lies into the air for the subjects of Magocha to consume until the lies took the place of the truth? This did not disturb him. What worried him was the meaning of the killings. Shingai knew the one person that could tell him the truth or something closer if he knew what was going on. When he thought of him, he felt a bit irritated and embarrassed at the same time. How was he going to talk to him when he had given him his back for a couple of months now? Shingai had stopped talking to Gotora when he had received the news of Shuvai's marriage.

He had grouped him together with Vandirai among the people he trusted the least in Magocha because he believed that they were working together. Vandirai had become his enemy because he had given away his girl for the love of riches!

Chapter 26

Shingai had been contemplating meeting with Gotora for two days. When he had finally made up his mind to go, a thought tickled him. What if Gotora was the killer? Gotora was a skilled fighter, but the people of Magocha did not know this. They only believed that he was the prince of witches in the kingdom. Nobody had suspected him because wizards and witches were not known for killing using weapons like what the recent killer in Magocha had done. His heart began to beat faster and louder. He thought he had solved the mystery. He needed to deliver the news to the king and Masimba without delay.

This came to his mind when he had just stepped outside the palace enclosure. He thought of first getting hold of Masimba who was still in his *gota* so that they could go together to present the news to the king. When he got inside the enclosure, he went to Mai Kundai's kitchen to ask for some water to drink before he looked for Masimba. When he entered the kitchen, the women and the other girls who were gathered in that room went quiet except for Kundai who had her back to the door and had not seen that Shingai had walked in. He did not hear much but the words that went like,"… because ... father … too much … for people that just rose from nowhere …"

The king's third wife shook Kundai's leg and in a panicking voice shouted,

"Be careful Kundai your foot is too close to the fire!"

Shingai saw that the fire was far from where Kundai's feet were. Kundai turned and saw him, then she quickly addressed him in an excited voice saying,

"Yah Shingi, I found you a new girl who is as beautiful as a forest flower this time. You will not have second thoughts about her because your heart is going to just jump into hers right away. She is too gorgeous."

Shingai had taught himself to stay calm even in stressful situations. It was clear that he had been the subject of discussion in that room before he had walked in. He did not need to let them know that he had figured it out. He had to play dumb. He was not worried about people talking lies about him behind his back because he was aware that everybody had people that spoke bad things about them during their absence, but there was something that struck him.

"I knew that no one else could sort out my issues the way you do. Could you please pass me a gourd of water to drink and may you also step outside so that you can tell me all about this new girl."

Kundai gave him the water, and the two of them went outside to talk. The story quickly changed from the new girl to her, giving him advice. She said that he had to seriously open his eyes to other girls because if he locked in his heart, the image of a girl who was now far away and had become another man's wife, he risked committing adultery and getting himself into serious trouble. Shingai told her that her advice had found the right spot in his ears.

What had worried Shingai was that Rubonga took Kundai's opinions seriously. Rubonga actually referred to Kundai as "my mother." Kundai had been named after VaKundai, King Rubonga's late mother. The king loved his mother dearly and was obedient to her. She had passed on when Kundai was aged six years. The loss of his mother had hit him hard. He mourned her for many days, and after that, he became more and more affectionate to little Kundai. He would share with her, things that did not make sense to her at her age. She became the only person who could restrain or pacify Rubonga when he got angry. All the queens knew this and would go out of their way to find favor with her. They did this because whatever she said to the king about them, he would heed to. So when Shingai became aware on that day, that there were some among the Royals who did not fully trust him and Kundai being one of them, he became concerned. He was confident that Kundai did not approve the trust that King Rubonga had in him. He once more remembered Gotora's words warning him to be cautious with Rubonga because he was a *svukukuviri* the two-headed snake.

Thinking about these words brought him back to the many things that he had heard from Gotora and that had turned out to be as he had said. Some of the issues had helped him in many ways. He thought of the fighting skills that the big hermit had taught him, which turned him into one of the most skilled and fiercest warriors in the kingdom. He became engulfed with confusion and regret. It became clear to him that he had taken a long jump to conclude that Gotora was an evil person, all because of his heart that had been broken to pieces by the evil daughter of Vandirai! He needed some time out before he rushed to the prince and the king with his theory that was now full of loopholes. By analyzing his suspicion more, he came to the realization that if he mentioned his knowledge of Gotora's fighting skills, this would actually raise more questions about his relationship with him that he would not be able to answer. The king and Masimba would ask why it had taken him long to tell them about it. He had kept many secrets between him and Gotora, which could spill out if he tried to prove his theory to the two. He concluded that he had almost thrown himself into the jaws of a hungry lion. The urge to visit Gotora grew, and he resolved to do so on the following day.

Shingai arrived at Gotora's home and found him drinking *mahewu*. He had already tilted the hard clay container so that he could strategically fill another gourd with the sweet and sour fermented drink. Shingai took his own drinking gourd and filled it. He sat down beside Gotora and took a couple of mouthfuls before he said anything. The big man did not change his expression. He neither showed that he was happy nor annoyed at Shingai's unexpected visit. Shingai then asked after his health, clapping his hands in respect. Gotora answered politely and carried on drinking his *mahewu* and chewing the residual solids of ground millet. Shingai struggled to find the words to break the tension, but he eventually just went for it.

"Sir, you said Vandirai is a good and understanding man, now if that is so, then where is my girl?"

Gotora turned his head and stared at him for a moment, then forced an expressive noise that was meant to imitate a sarcastic laugh but with the sound coming out of his nostrils. His face remained unchanged. He then responded.

"By the way, when did you employ me to shepherd your girl?"

Shingai just opened his mouth and froze, looking like a chicken gasping for air through the mouth on a hot day. He realized that he had used the wrong words, and he apologized.

"I am failing to find the right words to talk to you for I had given you my back for a long time. This was because I had gotten mad when I learned that my girl had decided to get married to some other man without warning me.

Gotora did another sarcastic laugh then he took out his tobacco and stuffed it into his nostrils before inhaling it. He rubbed his nose with the back of his palm and said,

"What kind of man are you that suffers a heartbreak like that? All this time, I believed that you were a grown man who had trained and loaded his mind with gravity, but it seems I was wrong. You should by now know that even a married woman living happily in her home can fall for another man and leave just like that. When such things happen, as a man, you should know that the woman was never yours because she would not agree to live with somebody that she doesn't want."

Shingai told him that he had learned about it the hard way, but he had now put it all behind him. He now just wanted to know about some strange things that were happening in Magocha.

In their discussion about the murders of Rubonga's security chiefs, Shingai realized that Gotora also did not know what had happened. Gotora said he did not even know where to begin and that throughout his life, he had not seen this type of murders. Shingai threw in Vandirai's name, but Gotora said it wasn't him. He had great respect for Vandirai's wisdom, but he did not believe that he was the one who committed the murders He suspected that a group of people from far away kingdoms were launching the coordinated assassins in retaliation to what Rubonga was doing in their territories. Gotora did not ask Shingai what Rubonga's views were on these developments. If he had asked him about it, Shingai would have suspected that the hermit might have had a hand in the murders and he might have been checking to see if he was a suspect. Shingai bade farewell to the big man and promised to visit him more frequently in the future.

After some days had passed, Shingai, Masimba, and Rubonga sat and agreed that they had failed to come up with a potential suspect who had killed the king's security chiefs. They ordered all the guards to travel in groups of twos or threes and to be alert all the time to avoid surprise attacks from the unknown assailant. This seemed to have worked because many months went by, and the kingdom did not witness such killings again. Still, Rubonga continued to preach vigilance to his men. He said that the enemy only needed a small gap to cause significant damage. Chakare and Ndukuyashe were promoted to fill in the positions left vacant by the passing of Mutoweshindi and Mangundu. The two king's guards were pleased by their promotion, especially Ndukuyashe.

Chakare was made the Chief of Security because he was older than Ndukuyashe. The king had known him for a long time, and he had faith in him. He was good at drafting duty roasters for the guards and supervising them while they guarded the king and his family. He would make his own plans without consulting anybody, and only Rubonga could query his plans or suggest adjustments. Ndukuyashe, on the other hand, was a muscularly built man. He was one of the warriors that Shingai relied on when they went for battles. He was moved from the battle warriors to the king's security team because getting past him was difficult. Although his whole body was muscular, it was his neck that seemed to be the toughest part. It was difficult to see where the neck ended and where the head started. His neck was as thick as his head. His jaws made him scary to look at. When he ground his teeth, children would say that he was hiding stones in his cheeks. His eyes were small, exposing his forehead bone, which made him look like he always wore a short brim cap. Shingai was happy to have these men around his king, for he was safer with them.

Chapter 27

A monkey possessed by the spirit of death will approach a lion and kiss it on the mouth. From the time that Shingai heard about Shuvai's marriage, he slowly developed a taste for alcohol. Earlier, Shuvai had told him how much she loathed the smell of an alcohol burp. He had then quit drinking alcohol. Now that the person who had made him an abstainer from the substance was out of his life, he no longer saw anything wrong with unwinding and drinking every now and then. Initially, he avoided it because of his work, planning and organizing military activities. However, as time went on, the yearning for alcohol kept growing, and so he drank; more and more. This did not amuse Gotora, who voiced his concern and implored Shingai to refrain from beer for the sake of his own integrity. Shingai casually assured him that he would do so, but in his mind, he knew he was not about to stop.

In those days Shingai had started seeing other girls, especially those that attended Prince Masimba's night parties during the full moon in Magocha. He had not found one that captured his heart, so he would flirt with one girl on this day and another on the next day, and so on. Kundai had tried to hook him up with a beautiful girl, but he was disappointed after speaking with her. He told Kundai that the girl had such a terrible breath, one would think she had goat poop in her mouth. On that day, he drank a bit more than usual, and he then decided to go to bed early while the party was still alive. He told Kundai that they would talk the following morning before he left. When he got back to the palace, he went to Mai Tongai's kitchen to get his supper. He knocked on the door, and it was opened. There was only Mukai in the kitchen.

"Good evening *mainini* Mukai. How was your day?"

"My day was good. How was your day? It seems you are back from the party rather early. Is everything okay?" Mukai asked.

"A-ah all is well *mainini*. My head just started aching so I decided to take an early night. There will be more of these parties for me to attend in the future. The full moon has just started. I'll be there partying again tomorrow. Where are the other mothers? I haven't seen any one of them this evening." Shingai ended by asking.

Mukai reminded him that the queens had gone for a funeral. The third queen's mother had passed, and so the other queens had gone to mourn with her. They were only going to get back to the palace the following morning because the king did not want them to walk back to the palace in the night.

Mukai asked Shingai to help her take down a woven basket that she could not reach from a top shelf. Shingai moved into the kitchen and asked where exactly the basket was, as he could not see in the dimly lit hut. He was surprised when Mukai's bosom tickled him on his bare spine.

"Right there, Shingi," she answered as she even got closer and pressed her breasts harder on his back. His mind spun in that short moment. At first, he wanted to tell her to move back, but then a little voice from his head whispered to him,

"But the squeeze from this bosom feels good, right!"

The little voice seemed to have been victorious for he then said to her,

"I can't see your basket."

He had now turned around and was facing Mukai. Mukai did not say anything, and Shingai was just shaking. His manhood was now as hard as a dry log. As he felt it, he wondered when it had gotten that hard. He moved his hands in front of him as if he was trying to find his bearings, but in earnest, he was searching for her breast. When he finally found it with his hands, Mukai took a deep breath as if she was running out of air. Shingai quickly knew that she was ready for him and could not control herself. As he laid both his hands on her breasts, he felt the taut teats pointing straight at his ribs. In no time their hands were all over each other, rubbing and squeezing.

They heard a sound that came from outside, and they froze for a moment and waited until it was clear. Soon after, they were on the mat that was on the floor. By the time their passion was over, Shingai felt all the alcohol leaving his system. They stood up and looked at each other without saying a word. Shuvai looked and found a garment to cover her bust. She had flung it away when Shingai was looking for her basket. She was blushing in the dark, as he barely managed to say to her,

"Do not worry about my food, I'll have it in the morning."

He finished speaking when one foot was already out of the door.

Lying alone on his bed and utterly sober in his *gota*, he was troubled. He could not sleep. He counted all of the poles and the purlins that supported the thatch roof of his *gota*. He noticed for the first time that the pitch of the conical roof was slightly off-center. Sleep decided to take a break from him that night. What he had done, ate him from within his heart. First, he blamed Mai Muneyi, the widow who had prepared the alcohol that he had drank before dusk. He then searched and found many other people to blame. Many as they were, none of them could hold enough blame to erase the crime that he had committed. With the number of girls that desired to have him do to them what he had done to Mukai, what sort of evil had blown in the winds headed his way for him to have ignored them all to fall in Mukai's hands? Mukai was someone's wife and not just of any other man, but wife to the despot King of Magocha!

Rubonga had given him, a mere commoner, the life of a prince. So in return for this favor, this is the gratitude he had to offer to his king? What if he had been caught in this act, how would he have explained it? These thoughts horrified him. He only found some comfort in knowing that they had not been caught and that Mukai would not share the incident with anybody because doing so would mean the end of both their lives. Shingai realized that Mukai had grown into a young woman without many noticing. Many still ignored her, taking her to be a little girl that had been given to the king as a wife.

By sunrise, Shingai had planned to clean his act and put his life in order. First, he would stop drinking alcohol as if his life depended on it. He would then find a girl that he would marry and start a family with. He had to be smart about that particular goal. He had to analyze his relationship with Rubonga and make a reasonable judgment, one that he would be sure not to regret in the future. Gotora had warned him several times to be careful about Rubonga, but the king trusted him a lot. He had done many things that had made Rubonga look invincible, and most of the king's plans to expand his influence depended on his work to be achieved. He decided to assess the situation for the next six months. If at any time he would sense danger, he would just take his girl or wife and run away from Magocha to settle in other kingdoms that were very far away. The option of running away had its own headaches. He was now known very well in many domains that Magocha had fought against or that were under Rubonga's dominion. Therefore if he were to run, the best for him would be to run to kingdoms that were much further from Magocha and those that he hadn't been to before. This he would only decide once the time was right.

It was true that Mukai had grown at the back of everybody's mind. All the Royals had become used to addressing her as "*Mainini* Mukai," from the time that she had joined them as a little girl. As time went on, nobody had noticed that Mukai was growing. She played with some of the king's daughters and listened to their tales and adventures in private spaces. The problem for her was that when it was time for the other girls to join the boys in games where they would play as "grown-ups," she would not go. She was not allowed to go outside the main enclosure. She would only hear about what went on outside by the princesses who were slightly older than her. She had tried to listen to the conversations between the queens, but she could not tolerate them or even understand their issues.

When she broke into her adolescence, she began to hear of tales about boys from the princesses as they shared their secrets and fantasies with each other.

Although she did not show it, she listened attentively, hanging on to every word they said. She heard about massages and how good it felt to be squeezed and caressed by boys, and she felt her body longing for that too. Rubonga did not do all this to her. He hardly even thought of her as his wife. She was beginning to believe what she had heard from some of the king's kids. The kids had heard their mothers proclaiming that she had not come to be the king's real wife but was there to fulfill a ritual that had been prescribed by a *n'anga.*

Like somebody who had no access to the outside world, each time she heard about boys doing this and that or being hot and all, she could only picture Masimba and Shingai. In her mind, these were the boys for her. Of all her imagination on what boys could be like, her picture would be of any one of the two boys or both of them. She had felt her heart drawing closer to Shingai, feeling sorry for him after she saw Kundai laugh at him for his loss when news of Shuvai's marriage was broken. On the day that Shingai had found her alone in Mai Tongai's kitchen, she had thanked her ancestors for looking down at her with great favor and thrown him into her open and willing arms.

When the two saw each other in the morning, they could not look at each other in the face. To the two, it felt like everybody knew what had happened the night before. They only got relieved after many days had passed without anybody showing that they knew about their secret. The discomfort between them began to fade slowly, but they did not put themselves in such compromising situations again. Shingai stopped drinking alcohol, and Masimba had a good laugh about it, telling him that he had definitely lost his mind. He went back to training himself on becoming a better fighter and to keep his body fit.

One day Rubonga summoned Shingai and Masimba to the family court where he was sitting and said to them,

"Boys, it seems like it has been a long time since you last went to Magondo. Do you think that the systems that we set up there are still in place? If people see that no one is coming to take a peep on them, the seeds of revolution begin to germinate in their minds, and before we know it, they will be rebelling against our dominion over them. If you were smart, you'd run there and just show yourselves to them and quickly come back. It is quiet in the kingdom these days, but we should not be too relaxed to the point of walking in the forest with our eyes closed."

The boys knew that what the king had said was right. The killings that had taken place in the kingdom had astonished and shaken them, so they needed to be cautious all the time. They did not waste time. After two days they were on the road. They needed to be back in Magocha before a month had lapsed.

Before the month had clocked, they were back in Magocha. The good news that they had brought did not find open ears to receive because of the bad news that they found waiting for them. They heard that the killer had struck again. People now believed that it wasn't just one person responsible for murdering the king's guards, but that it was a group of people that had been deployed to disturb the peace in Magocha. Three of the king's guards had been found dead at one spot with the trademark signature of the other butcheries; palms planted in the corpses' bellies! Evidence gathered showed that the killers had spoken to their victims before they killed them. The bottom lips of the bodies had also been cut off. Ndukuyashe claimed that he had told all the guards to avoid suspicious people in the night for the enemy was too slick. The enemy needed to be apprehended and interrogated in broad daylight. At the time that Shingai and Masimba returned from Magondo, seven of the king's guards had been slain in precisely the same manner. The killings had taken place over three days.

Once more, the two boys were at a loss for words. This was really strange and getting more and more worrisome. Some of the members of The Council of the Wise Eleven asked questions and made remarks that were laced with sarcasm to the boys.

"Prince Masimba and you Shingi, you are the new blood and you have sharper minds than us, this should not be taking too long for you to solve. What is going on?" One governor had said as he left without waiting to for a response from them. They just looked at one another and ignored him. All the guards and other warriors that were asked could not come up with any suspects linked to the murders. The *n'anga* could only confirm that the enemy had been getting stronger with each passing day and hence the king and his men really needed to be on the lookout all the time as their lives were in danger. Some of the *n'anga* maintained that those that possessed them were still refusing to share the information about the enemy with them. However, the gray-heads in the kingdom could tell that the *n'anga* were given the intelligence, but for some reason, they were afraid of releasing it.

What was clear for everybody to see but could not be mentioned publicly except by Prince Masimba was that the enemies were targeting the life of King Rubonga. Masimba made the observation and said it in the presence of the king and The Council of the Wise Eleven. On that day, the two boys had been allowed to sit in the meeting to assist the king with the analysis of all that was said. He stood up and said,

"Your Highness Shumba, the beast that is feared by all! To all of you respectable and wise governors who defend Magocha, we do not want to be like that stupid ostrich, which buries its head in the sand leaving its whole body exposed. Yes, what we have here are enemies to us all and to Magocha. I say this because even though these people are only killing the king's guards, their desire and ultimate target is to kill the king. I know that there are whispers that these enemies are coming from the kingdoms that we have put under our feet, but we must look at this one thing. How do these men know that the people they are killing are the king's security elements if they do not live in this kingdom? I do not want to believe that the spirit of Chitsere has rested upon one of you or that he was working with one of you and that person is now continuing with the work of eroding the Kingdom of Magocha. So Shumba, we may cast our eyes far and wide, but the enemy is right here in Magocha, and their primary mission is to take your life!"

Masimba sat down as soon as he had concluded his speech. The governors did not know how to react. They felt like clapping hands for him because they agreed with his observation. They looked at VaGondo giving him a cue to gather some words to respond with.

VaGondo rose and reiterated Prince Masimba's words and thanking him for being articulate and straight to the point that was on many people's minds.

Although Rubonga had known for a long time that the final goal of the assassins was to kill him, he could not help but feel amused and proud of the display of wisdom by his son. Such sense usually came from Shingai. Proudly looking at Masimba, he said,

"So what do you think we should do VaMupingamhuru?"

Masimba knew that whenever Rubonga called him by the clan name, he would be genuinely proud of him. He went on to suggest some precautions, including the imposition of a curfew to all the people living in the king's district. He suggested that groups of warriors would then be sent into random homes without warning. Those that would be found absent from their homes at those particular times without official notification to the high authorities would be sentenced for murder without hesitation. The selection of the warriors that would be doing the rounds would be left to the king and a few men of his choice because a dangerous worm had entered into the king's district. It was made known to everybody in the kingdom had that each person was a suspect to the violent crimes that were taking place in Magocha at that time. A person would only be regarded as clean when the real killers would eventually be caught. When he finished talking, Rubonga instructed the group to go, and he told them that he would summon some of them soon for some assignments.

Masimba did not stop his parties as the investigations and the hunt for the brutal killers carried on. The partygoers however, had to be at the venue before dusk and only leave at sunrise in observation of the curfew. He could not have stopped the parties even if he wanted to. As long as he was in Magocha during the full moon in summer days, he had to host the parties. It was the duty of a royal around Prince Masimba's age to regularly entertain the other youths in the kingdom. The teenagers looked forward to that period with great excitement.

That month, Shingai missed the parties because he was bothered by his failure to capture the killers. How could all his wisdom let down the people who had so much faith in him, including the king? One day he went into his *gota* just after dusk and closed the door behind him. His mind began racing in the dark. While thinking, sleep visited him, and before he knew it, he found himself in dreamland, standing face to face with Muthlomo. Muthlomo was not talking to him as she would usually do, but she looked depressed. Tears began to roll down her face. He did not know what to do. He could not even find one word to say to her. He drew closer to her, and suddenly, she became Mukai. He thought of asking Mukai where Muthlomo had gone to, but he could not speak. He was baffled. He tried to reach her, but she turned and began to run away from him. In that very moment, he woke up with his body soaked in sweat.

He went outside and looked, but there was no one in sight. He did not remember anything about Muthlomo except that he had dreamt of Mukai crying. He was intrigued. He listened, and the wind was filled with laughter and joy from the boys and girls that were having fun at the party. The moon was still up and bright in the sky. He was unsettled by the dream that felt so real. He thought that the vision was caused by a growing desire by his body to be close to a woman. But for Mukai, he had dug a hole in the ground and spat as a vow not to repeat the despicable deed. He was not going to venture into something that would leave him in the jaws of a lion. It is only a stupid antelope that escapes from a snare in its path, only to use that path again. His stint with Mukai had been for one night and was never to be repeated. He had been lucky that he was not caught in the act. His thoughts of not putting himself in the face of danger again superseded the idea of looking to satisfy his erotic needs, but it did not stop him from being bothered about why Mukai had been crying in his dream. Something didn't feel right. He looked towards Mai Tongai's kitchen and laughed. He knew that Mai Tongai was in her bedroom and Mukai slept in that same room with her. He went back into his *gota* and at least slept soundly.

On the following morning, as somebody who had had a strange dream about another person who happened to be nearby, Shingai sought to look at Mukai straight into her face when he went for breakfast. He almost choked on his saliva when he saw that Mukai looked sad and that she had been crying. He did not ask her because there were several people in the vicinity. He felt sorry for her. She had misplaced her heart. As much as she may have been amorously attracted to him, she did not need to let her heart stray out of bounds like that. Mukai was a beautiful girl who had grown up without being tarnished by the hanky panky boys from Magocha and would make a good wife but not for him, no. She was only going to be King Rubonga's wife! He knew he had to find a way to privately talk to her and set the record straight that there was no way the two of them were going to be lovers. She had to know that what had happened that night was just a moment of passion, but it was not right nor should it be repeated. She needed to know that crying and letting her heart trespass and graze in forbidden paddocks had to end, as it could cost her her life. He thought fast. He cleared his throat and drew her attention.

"*Mainini* Mukai, I'll come back to chop your firewood into smaller pieces for your oven before I go out."

"Oh, okay. That will be much appreciated. The boys who usually chop for me are coming tomorrow, but I could use just a little bit of sliced chunks now." She responded, as she quickly perceived that he had seen that she was worried.

Shingai had offered to chop firewood for her although he knew that there were boys assigned to that task for all the queens. He and Prince Masimba used to split wood for the queens from the time they were still little boys as a way to physically train their bodies in preparation for the initiation school. If the Royals saw him talking to Mukai during rest breaks as he axed the wood, they would not be suspicious of anything sinister going on between them.

Shingai was back in no time. He just took his ax and went straight to the heap of dry logs. The king's wives were sitting in the shade of a big tree at a reasonable distance from where Shingai and Mukai were such that they could not hear what the two were talking about. The queens seemed to be drawn deep in their own conversation. Mukai went to him with a gourd full of *mahewu* and gave him. He took three gulps and then stopped to wipe his mouth with the back of his right palm. He looked around and made sure that nobody could hear what he was going to say.

"*Mainini* Mukai, you know that you are my king's wife and that no one does any funny business with the queens unless he wishes to die. What happened that day was plain stupidity, and we must honestly thank our ancestors that nobody caught us in the act. Now I do not want you to be like the little child that cries for the food it ate yesterday. I want you to-"

"Shingi can you give me one moment to-"

"No *mainini*, there is nothing that you can say that I would be foolish enough to listen to. I was saying-," he could not finish what he was about to say, because she then started crying.

For a moment he felt like giving Mukai a forceful slap in the face, but at the same time, he felt sorry for her. She then quickly said,

"Shingi I said just listen to me for a moment, what you are saying is not-," he interjected her again.

"*Shhhh Mainini*, I know that you have not had any boyfriends before, but I know what girls do. Now let me finish what I am saying so that we can be safe otherwise by the end of the day we will be food for maggots. I am saying-"

"Shingi I am pregnant!" Mukai spoke with a raised voice, the crying gone, but the tears now gushing from her eyes.

Shingai heard the words, but they seemed to have ended only in his ears. His brain did not process them for he then said,

"A-ah, that is good. So why are you worrying yourself if you have been able to give my king a baby so soon? You just have to learn to love your husband, *mainini*."

Mukai saw that he was absolutely lost. At first, she thought that he was pretending, but he had no clue what was going on. She had to quickly update him because they had taken too long talking to each other. She did not want to be questioned by the other queens on what it was that she was talking about with him, so she said,

"Shingi, Mai Tongai already found out that I am pregnant, but she also thinks like you do. She thinks that King Rubonga is responsible for the pregnancy, but that is not true. You are the father of the baby that I am carrying Shingi. I have never slept with the king or any other man except for you Shingi."

Chapter 28

Even the cicadas seemed to have been silenced by the shock of Mukai's words. To Shingai, the whole world went dead silent, and pitch-black darkness filled his eyes for a moment. His heart beat loudly, and he thought he was dreaming, but then the strange part of the dream was that he could see the broad daylight! Dreamland did not have such bright lighting. He put his gourd down and could not find the strength to pick up the ax. In a short space of time, the human brain can travel to many places and do a lot of activities before coming back to reality.

Before he answered her, he had made many escape plans, and he had seen himself being killed by Rubonga in different ways also. He saw himself shooting and killing an unsuspecting Rubonga with his arrow. The last thought that came to him was to run away from Magocha as soon as he could. He saw himself getting up early in the morning and helping Mukai get over the wall. They then took various directions going to many kingdoms seeking asylum. Without doing this, the only other option was to be slain by Rubonga. With Mai Tongai aware of Mukai's pregnancy, it meant that any time the news would reach Rubonga's ears. He kept his eyes focused on the ground as if the earth would answer Mukai or provide the solution.

"So what do you think we should do Shingi? I am terrified of death. If those gates were not guarded all the time, I would have run back to my mother."

At that time a young girl walked towards them. Shingai sputtered.

"There is only one plan. We must run away from Magocha as soon as possible. Now, you need to stop crying and once more, please do not let anyone know about this. I will tell you what to do next. You must stop wearing that miserable face or else everything will come out before my plans are solid."

The little girl got to where they were and told Mukai that the queens had asked for some *mahewu*. Mukai went into the kitchen and brought a clay container frothing and spilling with the non-alcoholic brew and gave it to the little girl. She told her that she would be joining the queens in a short moment. Shingai did not carry on chopping the firewood. He said good-bye to her, and she left to join the queens after she had promised to be discreet about their predicament.

A man can promise a woman that everything shall be done as planned even though deep in his mind, he would be doubtful of how to do it. Shingai had told Mukai that the best option for them was to run away from Magocha, but he had not really looked at all the steps involved. Running would be simple for him as a young man who could go to far away places without asking for permission but not for him and a pregnant girl. Running would also be easier for somebody who knew where he would be running to. It would also be simple for a person who had adequate time to plan. This is what he spent much of his time working on over the following days. Losing Shuvai had assaulted his heart but getting the king's wife pregnant had killed him. At some point, he thought of taking his own life to cover up for the embarrassment and painful death he was going to suffer at the hands of Rubonga, but he quickly told himself that taking one's own life was for cowards. A real man would put up an intense fight and only die after losing a lot of blood. In putting up a fight, his fortunes might change, and he would save himself. Suicide would take away the small window of opportunity that would come from fighting.

On the days that followed, Shingai began to study the structure of the security wall once more. His ideas to make the wall impassable without using the three entrances on it had been adopted. He cussed at himself when he remembered it. It took a highly skilled rock climber to scale the walls from both the interior and exterior surfaces. The main gate was at the front, and it was used by all those who were allowed into the enclosure. There were two other entry and exit points that were used only by the king whenever he wanted to secretly enter or leave the enclosure.

The people who went into the palace walls for various assignments were expected to leave before sunset. All this proved to be difficult hurdles for Shingai and Mukai to go over before they could run away. Killing the guards at one of the king's secret gates seemed to be the best option. Three guards would not give him much resistance to eliminate. The trouble would be walking the long distance in a short time frame for the two to reach and hide in the caves of the distant mountains. They would only be a bit safe in the caves. He would need to kill the guards on the night that Chakare would be on duty to supervise the guards. Chakare had the ability to track animals and people, but he had a weakness. He was a sleepyhead. Shingai knew the time that he usually slept during his work hours.

His plans were disturbed when the killers struck again. Three of the king's guards who patrolled the perimeter wall of the palace were found slain in the morning. The unmistakable signature of the killers was conspicuous on the three corpses. Chakare was the supervisor on duty on the night of the murder. He claimed that he had chased four men that night. He said that the men had escaped and when he went back to check on his guards, he found three of them on the ground cold and dead. He said this happened well after the first rooster had cried. Chakare also claimed to have heard the four men discussing how pleased the king of Mazimbe would be when he finds out about the excellent job they had done in Magocha. The king and his wise governors then concluded that they now knew where their enemies were from.

Although many people believed that the enemies were from Mazimbe, Shingai and Masimba were still doubtful about it. The problem was that King Rubonga had expressed his firm belief conclusively that the foes were from Mazimbe and so if the two boys were to voice their doubts in his presence it would only serve to embarrass him in public. When they whispered to each other, the boys had noted that if it were true that Chakare had given chase to the four men and had heard them talk about the Mazimbe king, then they would have had done it deliberately to send him and the Magocha team on a wild goose chase. They believed that the enemies were from Magocha. Rubonga summoned his council, and the eleven governors went to him. Shingai and Masimba were once more called in to take seats in that meeting. The group then agreed to send Shingai on a mission with a group of warriors from which he would plant warriors in strategic positions near the Mazimbe eastern boundary. The warriors would then study the movements of their enemies and stop them in their tracks should they send assassins on a killing mission again. Shingai would then return to the kingdom once he was satisfied with the ambush. By sunset, he and his troops were ready to get on track.

Shingai was saddened and worried by this turn of events, but there was nothing that he could do. He did not even get the time to see Mukai, to update her on the latest development and how he planned to escape with her after the mission. He thought that the earlier he left, the quicker he would be back to execute his escape plan. He left Magocha with twenty-four warriors. He instructed them on how to perform their duty without being seen by anybody from Mazimbe. It was difficult for him to teach the warriors proficiently because he had a burning issue in his hands that his life depended on, that he needed to take care of. The group strolled, searching for tracks that should have been left by the enemies as they went back to their kingdom. The warriors were puzzled by how the suspects could have made off without leaving any traces of evidence on their way! This strengthened Shingai's theory that the enemy was from within Magocha. If the king were smart, he would have increased the search for the enemies in Magocha. At this time, he didn't need to bother himself with what the king needed to do because he was facing his own possible death from that king!

As he battled the thoughts in his head, it became clear to him that he had never even imagined being romantically involved with Mukai. Yes, he had looked at some of the king's wives and imagined how they would look if they were not wearing anything but not Mukai.

She was just a little girl that had come to stay with Mai Tongai. He had not seen that she had grown to be a young woman who could be married and who could have her own home. He wondered why he was saddened by the whole episode. He could just run off at that point and disappear because he was already far away from Magocha. Nobody would know where he would have gone to. This was a golden chance for him to start a new stainless life!

Just when he was getting excited about that possibility, the little voice in his head whispered, reminding him that the child Mukai was carrying was his. It told him that he had helped Mukai to commit the crime. It was not right for him to leave his child and its mother at the mercy of the cruel Rubonga. The truth was that if his offense was to be exposed before he would have escaped with Mukai, he would have to forget about the mother and child. Rubonga would never allow an illegitimate child from his queen to live in his palace. The only option was for him to return as soon as it was possible to free Mukai.

As the sun was tilting to the west, Shingai saw a group of twelve men approaching them. He could see that they were warriors because of the way they were dressed and the weapons they were carrying. The men were coming from the direction of Magocha, and they were carefully approaching, hiding behind trees and using hand signals to communicate with each other. He was about to tell his troops, but he quickly changed his mind. The forces were coming from Magocha so why would they be approaching stealthily? He just vanished from his team and found a spot that was higher than where his mates were seated. He waited with an arrow already sitting on his bowstring. The warriors went to his troops putting fingers on their mouth to stop the soldiers from panicking or greeting them. The troops were a bit startled at first, but they did not panic when they realized that the group was from their army. They pointed to the newcomers the spot where they had last seen Shingai. They carefully went there and found him gone.

"I said it. This guy has dog instincts," one of the senior warriors in the group said. At that point the warriors had crowded at one place, each one just looking sideways and backward like a group of animals anticipating a pounce from a lioness.

"The problem is that Cobra instructed clearly that we be bring him back alive, now how does one man apprehend Shingi? You'll see that many shall die before this man is captured."

The warriors agreed without opening their mouths but by nodding their heads and chorusing, "Ummnn-ummnn."

The colonel that led the new group then addressed the whole group.

"Comrades, the issue we have is that your mission here is no longer a priority and therefore it has to be aborted right away. The mission now is to apprehend Shingi so that we take him back to King Rubonga. The king and Prince Masimba are saying that Shingi is linked to the murders that have been taking place in Magocha and also that he has another serious crime that he committed. They want him to confess to the king and the people before he is sentenced and punished. So now that it is getting dark, for us to dip our bare hands into the hole to extract a snake that has gone in would be an act of glorified folly. It is my thinking that we get into smaller groups and begin to circle this small mountain. We must quickly force him to run towards Lake Doperakondo so that he won't have anywhere to run to. It is clear that he is not about to run back towards Magocha, but if he does that, then we will all owe our ancestors some strong brew."

The troops agreed that the arrangement was excellent. They did not want to search for a dangerous dead eye hidden in an unfamiliar mountain at night. They knew that he would clear them all if they were not careful. It didn't help that most of the troops were already demoralized. They had no issues with Shingai. They were more concerned about the increasing heavy-handedness that Rubonga was using on his subjects, which had left many of their relatives traumatized. In the comfort of the shadows, the people of Magocha whispered to each other that the killers had actually come to free them. If only they would succeed on their goal to kill Rubonga, then their troubles would dissipate. The people liked and respected Prince Masimba. They said he would make a much better king than his father. Most of the troops, deep down in their hearts, they were hoping that Shingai had escaped and ran away from Rubonga for good.

Listening to what the troops were saying, Shingai knew that the king was now aware of his crime. He had lived with the Royals for a long time, and many people regarded him as a member of the imperial family such that he had not perceived the hatred that these people had for the king. He had heard from Gotora that the subjects of Magocha loathed their king, but he had not taken it seriously enough. When he heard them planning to go around the small mountain and force him further west, he just assumed that it was all caused by their cowardice and that a large group was most probably on the way to apprehend him. He knew what he had to do. He would not interrupt them, but he would just let them go their way, and he would take his own direction. He could not even consider running to his enemies in the Western Kingdoms so he would instead head to the unknown southern territories. He had heard that there were other kingdoms there that Rubonga had not been to yet. He knew that Rubonga would not be venturing into those lands without him.

Chapter 29

After Shingai had walked for forty-three days without seeing any sign of human life, he trailed a shezhu that had followed him since that morning, flying from tree to tree above him. It was just before noon when he decided to follow the little bird. He did not like to follow shezhu because he knew that those little birds sometimes led people to danger. They were known to have led people to lions, or to some poisonous snakes. The great hunters claimed that a shezhu would only lead people to danger if at first, it would have led those people to honey and they would extract all the honey from a hive, leaving nothing for the little bird. After it had pestered him, Shingai had decided to follow it to see where it was trying to lead him.

He drew his bow and carefully followed as the bird made noises, frequently checking to see if Shingai was following. He was glad when it led him to a tree that had good honey. He was pleasantly surprised to see that the tree with the hive was just on the edge of a new field with crops. He waited until it got dark before he extracted the honey. While he waited, he helped himself to some sweet canes that were in the field. Most crops were about to dry up in the farm, but there were still plenty of plants that could be eaten fresh. He was not scared of charms that some people put on their crops because he knew that such charms would only affect the locals trying to steal the crops and not strangers passing by. He had heard of people that had attempted to pilfer in the fields of their neighbors and in the process, the thieves would get stuck on the crops. No matter how weak the plants were, the thieves would fail to free themselves until the farmer came and lashed the thieves with a special whip.

When night came, he extracted enough honey that he could carry and left some on the ground for the *shezhu*. He then slept near the field hoping that when daytime came, he would see the farmer and ask him to forward his request to the higher authorities of that land so that he could maybe settle in that kingdom. Nobody came to the field the following day, and he could not endure just sitting and waiting, so he decided to follow the path that led out of the farm. He saw more corn fields as he walked, but no people were working in them, so he kept walking. Like a skilled warrior, he soon became aware of people that were walking, some on his sides and others behind him. He noticed that they were not skilled warriors because what they thought was being sneakiness was actually not.

He reminded himself that he was not trying to defend himself nor fight these warriors. He was trying to find refuge from amongst the people of this land because he was not going to go back to Magocha. His best response was to act dumb and let the warriors believe that they were smarter than him. He sat in the shade of a tree and pretended to be sleepy. They circled him, and he faked some snores. The Warriors pounced on him and quickly bound him, whistling, shouting, and making other wild noises at the same time. They began to taunt him for being a spy and a thief. What puzzled him was that he could hear all that they were saying, but he was not sure where he had heard the language that they were speaking before. They asked him many questions, but he did not answer them. When they asked him more questions, he then responded in the language of Magocha, and they could not understand what he was saying. They then spoke of taking him to their king.

The warriors seemed to be just ordinary men, some physically active, and some not so much. Some had spears while the others carried knobkerries. Each seemed to be acting of his own accord and competing to say his opinion. They lacked discipline and did not have an apparent leader. From what they were saying, Shingai could tell that they had spotted him when he was following the *shezhu*. They watched him extract the honey and do everything else after that. He felt mad at himself for having been so off guard and putting his life at risk. He should have seen them first. What if they had been Rubonga's troops that had spotted him relaxed like that?

These strange warriors were quite different from the people of Magocha and those from the western and northern kingdoms. They were not groomed. He could smell the foul stench that radiated from their bodies due to taking infrequent baths. When they examined him, they talked about him being a nobleman, possibly a royal because he was clean and his garments were elegant and shiny. His garments were made up of mostly cheetah hides. At the time that he had run away, he had not discarded his semi-royal clothes, and now he realized that those garments were likely to put him at a disadvantage on his asylum-seeking mission. Most kings would be wary of accommodating a royal on the run as this could lead to a war with the king in pursuit.

This kingdom that he found himself in was different from Magocha. The king's home was not very different from the other homes that surrounded it. It had many houses, and the yard was clean and neat. There was no security boundary or wall around the home, and ordinary people could cross the king's yard as they wished. The king had only two guards that stayed close to him for most of the time. Shingai could tell that their main job was that of messengers of the king, and not to protect him. The subjects and the warriors seemed to give the king genuine respect. They did not kneel or even bow when the king walked near them. Shingai found it somewhat awkward that the king was not afraid of spring attacks from his enemies who could readily assassinate him. Did this king not know this? He thought to himself, "He who does not make enemies, does not need protection from enemies that he does not have!"

The king looked long at Shingai, and the people at the court went silent. He was older than Rubonga, and he had a protruding belly. His crown made of fur was small, and it sat inclined on one side of his head. He wore leopard skin garments and a lot of bangles on his hands, some made of copper, some wooden, and some made from various beads strung together. He did not carry a visible weapon on him from what Shingai could see. Sometime after he had stared at Shingai without lifting his eyes off him, he gave an order,

"Untie this man because he is not about to run away. Prepare some food for him quickly because I do not like to talk to hungry people."

In no time a plateful of freshly cooked food, mostly stewed chicken was placed in front of him. He enjoyed the home cooked meal, something that he had last had in Magocha. People murmured a lot of things as he was eating. He understood some of the words, but he did not show it. A warrior called out to the king loudly, informing him that the prisoner could not hear or speak their language, but the king acted as if he had not listened to the warrior.

"So where are you from, young man, and what are you doing here in Musita?"

The name "Musita" rang a bell in his mind, but he did not show it. He was familiar with the name, but he could not remember where he had heard it. A thought crossed his mind that disturbed him. What if he had landed into one of Magocha's enemy kingdoms? He had to answer the king's question, so he spoke in their language.

"I am coming from a kingdom called Magocha. I ran away from there because of a misunderstanding that I had with the king of that land. I am now looking for a place to settle."

The people were shocked to hear him speak in their language because the warriors who captured him had claimed that he could not understand what they were saying to him. They mumbled to one another, but only King Musita did not seem surprised. He then went to ask another question.

"And where exactly is this Kingdom of Magocha?"

Shingai told him that Magocha was a distant kingdom that lay to the North East of the king's residence. He said he had not been aware of Musita before he was captured. He had just continued to walk from the time that he ran away n pursuit of a place to stay among people. King Musita asked him many more questions that he answered satisfactorily, but he got stuck when he was asked where he had learned how to speak their language so fluently.

He could not find the appropriate answer, and the crowd did not believe him. King Musita then made his judgment. Because the prisoner had failed to provide a satisfactory explanation to the king's query on the language issue, he was going to remain in captivity. He would only be freed if he came up with a plausible explanation; otherwise, the king would be forced to judge him for the crime of espionage. He was to be sent to the holding cells in the meantime.

He was bound again and thrown into the cell where he was the only prisoner at that time. He was well taken care of, and therefore, he was not too worried about what the judgment was going to be like. For many days he was locked in the cell but as much as he tried, he could not remember where he had learned these people's language. At some point, he thought of telling the king that he had learned their language when he was under the sacred pools on the mighty Manyoka River. But he knew that this would draw more questions that he did not have answers to.

As his mind processed all this, he also thought about the crime that he had committed in Magocha. He wondered what might have been going on with Mukai and the child that she was carrying in her womb at that time. He did not take it lightly that somebody's child was going through all the trouble on her own while him being the responsible partner to the crime was out and semi-free. What consoled him was that according to Rubonga's warriors who had been sent to capture him, King Rubonga wanted him alive so that he could mete out the punishment he had for him personally. This meant that Mukai was only going to be sentenced after his capture by those that were looking for him. He had to escape from Musita. Shingai had not run this far to be kept in a better prison. He was a man on a mission!

Chapter 30

On one of those days, there was a big celebration for the people of Musita that was held to commemorate the construction of the first Musita granaries soon after the harvest. King Musita admired how other kingdoms were able to feed all their citizens during droughts using grain from the communal grain storage rooms. He had decided to do the same for his people. Many citizens attended the celebrations at the king's home. Shingai was taken out of his cell to join the others in the jubilation.

King Musita did not like it when people celebrated while some among them were sad. He said that this went against the wishes of his ancestors. Shingai was made to sit among warriors, facing those that were drinking and dancing. He ate, but he did not drink any alcohol. He had found his golden opportunity to escape. During the merrymaking, he would ask to be taken to the bush to relieve himself. He would be given a few drunken warriors to walk with him out. He would then run away from them. He would stop the drunks from following him by twisting each of their necks without killing them. He was not worried about his weapons because he would make new ones once he got to safety.

The party carried on with musicians playing drums and rattles. At the time that Shingai was about to ask to be taken to the bush, King Musita asked the crowd to be silent and pay attention to him for he had something to share with the gathering. Shingai frowned and made a faint snort. He needed to go, but he had to hold on for the king to say what he needed to say, and soon after that, he would carry on with his plan.

While the king was addressing the crowd, a gray-haired and wrinkled old woman rose and began to walk towards the warriors that were seated. She seemed to be purblind because of her old age. The king went quiet. It was forbidden for anybody to restrict women of such ages from doing whatever they wanted to do. It was believed that these people would have reached those points in life where they would soon join their ancestors, and therefore they also commanded the reverence of departed ancestors. The crowd broke into silence as everybody pinned their eyes on her. With one hand on her back and the other on her wooden cane, she walked towards Shingai and looked at him curiously, squinting her left eye. Shingai wondered what she was up to, but he kept his cool. She drew closer to him, and he could feel her warm breath on him and smell the stench of her sweating armpits.

The granny put her hand on top of his head and moved it down his occipital, then down on the back of his neck. She began to rub where his hairline ended and then suddenly she stood upright! Her cane was no longer resting on the ground. She threw it down, and the crowd craned out of curiosity. She began a high pitched and long ululation that puzzled the mob and soon after that she began to talk to the invisible loudly.

"Oh, I, daughter of the Moyo Clan.
Today I am blessed.
And why should I go on living?
Now that my eyes have seen my son!
Please receive my portion of gratitude.

And pass it to those that are above you.
Until it has been received by the highest authority!"

The old woman broke into another bout of ululation, and the crowd was further mystified. Shingai kept wondering what this old woman was up to. He worried that she could delay his mission to escape.

"They thought they were smart.
They said my son's life had been dissolved.
But nothing had they solved.
In my blood vessels, I could still feel his pulse.
Every day his breath blew on me.
Today my tears have dried.
You have demonstrated that your enemies could never fight you and win!
Yollolololoooooo-oo!
My arms are up in the air!"

The woman carried on talking to herself and addressing some immortal and invisible beings. When she was done, she bent to pick up her cane and doddered towards the king, who was quite relaxed and monitoring the activity from his throne. She went closer and knelt with her back straight and began to salute the king with applauds. She kept clapping until the king said to her,

"You may speak Mbuya Nyamukuta."

The crowd side-eyed her, not because they were frowning at her but because they were positioning their ears so that they could see her as well as catch all the words that were going to be released from her mouth before people added their own versions.

"My father, VaMusita, I am truly sorry that I disrupted your proceedings. My days of laughter among the living are now numbered. I think what I had been waiting for on this earth has just happened. That boy you see sitting there is my great-grandson, my late granddaughter Nyaradzo's son."

The old woman said as she pointed towards Shingai without lifting her eyes from the king's face.

"Nyaradzo was that daughter of VaMuzanenhamo Senior who died just after she gave birth to a baby boy and that child is the boy Shingai sitting overvthere. If you remember my king, his father is the man who came from Dangadema claiming that Shingai had died in Mazivandadzoka during that year of the severe outbreak of rats!"

The crowd went into a tumult, some pointing, some putting their hands on their mouths, while some shook their heads. Shingai thought he was dreaming. He remained seated, looking at the old woman. The king allowed some time for the people to express their shock and amazement before he lifted his head towards the drummer, who gave his drum three heavy beats and the crowd went mute at once! Shingai's uncle Muzanenhamo Jr. and his father, VaMuzanenhamo Sr. rose and went to him and looked at the back of his neck and they too just put their hands on their mouths in disbelief. Shingai was troubled. He wondered what it was that was at the back of his neck that he was not aware of. What he did not know was that Mbuya Nyamukuta had made two tiny tattoo marks at the back of his neck when he was still a newborn. She knew that the tattoos would stay on for as long as he lived and would not change as his body matured.

King Musita knew bits and pieces of the story, so he allowed the Muzanenhamo family to take Shingai home for them to catch up and celebrate his return. He said that Shingai was a grandchild of the Kingdom of Musita and therefore he had the freedom to settle anywhere amongst his kinsfolk in the kingdom. He requested to be informed if there were things that the boy could help with, in the development of Musita. Shingai thanked him for his generosity, and bade him farewell. He was given back his weapons. The rest of the people stayed on to enjoy the party after the Muzanenhamo family had left. Shingai had a lot that he wanted to know, especially about his early days from his newly discovered family. His smile grew wider when he realized that it had been a long time since he had been that happy.

Shingai's grandparents and uncles did not waste time. They threw a welcome party for the return of their once lost grandchild. The feast was held five days after he was discovered at King Musita's home. It was held at VaMuzanenhamo Sr.'s homestead. His grandfather slaughtered a big ox for the guests, and the relatives that came from all over the kingdom for the party. Yes, many relatives attended, but the majority of guests were the neighbors. Different dishes were prepared, and there was plenty of alcohol. The people ate and were having a good time. Muzanenhamo Jr. stood up to speak to the people before many of them had guzzled in too much alcohol. It took some time to get the people to pay attention to him. The musicians were the first to be ordered to stop their music. Muzanenhamo then found a spot that was elevated and stood there, clearing his throat before he spoke. He greeted the people and cleared his throat again, and then he began to address the crowd.

"My friends and relatives, we thank you so much for coming in your numbers to celebrate with us as we welcome our beloved grandchild who had been lost. We are sincerely honored to host you. Even though he is coming to take our wives right here in our home, we do not mind him. We are, in fact, quite pleased that we now have a proper beneficiary to our wealth. He is our undoubted relative. We have many sons here in our home; true sons of the Shumba totem but you know very well that only our wives know who amongst them are truly from the Lion Clan. But for those that are born from our sisters' wombs; we are definite that they are our true relatives!"

The people laughed, some teasing the younger Muzanenhamo boys. A drunkard called out from the crowd, asking to be given a gourd of beer so that he could cool his dry throat. He suggested that the others could catch up with him once they were done listening to Muzanenhamo's comedy show. Nobody gave him their ear so he just loudly snorted and mumbled. Muzanenhamo then carried on.

"You all know that nobody doubts the maternity of a sister's child. Even if the father of the child is not the one claimed by the sister, we are not concerned about that. We just know that the child is our relative. Shingi my nephew, you can do as you please in this home. Nobody will restrict you. Even if you need a place to build your own home, all you need to do is to just point at the place, and it will be done. We welcome you to our family with our open arms. I thank you all. Our musicians, you may carry on serenading all our beautiful guests."

The crowd clapped with some men whistling as the women ululated in elation. The party came alive. The young women that were serving the food and drinks were all over the place. A number of them exaggerated their mannerism in an attempt to get noticed by the man of the moment.

Shingai was enjoying his newfound freedom, but his happiness had a limit. There was still something not in place. The thought of Mukai and what could have become of her would quickly suck whatever little joy he had. He found it rather strange that he kept thinking about Mukai even though he was not in love with her. So what is it that was bothering him? Could it have been that he knew the baby that Mukai carried was his? What he was sure of was how much regret he had for having involved a young girl in an act that could result in her losing her life! From the time that he had graduated into a warrior of Magocha, he had never done such an act of cowardice like running away without Mukai. It was not right. A true warrior does not do that, and he should not have run this far. He should have found a nearby place to hide and then executed his escape with Mukai.

Now, all this was ringing in his head, but he was so far away from Magocha to do anything about it. He had found an excellent place to settle among his kinfolk, so what was more important? Another issue that troubled Shingai was that his relatives spoke a lot about his mother, who he now knew was called Nyaradzo, but they did not talk much about his father, a man they said was of the Monkey Clan. They had mentioned that he had taken another wife from his kingdom, Dangadema. He wondered why his uncles seemed to not know much about his father. A part of him began to entertain the idea of going to look for his father.

While in deep thought, he heard the unmistakable voice of his grandmother, VaNyamukuta calling him to her.

"Come and hold my hand so that we can take a short walk Shingi."

He rose quickly and went to her. The old woman hooked her weak left hand on to his right hand, and the two slowly began to walk away from the jubilant crowd. Shingai thought she had grown a lot older from the first time he saw her and she had also lost a considerable amount of weight. She had thrown more than half of her weight onto his hand, but he could hardly feel it. He thought if a whirlwind had twisted near her, it could have lifted her off the ground and spun her in circles. They walked up to a shade that was cast by the big tree that stood at the edge of the yard. This was their first time finding time to talk to each other without a third participant actively paying attention to their conversation. Shingai had a lot that he wanted to ask Mbuya Nyamukuta, but he felt it was insensitive for him to be seen as bothering an old woman.

The old woman then began to talk.

"My son, being here with you, fills my heart with such great joy. You see, your soul had been tormented from the time you took your first breath up until the time I saw you at the king's palace a few days ago. It is true what our wise elders said about ancestors never being in a hurry to answer our pleas. Your mother left me a heavy load that I have carried all this time in the form of a secret that I never shared with anyone, even my first-born son, Muza Sr. the father of your mother. As the years went by, I too grew older and older, and my heart constantly missed beats each time I thought of what I was going say to those that live in the winds if were to go there without having seen you. Your father, the one who raised you when you were little, came here to tell us that wild animals in the big Mazivandadzoka forest had savaged you. I did not believe him when he said that, but what could I do?"

The old woman went quiet for some time, focusing her eyes on the ground as she drew lines with her cane. Shingai did not have a clue of what she was trying to say or where she was heading.

"The heart of a wise man is secured in his rib cage, but that of a foolish one is kept in his hands for everyone to see. The words that I am about to share with you today are precious and therefore when you receive them, you must not share them with anyone until you see it fit for the world to know."

She took another break and went silent with her eyes still focused on the marks she was drawing on the ground as she spoke. He lifted his head to check if they were still on their own, and he saw that nobody was about to join them. The feast was keeping the other people busy. For a moment he became impatient, wishing that the old woman would be faster in saying what she needed to say. But then he quickly reminded himself that he was not in a rush to go anywhere, so he calmed down.

"It is all in my ears Mbuya. You must trust me for I shall do exactly as you have asked me," he said this while trying to look at her eyes, but she did not lift them from the spot that her cane poked.

"Now listen clearly. The man that you hear people referring to as your father, Chafunga of the Monkey Clan, is not your father. Your father is of the Moyo Clan, and he is known as King Zihwe of Dangadema."

Mbuya Nyamukuta then lifted her head, wanting to see how much she had shocked him, but to her surprise, he did not even flinch. He was quiet and just looking at her. What had struck him as funny, though, was that his father was a king. He said to himself, "So all the time that I was treated like royalty in Magocha, it was actually in order because I am of royal blood!" He slipped into daydreaming, seeing himself plan with his father's army to go and free Mukai and his child from Magocha. He suddenly asked without thinking carefully.

"Is he even a real king, this father you are talking about? And is Dangadema even a proper kingdom or is it just one of those places where even if three people get together, one of them claims to be king of the other two?"

Mbuya Nyamukuta gave him a long stern look, but she did not answer him. He quickly brought himself back to what she was telling him for he realized that he was getting carried away.

She then realized that Shingai was not bothered about who his father was because he had lost memory about Chafunga and how he had lived with him. As she was about to continue, he thought of something and interjected her speech,

"By the way, you said my father is known as, King who?"

"Oh, so that he is a king is what has caught your attention? Now do not get lost, young man. You have to hear what I have to tell you and after I am through, you may do as you please with that knowledge."

"No Mbuya, the name that you mentioned sounds very familiar. I think I remember it being mentioned by someone on one of our war escapades, eh-eh, I think I recall King Mutambanemoto saying to me that I was a son of Ziwere or something like that."

"Son of Zihwe?" She quickly added, looking at him in surprise.

"Yes, that is exactly what he said."

She looked at him again then said,

"When I say nobody knows about this, do you really get me? I am truly shocked to hear you say that a king from a faraway kingdom like that knows about such a secret. Who could have told him? Anyway, what happened is this, your father; King Zihwe raped your mother after he found her taking a bath in a river. Nyaradzo conceived but neither your father the king nor Chafunga her husband knew about it. Your mother must have feared that if the news about the pregnancy had broken, she could have been killed or forced to marry the cruel king. This is now just my speculation of what could have taken place because she just whispered to me a little bit before she rested for good. What she stressed on was for you to be told this after you had grown into a man and that you had to be brave in your life as your name implies. She is the one who gave you the name Shingai because she said you needed to brave to face and survive the life that was before you."

Slowly tears gathered in his eyes. He felt sorry for his mother, and at the same time, he felt rage for his rapist father. He could not quickly think of what to do about it. He hated all kings. To him, all kings were hardhearted and corrupt. Even king's like VaMusita was just being nice for nothing. They were all disgusting. He thought of Rubonga's cruelty and realized that he was on the same wavelength with Zihwe, terrible, and heartless human beings. If they had hearts in their chests, then those hearts were made of soapstone. What kind of a king would rape a woman except for one with cold blood like a reptile? He felt angry at all kings. The list of his enemies was growing. Rubonga and Zihwe had to be killed so as to free many people. At that moment he questioned the powers of the ancestors in the winds. If they possessed special powers, then why was it that those who seemed to be working with the evil spirits appeared to have the upper hand all the time? His tears fell, and he did not attempt to stop them. She held on to his arm and massaged it, but she let him cry. Moments later, he wiped the tears after telling himself that a man's tears were precious and were best let out in the cover of darkness.

"As I was saying earlier my grandson, these words that I have shared with you, I was told by your mother on the day you were born, and she asked me to pass them on to you. I have done my part. Tonight I know that I'm going to have a peaceful sleep. Even those messengers who are usually sent to me through my dreams and through spirit mediums will not be coming tonight. Now you have to be strong and do what needs to be done."

Mbuya Nyamukuta gave Shingai a tight embrace. He could feel and hear her heartbeat. She looked into his eyes, and he looked back at her. He saw that her countenance had changed. Yes, all the signs of her age were still evident on her face, but she now looked at peace, and her eyes were twinkling like precious stones. The sun was now low in the western horizon turning to a dark reddish color. Some of the older guests were getting ready to take the various paths that led out of the Muzanenhamo yard. The old woman and her great-grandson walked back to join the crowd. They met Muzanenhamo Jr. and joked about who between him, and Shingai was the better husband to Mbuya Nyamukuta. Some people bade farewell to the old woman, but some guests were determined to stay until all the food and drink containers had been emptied. The young women that had hovered around Shingai were disappointed that Mbuya had pinned him to herself for most of the day. Mbuya Nyamukuta asked for some beer, and she was given a gourd full of brew, and she guzzled it all without taking a break. She then wiped her mouth with the back of her hand and asked Shingai to take her to rest in her hut for the night. Darkness had covered the whole kingdom by now. Shingai said to her,

"Sleep well, my sweetheart. Let's see each other early in the morning."

She just laughed without answering him and continued into her hut. He was also tired by the day's activities, and he needed to digest all that she had told him, so he found his way into the room that he had been allocated as his *gota* during those days.

The rooster flapped its wings and slammed them three times on the sides of its body before it let out a loud cry to announce the arrival of the coming day. Immediately after that, a high pitch cry of a woman was also heard. In no time two other women had joined the wailing. By the time that Shingai stepped out of his hut into the yard, the tumult had spread to all the women at

Mbuya Nyamukuta's home. He went straight to his uncles' houses and found them standing at their doors. Their women had rushed in the direction where the first cries had been heard. In no time, the men knew what had taken place. One woman ran around the yard, lamenting.

"Why have you done this, oh, ancestors of the land? Why have you lashed at us with such a painful whip? Does it really make sense to you to leave this village without its shade in this blistering sun? Why have you taken away our shade and with all the joy that had filled her from seeing with her own eyes, the son of her granddaughter Nyaradzo you thought it was the best time to take her? Oh great one, why have you left me? Why did you not take me, a useless animal in the village and let Mbuya live…"

The men then quickly kindled a bonfire and sat around it.

"A-ah, at least the old one has rested now," many were heard saying.

Another man lamented,

"Ummnn, boys, you know when old people are about to go they just bid you farewell, and you won't even suspect it. You know a couple of days ago she came and sat on a bench in my hut, something that she had last done a long time ago. She said, 'I've come to have a meal in your house today.' I thought that it was just one of those blessed occasions for me to have her in my house, but little did I know that she had come to say goodbye to me!"

Shingai was grieved. How could a person who he had spent the previous day talking to and who had been in good health, just die in the early hours of the following morning? He, however, quickly came to terms with it when he remembered his conversation with her and realized that she had known that her time as a mortal was coming to an end. One of his uncles asked him as they sat around the fire.

"Hey Shingi, you spoke to the old one for a long time before sunset, what were you talking about?"

All the men lifted their eyes to him sorrowfully expecting divine words that she may have left him with.

"A-ah, she was just telling me many things about what my mother used to do when she lived amongst you. She had said that she wanted a quieter place, so we had moved to stand under the shade of that big tree."

The men affirmed with a chorus of groans and went ahead to talk about many other memories of the late family pillar.

The sun rose after many people from the surrounding homes had flocked to Mbuya Nyamukuta's home. The women arrived and threw themselves on the ground wailing. Each time when new mourners arrived, the wailing would start over. Those that would have stopped crying would join the new arrivals in expressing their grief. The late widow's sons quickly ordered their sons-in-law to slaughter a big cow and prepare the meat for the mourners. Later on, the men made a queue as they went into the hut where the body of the deceased lay, surrounded by sad sniffling women. Shingai joined the other men and was surprised to see Muthlomo sitting among the mourning women. She was not as dazzling as she would usually look, but he could see clearly that she was different from all the other women in the big hut. When he got out of the rondavel, she followed him and started talking to him. He found it strange that he did not suffer from the dizziness that would usually engulf him, as he would speak to her.

Muthlomo began by saying,

"The time is now upon you Shingi. You learned a lot, with us watching you. You have done a lot on your own even though we chose you just after you were born. You heard what your grandmother had to say. Her words are not different from what we always tell you. You were chosen, and you must lead a great kingdom that includes a group of other kingdoms headquartered at Dangadema. What your father Zihwe is doing in that kingdom goes against everything that must be done in that land. We sent you to Magocha to learn about the good and the bad in that kingdom. You lived with the royals and assisted them in many ways with running the daily affairs of the kingdom. You must know what to do with all the wisdom that you attained while you were there. We shut down your memory of all that happened to you when you were a little boy up until Magodo found you, but we shall restore all those memories to you soon."

Shingai responded quickly.

"Now, with all this power that you have, why do you let me go through all these troubles? Why don't you do everything on your own? Or better still, why don't you just tell me how to do everything that you want me to, and I will just follow your orders as you give them to me?"

"That is not how it's done Shingi. We help you or visit you on rare occasions. All you have to do is just use the experiences that you have gathered to guide you on how to live and make decisions. If you sleep like a log thinking that you have somebody looking over you all the time, then you must not be surprised if you wake up in the middle of a big fire or in the spirit world.

"Now listen carefully. You must go into Mazivandadzoka and walk until you find a place called Bvuterevadzimu. As you walk, you must look out for a *Mhondoro*, the sacred lion that will be on top of large boulders. That *Mhondoro* will walk, and you shall follow it, keeping a good distance between it and yourself. It will lead you to a place where you will see three tall mountains with a big lake between them. The mountains are called Nyamutatu. If you find the water in the lake tranquil, you must drink it and then use it to bath your whole body. If the water is not calm, do not touch it. You should stay and wait for it to be peaceful. When you are done with that process, you will see what will happen. Remember to be smart about everything. Watch your every move for you shall be alone for most of the time. This area is very sacred, so you must be careful about what you do and say while you are there. You must do this soon. Do you hear me?"

Shingai almost burst into laughter. He wanted to talk back and ask her questions, but in that instant, Muthlomo turned and walked back into the hut with mourners. He was a bit shocked and called out to her,

"But please just come back and repeat what you said for I do not remember most of what you told me!"

He did not get an answer. A wave of anger went through his blood vessels, but he could not tell who it was directed at. He looked around and saw one of his younger uncles, son of Muzanenhamo Jr., and he asked him.

"Excuse me, *sekuru*. Who was that woman that I have just been talking to right here?"

"Do you mean aunty Mai Munashe?"

"Yes, that one. How can I see Mai Munashe?"

"Let me get somebody to fetch her for you," the young uncle said as he looked around for somebody to send.

When Shingai saw the aunt that came out, he knew that he had not talked to her. He was embarrassed when he asked her if they had spoken to each other in the past few minutes. She said she had not spoken to him but had just passed by where he was standing. He apologized and blamed his confusion on grief. He waited for some time until a new group of men that had come for the funeral were taken into the big hut where the corpse lay, then he joined them. He wanted to go to where Muthlomo was seated so that he could confirm his assignment. He was surprised to find that she was not in the hut. He got out and thought intently. The fact that he had managed to hang on to Muthlomo's presence excited him. This was unusual. He still remembered the whole conversation that he had with her. This definitely meant something. He became curious about going to the place that she had instructed him to go because he wanted to see what it was that she had said would happen!

Chapter 31

When Shingai considered the words Mbuya Nyamukuta and Muthlomo had said, he decided to act fast. Muthlomo had told him that his time had come, so there was nothing to hold him back. Yes, the name Mazivandadzoka had deterred him because of the possible hurdles of the journey ahead, but he knew that the sweetest honey is often extracted from the most toxic bees. He had to be brave. It had taken bravery for him to survive most of his life and therefore, his trip to Bvuterevadzimu had no other means but wadding into the dark forest. When king Musita released him, he had been given back his weapons, and he had sharpened them in the few days that had passed. All he needed to do was to vanish with no one knowing where he had gone.

By midnight he was heading towards the eastern boundary of Mazivandadzoka. He walked swiftly, sometimes breaking into a trot to get as far away as he could from Musita. By sunrise, he had covered a distance that would take the average man two days to walk. The heat became unbearable for him to keep walking, so he found a place under shade to rest, intending to proceed towards sunset. He had skipped meals because he was snacking on wild fruits as he walked. He sat in the shade and thought about his life and his current predicament. In the process, he fell asleep. He did not know how long he had slept, but he woke up shouting,

"No, it's not like that!" He rose and looked all around him, but there was nobody in sight. The sun was up in the clear sky. He had just been dreaming. He dreamt Mbuya Nyamukuta pulling his hand and asking him why he was running away from her.

At first, he dismissed it as just a dream, but when he considered how she had discovered him at King Musita's home, he became conscious that the late old woman was in no way just an ordinary granny in the village. There was something that she was trying to say to him. He wondered if Muthlomo was trying to create animosity between his grandmother and himself. His *mbuya* was attempting to stop him from running away from her, but Muthlomo was saying that his time had come and he had to do something about it! This thought split him in the middle. Time ticked as he tried to weigh his options. Who was he going to listen to and who was he going to ignore? He looked around thinking and wishing that he would see Muthlomo, but she did not appear.

"This is what she does!" He said to himself. Muthlomo only appeared when she wanted to instruct him something but not when he desired to see her. He looked back on how he had left Musita. He saw that the people of Musita were his actual relatives. His grandparents and uncles had shown him nothing but pure love. They had told him that he could settle for as long as he wanted among them. The people of that kingdom received him well when they became aware of who he was to them. Even King Musita himself understood his plight.

Musita had become his new home, not the other kingdoms that he did not know of nor where he had left running for his dear life. Thinking of this made him want to go back to Musita. Only a fool plants thorns in the path that he would need to use again in the future. He had acted like a fool for not letting his kinsfolk know that he would be going away but for a bit, but coming back to live with them. By the time that he convinced himself thoroughly that he needed to go back and say a proper goodbye, he was already en route back. As he thought about it more and more, he then realized that he had left his *mbuya* in her hut and not at her final resting place, something that was a taboo. Muthlomo had emphasized to him that he should always use his head to make wise decisions. It then became clear to him that his *mbuya* was trying to communicate this to him. The body of such an important old woman needed to rest at a particular place as her spirit would be very close to becoming an ancestor. Angering of ancestors was known to invite untold suffering to the lives of the offenders.

When he got back to *sekuru's* home, it seemed like nobody had noticed his absence, so all the plans went ahead without unpleasant explanations. The old woman was to be buried on that same day. Many people had come from various villages of the kingdom to send her off. On this day, nobody was to be seen or heard wailing, for this risked invoking the ire of those ancestors who would have come to fetch the soul of one of theirs. Shingai heard later on that a man who was said to be Mbuya Nyamukuta's brother had marked the site of the grave. As required by law, for all the procedures that took place at the funeral, that man had to be informed or consulted first. King Musita was also in attendance, and he was frequently updated on the progress of the funeral although all he did was just to nod in agreement. He had the last word as the leader of the land, telling people the number of days that they were expected to stay at home without carrying out any heavy workloads as a way of paying their last respects to the departed strong woman of the land.

Shingai's heart was now burning with the desire to go to Bvuterevadzimu. He struggled to find a convincing reason to tell his grandfather about it. Eventually, he went to him and told him that he needed to see where he could build his home and the piece of land he needed to clear in order to start farming. VaMuzanenhamo Sr. then told him that such issues had to be put on hold until the new moon when people would then be done with the official mourning period for an esteemed departed elder in the kingdom. Shingai was disappointed that there was nothing he could do but wait for the new moon. When the period lapsed, his grandfather showed him a beautiful arable piece of land that was close to the stand where he was to build his home. He marked the boundaries with wooden pegs, and he seemed pleased with it. The following morning, he went to his grandfather, and after the morning greetings, he went straight into his issue.

"*Sekuru*, I am here with another issue."

"A-ah, you may go ahead and say what it is that you want to say. You know one cannot use a war shield to block words," the old man responded without taking his eyes off the ax handle that he was carving.

"*Sekuru*, I want to disappear from this kingdom for probably several months, but I shall be back."

The old man did not stop what he was doing. Shingai thought he had not heard him, but as he was about to rephrase and speak louder, the old man responded.

"All your words are in my ears, speak on my son."

Shingai told him that he needed to settle some personal issues and that he did not want anybody else to know about. When he finished speaking, his grandfather continued to work on his carving quietly. Shingai thought that the old man was putting all his focus on the ax handle and nothing else. He chipped, blew the shavings off, and looked at his workmanship with a lot of satisfaction. Shingai knew that he could only wait for his response patiently. He stared at the man and his work, quietly. The answer finally came some moments later, after VaMuzanenhamo took out his ground tobacco container and inhaled some tobacco. He put a little bit of it on his open left palm and then pinched two doses, stuffing them in his nose and inhaling hard.

"Son, I do not have much to say. If all that you are planning is what you were instructed by Mbuya Nyamukuta, then I shall not add nor take anything from that. I told you that this kingdom is your home. You are my child's child, and therefore, you are my child. In all that you do, do not stray from the meekness that I saw in you. You must always put your anger on a leash, or should I say you must not let your anger forge ahead of your brains. Many things are not as they appear. He who has eyes in the brain is the wise man, and surely the evil ones find it difficult to ambush him. If you have found favor with those that live in the winds, then we shall absolutely see you again."

"Thank you, *sekuru*. Your words are profound. Truly they shall find a big place in my heart."

With these words, Shingai left the old man to his work as he went to prepare for his long journey.

When he left no one saw him. Nobody followed him, and he walked without the haste of his previous attempt. Even his heart was a lot calmer. He walked for many days, getting deeper and deeper into Mazivandadzoka. He carefully looked at the small rocky hills, but he did not see the sacred lion that he was looking for. He saw a lot of other lions lying on rocks but not the *Mhondoro*. One day he got to an area that triggered his dizziness as he walked. He felt like he was just going in circles. The sun seemed to be rising from every direction, making him feel completely lost and wandering aimlessly. Strangely he found the moon to be consistent and so he ended up traveling at nighttime. As he kept walking without seeing any sign of the *Mhondoro*, he began to think that the Muthlomo mystery could be a figment of his imagination and that he could have been losing his mind. This thought of losing his mind scared him. How could one know if their brain was malfunctioning? He carried on walking, but he was still worried about his mental status. As he tried to figure it out, he saw huge boulders on a knoll. He had walked quite a long distance focusing on his burdened mind, so he decided to rest for the night near the hill. He climbed on top of one of the rocks so that he could search the area around him for more boulders.

When he got on top of the boulder, he heard the roar of a lion. He quickly drew his arrow and was ready to end the life of the probable predator. He saw that the lion had a deep dark mane and fur, so he knew it was a *Mhondoro* and possibly the one he was looking for. Mixed emotions ran through his head. First, he was happy that he had found what he was looking for. But after recalling Muthlomo's instructions, he became sad. Muthlomo had said that he would see the lion sitting on top of a rock! The lion roared again and began to walk in the direction that Shingai had come from. Instinctively he followed it. He was exhausted from all the walking he had done, but he just had to drag himself along, following the *Mhondoro*. The sun seemed to have stopped moving. He kept walking, but the sun remained on the same spot. It was still an eerie broad daylight hour round him even after he had walked for a long time.

He was also surprised to see the appearance of many mountains in an area that had seemed to have plateaus all around when he had previously passed through. Eventually, the sun seemed to be moving again, and the lion roared five times. Shingai briefly glanced behind him, and when he turned back to look at the lion, it was gone! He looked everywhere around him, and further ahead but he did not see any sign of it. As he assessed the terrain, he saw three steep mountains grouped together, and at once, he knew that those were the Nyamutatu Mountains that Muthlomo had mentioned. There was a lake between these mountains, and so Muthlomo was real after all.

He was sure that he had now stepped into the sacred area of Bvuterevadzimu. Everything he was to do from that point on required him to inform the ancestors with utmost reverence. Even when he needed to perform essential and natural activities like offloading used food from his gut, kindling a fire to prepare food, eating wild fruits, hunting, or getting down to sleep. All these activities required him to ask for permission from the ancestral spirits. He would plead and immediately proceed, for the immortals did not answer him directly. He had plenty of dried meat in his sling bag, so hunting was not top on his list. He was not too keen on shooting and killing the wild animals in that area. From legends that he had heard, it was believed that most of the animals that were found in such sacred areas were actually human ancestors in disguise. The spirits of the dead authorities would take refuge in different animals. He would clap his hands respectfully, saluting the souls before he did anything like a dowry negotiator would do during a bridal price-payment ceremony. He was scared, but he had to do all that Muthlomo had prescribed for his mission to be successful.

The Nyamutatu Mountains were three steep mountains that seemed like three petals of a flower joined together at the bottom, although the joints could not be seen from above because of the lake that lay between them. From afar, they looked like identical high-pitch thatched roofs of rondavels. Two of the mountains sat on the west side and had the exact height. The one that lay on the east was slightly taller than the other two. Most of the time, a thick fog covered the middle part of the mountains. As Shingai stood before these mountains, the whole area was clear except for the central part of the three peaks, that was covered in fog. He had no doubt that this was the area Muthlomo had sent him to.

After performing the formalities and seeking permission from the spirits that filled the air, he proceeded towards the center of the mountains. While he was still far, he saw that there was a big lake on the south of the hills that did not have fog on top. Out of fear of the foggy place, he tried to convince himself that Muthlomo had meant for him to bath in that big lake. But then he gained courage, and he convinced himself to first go and see what was at the center of the

Nyamutatu Mountains. He found a way around the lake until he found a narrow passage that led him through to the middle of the mountains. As soon as he stepped into the fog, it completely covered him, and he could no longer see where he was stepping. He thought of quickly turning back to run out, but when he turned, he could not see anything. He was now terrified. He thought of breaking into a loud cry, but he then decided not to alert any nearby danger with his foolishness, so he remained quiet.

Soon he was no longer sure where north and south were. He no longer knew the direction he had come in from! He sat down shaking and clapped his hands as he began to talk to the omnipresent inhabitants of the sacred land that he sat on.

"Owners of the land,
Owners of the forests
You, owners of all the rivers and lakes
All the beasts fear you
I know that your ears are inclined to me
You all know that I know nothing of this land
Smile oh Great ones, smile at your son
Guide him to where he should be
It is that strong desire to fulfill your missions that has brought me here
Now guide your calf and instruct it softly on your requirements
When you look at me, I know you see your seed
I am now just waiting for you to tell or show me the way."

After he had said these words, he listened carefully with the hope of hearing a voice responding to him. But he did not hear anything. This was a hard herb for him to swallow. "Imagination has no limits," he thought to himself. What if no one had heard him speak? What if the ancestors were busy snoring? These thoughts scared him. He did not want to think of such, for it could upset the spirits. This was not the time to be angering the all-powerful spirits as he could instantly just perish without knowing what would have struck him. He needed to quickly distract himself from such foolish thoughts, so he thought of food. He should have been hungry, but he was not. He knew that it was still broad daylight outside and so he would not be able to sleep. He decided that once the fog cleared, he would leave this miserable place and get away, as far away as he could, without wasting time. He kept on asking himself many questions that he could not answer.

Sleep is known for visiting even kings sitting on their thrones during important court sessions. Shingai woke up to find himself in a cave that had an interior similar to a house. The cave had a big opening such that, from where he lay, he could see many stars up in the sky. In front of him was a bonfire with burning flames, but the wood in the flames did not seem to be getting consumed by the flames. The twinkling stars that he saw in the sky above were also unfamiliar to him, so he could not tell where he was. The Milky Way was not in the sky. It was now very dark outside, and the fog seemed to have gone. He looked for his weapons and found them neatly on his side. The silence that was around that place scared him. He thought he was dreaming, and he let out a short laugh. He pinched himself twice and felt pain, then he knew that he was not dreaming! He took his weapons and rose to leave the cave. He had to leave this place. As he took a few steps towards the big opening in front of him, he began to hear enigmatic noises that sounded like voices in the winds. Shingai could not make out a single word from these sounds, and so he stopped.

His mind raced. Reason found him and convinced him to stay where he was. If whoever had brought him where he was wanted to destroy him, there was nothing that was going to stop them for they had brought him there without his faintest knowledge. It was not by his wisdom that he was alive but the clemency of some being unknown to him. This led him to quickly give thanks to the ancestors and owners of the sacred place for what they had done for him. He sat down until it was daylight. His blood almost clotted in shock when he saw the human skulls that surrounded him. The bones were neatly placed on the rough surfaces of the cave walls, facing the center of the cave. His hair follicles tightened as he looked around the cave. The fire had gone out.

"Okay, so this is where I shall perish. My skull is going to find an empty spot to rest among all these here," he thought to himself as his body shook uncontrollably.

He quietly picked himself up, not wanting to send out any vibrations from his footsteps. Between the three mountains, lay the sanctified lake that had taken the color of the clear sky above. He began to walk out of the cave and down to the lake. Before he had gone far, a fog rose and engulfed him completely. He looked behind him and saw that the fire in the cave had been rekindled. He walked back to the cave, his imagination creating an image of the skulls teasing and laughing at him as he walked back into the cave. He just had to be brave. He stepped into the cave and sat down. To his surprise, the fog instantly cleared. He tried to think about food, hoping to wake his appetite up but it did not work. He still had his sling bag full of dried meat.

This happened for five consecutive days. Shi̇ngai's appetite finally returned, and he ate a bit of the dried meat. He became accustomed to the skulls in the cave. On the sixth day, he was able to walk all the way down to the banks of the lake with no fog in sight. Finally, it seemed like he was about to perform the drinking and bathing in the lake as directed by Muthlomo, but when he got really close, he noticed that the water from the lake was actually boiling! He had to be patient, and he was now prepared to see how long it would take him. Fortunately, on the following day, he found the water calm, and he was able to drink and bath from the water in the sacred lake after he had appeased the ancestors. Nothing happened to him after the ritual, but he did not wait to find out. He found his way between the other mountains and walked through, occasionally throwing his eyes back to make sure that he was on his own. He walked faster and faster and ended up running because he did not want to be caught by the fog again. The mist did not pursue him. When he got out of the mountains, he looked back again and saw that the thin vapor had risen above the lake again and it seemed to be contained by the three peaks. He kept walking and wondering what it was that had changed on him, but he could not feel anything new about himself. He just went on walking in one direction and kept on going that way.

He did not stop walking even when the sun had set. The weather was cool. He did not sweat, in spite of how fast he was walking. Shingai then realized that from the time that he had gotten into the sacred land, he had not felt hot or cold. The weather was just fine all that time even though it was harvest time and the sun was known to be scorching most of the time. He wanted to rest only after a new day had begun. He needed to get out of the sacred place. It was too tense for him to be in that area for his liking. He still could not workout his bearings because of the strange stars above. When he crossed a little stream that was on his way, he felt a warm breeze greeting him. He suddenly began to feel the fatigue kicking in. He looked up, and he saw the familiar stars shining on him. *Hwevazuva*, the brightest morning star was rising in the east. When he looked back where he had come from, the terrain was no longer the same. The river was still there, but the whole area did not look the same. This did not bother him. He was not about to investigate. All he needed to do was to get as far away from that sacred area as he could.

Shingai only managed to rest when the sun was way up on the eastern horizon. He shot a duiker to treat his sudden craving for fresh game. While skinning the little antelope, he thought of the first one that he had shot as a young boy and that he had given to his stepmother Marujata. His heart skipped a beat when he thought of the name "Marujata." He immediately realized that his memory had been restored! He began to think of the Dangadema people and how he had left that kingdom running away from his father, Chafunga. For a moment, he stopped skinning his duiker, and just smiled, enjoying the pleasure of his restored memory. He still remembered his experiences in Magocha. He remembered being horribly sick and walking in the rain until he collapsed. He remembered Colonel Magodo and the man that gave him porridge and how they took him with them to Magocha. Muthlomo was still visible in his mind. It became clear to him that the Bvuterevadzimu episode had something to do with his memory restoration. His time had really come, now that he had complete memories of his life. It was time for him to decide on how he was going to direct his life. He found it funny that the people of Magocha had totally believed that he was a son of the deep sacred pools of Manyoka River.

The sun was sitting right in the middle of the blue sky without sharing the big open space with even a single cloud. It scorched on everything below it. Mirages filled the whole plain below. There were a few trees in the vicinity with plenty of tall and dry grass on the ground. Even the birds had taken refuge from the blistering sun in the trees except for two bateleur eagles that were flying high in the sky. The southeasterly breeze would now and then cool down the temperatures briefly before being overpowered by the unforgiving sun.

Shingai had sat down in the shade of one of the leafy trees, leaning on the trunk and gazing out in the distance. His eyes were opened, and he was looking ahead of him but seeing nothing that was in front of him. He was looking at what lay ahead of him in his life. The problem was that he could not get his mind to focus on one thought at a time. He would think of Magocha, then he would be taken to Dangadema and of all he could see, some things had already happened. Sometimes his mind would take him to Musita, and while there he would think about Shuvai. The thought of Shuvai would invoke a flash of anger, but his thoughts would wind up on Mukai. Thoughts of his future settled on Mukai!

Shingai was trying to create his game plan from where he sat. Muthlomo and Mbuya Nyamukuta had advised him on many things, but they had put a lot of emphasis on him using his head carefully in all that he did. His life was now right in front of him. His mind began to crack on three apparent issues that he needed to choose from or execute first. He could just go back to Musita and build his home as well as to find someone to cook for him and to raise a family with. He could offer to help to train and organize the Musita army. This was easy to do, and he would not have issues with his ancestors, for he would live a peaceful life! Musita was a pleasant kingdom. The citizens were happy people with good hearts, unlike the people of Magocha and Dangadema.

Shingai had heard that his real father was King Zihwe of Dangadema. In his days in that kingdom, he had seen King Zihwe, but he now had a faint memory of him and would not be able to recognize him if they were to bump into each other. Muthlomo had told him that the spirit council had chosen him to take up the throne of Dangadema. This option made him laugh. He believed in what Muthlomo said, but he could not imagine himself as king. He could go to Dangadema to claim the rights to the throne. This meant that he would have to go and wage war against his father, King Zihwe, that is if Zihwe would be the one still ruling. A tiny part of his heart desired to see how King Zihwe would respond to him if he were to know that he was his son.

Even if he were to be welcomed by his father, did the king not have other sons who may have been waiting patiently to sit on the Dangadema throne after Zihwe? But Muthlomo had told him that Zihwe was running the kingdom in an unacceptable manner and this had angered the ancestors. The ancestors had then chosen him to be the rightful leader. It was definitely not going to be easy for him and Zihwe to get along. Even if there was a new king in his place, he was just going to have to fight with Zihwe's successor. Shingai had left Dangadema a long time back when he was still a little boy so not many people would remember him or know about him. He knew about the land, but he no longer remembered how the wars were fought. He did not have a clue of how the army in that region was organized. Thinking about all this made him realize that the Dangadema issue was not a mean feat.

Thirdly, Magocha kept beckoning him. Not that he was unafraid of what he had done there, but he had grown in Magocha. Most of what he knew in his life, he had learned and experienced it there. Most of the people that he knew were from Magocha. Most of his happiest days had been in that kingdom. The person whom he had loved with all his heart, he had met in Magocha. Even most of his dreams were still set in Magocha. All this did not draw him there as much as the curiosity to know what had become of Mukai. He had committed a grave crime, unheard of in the memories of the living people of Magocha. Although Rubonga had made it known that he wanted to kill him, Shingai had lived with him, and the king treated him like his own son for many years. However, Mukai had conceived his child, so he wanted to see how he could smuggle her and the child, out of Magocha and head to settle in Musita.

The desire to see his child grew stronger in his mind. Nine months had not passed yet from the time that he had run away from Magocha, but he knew that at the time of his running away, Mukai had already been carrying the baby for some months. This meant that there must have been a child from his seed back in Magocha by now. He knew that Rubonga would not kill Mukai before Shingai's attempt to rescue her and the baby, and he also knew that it was in Rubonga's nature to want to make his enemies suffer in public. This caused many people to fear Rubonga and to refrain from displeasing him.

A flying insect with black and white legs that bites and sucks blood from cattle and other animals landed on his bare back, but he did not feel it. When it stung him, he tried to reach for it with his open palm, but he could not reach it. He had to rub his back on the bark of the tree trunk that he was leaning on to scratch the itchy sting. He had not seen what had stung him, but he suspected it to be a stinging ant. He returned to his thoughts and decided that he would first go to Magocha to investigate on the welfare of Mukai and make a plan on how to make her vanish from the security stonewall that fortified Rubonga's palace. If he would be able to do this, he would then quickly return to Musita to build and settle among his mother's kinsfolk. One day, long after that, he would visit his friend Prince Masimba, knowing that Rubonga would be long gone.

Shingai had on his plan, his first port of call once he got back to Magocha. When he thought of this, sleep had already taken him to another place. He woke up as he gave a fast slap on his thigh where the stinging insect had pierced him and was sucking his blood. He got it, this time and both his thigh and palm were red with the blood that the insect had sucked. He looked at the insect and knew that there must have been buffalos close by. The sun was speeding down to take cover on the western horizon. He looked for the buffalos because he knew they would be going for a drink. He also needed to drink some water and to fill his water gourd before he started walking. He preferred walking at night, as it was much more relaxed during the hot season.

Chapter 32

The sun had turned deep red on the western horizon; one could not look at it without getting stung in the eyes by its rays. The calm waters that flowed slowly in the river below could not resist mirroring the beautiful reddish color of the atmosphere. Many birds had already perched in their places of rest for the nighttime, except for the wild geese that happily flew above the water and a few others that were trying to get their last catch of little fish on the banks of the river. The wind seemed to have also retired for the day for the leaves and grass had become still. In that peaceful silence, Shingai emerged from the tall grass that was on the banks of the river, and he took a moment to marvel at the beautiful scenery that lay before him. He remembered the days that he had seen such sights, and then he gave out a smile.

Shuvai loved to watch the sunset. She would complain and remark that the creators should have made the sunset period a lot longer than the few moments it was available. Shingai agreed with her. As he thought about Shuvai, his heart grew cold and erased his smile. He imagined that Shuvai probably had two kids already. These memories of her were just showing up to ruin his plans! He thought to himself. His mission was to rescue Mukai and not Shuvai who was long gone. The baby never stopped crying just because it had been reminded about food that it had eaten a long time back.

As he thought about it, he realized that darkness was fast setting in. He needed to swim to the other side of the river. He waded into the water, breaking the calm surface as his movements sent ripples in all directions. He was careful to swim calmly, peddling his hands and feet below the surface of the water like a dog. He had mixed crocodile fat that he kept in his sling bag with a liquid that he had extracted from fresh *mutondo* bark. He then applied the mixture on to his belly, rubbing it hard into his skin with his palms. The combination was said to repel crocodiles. This had become his norm whenever he swam in deep and murky waters, although he knew of some people who had fallen prey to the giant reptiles even after they had applied the potion. Angering one's ancestors could neutralize the powers of even the most potent medicine.

He pulled himself out on the other bank of the river and walked about seven steps, then suddenly he was hugged tightly from behind and thrown to the ground. Before he could free himself, he felt something sit on his back, his hands bound by what felt like a big hand. Another big hand shoved his head into the ground, and he could not turn it. He tried to violently free himself, but he was gripped too tight to move! In that short space of time, his mind raced. How is it that he had been caught so soon like this? Could it have been Rubonga's people who had been planted all over knowing that he would be back? His mind also wanted to perceive where the first blow would strike. Would it be a stabbing? In that same moment, he was planning on how to free himself. Was this even a person or it was some creature that was attacking him? When a familiar odor was emitted by his attacker, he relaxed and laughed.

Gotora released him and joined in the laughter.

"But how did you know that was me?"

"A-ah, old blood, is it not true that you have not taken a bath yet?" Shingai responded before breaking into laughter again. They shook hands firmly and embraced each other as they stood up.

"I saw you before you even went into the water. Nothing can come after me and try to prey on me before I am aware of it. Otherwise, are you well? Word here was spread that you had perished, but not many people believed it. But you young man, you are something else. After your daredevil act of pricking a mad lion on its tongue and then running off, you still have the audacity of stepping back on Mupingamhuru's soils?"

Shingai sighed before he responded.

"A-ah my old man, life as a mortal is difficult to explain. This flesh of ours is the source of all mankind's problems. I am not here for much."

The hermit looked at him without saying anything for some time, then he said,

"Let us go into my house, and we will talk from there."

In the dark night filled with sounds of mostly insects and frogs croaking in various tones, old Gotora was taking a bath behind a shrub that was near his hut. Shingai was sitting in the rondavel. From the time that they had become close friends, this was his first time inside Gotora's hut. The many times he had visited, the two would sit and talk outside. He looked at the pitch of the roof and ran his eyes down looking at each set of purlins that ran in circles, starting with one that had the smallest circumference at the top to the big one at the bottom of the roof. The round wooden poles that supported the thatch were straight and had their barks peeled off. The poles had turned smooth black from the soot. He was surprised at how neat the roof was, despite the smoke that had transformed the whole interior of the roof to black. A lot of different things were hung on two of the lowest purlins. Among the items, Shingai saw a dried hand of a baboon and a whip made out of a hippo tail. He also saw a collection of bird feathers bound together and hung on a purlin. When he saw skins of big snakes and the skin-shed of a king cobra, a chill ran down his spine, and his hair stood on edge. He had never been in a house as bizarre as Gotora's hut.

There were two benches built of clay, mounted onto the wall of the hut. The seats were placed symmetrically, although one was smaller. Shingai was sitting on the smaller one that could fit two grown men. He doubted if anyone other than Gotora had sat on that bench. On the bigger bench was a heap of baskets and gourds of different sizes, probably containing a lot more mysterious objects. He could not see the other things because the light from the fire illuminated mostly the dark roof. A cooking pot was simmering on the fire. Shingai could not get over the savage stench that was in the hut. He could not tell where the smell was emanating from. From the time he had entered the hut, he had started coughing and hoped that he would become accustomed to the stench. He was troubled. Was he going to be able to eat what Gotora was cooking?

Shingai moved from the bench to sit on a stool closer to the fire so that he could ward off the mosquitoes that were biting him. He had forgotten to apply some insect repellent from a tree that emits a thick milky fluid when cut. He knew Gotora would definitely have something to repel mosquitoes because he resided close to a slow flowing river, so he would ask for some later. Gotora eventually came into the hut and began preparations to cook. Shingai offered to help with the cooking, but Gotora declined his offer. Shingai was relieved by this because he could not have stood cooking while inhaling the foul aroma in the hut. He just had to be brave enough to stomach the food and keep it in his belly.

"So tell me, young man, why exactly have you come back to Magocha?"

Gotora asked while he dished *sadza* made from *masekesa* meal. Shingai delayed his response. His eye was inspecting the food that the big man was dishing. It was bad manners to ask a host what type of food they had prepared. The host would ask if they doubted that their guest would be okay with the food being served. He was a well-mannered young man, and all he could do was look!

"Did you not hear my question?"

"Ho-o, no, a-ah I heard you but ummnn- "He did not complete his answer.

"And?"

"I did not come back for much. After I ran away, I went very far away and got to a kingdom where I found my real relatives. I got to my mother's home kingdom. My grandparents and uncles are still alive, and they gave me a beautiful place to build my home and farm."

"Oh, is it? So why have you come back here? Why would you leave such a beautiful place to come and throw yourself into the hands of the man who wants to kill you?"

Gotora looked really puzzled. He added,

"I have always known you to be a level-headed person but just explain to me your reasoning behind this."

"My old man, I committed a heinous crime. I do not blame my king for having been infuriated by my act to the point of wanting to separate my soul from my body. What's hurting me the most, and that keeps me bothered is that I did not create trouble for myself alone, no. I created trouble for somebody's daughter and left her in a difficult situation. Even though she assisted in creating the trouble, it cannot be equated to me as a man and the older of the two of us. That girl is only a little chick that grew up caged. She does not know anything or how women should act when the spears of men aim at them. She never had anybody teach her how or what to do when desire would have overcome her." Shingai said and sighed.

"After some time of deep thinking about it all, my heart told me that I would never ever live peacefully again if I were to leave the girl to suffer at the hands of Rubonga. As we are talking now, there is a high possibility that Mukai has given birth to my child in that fortress. This is what I have come to try to establish. If Rubonga sent Mukai back to her parents' home, then I will just go there and convince her to flee with me. I will take both her and my child to my kinsfolks' kingdom. If she is still trapped and suffering in Rubonga's home, then I will plan to fish them out and run. I know that this is going to be pretty hard to do, but my determination shall be the spike. I have come to you first because you are the only person in Magocha who can volunteer any information on my mission freely. I don't want anybody but you, to know that I have set my foot in this kingdom."

As he was speaking, Gotora continued to nod his head slowly, eating his *sadza*. Shingai remembered later that he had expected the food to be disgusting, but it actually tasted good! The *masekesa sadza* had a sour taste that triggered the production of saliva from his inner cheeks and near his bottom molar teeth. However, what he had enjoyed most, was the dried meat in peanut butter, sprinkled with mild powdered chilies. He could still detect the horrible stench in the hut, but it was getting less intense. With his mouth full of dried meat, Gotora then said,

"Ummnn yah, it is true that your mission is a heavy one. I do not know where to begin, but perhaps let me just begin by filling you on what took place in Magocha while you were gone. You will then tell me how you plan to go about it only after I have told you everything."

Gotora related to Shingai a lot of the events that had taken place, starting from the warriors that were sent to follow and apprehend him, and how they were thoroughly beaten up in front of civilians for their failure to bring him back to Magocha. He told Shingai about the price that had been put on his head for anybody that would bring evidence leading to his arrest. The man that would bring such proof had been promised immense wealth that would include a herd of fifteen cattle. Whoever would bring Shingai's head, would be elevated to become a member of The Council of The Wise Eleven in addition to the other rewards. This person would also be given Ruvarashe, the king's daughter who comes after Kundai, to marry without paying the dowry for her.

Shingai broke Gotora's narration with laughter, but old Gotora did not seem to have been amused by the king's ridiculous offer. Gotora went on to tell him that even with all these incentives, only a few men had shown interest in wanting to go after him. Many had whispered to each other that following Shingai and trying to capture him was not different from being sent to fight or hunt a lion with bare hands. Some had been charmed by the chance of acquiring quick wealth, but they had not gone far with that ambition.

The story that fascinated Shingai on what took place while he was gone was the return of Gwari, son of Governor Revesai's brother. Gwari was a young man of Shingai and Masimba's age. They had attended the boys initiation school at the Pengapenga Mountains together and he had become close to Shingai. He had performed well as a fighter at the school, and it was almost definite that he was going to be drafted into the Magocha army. What then happened was that, when the group had returned from Pengapenga, Gwari had not stayed long in Magocha as he went to live in Bengwa with his mother's kinsfolk after the break up of his parents. Governor Revesai had had constant quarrels with his young brother over the way he beat up his wife. Gwari saw all that was happening and had grown fond of his uncle, the governor for being a rational man. Over time, he began to spend more time at the Revesai's, sharing a *gota* with the governor's eldest son. When his parents divorced, Gwari went with his mother to the Kingdom of Bengwa. He did this so that he could help her with work and look after his younger siblings. The killing of his uncle happened when he was already living in Bengwa. His father also just disappeared from Magocha.

Now Gotora was saying that Gwari had come to visit his *bamukuru* who he was so fond of to show him his wife, but he found out that the whole family had perished. Some neighbors told him that he was lucky to be alive for if he had been present at the time of the killings, he too would not have been spared! According to Gotora, people were saying that after hearing about the sad demise of his people, he just vanished from Magocha, and that he is the one who had returned to live like a dissident, killing anyone that seemed to be guarding Rubonga. Many unofficially claimed to have seen him at places where the warriors would be found slain the following morning.

"Some people claim that you and Gwari are working as a team carrying out the gruesome murders." Gotora said as he took a break to drink some water.

"Now Gwari has caused a lot of sleepless nights at the palace. The whole royal family is worried sick about their lives. He is eliminating the guards, and his signature is still consistent."

Shingai kept listening, marveling, and fascinated by the Gwari dimension. He wondered how he had failed to connect Gwari to the murders. Gotora ended by saying,

"Now, here is how things stand in Magocha. Many warriors have been sent out into the kingdom to hunt for Gwari, so they are everywhere. Wherever you plan to go, you must know that the path is infested with warriors ready to kill without checking first who they will be attacking. Anyway, that aside, here is what happened to your Mukai. When Rubonga saw that much time had passed without any news of your whereabouts and that Mukai's belly had grown big, he summoned many people to the tree of smoke.

"When the people had gathered, Gezi was called first, and he went dressed in his religious garb. He was told that he had used fake medicine to lock the queens' genitals to prevent them from sleeping with other men because the medicine had not worked on Mukai. Because of this, Ndukuyashe decapitated him in an instant with his razor-sharp machete. People lowered their heads with many women horrified by the act. Several men murmured that Governor Revesai had been vindicated and avenged. They went quiet when Rubonga stood up. Rubonga breathed fire as he spoke, complaining that he had bred a poisonous snake in his own home. He said that he did not care or fear because no poison could defeat him or put him down; therefore he wanted to teach a lesson to all that would harbor ambitions of trying to bring him down. As he was speaking, his warriors brought Mukai, dragging her to the center of the court. Rubonga then called out saying 'It is common knowledge that the young one of a snake is a snake, and the young one of your enemy is your enemy!'

"Rubonga then said that he no longer cared that you had raped his wife. He said that his young wife had not committed any crime, but he had to kill the little snake that you had stuffed into his wife's womb so that the breed of this snake would not bring trouble to him in the future. Without people expecting it, Rubonga drew out his dagger and slit open Mukai's belly, and all the insides fell out. The crowd broke into a loud cry, and Mukai fell down and died shortly. Some of her limbs were seen jerking, but she was gone. Some say they saw the fetus jerk for a little bit. All the men just stared with their mouths wide open. No one attempted to confront him. Even his warriors seemed to have been shook by what had just happened. Rubonga walked like a baboon heading back to his palace, leaving the women wailing while holding their wombs and some holding their heads. Masimba remained seated, dumbfounded as he stared at the messy heap of what was once his *Mainini* Mukai."

By the time Gotora ended his narration, Shingai was already up and heading for the door. He unsuccessfully tried to stop him. He wanted to follow him but decided otherwise, for he knew that there was not much that he could do. He knew that all that was left was for Shingai to do as he pleased. As he heard the sound of splashing water, he knew that Shingai was heading deep into Magocha.

Chapter 33

The red sun rose in the cool morning breeze. A lot of birds filled the eastern horizon seeming to enjoy the energy of the morning. White smoke could be seen rising from the walls of Rubonga's palace indicating that the girls who ran chores for the queens and the king's family had already returned from fetching water and they had already kindled fires. From the summit of Chineninga Kopje, it was not possible for one to see what was going on inside the security wall around the king's home, but for Shingai who had lived in that home for a long time, he did not need to see what was going on at this time. He knew the routines. The sun rays hit on his forehead, but he kept staring in the east, his mind spinning in reflections. When it rose a bit, the light became unbearable in his eyes so he could not keep staring in that direction.

Shingai had been sitting on the summit of the sacred mountain from the time he arrived from Gotora's home in the night. He had decided to camp on this mountain for he knew that it was a no go area for the people of Magocha. There was nobody who was not terrified of getting near that sacred castle kopje. Even among all the warriors that were searching for him and Gwari, none would be brave enough to look for him in that mountain. Only strangers to Magocha were said to have gone into it and had come out unscathed. Most strangers would not risk invoking the wrath of the spirits of any kingdom by just going up mountains that were near residential areas without first asking the locals if the particular mountains had souls or not.

When he was on the way to Chineninga from Gotora's home, he began to work out his action plan. First, he convinced himself that he had to quickly kill Rubonga. The king had to pay for his evil deeds. Secondly, he no longer cared if he was going to be killed in the process of doing this. There was no living person who was going to convince him to abort his mission. Thirdly, if his ancestors and those of Magocha would decide to punish or kill him for choosing to camp in Chineninga, a place that the departed and revered kings of the kingdom slept, then it was up to them. He did not care. He had been badly hurt, and all he could think of was to spill Rubonga's blood! He needed a solitary abode where he would plan on planting his snares to achieve his goal. The plan had to be foolproof. He had all his weapons on him, so he was ready to face anything. When he got to the foot of Chineninga, he had not even spared time for the ritual introduction of his intention to the sleeping kings. He just went up and found his way to the summit, and he sat there thinking. The motion picture of how Mukai was killed kept playing vividly in his mind, and he could not plan anything. His anger and hurt kept rising and taking prominence in all his thoughts. Rubonga had to be killed!

The sun rose higher, and he remained seated on the mountain top, trying to imagine what was going on inside the security wall in the east. He only climbed down a bit lower to inspect and familiarize himself with the area that he had chosen to camp. From the time that he lived in Magocha, he had never climbed that mountain. He had avoided the side of the hill where the burial caves of the departed kings and other high-ranking royals of Magocha was located. There were plenty of rock rabbits in the kopje, and these would provide him with a good supply of food. The presence of rock rabbits also warned him of the existence of black mambas and other big poisonous snakes, so he needed to be extra careful.

When six days had passed with him still on the kopje, he was able to come up with a well-thought plan of how he was going to kill Rubonga. From what he had heard from Gotora, it was clear that for him to get to Rubonga, he needed to cross two boundaries only. The warriors had been instructed to guard two circular borders around the king's palace with the outer one being bigger. Ndukuyashe and Chakare had created the boundaries so that the enemies could be fought off before they got too close to the king. Although the outer perimeter was more extensive, it was the more porous one. Chakare was in charge of monitoring the troops that guarded it. Ndukuyashe was responsible for the last and inner frontier. Shingai was not concerned about Masimba because he had nothing against him. Yes, Masimba was not going to stand by and let his father be killed, but he had planned to only take care of it if and when that time presented itself. All he wanted to do was to capture wicked Rubonga and cut his limbs off slowly so that he would feel the pain that Mukai and her baby had felt.

He had to find Chakare and kill him without trying to fight all the troops that were under him. The death of Chakare would cause a lot of confusion amongst the warriors that were under him. Soldiers without a leader, scatter. This weakness was good for him. It proved to him that the strength of the mighty

Magocha army had deteriorated in his absence. Now the troops were only taking command from Chakare and Ndukuyashe. The death of the commander of a boundary meant the end of that boundary and the increased vulnerability of the king! Gotora had also told him that most of the troops were now demoralized and were just being forced to guard the king because they too feared to die for what they did not know. If he would quickly eliminate Chakare, he would then only have Ndukuyashe to kill before he got to Rubonga.

Thinking about this made Shingai proud for a moment. He smiled and asked himself why Gwari had not thought of this plan earlier on. His blood streamed faster in his blood vessels when he thought of Gwari, the dissident. However, he had not asked himself what would happen if he were to bump into him. He was troubled a bit. He knew that Gwari was a rational young man, but what he was not sure of was if Gwari had known that he was not an enabler when Rubonga killed Governor Revesai. Would Gwari ever know and understand that the killing of his uncle had also hurt him? Shingai just decided that he would only see what would happen if he met Gwari. If Gwari chose to fight him, then he would gladly accept the challenge, and they would square it off like men.

As Gotora had told him, Chakare had planted many troops around the king's home. His soldiers were guarding the area around the outer boundary up to the security wall where Ndukuyashe's border ended. Shingai knew that most of Chakare's warriors were cowards that had been forced to take the assignment. A number of them were said to have already run away from their posts to secure refuge in other areas. He did not want to kill many people for they had not wronged him. His targets were Chakare, Ndukuyashe, and Rubonga. He knew what he had to do.

Towards sunset, Shingai stealthily approached Chakare's warriors. The warriors surrounded the area before the king's palace. They guarded in groups of between three to five warriors. The warriors would take turns to patrol the area while others would be resting. Shingai saw a group of three warriors talking to one another. He went carefully to them, and they only saw him when he was right in front of them. As they swiftly scrambled to get their weapons, he warned them not to be be stupid. They obeyed and just stood there, two of them with their mouths open in shock. They were visibly shaking.

"I am not hunting after you, gentlemen. I do not have a problem with any one of you, and I also do not believe that any of you has an outstanding issue with me, right?"

"None of us," two of the warriors answered at the same time. Shingai stayed charged at them silently for a few seconds. Fear was written all over their faces. He looked scary and savage with the mixture of ashes and blood that he had applied on his face and body. They knew that he was a skilled fighter that no ordinary warrior dared to fight.

"Where is Chakare?" He asked with a raised voice. The warriors looked at each other, hoping that one of them would volunteer to speak first. The warrior that seemed to be the eldest of them took the responsibility and said,

"Ummnn, we only see Chakare when he comes for inspection and to inquire if we have seen any suspicious people. He does not have a set time that he comes. No one knows his schedule."

Shingai nodded slightly then said,

"You, run this way, you run that way and tell everyone that you meet that I said, 'If you are not Chakare, Ndukuyashe, or Rubonga you are not my enemy, and I am not yours. You will only become my enemy if you place your sorry self between those people and myself. Then I will not hesitate to separate your head from your neck. Do not be used by people that are left with only a few more days to breathe. The wise among you should immediately get out of the way.' Do you hear me!" He was seething with anger when he finished speaking, and this made the warriors even more scared.

"We heard you, My Lord!" They all answered at the same time.

"Now, run! If you turn around just be prepared to receive an arrow through your heart."

The two younger warriors broke into a sprint going in opposite directions. Shingai then asked the older warrior to go back to his home. Even though he was not instructed to run, he found himself bolting towards his compound.

The whistling and hullabaloo that filled the air in the king's district that night indicated that his plan had worked. Many warriors were loyal to Magocha and would have executed their duties well, but at that moment, only a few of them were willing to die for Rubonga the despot. It was going to take long for Chakare and Rubonga if they were to try to reign in the panicking warriors.

On the following day, Shingai went down to hunt for Chakare. He knew that Chakare was well prepared for him. Fighting a giant like him required smartness and killer instincts. He didn't want to pounce on him in the dark without warning, and he needed to avoid killing the wrong person by mistake. He needed him to see who it was that would be ending his life.

He walked in a densely vegetated area to avoid being spotted, and as he walked, he heard the sound of a person running. He looked down and focused on a spot in the clearing and opened his ears to listen carefully to establish where the person was running from. He hopped into a tree to see further, and from up there, he spotted a warrior running in the bushes. He climbed down and ran to intercept him. He hid behind a big tree trunk and waited for the warrior to get closer and then he jumped in front of him. The warrior was shocked and broke into a loud cry, but he could not run away from Shingai. Shingai tried to stop him from shrieking, but he kept screaming. He then landed him a bolting clap in the face of the warrior and phlegm came out his nose spreading on to one of his cheeks. At this point, the warrior's eardrums could only hear a ringing sound similar to that of a crying cicada.

"I said, shut up!" Shingai shouted. The warrior went dead silent, and then he knelt before him.

"Stand up! I'm not your king that you should kneel before. Why are you running like a mad man?"

The warrior did not answer. He kept kneeling with his face down, afraid of looking at Shingai. Another sudden clap landed on the same cheek that had been struck first. Shingai thought he heard the echo of the slap being thrown back to him from a nearby castle kopje and he felt good.

"Answer my question now before I make you food for the hyenas! Where are you running to or who are you running away from?"

The warrior had now raised his head and was looking at him. His mouth was full of blood.

"Everyone is just running, some looking for places to hide, others going to their homes to check on their families, some are-"

"What do you mean everyone? What exactly is going on and who are they running from?"

Shingai was now getting confused. He was no longer listening because he was now trying to think of what could have been going on before the warrior had given a clear explanation. Could it be that an enemy kingdom had invaded and war had broken out in Magocha? He did not like these sorts of surprises, and this could ruin all his plans.

"Hey, can you speak up quickly!" Shingai commanded as he faked the release of another clap. The warrior did not point out that he had not stopped talking, but it was Shingai who was no longer paying attention to what he was saying. He just carried on saying,

"People are giving different versions of what is going on in the kingdom, and nobody now knows who has the correct version. It is being said by some that you intend to kill all of the king's warriors; some are saying that you have already butchered many of the warrior's families. Some are saying that you have come to free the people from King Rubonga's bondage. Then others are saying that you and Gwari have brought a legion of assassins to fight the Magocha army. What has made me run to my family is that, early this morning our commander Chakare was found dead. It has not been made clear on whom between the two of you has killed him. As we are speaking right now, some of the warriors that were guarding the inner circle under Ndukuyashe have also started running."

Shingai went quiet looking at the warrior, but his mind had taken him somewhere else. He came back to find the warrior still kneeling and looking at him. He ordered him to run to his family and not to look back.

The warrior answered when his heels were already tapping on his spine as he ran. Shingai made a sigh of relief. He had not expected the impact of his plan to be that extreme. Rubonga's troops had been gripped by untold terror. He remembered that these people did not care whether it was a time of great suffering or not; they still found pleasure in exaggerating stories. People did not want to appear ignorant of what was going on. The people of Magocha loved to be the bearers of breaking news in the kingdom. It seemed there were silent awards given to those that broke the latest news. Even with just bare skeletons of stories, by the time they would be shared to others, the stories would have gathered a lot of fat. It was not easy to establish the truth at such a time. What sent some chills down his spine was that Gwari had gotten to Chakare before him! It was good that the people he intended to kill were being eliminated, but he still felt a bit jealousy that Gwari seemed quicker than him at planning.

Chapter 34

The sun was blistering throughout the kingdom of Magocha. There was no breeze blowing at intervals to bring some cooling relief to the organisms that lay under the scorching sun. Even the ever-happy birds had taken a break from flying and chirping. The few clouds that were moving slowly in the sky provided the much-needed shade here and there.

Shingai walked sneakily and slowly in the cover of the foliage. His ears were wide open and stood like those of a dog that has heard a strange sound in the grass. He had moved into a dangerous zone where many houses surrounded King Rubonga's fortress. He was aware that there could be some warriors that were waiting for him, and so he would frequently go up a tree to scan the view ahead. For some time, all he could see were just homes of the warriors that created the buffer zone between the palace and the ordinary citizens. He circumvented the homes and carried on drawing closer to Rubonga's palace.

From up a tree, he saw a group of warriors sitting under the shade of a big tree. They were a bit distant from where he was so he could not tell who they were or hear what they were talking about. He did not want to start a fight with them because they could overpower him because of their advantage in number. He climbed down and began to walk carefully, avoiding the dry leaves that covered the ground.

Suddenly he heard what sounded like a spear that had been thrown at his right side. He quickly turned in that direction, his bow already drawn. His eyes were slow. The spear shot into the ribs of a big man, who fell down in that instant. At that same moment, an arrow whizzed and took out another big man close to where the first stood. The big man bellowed like a bull that had taken a blow from another during a fight. Shingai quickly lowered himself onto the ground and shrank as he moved like a reptile in the grass to take cover behind a tree. He turned to look on the other side, and his eyes met those of yet another giant who was taking aim at him with a spear. Shingai quickly let go of his arrow, aiming it at the giant's neck. To his surprise, his arrow just managed to cut the giant slightly as he was in the motion of falling down from another arrow that had been shot by a mysterious archer.

A short silence ensued, and Shingai looked up to see who the mysterious archer that had saved him was. He did not see him, but he was confident that it was Gwari. While he was still searching, he picked up voices of people that were heading towards him. These were warriors and rather unfortunate ones, for they had not managed to ambush him and he was ready for them. The warriors got near him, and he twisted and broke their necks with his bare hands, one by one. He stabbed some with his dagger ripping their rib cages.

He fought like a hungry lion. More warriors came out to attack him, and he quickly grabbed one of them and used him as a live shield, absorbing the spears that were aimed at him. When the live shield had taken three spears, he became heavy, and Shingai knew that he had died. He let him go as he swiftly leaped on to another warrior like a leopard and stood on his shoulders. From there he shot three arrows in quick succession. Two arrows downed two warriors, but the third one landed on the bum cheek of another who had turned to run and so he fled with the arrow stuck deep into his rump. Shingai then sent the blade of his dagger into the neck of the warrior that he was standing on, just behind the collarbone and the warrior fell down. Shingai pulled out his knife and drew another arrow before turning around slowly as he inspected the area to see if there were still any assilents. All this happened in an instant.

No one had remained. The warriors had seen what he had done in a short space of time, and none of the survivors had dared to lose their lives just like that. The surviving warriors had run and jumped over the low bushes that were ahead of them, getting as far away as they could from the killing machine. Shingai felt proud of how he had fought. He began to extract his arrows from the dead warriors. After that, his instincts told him that somebody was watching him. He swiftly turned around with his arrow drawn, but he did not see anybody. He then thought of checking the type of spear and arrows that had killed the giants. He knew the weapons of many skilled fighters in Magocha so those weapons could tell him the warrior that they belong to. He had no idea what Gwari's weapons looked like for he was no longer using the same weapons that they had used at the Pengapenga Mountains. He was surprised to find that the weapons had already been pulled out from the carcasses of the giants!

He looked closely at the giants, and he recognized them. They were Rubonga's mercenaries, the ones that he had sent to kill Shuvai and Vandirai. The giants had painted their faces and bodies with green and brown colors to blend in with the vegetation around them. Shingai thought that Muthlomo had probably sent

Gwari to look after him. He saw that if it had not been for Gwari, he would have ended that day as food for ravens and hyenas. He sensed that someone was looking at him again. He turned and aimed his arrow in the direction that he suspected his tail to be. His eyes ran into somebody that he had not expected to see at all. It was Lord Vandirai that had been looking at him! Vandirai was carrying a quiver full of arrows on his back and a spear in his hand. Shingai was totally astonished. He knew that Vandirai was not allowed to carry weapons by Rubonga. When he saw that Vandirai was not about to fight him, he lowered his arrow and stared back at him. Vandirai kept staring at him but did not say a word to him. So Vandirai had saved him from the assassins!

The old artful cripple then turned around and limped away without looking back. Lord Vandirai was not using his walking stick. Shingai remained standing and looking at him as he walked away. He cussed at himself for not thanking him for saving his life. He wished he had at least greeted him. If only he had exchanged pleasantries with him, then he could have also asked him why he had helped him. His mind began to spin. Could it be that Vandirai was working with Gwari? Would it not be better for the three of them to join forces and fight as one since they had a common enemy? How come he had not met Gwari? Was it even true that he was in Magocha and killing Rubonga's troops?

He almost ran after Vandirai to ask him about all this but then he restricted himself. He reminded himself that his war was just to avenge the killing of Mukai and her child by Rubonga and nothing more. Other people had to fight their own battles, and he was not about to stop them. He also reminded himself of the cruelty that Vandirai had shown him when he married off Shuvai to a man she probably did not love as a way to prevent her from marrying him. When he thought of Shuvai, he became happy and felt vindicated for not thanking or greeting Lord Vandirai. It served him right! A lot had been done that day, and it was enough. He waited for darkness before he moved back to his camp on Chineninga to strategize on his next move.

Chapter 35

Rubonga was sitting on his throne, his right cheek resting on his left hand while his right hand hugged his chest with his fingers patting on his left ribs. He nodded his head to the beat of mbira and shackles that were being played softly by his musicians. The musicians had started playing his favorite songs early that morning. The serenades had been going on for some time now. The melody seemed to tranquilize the king from the myriad of problems that had multiplied in those days. For a long time, happiness had fled from the palace of Magocha.

The queens and princesses were now taking up some of the chores that they never used to do because the number of girls assigned to the palace to tend to them was depleting. The girls' parents were getting scared that their kids would be caught in the crossfire of the fighting and killing that was taking place in the kingdom. Masimba had finished eating his lunch, and he had joined his father at the family court. All the Royals were up, with each one of them minding their own business except for the little kids that did not have the slightest idea of the deadly threat that their father faced from his foes.

Rubonga looked at his little sons that were playing bullfight, head-butting each other, and moving on fours. The boys seemed to be totally enjoying their playing. He wished he was still at their age. Things were not going well for him. He was still having all his meals but only so that he could gain energy to move around, otherwise, he had long lost his appetite. He rarely had the desire for any food. Many times in those days, he would be seen having conversations with himself. Prince Masimba was now chairing the meetings of The Council of Wise Eleven, which at that point, only had a few governors that were still loyal to King Rubonga. Many of the citizens were no longer comfortable walking near the palace. In that year and for the first time in a long time, the sixteen-year-old boys of Magocha did not attend the initiation school because there was no one organizing that event. All the warriors' efforts and focus were to keep the king and the rest of the royal family safe from the assassins.

As the musicians played their music, Prince Masimba drank some alcohol from a hard-burnt clay container. He did not use a gourd because he was the only one drinking, and he liked drinking straight from the clay container. Suddenly, the musicians stopped playing their instruments all at once, and at the same time, the king and the prince rose. They all looked in the direction of the main entrance into the enclosure. The guards at the gates were dumbfounded and just stood still. At first, Rubonga thought that his enemies had finally gotten to him, but soon he saw something that he had only seen when he was still a young boy! A band of ancient men and women were approaching the king. The group was composed of thirteen old men and eleven old women. An old woman who was addressed as "the Big Aunt of the Lion Clan" led the group.

As the group headed for the king's family court, the Big Aunt was continuously cussing at Rubonga while the other members were snorting loudly and some bellowing inaudible words. The old people, all dressed in black, appeared to be possessed by some spirit. Some of them were wearing weird headgears even though they were not *n'anga.*

"Son of Mupingamhuru! You are a bad man. Who do you think you are to disturb the peace of these old bones of Magocha and those who have been sleeping for a very long time? All this because of the stinking habits that you picked up from your appalling mother?" The Big Aunt belched and hysterically shook her head, and then she carried on her assault.

"Son of a witch! Son of a mother who sucks blood even from newly born babies. What is this that you have brought upon the people of this land, that has shaken the roots of the mountains of Magocha? How much more blood do you need to spill for you to be full? Is it that you do not have even a little half-witted ancestor to advise you?"

The Big Aunt then froze and looked at Rubonga for some moments then she broke into a sharp but short laugh. She then slowly shook her head and made a snorting sound from drawing air into her mouth, expressing what seemed to be between sympathy and disdain for the king. She then cursed,

"Shame, you probably think that the ancestors of this land are sleeping, sorry young man, you are still a mere mortal. Yes, I can see that your blood is about to clot inside you, but remember that you are going to face the wrath of those who dwell in the winds when they finally judge you. Now, look at the trouble that you have brought for your children!"

The other old women took down the clay pots that they were carrying on their heads and took out what appeared to be like ashes and began to sprinkle them on the ground. The old men also took out beer containers and poured beer on to the ground.

Nobody tried to stop them nor to ask what they were up to. Everyone that was in the enclosure just stood and looked in bewilderment at what was going on. Even the little boys that were playing mighty bulls had run to seek haven from their mothers. The Big Aunt took out her ground tobacco and pulled one sniff, then broke into a series of sneezes. She started jerking her limbs ecstatically, and the muscles on her face began to stretch her skin, making it twitch in different places. At times, it looked like The Big Aunt would be laughing, then it would change to look angry, then it would appear like somebody who is about to throw up. She walked towards Rubonga, looking deep into his eyes. The curious people thought she was going slap the king, but when she got close to him, she pointed at him with her wooden staff. Masimba moved closer to his father, but Rubonga stopped him by raising his open right-hand towards him. The Big Aunt then whispered to him saying,

"You know exactly what you did that is infuriating the great ancestors of this land. It is not just the innocent blood that you are currently spilling, but there is something that you did a long time ago that has come to eat your insides. If you were smart, you would run away from this land while you still can because what you ate then, is now ready to come out and nobody is going to be able to stop it."

After those words, she suddenly spat on his face, and the spit slowly rolled down his face, but he did not wipe it off. Masimba looked at his father, expecting him to blow his head off with anger, but he did not move.

The words that had been layered on him were heavy. They had not just sat deep in his heart, but they had also clung onto his whole body. The group hummed a strange tune as the Big Aunt led the ancient citizens out of the fortress.

Rubonga noticed that Masimba had been troubled by the events of that day. He knew that his son was aware that the elderly were revered in Magocha but that they also had their limits in regards to what they could say or do before the king and the royals. The group that had visited the palace on that day had performed a ritual that only a few in the kingdom knew about, but he had not told his son about the ritual. When he turned to look at his son, Masimba shot a question at him.

"What is going on my father? What have these people come to do, and what is the meaning of it all? Why did they say you must run away, father?"

"I will tell you one day. Don't you know that kingship is a circle that rotates? Don't you want to be king one day?"

Rubonga could see that his son had suspected that there was much more that had happened in the past that he had not shared with him. Masimba looked sad as he just left and went straight to his *gota*. The musicians began playing their instruments, but Rubonga stopped them. He told them that it was enough for that day and that they could go to their homes and rest.

Those that saw King Rubonga walking about saw a man who seemed to be well. Yes, he was still physically fit, but the man was emotionally eroded. As for sleep, it had packed and left a long time back. He had known much earlier than most people, from the time that the assassins had first struck, that he was their primary target. He tried to counter these attacks without success. This resulted in a maggot finding its way into his head, and it was now feeding ceaselessly on his brain. His family could see how he was suffering. They were hurt and worried about him, but they could do nothing to assist because he planned all his affairs on his own. He shared some of his concerns with Princess Kundai, but she did not know what to do either. As a spoilt father's daughter, the princess became more arrogant and filled with pride because she knew that her father loved her most, but at that moment, it did not take away the pain of seeing her father agonizing.

When Rubonga saw that Masimba had developed fear and uneasiness with what was going on and that he had begun to look at him with a suspicious side-eye, he became even more depressed. One skill that he had sharpened from the time that he had become king was his mind-reading skills. He knew how to quickly tell what was going on in many people's minds without them being aware. He liked to know the thoughts of his subjects, but mostly he wanted to know the feelings of those close to him, such as other royals or his wise governors. This made him keen on hearing even the most foolish rumor doing the rounds in his family or among his top leaders in the kingdom. He had developed the skill of sending his ear to people conversing while he would appear to be focusing on a totally different issue. He paid attention to minor issues, analyzing how they could destroy or consolidate his grip on power. This helped him to efficiently run his tyranny and to sit firmly on his adversaries' chests.

He was aware that the enemy could find a crack to insert a wedge from amongst his family if he was not careful. He quickly saw the danger that could come if Prince Masimba was to try to find more information on what the Big Aunt of the Lion Clan had said. He would unearth a lot of his corrupt activities from a long time back. He was not stupid, and he had to quickly figure out who Masimba was going to try to squeeze this information from. All the king needed to do when that person was found was to make sure that their tongue would be cut off. He was not short of ways to execute that. He was slightly relieved that Masimba seemed to have quickly found a confidante in Princess Kundai because he was sure that Kundai would not hide issues from him.

Rubonga summoned his commander Ndukuyashe and said,

"VaNduku, I want you to look for very clever warriors amongst your boys that you know are skilled trackers. There are too many enemies roaming in Magocha. You know that the enemy is not restricted to those that are murdering our people, but that there are some in the kingdom that are taking care of those killers, some by cooking for them?"

"It is all in my ear Your Highness," Ndukuyashe responded almost looking directly into Rubonga's eyes, a taboo in Magocha, but he needed to be absolutely sure he was getting what the king was saying to him.

"Now, I want those boys to keep their eyes on this boy, your prince, Masimba so that they know who he talks to and where he goes. I want this to be quickly done, you hear me?"

"It is all in my ear, Your Highness."

"I know that sometimes he roams around alone, but with the way things are in the kingdom, it is not advisable for a royal like him to be taking such risks. You must make sure that he is well protected. Now you should do this without him knowing about it because if he does, he will panic and we will lose him completely. Do you hear me clearly?"

"It is all in my ear, Your Highness."

Now go plan and let me know how it goes!" Rubonga ended up slaping his thigh for emphasis.

Ndukuyashe did not waste time. By the time the sun was setting on that day, his boys were all kitted up and ready for the assignment. Rubonga was pleased that he had managed to think and organize such a great plan at a time when his mind was extremely fragmented. He trusted Ndukuyashe, and he knew that in his mind, there was nothing superior to being obedient to his king and making him happy.

That night, Prince Masimba rolled and rolled on his bed in his *gota*. When he was younger, he had heard some people talking about what a bad and cruel man his father was, but it was just one of those incidences that he caught the people talking in cryptic proverbs and riddles. He knew that his father was feared by many and was not one that people could quickly get used to. He truly loved his father, and he admired and wished to do many things that he had done as the king. He counted him among men as his chosen role model. Prince Masimba also knew that many of his relatives, especially his uncle Vandirai loathed his father because he had failed to sit on the throne of Mupingamhuru, which he desired so much. His *bamunini* Vandirai had tried to use witchcraft to topple the king from his throne, but he failed dismally. So what was this that the elders of Magocha were now saying? It did not make sense. It bothered him that his father had not stopped the senile lot from doing all the nonsense that they were up to on that afternoon.

The prince reflected on the sentences that his father had said when people such as Governor Revesai and Mukai were atrociously killed, and he thought that this must have been the reason that had angered the elders. He had not liked the judgments himself, and definitely, they could not have amused the elders! However, this did not erase the other accusations that the elders had proclaimed. He needed to know about all it. He could tell that many things had taken place in the past that his parents had kept from him. He wondered why they had not told him about it, but they always told him other things to be wary of as he was going to be king after his father. How was he going to be a strong king when he was not aware of what sat on the foundation of that throne? How come all this was coming out at a time that the king had been reduced to just a crown bearer without much control of his kingdom because of his enemies who seemed to be getting more powerful and daring as each day passed? Could it be that the enemy was influencing the elders? The more he thought about it, the more he became curious about finding out what those dark secrets were about. Eventually, he was able to sleep, but by that time, the first cock had crowed to introduce the new day to the world. The mystery followed him to dreamland and troubled him further, creating more questions than answers for him.

Chapter 36

Masimba abruptly sat up on his bed in shock. The sun had already risen, and the day was getting hotter. Many people had already had their breakfast. He stood by the door of his gota, rubbed off sleep dust from his eyes, and yawned as he stretched. The cool breeze outside hit his face and freshened him up, making him more alert and present. His dreams had troubled him, although he did not remember much about them. One thing that had remained vivid from his dreams was the amount of fun that he had with Shingai. He dreamt of the two of them as young boys having lots of fun. He thought of his old friend and missed him. Although from a young age, Rubonga had warned Masimba not to be complacent when around Shingai, but he had not taken it to heart. Shingai had become his mother's son, and he always had pleasant thoughts of him from the time that he had run away from Magocha.

Incidentally, as Masimba set his foot outside the stonewall to get some air, he heard the familiar whistling sound of a little bird that he and Shingai used to imitate when they were looking for each other. He vividly remembered the first time they used the code. These were the days they began seeing girls. They carried on using the code even when they went for various military expeditions. Only the two of them knew what the code meant. They had vowed to not let anybody know what the sound meant to them. On that day, he knew that what he heard was just a little bird enriching the melodies of nature. The little bird invoked a thought in him to look for Shingai, who some were claiming to have returned to Magocha intending to kill King Rubonga. Masimba realized that if he acted fast and got to Shingai before he got to his father, he could probably convince him to abort his mission because he had a great deal of respect for him! Those that spoke in those days claimed that Shingai had drawn very close to the palace. If the prince could get hold of Shingai quickly and convince him, the two of them could maybe join forces against Gwari, or they could even ask for forgiveness from Gwari on behalf of the king.

After two days had passed, Prince Masimba started searching the places that he thought he might see Shingai, whistling their code but getting no response. He did not lose hope; instead, he became more resolute as each day went by. While he was doing all this, he did not notice that he had grown a long tail. Ndukuyashe's boys followed him carefully from a safe distance as he went about. Masimba thought he was losing the Ndukuyashe boys just after he would have left the stonewall enclosure, but he did not know that the boys were acting dumb deliberately. Ndukuyashe planted many boys to carry out this task diligently. By the time that the prince would return to the palace, Rubonga would have had all the information on all his activities of that day. Each time he would return to the castle, he would look for Kundai, and they would talk about a lot of things, something that had been a recent development. The brother and sister had gotten closer than they were growing up. When the other royals saw them talking, they assumed that they would just be talking about Masimba's girls.

Near the summit of the sacred mountain, Shingai applied pigments made from leaves and mud to his face and body, then he picked up his weapons. His mind was now focused on going straight to annihilate King Rubonga and anybody who was going to attempt to stop him. He descended from Chineninga and followed the canopy bushes as he headed to the palace. He knew the weakest point on the security wall because he had studied the wall meticulously when he was planning on fleeing with Mukai during his last days in the palace. Many of the warriors on Rubonga's security team believed that the spot on which the wall was connected to the rocky cliffs was the hardest point for anybody breaking into the enclosure, but Shingai had seen a weakness there. Before he had gone far, he heard the sound of their code whistling, and he immediately stopped in his tracks, chest forward, and one foot balancing by the toes. He listened once more, and he knew that it was Masimba whistling and not the little bird. Masimba was looking for him.

He did not quickly return the code to indicate that he had heard him. He thought that the prince must have been in the company of warriors sent to apprehend him. This was a plan to trap him. He carefully moved, looking for a place where he could fully see Masimba. He drew his arrow and checked around. He saw that Masimba was alone and did not have a weapon on him ready for attack. He ran and hid behind a tree, and from there, he returned the whistle. He then ran from there to another point where he could see Masimba, but Masimba could not see him, and he stopped. Masimba ran to where the sound had come from. He got there and looked everywhere and even up the tree, but he did not see Shingai. He whistled again and heard the response coming from another point. He ran in that direction but still when he got there, there was no sign of Shingai. They kept doing this, Shingai wanting to determine what his friend was really up to. When he became satisfied that Masimba was not about to harm him, he whistled back and remained in that spot but drew his bow and aimed at Masimba.

Masimba gaily approached him not even worrying about the arrow that was desperate to spring straight into his chest. When Shingai saw that he was not afraid of the arrow and that he was approaching fast, he once more looked in all directions to check if there were indeed no warriors waiting to spring from the grass. He did not see anybody, and he was satisfied. In the distance, Ndukuyashe's boys could only see Prince Masimba running from tree to rock, to another tree like a madman, so they took cover in the bushes and watched from afar, not knowing what to do.

"Shingi, my brother, it's just me. I am on my own, lower your arrow!"

Masimba was happy, and he smiled as he spoke.

"Hey, I said lower your arrow, it is only me here," by now he had reached where Shingai stood. Shingai was the unsettled one. He was very fond of Masimba, but at that particular time, he did not trust anyone but himself. He then lowered his arrow and put it back into his quiver.

"Now, son of my mother, can you give me five," Masimba brought forward his hand for a handshake. Shingai ignored the open palm, but then embraced him tightly for some time. The two then shook hands.

"My heart has been so relieved today you won't understand it, my eyes have seen the real Shingi once more! Ummnn, this is what they mean when they talk about being favored by the dwellers of the winds."

"Don't say that my friend, I am the happiest one today. I did not think you would want to ever see or talk to me again because of what I did to the Cobra just before I fled from Magocha."

The two burst into laughter for some time and then went to talk about other issues. During their conversation, Shingai suddenly drew his bow and arrow, saying he had sensed that they were being watched. They turned and sent their eyes searching the whole area around them, but they could not see anyone. They concluded that it was probably the little animals moving in the long grass. However, they decided to move to a strategic spot where they could see from a distance if anybody sought to approach them. They sat beside a big boulder and talked a lot more, updating each other on developments that had taken place when they had separated. The conversation carried on for a long time, punctuated with laughing and high-fives. Shingai even forgot for some time that even though he was hunting for Rubonga, Rubonga and his people were also hunting for him!

Masimba came up with a plan. It was actually a plan that he had thought of a few days back, so he said,

"Now look here, son of my mother, spilled water cannot be collected and placed back into the container by hands like we do with grain. Yes, Mhungu was absolutely wrong to kill *mainini* Mukai and the child, but even you will agree with me that he had strong reasons for being mad about the issue. *Mainini* Mukai is gone, and she is not coming back. Even if you kill the king, you'll have just done it, but it will not bring back those that have left. Now, like I'm telling you, I know my father because I have lived with him all my life. There is something that man did that is eating his live heart out. It won't be a surprise if you hear in three months that he has just collapsed or that he was found lying dead on his bed in the morning. He is now almost hollow inside. I am not happy that this is what is going on, but the man is struggling Shingi. Nobody knows what to do to help him, and in the whole palace, everybody is just hanging their heads in worry and sorrow for the king's health.

"As I said before, a group of gray-haired elders of Magocha came to the palace chanting words that we could not clearly decipher. It appears to me that his days are about to be cut. He may soon lose his marbles and will then not be able to execute his royal duties, and when such happens, the throne will have to find another occupant. These days, the main courts cannot be in session if I am absent. Now since you said that you also have a kingship that is waiting for you to take over, would it not be a good plan if you stopped your fight against the Cobra so that you go back without anyone knowing and build your home in your mother's land? When the time comes, you will rise and take your kingship, then the two of us can work together to build and run our kingdoms in humane ways that are appreciated by the departed senior ancestors. This is what I think we should do, what do you think about it?"

Shingai kept his head down, staring into the ground and thinking. He remembered the words of his *sekuru* VaMuzanenhamo that in all issues, anger should take the back seat. Masimba's plan was good. Yes, fighting and killing Rubonga could avenge the killing of Mukai and his child that he never got to see, but after that, then what? He had genuine love and respect for Masimba, and if he were to become the king of Dangadema, he would need to exchange notes with other progressive kings, of which Masimba would be one! Magocha was distant from Dangadema, but there were many things that he would need to learn and borrow from there to apply in his own kingdom. He looked up, sighed and then responded,

"If it wasn't you that had delivered this message, trust me, I was not even going to listen for a second. Magocha is the home that raised me, and it should not be decimated while I watch or add my hand to its destruction. Instead of destroying, let us build. Let me plan to vanish from Magocha once more and focus on other things. Do not worry about me. When these murky waters settle, you will see me. But you also need to take care of yourself, my brother. You see, if Gwari, who is said to be committing these killings gets to you, he may harm you."

"Shingi my brother, you have just removed the heavy rock that has been sitting on my back! I do not know what to do for you to thank you. But you do this for me; take these princely garments of mine so that when you come back here, you will be wearing them. All those that will see you wearing them will know that we are one and also even as you are going now, those that might have planned on ambushing you will not be able to do so because of the royal garb. I'll need to wear your garment so that I may be decent enough to walk back to the palace. If what they say about Gwari is true, then let us just leave it to those who live in the winds. What I know is that, if he really is out there and wanted to kill me, he would have done that already. He must just be after killing father and not me. Nduku's stupid little guards are going to be shocked today when they see me dressed as a commoner."

They laughed at the description of Ndukuyashe's guards. They exchanged their garments and shook hands tightly before Masimba left.

Masimba broke into a sprint and went under the bushes, whistling their code joyously as he went. Shingai kept looking at him and just smiled, shaking his head in amusement. Masimba had not changed. All he cared for was only happiness. Shingai kept looking at him, and suddenly he was puzzled by what he saw. Masimba ran from one bush and headed to another. The bushes were some distance apart, and the area between them was covered by tall, dry grass.

Out of the grass rose six or seven men. Being on the upper ground, Shingai could see that the man who was in front was Rubonga. For a moment he thought that Masimba had set a trap to catch him, but before he began to run, he was traumatized to see Rubonga drawing his arrow and sending it into Masimba's ribs. Masimba went down like an antelope shot in mid-air. Rubonga was handed his knobkerrie by one of his guards, and he ran straight to the injured Masimba and gave him one blow of the knobkerrie. He raised it again to deliver a second blow, but at that moment, he dropped his weapon and broke into a loud cry as he picked his son up. Rubonga roared so loud that the whole valley was filled with echoes thrown back from the several castle kopjes surrounding it. Blood was gushing out of Masimba's body, and he wasn't saying a word. He was just looking at his father, and at the same time, his eyes were shutting slowly. All that did not erase the smile that he always wore on his face.

Shingai blew a lid, and all he could see in his eyes were hot flames. He sprinted to where Rubonga was and slit the throats of two unsuspecting warriors. When two other warriors took a glance at him, they decided to tap on their spines with their heels as they disappeared into the bigger bushes. The other two could not figure out what was going on, and so they remained standing and confused. Shingai went on and snatched Masimba from his father and tried to call him.

"Masimba, Masimba! Hey Masimba, come on my brother, what is going on? Talk to me please, Masimba!"

Masimba did not respond. Shingai kept holding him, wiping off the dust and grass that had stuck all over him. He broke into tears and sorrowfully cried out loud as he slowly placed him on the ground. Rubonga resumed crying, with his hands on his belly and looking at Shingai and Masimba. For a moment the king hoped that Shingai was going to miraculously bring his son back to life. Rubonga began to talk as he cried.

"Am I dreaming, people? What is the meaning of all this? Who can finish me now for my heart is gone? Oh people, come and witness this lie here. Not Masimba, no. He is just sleeping and will soon wake up. Oh my father VaMupingamhuru, please talk to me."

Shingai kept his head down, trying to deny that this had actually happened. What he had not known was that when Ndukuyashe's boys had seen him talking to Masimba, they had all run back to the palace to report to the king. Nobody agreed to stay behind watching for they feared that if Shingai had spotted them, he would not have spared them. They described to Rubonga what he was wearing and so when they had returned with the king and saw Masimba running dressed in Shingai's garment, they all thought that they had gotten their prey.

As he remained kneeling, with his face down, Shingai was suddenly almost floored by a heavy fist that landed on his forehead. He lifted his head swiftly in time to dodge a second one and sprung on to his feet. He saw that Rubonga was ready to fight as he was moving towards him. His eyes were red.

"You are the reason why this has happened. You are the one who has killed my son, so you should also know that your end is now."

Shingai responded on his feet,

"Oh, okay, I've been looking for you too. You must absolutely kill me because if you don't, then you must know that all that you see now is your last view of the world."

Before he had finished talking, he had already landed two blows on Rubonga's jaw. The king spat blood. Shingai tried to land another one, but the old one was prepared, and he countered, missing Shingai's face at his first attempt but the second landed on his chest, and the boy staggered, almost completely losing his balance. The men fought fiercely. Shingai wondered what Masimba had tried to imply when he said that the king had become weak physically. It got to a point where Shingai's blows were raining on Rubonga's face relentlessly. The king was forced to move backward in short paces as if he was following the rhythm of the fists landing on his face. Suddenly he was able to abruptly stop backtracking and went for Shingai's throat with both his hands. He turned him and made him face away from him before he tightened his grip on the boy's throat. Shingai felt dizzy, and his blood felt as if it had stopped moving. He shook himself, but Rubonga did not let go. He used a lot of energy to keep his grip on the boy, and so he too was gasping for breath.

The two warriors that had remained thought that life was ending for Shingai. They were surprised when they saw him gain energy from nowhere and he began to slowly turn in slow circular motions at first, then he picked up speed. He went round carrying Rubonga with him, but Rubonga maintained his grip on to his throat. Shingai held his left fist into his right hand, and he began to hit Rubonga in the ribs with his left elbow. He put his full force, and Rubonga began to loosen his grip on his throat. The king let go entirely and became vulnerable again. Shingai was furious, having missed death by a whisker. He assaulted Rubonga in ways that he could not see or tell. Shingai jumped high into the air and swung his right leg to hit Rubonga on the head with his right heel, sending him straight to the ground. By the time he landed, Shingai had sat on his chest, delivering a series of blows everywhere on the ailing king's face. The king was no longer blocking the punches. His two front teeth shook. Shingai looked for his dagger so that he could finish off his man, but at that same time, he saw Vandirai walking in front of him. When he raised his head to see what he was up to, Vandirai hit him on the head with his club. Shingai saw stars in broad daylight and he passed out.

Chapter 37

Shingai felt a sharp pain on his neck, then he opened his eyes. It was dark outside. He tried to raise his hand so that he could reach for his neck to massage it, but he failed to move his hands. He decided to move his legs, and he failed too. He felt his blood flowing, and his sense of touch was activated all over his body. He figured that his whole back was pressed hard on to a tree trunk for when he moved slightly, he felt the bark of the tree scratching his bare skin. He thought he was in the middle of sleep paralysis, but slowly, he began to recollect his last memories. The bloody fistfight that he had had with Rubonga returned to his mind, and he remembered how Lord Vandirai had struck him with a club on the head. From there, he had blacked out. When he thought of this, he tried to move his limbs, but once more he failed. He realized that he was tightly bound on to a tree! As he fully regained his consciousness, he could tell that there were people near him from their breathing. He did not know who they were.

Time went by slowly until signs of light became visible in the east. Shingai did not know how long he had been out for and what had happened during that period. The roosters took turns to cry as the sunrays chased the darkness off the land. Shingai began to see that four warriors were guarding him and another prisoner that he could not identify yet. The warriors were standing a couple of meters away from him and the other prisoner. They were armed with spears and bows and arrows. As it grew lighter, Shingai was surprised to see his fellow prisoner. Anger flushed in him, but he could not break free. Lord Vandirai was tied on to a tree next to him, and he looked at him with reddened eyes. Shingai looked back at him with eyes full of hate. They froze like that for some time without talking to each other.

Shingai was puzzled. How could it be that the person who had disturbed his plans become a prisoner too? He concluded in his mind that Rubonga and his brother had joined hands and they were up to no good. There was something that they wanted from him. It was going to come out. What gave him a glimmer of hope was that, if Rubonga had wanted to kill him, he would have done so at the time that he was out cold. They had to kill him while he was still bound otherwise if they were to make the mistake of untying him, he would kill a couple of them before they would be able to kill him.

Vandirai began to talk to the warriors saying,

"Hey you boys, do you really think that you still have a king in Rubonga? Is that why you keep on taking silly orders from him? Can't you see that it is only a matter of a few days left before he takes his last breath? If you were smart you would run now because if you delay, soon you'll find yourselves sitting before the courts of the spirit world, do you hear me? The warriors just looked at each other and remained silent. Shingai could tell that deep down they agreed with what Lord Vandirai was saying, but they feared that among them, were those that would report them to Rubonga. He also wondered what it was that Vandirai was talking about.

"Did you not hear my words, boys?"

Vandirai asked again, looking at the warriors menacingly. The warriors still remained tight-lipped but looking at each other for cues. Shingai could see that one of the warriors had begun shaking and was fidgeting with his spear. The warrior cast his eyes on him and then announced to his colleagues that he was taking a break to relieve himself.

Lord Vandirai once more warned the uneasy warriors.

"Look what your clever friend has just done to you. Do you think he is still relieving himself?"

This time the warriors did not get to respond because three arrows had stabbed them almost at once. Not one of them was able to talk or cry out loud. They just fell onto the ground and passed out. Two were shot in the neck, and one was shot in the ribs. Shingai was shocked by what had happened. He set one of his eyes to the fallen warriors and the other on Vandirai. Lord Vandirai did not show any signs of shock or panic. He remained silent. Shingai then saw a person emerge, heavily disguised with charcoal marks on the face and leafy branches all over his body. He did not clearly see the mysterious man for he swiftly moved and hid behind the tree that Vandirai was bound to. At that moment, the man ran back and vanished into the woods. The man was like a shrub that had grown arms and legs. Vandirai soon began to stretch himself shortly after the mysterious man had freed him. Shingai perceived that Lord Vandirai and Gwari were working together.

He also thought that Vandirai was about to finish him at that point. Vandirai limped towards the area where the mysterious man had disappeared from and then limped back with a bow in his hands and arrows in a quiver. Shingai looked at him, thinking that death had finally caught up with him. Vandirai then cleared his throat and spoke to him.

"You see son, the Mupingamhuru battles are for the Mupingamhuru family, and therefore they should be fought by those of Mupingamhuru. Now, where do you come in? Leave us to solve our own family issues. You have no idea what this blood that you desire to spill can do to you and all your family members, even if you do not know them. Very soon, you will see a group of warriors that shall come here to take both you and me to be killed in front of Rubonga. What has actually delayed this process is that Rubonga has been summoned by the Council of Elders court, presided by the gray-haired ones of Magocha. They are busy rebuking the king. His wish was to have us killed in the absence of the elders, but it is being said that the elders have refused to return to their homes. Can you hear those people approaching? I will not wait any longer, and I shall not free you just yet. You will be freed because today, the sun shall not set while Rubonga is still breathing. You will witness what I am saying."

The last of Vandirai's words were said while he was already limping away from Shingai into the forest. This heaped more confusion on Shingai. He had heard what Vandirai had said, but it had not suddenly absolved him of being the cruel man that Shingai deeply resented. He still did not trust the conniving, cunning, and bitter old royal. If he was a genuinely honorable man, why had he not freed him and then sought to tell him his tales later? And if whatever he was planning was to fail, did it not simply mean death for him? He just shook his head in confusion.

The Warriors arrived at the scene and were horrified by what they saw. They were puzzled to see that Vandirai had escaped and that the warriors guarding them had been killed, but Shingai was still bound to the tree. They craned from a distance like one would do when inspecting a lion that had fallen into a pit trap so that they could see if he was still bound or if he wanted to spring-attack them. When they eventually got to him, he did not threaten to fight or to resist them. The warriors showed him respect. He could tell it from the way that they looked at him, and they did not ill-treat him. He learned from what they were talking about, that as soon as Vandirai had struck him with his knobkerrie Rubonga's two warriors that were watching the proceedings apprehended the old prince. They said he had not resisted the arrest as if he had planned for it to happen that way. At the time that Shingai had passed out, the warriors had removed Prince Masimba's royal robes that he was wearing and had made him wear his little skirt.

Shingai was sat right on the center of the court at the tree of smoke. The people stood, and some craned to see him. Ndukuyashe bellowed an order for everybody to sit down and listen. On that day, many people of different ages from the districts and villages of Magocha that were near the king's residence had attended the court session. The wind had carried to all corners of the kingdom that King Rubonga had killed his own son, Prince Masimba thinking that he was finishing off Shingai. They had also heard that the king wanted to twist the narrative so that the blame would be heaped on Shingai and Lord Vandirai.

People had received this news, and out of curiosity, they tracked to the king's village. The wind had also carried news of the public rebuke of the king by the Council of Elders. This meant that the elders could strip the king of his title and appoint one of his sons, even from the little ones to take his place until the spirits would eventually ordain the substantial occupant of the Mupingamhuru throne. When word got to some, it had been totally distorted to claim that it was actually Rubonga who had been killed. Because of this, many people had chosen to witness it with their own eyes and ears.

Rubonga had not gained his strength after his fight with Shingai. He was sitting on his throne with his head leaning on the trunk of the tree of smoke. For most of the court session on this day, he held his jaw and mouth with his left hand. Doing this somehow reduced the severity of his aching teeth that had been knocked by Shingai. Shingai was bound on his hands and legs, and he sat in the middle of the court where the body of Prince Masimba lay covered with a black cloth. He was facing Rubonga. Rubonga tried to stand up, but his aching body begged him to keep his limbs rested. All the royals that were present were wearing long faces of grief. When Shingai's eyes met with Kundai's, for a moment, he felt sorry for her. The death of Masimba had devastated the whole royal family.

Suddenly Shingai heard loud murmurs coming from behind him. He tried to turn, but then he saw Lord Vandirai passing beside him, heading to Rubonga. The warriors wanted to stop him, but one of the old men from the elders' council told them to leave him to do as he wished.

"The seed that you sowed has ripened today, *mukoma*! When you destroyed my family, you thought you were smart, right?" Vandirai spoke loudly so that everybody could hear him. The crowd went dead silent and listened. Shingai and most of the warriors wondered what Lord Vandirai's courage was based on, for him to be so brave as to dangle himself in front of a merciless killer without any weapon to defend himself except his bare hands. Without anybody noticing, for all eyes were sitting on Vandirai, Rubonga reached for his spear with his right hand. When he tried to hastily throw it at Vandirai, his hand was suddenly pinned on to the tree trunk by an arrow that whizzed over people's heads. Rubonga roared in pain, and the crowd was perplexed. They did not see who had shot the arrow. At that moment, the mob heard a yelling sound that emanated from a bush that went running into the center of the court.

"Iyiyiyyiyiyiiiiii! Iyeeeee, Iyiyiyiyi!"

All eyes shifted and rested on the shrub with legs. Suddenly a person emerged and pulled off all the little branches from their body, and everybody's jaws dropped because of what they saw!

Shuvai stood with a bow stretched, and her arrow pointed right at Rubonga. Rubonga's eyeballs shot out. His right hand was firmly pinned to the tree trunk so he could not move. Lord Vandirai called out again,

"You thought you were smart by killing all my sons so that my family would not be avenged, now here is the person who has proved your foolishness!"

Vandirai limped proudly and sat near the revered elders.

One of Rubonga's guards ran into the arena intending to stab Shuvai with a spear, but the people were dumbfounded by what happened next. Shuvai promptly beat up the man using just one hand, and in no time she had stabbed him dead with a dagger. She ripped his gut, cut off his wrists and lips. She shoved the lips into his open belly and planted the wrists through the opening. The crowd made breathtaking sounds as it immediately became clear that Shuvai was the mysterious killer that had terrorized Rubonga and his security guards! Rubonga's eyeballs were still in denial as he struggled to come to terms with what he was witnessing. Shuvai had once more pointed her arrow on the wretched king. As people were also still dealing with Shuvai's shocking acts, marveling at what nobody thought could ever be achieved by a girl; Ndukuyashe rose and put himself between Shuvai's arrow and his king.

Shuvai slowly relaxed her bowstring and put her weapons down to face the veteran warrior. The warrior rolled his fingers into rocky fists and sprung about like a boxer. While he was hopping up and down like that, Shuvai landed three quick claps on his cheeks. She was so fast that some people did not process what had just happened. Ndukuyashe stopped hopping and touched his cheeks in shock. The multitude began to cheer Shuvai, and the sore warrior was infuriated. He tried to pounce on her and land a strong punch on her face, but Shuvai easily evaded the punches. She then began to kick him on his face so fast until it was tenderized and bloodied, to the amusement of the crowd. The warrior failed to land even one blow on Shuvai. She faked some kicks, and he opened his legs. She then shot herself between his legs and stood behind him. She used his shoulders to shove herself up and sat on his shoulders before she lowered herself and choke his throat with her legs. His windpipes were blocked. The big man tried to remain on his feet, staggering from side to side but eventually falling to the ground.

Shuvai then released him and stood, giving her back to Rubonga, who was still groaning in pain and stuck to the tree. Ndukuyashe rolled on the ground to the side where the men were sitting and snatched a spear from one of the men. He then threw it with so much power towards Shuvai. She just moved her upper torso out of the spear's way, but her legs remained firm on the ground. The spear went straight into King Rubonga's chest and finished him at once. The people chorused a cry of shock, and many put their hands on their mouths, some covering their eyes.

Shuvai turned around and saw her *bamukuru* hanging his head on the side, blood still oozing out of his chest. As she looked at the rather sad sight, she heard loud voices from the crowd. From the voices, she picked Shingai's shouting to her,

"Shuvai look out!"

She turned and saw Ndukuyashe throwing another spear at her. Once again, she just stepped on the side and grabbed the spear with her right hand before it passed her. People were thrilled. She walked towards Ndukuyashe, lifted the spear high in the air, and forcefully stabbed it into the ground an inch away from his belly. He had already closed his eyes, thinking he was at last dead.

Shuvai used her dagger to cut loose the ropes that bound Shingai. Shingai stood up, and the two looked at each other. Shuvai slanted her head to the side and smiled at him saying,

"So you just couldn't wait for me my darling, even though we had a binding vow?"

Shingai blushed. He did not know where to begin.

"So was it really you who has been doing all this? Wow, you are bad news! So where does your husband think you are and what does he think about all this?"

"A-ah, Shingi dear, so you of all the people actually believed those lies, hmmnn, Shingi? It was just father's way of misleading *bamukuru* and his people. But I do understand how it must have been for you. It was quite a difficult situation. You see, we had been planning many of these things for a very long time; from the time that *bamukuru* Rubonga ordered arsonists to burn my whole family to death in the rondavels that they were sleeping in."

They looked deep into each other's eyes, and they embraced. The whole crowd was looking at them and feeling their love. The men clapped their hands and whistled as the women and girls broke into continuous ululation. Ndukuyashe rose, and people began to boo and jeer at him. His anger once more got the best of him as he snatched another spear and tried to aim it at Lord Vandirai, who was talking with the elders. He was stopped in his tracks when a stray arrow landed on his throat, and he fell dead. The people followed the path where the arrow had come from and saw Gotora the giant hermit laughing, something that they had never seen him do before. The people laughed and were happy to see that the stubborn Ndukuyashe had finally passed on, and they were also delighted to see Gotora laughing. Soon after that, Gotora disappeared into the covers of the forest.

Princess Kundai left her father and went to Shingai and Shuvai and stood looking at them for a moment. She then embraced both of them tightly. Shuvai and her immediately broke into sobs. After they had calmed down, Kundai said,

"*Mukoma* Masimba has left us, but he told me many things in the past few days that we were not privy to growing up. Please forgive us, my people. I love you."

She then walked back to where her mother and the other queens were sitting and sniffling, with tears still rolling down her cheeks.

The Big Aunt of the Lion Clan rose, and the crowd went quiet. She looked into the sky for some time and then looked at the gathering and said,

"Men, you can now make plans to prepare where Rubonga shall sleep. He shall not be buried in the Chineninga caves. Only Prince Masimba shall be buried there. Prepare a good place where the two shall sleep tonight, for a big storm is coming."

She then looked at Lord Vandirai and said,

"VaMupingamhuru, you may now dismiss your people so that they can return to their homes. Remember that somewhere on this tree, are lightening's eggs."

By the time the old lady finished speaking, raindrops had started falling. The people rose and went on their way, many going to their relatives' homes in the king's district for the night. Amid the women that were walking away, Shingai saw Muthlomo also walking away with them but looking at him. She nodded once, and he returned the nod. Shingai held Shuvai's hand, and they both started walking towards the palace.

44352485R00265

Printed in Poland
by Amazon Fulfillment
Poland Sp. z o.o., Wrocław